Ghana Must Go

Taiye Selasi was born in London and raised in Massachusetts. She holds a BA in American Studies from Yale and an MPhil in International Relations from Oxford. 'The Sex Lives of African Girls' (Granta, 2011), Selasi's fiction debut, appears in *Best American Short Stories 2012*. She lives in Rome.

GHANA MUST GO

Taiye Selasi

VIKING
an imprint of
PENGUIN BOOKS

VIKING

Published by the Penguin Group

Penguin Books Ltd, 80 Strand, London WC2R ORL, England

Penguin Group (USA) Inc., 375 Hudson Street, New York, New York 10014, USA

Penguin Group (Canada), 90 Eglinton Avenue East, Suite 700, Toronto, Ontario, Canada M4P 2Y3
(a division of Pearson Penguin Canada Inc.)

Penguin Ireland, 25 St Stephen's Green, Dublin 2, Ireland (a division of Penguin Books Ltd)

Penguin Group (Australia), 707 Collins Street, Melbourne, Victoria 3008, Australia
(a division of Pearson Australia Group Pty Ltd)

Penguin Books India Pvt Ltd, 11 Community Centre, Panchsheel Park, New Delhi – 110 017, India

Penguin Group (NZ), 67 Apollo Drive, Rosedale, Auckland 0632, New Zealand
(a division of Pearson New Zealand Ltd)

Penguin Books (South Africa) (Pty) Ltd, Block D, Rosebank Office Park,
181 Jan Smuts Avenue, Parktown North, Gauteng 2193, South Africa

Penguin Books Ltd, Registered Offices: 80 Strand, London WC2R ORL, England

www.penguin.com

First published in the United States of America by The Penguin Press, a member of Penguin Group (USA) Inc. 2013
First published in Great Britain by Viking 2013

001

Copyright © Taiye Selasi, 2013

The moral right of the author has been asserted

Excerpt from 'Approximations'. Copyright © 1962, 1966 by Robert Hayden.
From *Collected Poems of Robert Hayden* by Robert Hayden, edited by Frederick Glaysher.
Used by permission of Liveright Publishing Corporation

'a word forgot to remember what to forget . . .' by Renee C. Neblett. Used by permission of the author.

Printed in Great Britain by Clays Ltd, St Ives plc

A CIP catalogue record for this book is available from the British Library

HARDBACK ISBN: 978–0–670–91986–4
TRADE PAPERBACK ISBN: 978–0–670–91987–1

www.greenpenguin.co.uk

Penguin Books is committed to a sustainable
future for our business, our readers and our planet.
This book is made from Forest Stewardship
Council™ certified paper.

ALWAYS LEARNING   **PEARSON**

for Juliette Modupe Tuakli, M.D.

Not sunflowers, not
roses, but rocks in patterned
sand grow here. And bloom.

—ROBERT HAYDEN,
"Approximations"

A word forgot to remember
what to forget
and every so often
let the truth slip

—RENEE C. NEBLETT,
"Snapshots"

Pronunciations

	PRONUNCIATION	MEANING	ORIGIN
ACCRA	ah *krah* (as in afar)	Capital city of Ghana	Ghana
BABAFEMI	bah bah *feh* mee (as in absolutely)	"Loved by his father"	Nigeria
EKUA	eh *kwee* ah (as in Evita)	Girl born on Wednesday	Ghana
FEMI	*feh* mee (as in Emmy)	Short form of Babafemi	Nigeria
FOLA	*fo* lah (as in cola)	Short form of Folasadé	Nigeria
FOLASADÉ	fo lah *shah* deh (as in absolutely)	"Wealth confers my crown"	Nigeria
IDOWU	*ee* do woo (as in peekaboo)	Born after twins	Nigeria
KEHINDE	*ky* in deh (as in yesterday)	Second-born twin	Nigeria
KOKROBITÉ	ko kro *bee* teh (as in absolutely)	Coastal town near Accra	Ghana
KWEKU	*kway* koo (as in Quaker)	Boy born on Wednesday	Ghana

PRONUNCIATIONS

	Pronunciation	Meaning	Origin
LAGOS	*lay* goss (as in famous)	Largest city in Nigeria	Nigeria
NIKÉ	*nee* keh (as in ginseng)	Short form of Adeniké	Nigeria
OLUKAYODÉ	o loo *ky* o deh (as in only Saturday)	"God brings happiness"	Nigeria
PHILAE	*fy* lee (as in highly)	Southern limits of Egypt	Greece
SADÉ	*shah* deh (as in André)	Short form of Folasadé	Nigeria
SAI	*sy* (as in sigh)	Surname	Ghana
SENA	*seh* nah (as in henna)	"Gift from God"	Ghana
SOMAYINA	so mah *yee* nah (as in Serafina)	"May I not travel alone"	Nigeria
TAIWO	*ty* wo (as in Cairo)	First-born twin	Nigeria

FAMILY TREE

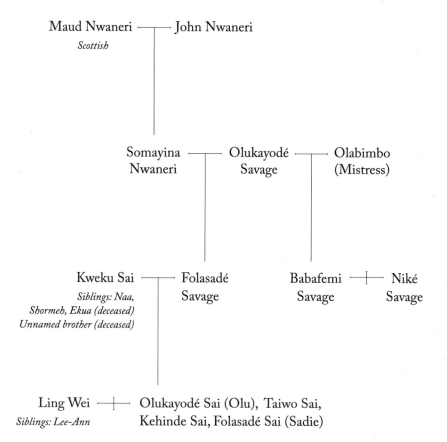

Maud Nwaneri ——— John Nwaneri
Scottish

Somayina —— Olukayodé —— Olabimbo
Nwaneri   Savage   (Mistress)

Kweku Sai —— Folasadé   Babafemi — Niké
Siblings: Naa,   Savage   Savage   Savage
Shormeh, Ekua (deceased)
Unnamed brother (deceased)

Ling Wei —— Olukayodé Sai (Olu), Taiwo Sai,
Siblings: Lee-Ann   Kehinde Sai, Folasadé Sai (Sadie)

Part I

GONE

1.

Kweku dies barefoot on a Sunday before sunrise, his slippers by the doorway to the bedroom like dogs. At the moment he is on the threshold between sunroom and garden considering whether to go back to get them. He won't. His second wife Ama is asleep in that bedroom, her lips parted loosely, her brow lightly furrowed, her cheek hotly seeking some cool patch of pillow, and he doesn't want to wake her.

He couldn't if he tried.

She sleeps like a cocoyam. A thing without senses. She sleeps like his mother, unplugged from the world. Their house could be robbed— by Nigerians in flip-flops rolling right up to their door in rusting Russian Army tanks, eschewing subtlety entirely as they've taken to doing on Victoria Island (or so he hears from his friends: the crude oil kings and cowboys demobbed to Greater Lagos, that odd breed of African: fearless and rich)—and she'd go on snoring sweetly, a kind of musical arrangement, dreaming sugarplums and Tchaikovsky.

She sleeps like a child.

But he's carried the thought anyway, from bedroom to sunroom, making a production of being careful. A show for himself. He does this, has always done this since leaving the village, little open-air performances for an audience of one. Or for two: him and his cameraman, that silent-invisible cameraman who stole away beside him all those decades ago in the darkness before daybreak with the ocean beside, and who has followed him every day everywhere since. Quietly filming his life. Or: the life of the Man Who He Wishes to Be and Who He Left to Become.

In this scene, a bedroom scene: The Considerate Husband.

Who doesn't make a peep as he slips from the bed, moving the covers aside noiselessly, setting each foot down separately, taking pains not to wake his unwakable wife, not to get up too quickly thus unsettling the mattress, crossing the room very quietly, closing the door without sound. And down the hall in this manner, through the door into the courtyard where she clearly can't hear him, but still on his toes. Across the short heated walkway, from Master Wing to Living Wing, where he pauses for a moment to admire his house.

It's a brilliant arrangement this one-story compound, by no means novel, but functional, and elegantly planned: simple courtyard in the middle with a door at each corner to the Living, Dining, Master, and (Guest) Bedroom Wings. He sketched it on a napkin in a hospital cafeteria in his third year of residency, at thirty-one years old. At forty-eight bought the plot off a Neapolitan patient, a rich land speculator with Mafia ties and Type II diabetes who moved to Accra because it reminds him of Naples in the fifties, he says (the wealth pressed against want, fresh sea air against sewage, filthy poor against filthier rich at the beach). At forty-nine found a carpenter who was willing to build it, the only Ghanaian who didn't balk at putting a hole in a house. The carpenter was seventy with cataracts and a six-pack. He finished in two years working impeccably and alone.

At fifty-one moved his things in, but found it too quiet.

At fifty-three took a second wife.

Elegantly planned.

Now he stops at the top of the square, between doorways, where the blueprint is obvious, where he can *see* the design, and considers it as the painter must consider the painting or the mother the newborn: with confusion and awe, that this thing which sprang to life there inside the mind or body has made it here to the outside, a life of its own. Slightly baffled. How did it get here, from *in* him to in front? (Of course he knows: with the proper application of the appropriate instruments; it's the same for the painter, the mother, the amateur architect—but still it's a wonder to look at.)

His house.

His beautiful, functional, elegant house, which appeared to him whole, the whole ethos, in an instant, like a fertilized zygote spinning inexplicably out of darkness in possession of an entire genetic code. An entire logic. The four quadrants: a nod to symmetry, to his training days, to graph paper, to the compass, perpetual journey/perpetual return, etc., etc., a gray courtyard, not green, polished rock, slabs of slate, treated concrete, a kind of rebuttal to the tropics, to home: so a homeland re-imagined, all the lines clean and straight, nothing lush, soft, or verdant. In one instant. All there. Now here. Decades later on a street in Old Adabraka, a crumbling suburb of colonial mansions, whitewashed stucco, stray dogs. It is the most beautiful thing he has ever created—

except Taiwo, he thinks suddenly, a shock of a thought. Whereon Taiwo herself—with black thicket for eyelash and carved rock for cheekbone and gemstone for eyes, her pink lips the same color as the inside of conch shells, impossibly beautiful, an impossible girl—sort of appears there in front of him interrupting his performance of The Considerate Husband, then goes up in smoke. It is the most beautiful thing he has ever created *alone,* he amends the observation.

Then continues along the walkway through the door into the Living Wing, through the dining room, to the sunroom, to the threshold.

Where he stops.

2.

Later in the morning when the snow has started falling, and the man has finished dying, and a dog has smelled the death, Olu will walk in no particular hurry out of the hospital, hang up his BlackBerry, put down his coffee, and start to cry. He'll have no way of knowing how the day broke in Ghana; he'll be miles and oceans and time zones away (and other kinds of distances that are harder to cover, like heartbreak and anger and calcified grief and those questions left too long unasked or unanswered and generations of father-son silence and shame), stirring soymilk into coffee in a hospital cafeteria, blurry-eyed, sleep-deprived, here and not there. But he'll picture it—his father, there, dead in a garden, healthy male, fifty-seven, in remarkable shape, small-round biceps pushing up against the skin of his arms, small-round belly pushing out against the rib of his top, Fruit of the Loom fine rib A-shirt, stark white on dark brown, worn with the ridiculous MC Hammer pants he hates and Kweku loves—and try though he will (he's a doctor, he knows better, he hates it when his patients ask him "what if you're wrong?"), he won't shake the thought.

That the doctors were wrong.

That these things don't "sometimes happen."

That something *happened* out there.

No physician that experienced, never mind that exceptional—and say what you want, the man was good at his job, even detractors concede this, "a knife-wielding artist," general surgeon without equal, Ghanaian Carson, and on—could've missed all the signs of so slow-building a heart attack. Basic coronary thrombosis. Easy peasy. Act fast. And there would have been *time*, half an hour on the low side from everything Mom says, thirty minutes to act, to "return to his training," in the words of Dr. Soto, Olu's favorite attending, his Xicano patron saint: to run through the symptoms, to spit out a diagnosis, to get up, to go inside, to wake up the wife, and if the wife couldn't drive—a safe bet, she can't read—then to drive himself to safety. To put on slippers for God's sake.

Instead, he did nothing. No run-through, no spit-out. Just strolled through a sunroom, then fell to the grass, where for no apparent reason—or unknowable reasons that Olu can't divine and damned to unknowing can't forgive—his father, Kweku Sai, Great Ga Hope, prodigal prodigy, just lay in pajamas doing nothing at all until the sun rose, ferocious, less a rise than an uprising, death to wan gray by gold sword, while inside the wife opened her eyes to find slippers by the doorway and, finding this strange, went to find, and found him dead.

An exceptional surgeon.

Of unexceptional heart attack.

With forty minutes on average between onset and death, so even *if* it's the case that these things "sometimes happen," i.e., healthy human hearts just "sometimes happen" to cramp up, willy-nilly, out of nowhere, like a hamstring catching a charley, there's a question of the timing. All those minutes in the gap. Between first pang and last breath. Those particular moments Olu's great fascination, an obsession all his life, first in childhood as an athlete, then in adulthood as a physician.

The moments that make up an outcome.

The quiet ones.

Those snatches of silence between trigger and action when the challenge of the minute is the sole focus of the mind and the whole world slows down as to watch what will happen. When one acts or one doesn't. After which it's Too Late. Not the *end*—those few, desperate, and cacophonous seconds that precede the final buzzer or the long flatline beep—but the silence beforehand, the break in the action. There is always this break, Olu knows, no exceptions. So, seconds just after the gun goes off and the sprinter keeps driving or pops up too soon, or the gunshot victim, feeling a bullet break skin, brings a hand to his wound or does not, the world stopped. Whether the sprinter will win or the patient will make it has less to do finally with how he crosses the line than with whatever he did in these still prior moments, and Kweku did nothing, and Olu doesn't know why.

How could his father not realize what was happening and how, if he realized, could he stay there to die? No. Something must have *happened* to debilitate, to disorient, some strong emotion, mental disturbance, Olu doesn't know what. What he does know is this: active male under sixty, no known history of illness, raised on freshwater fish, running five miles daily, fucking a nubile village idiot—and say what you want, the new wife is no nurse: it is futile to blame but there might have been hope, chest compressions done right/had she just woken up—doesn't die in a garden of cardiac arrest.

Something must have *arrested* him.

3.

Dewdrops on grass.

Dewdrops on grass blades like diamonds flung freely from the pouch of some sprite-god who'd just happened by, stepping lightly and lithely through Kweku Sai's garden just moments before Kweku appeared there himself. Now the whole garden glittering, winking and tittering like schoolgirls who hush themselves, blushing, as their beloveds approach: glittering mango tree, monarch, teeming being at center with her thick bright green leaves and her bright yellow eggs; glittering fountain full of cracks now and weeds with white blossoms, but the statue still standing, the "mother of twins," *iya–ibeji*, once a gift for his ex-wife Folasadé, now abandoned in the fountain with her hand-carved stone twins; glittering flowers Folasadé could name by their faces, the English names, Latin names, a million shades of pink; glowing sky the soft gray of the South without sunlight, glittering clouds at its edges.

Glittering garden.

Glittering wet.

Kweku stops on the threshold and stares at this, breathless, his shoulder against the sliding door, halfway slid open. He thinks to himself, with a pang in his chest, that the world is too beautiful sometimes. That there's simply no *weight* to it, no way to accept it: the dew on the grass and the light on the dew and the tint to that light, not for a doctor like him, when he knows that such things rarely live through a night; that they're in but not long for the world as he's known it, a brutal and senseless and punishing place; that they'll either be broken or break away free, leaving loss in their wake. That the N.I.C.U. had it right.

They don't promote naming in the N.I.C.U., as he discovered during his third-year pediatrics rotation, that heartbreaking winter, 1975, with his mother just dead and his first son just born. If some ill-fated infant wouldn't last through the weekend, they discouraged its parents from picking a name, scrawling "Baby" with the surname on the incubator label ("A, B, C Surname" on for multiples). Many of his classmates found the practice uncouth, a sort of premature throwing up of hands in defeat. These were Americans, mostly, with their white teeth and cow's milk, for whom infant mortality was an inconceivable thing. Or rather: conceivable in the aggregate, as a number, a statistic, i.e., x% of babies under two weeks will die. Conceivable in the plural but unacceptable in the singular. The *one* gray-blue baby.

The late Baby Surname.

To the Africans, by contrast (and the Indians and West Indians and the one escapee Latvian for whom Baltimore was comfortable), a dead neonate was not only conceivable but unremarkable, all the better when unavoidable, i.e., explicable. It was life. To them the nonnaming was logical, even admirable, a way to create distance from existence so from death. Precisely the kind of thing they always thought of in America and never bothered with in places like Riga or Accra. The sterilization of human emotion. The reduction of anguish to Hallmark-card hurt. The washing, as by sedulous scrub-nurse, of all ugliness off grief's many faces.

Faces Kweku Sai knew.

To him, who could name grief by each one of her faces, the logic was familiar from a warmer third world, where the boy who tails his mother freshly bloodied from labor (fruitless labor) to the edge of an ocean at dawn—who sees her place the little corpse like a less lucky Moses all wrapped up in palm frond, in froth, then walk away, but who never hears her mention it, ever, not once—learns that "loss" is a notion. No more than a thought. Which one forms or one doesn't. With words. Such that one cannot lose, nor ever say he has lost, what he does not permit to exist in his mind.

Even then, at twenty-four, a new father and still a child, a newly motherless child, Kweku knew that.

Now he stares at the glittering, arrested by beauty, and knows what he knew all those winters ago: that when faced with a thing that is fragile and perfect in a world that is ugly and crushing and cruel the correct course of action is: Give it no name. Pretend that it doesn't exist.

But it doesn't work.

He feels a second pang now for the existence of perfection, the stubborn existence of perfection in the most vulnerable of things and in the face of his refusal—logical-admirable refusal—to engage with this existence in his heart, in his mind. For the comfortless logic, the curse of clear sight, no matter *which* string he pulls on the same wretched knot: (a) the futility of seeing given the fatality of beauty, much less of beauty in fragility in a place such as this where a mother still bloody must bury her newborn, hose off, and go home to pound yam into paste; (b) the *persistence* of beauty, in fragility of all places!, in a dewdrop at daybreak, a thing that will end, and in moments, and in a garden, and in Ghana, lush Ghana, soft Ghana, verdant Ghana, where fragile things die.

He sees this so clearly he closes his eyes. His head begins throbbing. He opens his eyes. He tries but can't move. He is glued there, overwhelmed.

The last time he felt this was with Sadie.

4.

Winter again, 1989.

The delivery ward at the Brigham.

Fola propped up in the hospital bed, still bloody from labor and clutching his arm.

The twins, nine years old, fast asleep in the lounge in those ugly blue chairs with the yellow foam stuffing, arranged as they always were, locked into place like some funny wooden Japanese logic-game puzzle: Taiwo's head on Kehinde's shoulder and Kehinde's cheek on

Taiwo's head, a girl and a boy with the same amber eyes throwing sparks from their otherwise gentle young faces.

Olu eating apple slices, already so healthy at fourteen years old, reading *Things Fall Apart*, the single visible sign of his mounting distress the rote up-and-down bounce of his femur.

And the newborn, yet unnamed, fighting for life in its incubator. Losing.

Baby Sai.

In the rancid delivery room.

"What's wrong with Idowu? Where are they taking her?"

She clutched his bare arm. He was still in his scrubs, nothing else, arms uncovered. He'd been stitching when she went into labor (too soon). A friend at the Brigham had had him paged over the intercom, and he'd run through the snow from Beth Israel here with the swirling flakes clouding his vision as he ran, and the words, two words, clouding his thinking. *Too soon.*

"It was too soon."

"NO."

Not a human sound. Animal. A growl rumbling forth from the just-emptied belly. A battle cry. But who was the enemy? Him. The obstetrician. The timing. The belly itself. "Folasadé," he murmured.

"Kweku, no," Fola growled, her teeth clenched, her nails piercing his goose-pimpled skin. Drawing blood. "Kweku, no." Now she started to cry.

"Please," he whispered. Stricken. "Don't cry."

She shook her head, crying, still piercing his arm (and other pierceable parts of him neither perceived). "Kweku, no." As if changing his name in her mind now from Kweku, just Kweku, to Kweku-No.

He laid his lips gently on the crown of her head. Her crowning glory, Fola's hair, reduced by half by fresh sweat. A cloud of tiny spirals, each one clinging to the next in solidarity and smelling of Indian Hemp. "We have three healthy children," he said to her softly. "We are blessed."

"Kweku-No, Kweku-No, Kweku-*No*."

The last one was shrill, nearing rage, accusation. He had never seen Fola unraveled like this. Her two other pregnancies had gone perfectly, medically speaking, the deliveries like clockwork, instructional-video smooth: the first one in Baltimore when they were still children, the second here in Boston, a C-section, the twins. And now this, ten years later, a complete accident, the third (though they were all complete accidents in a way). She was different with this one almost right from the start. She insisted upon knowing the gender at once. Then insisted he not tell anyone, not even the kids, not (a) that she was expecting and then (b) what it was. Both became obvious that evening in summer she returned with four gallons of pastel pink paint. She chose the name without him, for "the child who follows twins." This didn't so much surprise him. She'd become kind of precious about her Yoruba heritage after becoming *iya-ibeji*, a mother to twins. He didn't like the name, the way *Idowu* sounded, and less what it meant, something about conflict and pain. But he was relieved that her choice wasn't something more dramatic, like *Yemanja*, the way she'd been acting. Building shrines.

And now this. Ten weeks early. There was nothing to be done.

"You have to do *something*."

He looked at the nurse.

A drinker, he'd guess, from the paunch and rosacea. Irish, from the trace of a South Boston *a*. But no trace of bigotry, which often went with this, and gentle eyes, grayish-blue, glistening. The woman managed to frown and to smile simultaneously. Sympathetically. While Fola drew blood from his arm. "Where did they take her?" he asked, though he knew.

The nurse frowned-and-smiled. "To the N.I.C.U."

. . .

He went to the waiting room.

Olu looked up.

He sat by his son, put a hand on his knee. Olu abandoned Achebe and looked at his knee as if only now aware it was bouncing.

"Watch your brother and sister. I'll be right back."

"Where are you going?"

"To check on the baby."

"Can I come with you?"

Kweku looked at the twins.

A funny wooden Japanese logic-game puzzle. They slept like his mother. Olu looked at them, too. Then pleadingly at Kweku.

"Come on then."

They walked down the hospital hallway in silence. His cameraman walked backward in front of them. In this scene: a Well-Respected Doctor goes striding down the hallway to save his unsavable daughter. A Western. He wished he had a weapon. Little six-shooter, silver. Two. Something with more shine than a Hopkins M.D. And a clearer opponent. Or an opponent less formidable than the basics of medical science. The odds.

Presently, Olu. "What is it?"

End scene.

"Nothing." Kweku chuckled. "Just tired, that's all." He patted his son's head. Or his son's browbone more accurately, his son's head having moved from where he remembered its being. He looked at Olu closely now, surprised by the height (and by other things he'd seen but never noticed before: the wide latissimus dorsi, the angular jawline, the Yoruba nose, Fola's nose, broad and straight, the taut skin the same shade as his own and so smooth, baby's bum, even now in adolescence). He wasn't pretty like Kehinde—who looked like a girl: an impossible, impossibly beautiful girl—but had become in the course of one week-end, it seemed, a really very handsome young man. He squeezed Olu's shoulder, reassuring him. "I'm fine."

Olu frowned, tensing. "The baby, I meant. What is it? The gender?"

"Oh. Right." Kweku smiled. "It was a girl," then, "It's a girl," but too late. Olu heard the past tense and glared at him, wary.

"What's wrong with the baby?" he asked, his voice tight.

"The curse of her gender. Impatience." Kweku winked. "She couldn't wait."

"Can they save it?"

"Not likely."

"Can you?"

Kweku laughed aloud, a sudden sound in the quiet. He patted Olu's head, this time finding his hair. His elder son's appraisal of his abilities as a doctor never ceased to amaze or delight him. Or appease him. His *other* son couldn't have cared less what he did, irrespective of the fact that they lived off his doing it. He didn't take this personally. At least he didn't think he did. At least he didn't show it when his cameraman was around. He was an Intelligent Parent, too rational to pick favorites. A Man's Man, above petty insecurities. And a Well-Respected Doctor, one of the best in his field, *goddammit!*, whether Kehinde cared or didn't. Besides. The boy was un-impressable. Per-petually indifferent. His teachers all said the same year after year. Pre-ternatural ability, exemplary behavior, but doesn't seem to care about school. What to do?

Kehinde doesn't care about anything, Kweku told them. *Except Taiwo.* (Always except Taiwo.)

"No," he answered Olu, his laugh lingering as a smile. Olu's eyes lingering on the side of his face. Then falling away. They walked far-ther down the hallway in silence. Suddenly, Olu looked up.

"Yes, you can."

. . .

All these years later when Kweku thinks of that moment, he can picture the look on his fourteen-year-old's face, when Olu seemed to become—in the course of one instant—an infant again, raw with trusting. The boy was transfigured, his whole face wide open, his eyes so undoubting that Kweku looked down. His elder son's appraisal of his abilities as a doctor broke his heart (for a second time. He hadn't felt the first). He shook his head weakly and looked at his hands. His fingers still frozen from running through the snow. He was teetering on an edge, though he didn't know which, some strange gathering force building within and against him. "She doesn't have the heart for it—" he started, then stopped. They'd reached the glass door to the nursery.

Kweku peered in.

There it was.

On the left.

Three and a half pounds, barely breathing, barely life.

With all kinds of patches and tubes sticking out of it, it looked like E.T. going home.

Olu pressed his hands to the Plexiglas window. "Which one is it?" he asked, cupping his hands around his eyes. Kweku laughed softly. Olu didn't say *she*. Only *it*, *one*, *the baby*. Little surgeon in the making. He pointed to the incubator, the handwritten tag. "That one," he said. "Baby Sai."

It was the simplest thing, really, just the littlest slip (*Sai*), speaking aloud as he tapped on the glass, but he'd been teetering already on an edge when it happened, when pointing to the incubator he spoke his own name. And the two put together, like combustible compounds— the sound of his name breathed aloud in the space and the sight of the neonate fighting for breath—suddenly somehow made "Baby Sai" his. It was his.

She was his.

And she was perfect.

And she was *tiny*.

And she was dying. And he felt it, felt this dying, in the center of his chest, the force gathered, raw panic, overwhelming his lungs, filling his chest with a tingling, thick, biting, and sharp. He heard himself whisper, "There she is," or something like it, but with the constriction of his larynx didn't recognize his voice.

Neither did Olu, who looked up, alarmed.

"Dad," he whispered. Stricken. "Don't cry."

But Kweku couldn't help it. He was barely even aware of it. The tears came so quickly, fell so quietly. *She was his.* That precious thing there with her toenails like dewdrops, her ten tiny fingers all curled up in hope, little fists of determination, and her petal-thin skin, like a flower that Fola could name by its face. Fola's favorite already. And she. Waiting, hopeful, still propped up in bed, sweating, bloodied. His, too.

You have to do something.

He had to do something. He wiped his face quickly with the back of his arm. The salt stung the wound there. He squeezed Olu's shoulder. Reassuring himself.

"Come on then."

The next ninety-six hours he stayed: in the staff lounge, befriending bleary interns who slept there as well, consulting colleagues, researching treatments, obsessively reading, barely sleeping, until his opponent was defeated. Until the newborn was named. And not *Idowu*, that goat-meat-tough name Fola loved for the long-suffering child born directly after twins. He picked *Sadé* when they brought the child home from the hospital on the grounds that two Folas would become too confusing. His first choice was *Ekua*, like his sister, "born on Wednesday," but Fola had established sovereignty over naming years back (first name: Nigerian, middle name: Ghanaian, third name: Savage, last name: Sai). Sadé picked *Sadie* when she started junior high on the grounds that her classmates pronounced Sadé like that anyway. But a nurse picked *Folasadé* in the first place, inadvertently, that last night at the Brigham.

Another accident.

He was alone in the nursery with the infant after midnight, in the scrubs from the appendectomy at Beth Israel days before, fully aware that some parent passing the Plexiglas window might mistake him for a homeless man and very well should. The bloodshot eyes, the matted hair, that half-crazed look of consuming obsession: he looked like a madman, a madman in scrubs, gone broke trying to win against the odds. (He had no way of knowing he would one day become this.) The nursery was dark, save the lamps in the incubators. He rocked in a chair with the girl in his lap. The girl had been asleep for over an hour at this point but he carried on rocking, too exhausted to stand. The chair was too small, one of those tiny plastic rocking chairs that hospitals put in nurseries, apparently for neonates themselves.

The Irish-looking nurse with the paunch and the rosacea appeared in the doorway with her clipboard and paused. "You again." She leaned against the door, frowning-smiling.

"Me again, yes."

"No, no. Please don't get up."

She entered without switching on the overhead fluorescents, kindly sparing them both the sudden violence of light. She made her rounds quietly, scribbling notes on her clipboard. When she reached the little rocking chair she looked down and laughed.

The infant's hand, with its five infinitesimal brown fingers, was attached to Kweku's thumb as if holding on for life.

"You must really love her," she said. Boston accent. *Luff-ha*. "You're here more than I am, I swear it."

Kweku laughed softly so as not to wake the baby. "I do," he said simply. "I do."

The two words returned him to Baltimore, to his wedding day, to Fola, young, resplendent in maternity dress in that low-ceilinged chapel, red carpeting, wood paneling, their first night of marriage, ginger ale, plastic flutes. Whereon two other words came sort of floating like little bubbles to the surface of his thoughts. And popped. *Too soon.* Had they married too soon? Become parents too soon? If so, what might that mean? That it wasn't "really love"?

The nurse, still in Boston, turned off the lamp in the incubator. Kweku, still in Baltimore, closed his eyes, rocked back and forth. "But I *do* really love her." The nurse didn't hear this. She checked the label on the incubator. Baby Sai. No given name.

"What's ha' name?" she asked him, pen poised over clipboard.

"Folasadé," Kweku mumbled, too exhausted to think.

"That's pretty. How do you spell that?"

Without opening his eyes. "F-o-l-a-s-a-d-e."

It didn't even occur to him what the nurse was actually asking until the confusion at the discharge desk. "No Idowu Sai." A different nurse now, smacking her gum in irritation, slapped the folder on the countertop and pointed. Acrylic nail. Kweku took the folder and looked at the writing. *First name: Folasade. Last name: Sai.* The nurse, smiling, smug, blew a bubble, let it pop.

"Fola-say-dee Sai. Is that your kid? Fola-say-dee?"

5.

The last time he felt this was with "Say-dee," this sense of epiphany, this same unsettling sort of discovering that he's gotten it *wrong*, that a thing he has looked at countless times and found unremarkable, discountable, is in fact beautiful, has been beautiful all the while. How had he missed it? The just-barely-born infant, the just-barely-breathing neonate, hands clenched in hope, not bizarre-looking, alien, as he'd once thought of newborns (even Olu, Taiwo, Kehinde), but glorious, worth the fight. With the accompanying consternation: sudden cinching in the chest, on the left, where he feels dying and other gathering forces, less: blind-but-now-I-see, choir of angels, hallelujah, more: but-what-does-it-all-amount-to-in-the-end, a sharp, a shrill frustration.

Or what he thinks is frustration.

He once read that frustration is self-pity by another name.

Whatever you call it.

The last time he felt it was with Sadie: frustration/pity, that the world is both too beautiful and more beautiful than he knows, than he's *noticed*, that he's missed it, and that he might be missing more but that he might never know and that it might be too late; that it *can* be too late, that there is such a thing, a Too Late in the first place, that time will run out, and that it might not even matter in the end what he's noticed, for how can it matter when it all disappears?

Or a sort of spiral of thoughts in this general direction that comes to a point at that final defense, i.e., how can he be faulted for all that he's missed when it's all wrapped in meaninglessness, when everything dies? He is pleading his innocence (*I didn't* know *what was beautiful; I would have fought for it all, had I seen, had I known!*), though with whom he is pleading, in the sunroom as in the nursery, remains for the most part unclear. And something else. Something new now. Neither righteousness nor blindness nor blind indignation nor pity.

Acceptance.

Of death.

For he knows, in a strange way, as the spiral comes to rest at *when everything dies*, that he's about to.

He knows—as he stands here in wifebeater and MC Hammer pants, shoulder against sliding door, halfway slid open, sliding deeper into reverie, remembrance and re- other things (regret, remorse, resentment, reassessment)—that he's dying.

He knows.

But doesn't notice.

It is knowing, not knowledge. Inconspicuous among his other thoughts. Not even a "thought." A sound traveling toward him through water, not rushing. A shape forming far off out of negative space. A bubble just beginning its ascent into consciousness, still ten, fifteen minutes from awareness, behind schedule, all the facts being returned to their upright positions, attendants preparing the cabin for arrival. A woman. The voice of a woman. The love of a woman. Love for her and from her, a woman, two women. The mother and lover, where it begins and is ending, as he's always suspected it must. (More on this in a moment.)

At the moment he is on the threshold, transfixed by the garden.

How in the world has he missed this?

6.

In nearly six years of looking—every morning from this sunroom with its floor-to-ceiling windows and architectural-glass roof, pausing mid-sip of coffee and Milo (poor man's mocha) to shift his *Graphic*, distracted, sucking his teeth at the view, thinking he should have insisted upon the pool and the pebbles, that the "love grass" wants water, that this is the trouble with green, that he hopes his bloody carpenter Mr. Lamptey is happy now—he's never once seen it.

His garden.

Never could.

He didn't want a garden. He couldn't have been clearer. Nothing lush, soft, or verdant; all the lines clean, etc. (In fact, he didn't want the things that he associates with gardens, like Fola or the English, on his property, in his sight.) He wanted pebbles, white pebbles, a wall-to-wall carpet of white like fresh snow, a rectangular pool. With the sun glinting brilliantly off the white and the water, the heat kept at bay by a concrete overhang. This is what he'd sketched in the Beth Israel cafeteria, sipping cheap lukewarm coffee, stinking of disinfectant and death. A chlorine-blue box on a beach of bleached-white. Sterile, square, elemental.

An orderly view.

And the life that came with it: getting out of bed every morning, coming to sit in his little sunroom with the paper and croissants, sipping fresh expensive coffee served by a butler named Kofi to whom he'd speak in a British accent (somewhat inexplicably), "That will be all." All his children sleeping comfortably in the Bedroom Wing (now the Guest Bedroom Wing). A cook cooking breakfast in the Dining Wing. And Fola. By far the best part of the view in her Bic-blue bikini swimming the last of her morning laps, Afro bejeweled with droplets, rising dripping from the water like Aphrodite from waves (somewhat improbably; she hated getting her hair wet), and waving.

Stick figures on napkin.

She: smiling, dripping, waving.

He: smiling, sipping coffee, waving back.

Instead, he's come to sit here all these mornings with his paper and his breakfast (poor man's mocha, four fat triangles of toasted cocoa bread), beset on all sides by the floor-to-ceiling windows and the vision of a carpenter-*cum*-mystic.

That bloody man.

Mr. Lamptey.

The carpenter. Now the gardener. Still an enigma. Who built the house in two years working impeccably and alone, smoking hash on the job, rolling blunts during lunch, singing prayers of contrition for any harm done the wood: who came to work in swami clothing (saffron, barefoot, hip-slung tool belt) looking less like a sage than an elderly stripper with his hammer and chisel and bare chiseled thighs: an ancient soul in a younger man's body with infant eyes in his old man's face, some seventy odd years old with his cataracts and six-pack: who sabotaged the sunroom and denied Kweku his view. But who understood the *vision*: simple one-story compound. The only carpenter in Accra who would build it.

All of the other high-end architect-contractors had their own ideas (same *one* idea) of how a house should look; namely, as gaudy and gargantuan as financially possible, with no reference to any notion of African architecture whatsoever. Kweku tried to explain this as politely as possible in one overly air-conditioned office after another: (a) that his house as envisioned wouldn't appear "out of place," as the contractors suggested ("This isn't the States"); (b) that Accra had always welcomed brave modernist architecture, just look at the futurist genius of Black Star Square; (c) that a compound around a courtyard was in fact a classically Ghanaian structure, expressly suited to Ghana's environment, which their show homes were not. Those were storehouses—not "homes"—for the stockpiling of purchases: tacky paintings, velour couches, plastic flowers, pounds of kitsch, Persian rugs, velvet drapes, chandeliers, bearskin throw-rugs, all completely out of context in the tropics. And cheap. No matter how massive they made them, with their three-story foyers and pillars and pools, the homes always looked cheap.

To which the contractors responded as politely as possible that he was free to leave their offices and never return. After the seventh such encounter Kweku tucked his little blueprint (the then-thirteen-year-old napkin) in the pocket at his heart and walked in no particular hurry out of the office, down the staircase, out the entrance, onto High Street.

Into brilliant glinting sun.

The humidity welcomed him back, open arms. He stood still for some moments, obliging the hug. Then hired a taxi to take him to Jamestown—the oldest part of Accra and the smelliest by far, a fetid seaside slum of corrugated tin-and-cardboard shanties in the shadow of the country's former Presidential Palace—where, braving the stink (re-dried sweat, rotting fish), he inquired in rusty Ga about a carpenter.

⌇

"A carpenter?" someone said, and hissed to someone else.

"A carpenter . . ." murmured someone else, and pointed down the alley.

"Carpenter?" The pointed-to someone laughed loudly, then shouted out, "The carpenter!"

An old woman appeared.

"The old man," she said, sucking what teeth she had left. A wave of quiet yeses rose and washed across the slum. "*Yes*. The old man who sleeps by the ocean." "*Yes*. The old man who sleeps in the tree." The woman sucked her teeth again, impatient with the addenda. "The old man," she said. "Get the small boy."

A girl appeared.

She'd been standing behind the woman, who was of such considerable width that she'd obscured the girl entirely, knobby braids and knees and all. Now she sprinted off obediently before Kweku could ask the obvious, e.g., if an "old man" was the answer or why he slept in a tree or what a "small boy" had to do with it. He supposed he'd find out. He leaned against the cab, wiped his face, crossed his feet. It was too hot to wait in the car sans A/C. The driver sat contentedly eating freshly smoked fish, the pride of Jamestown, blasting Joy FM Radio, "Death for Life." Reggie Rockstone, all the rage in Accra.

Not sixty seconds later the girl sprinted back, holding what looked to be her brother by the brittle-thin wrist. The boy was smiling brightly, possessed of that brand of indomitable cheerfulness Kweku had only seen in children living in poverty near the equator: an instinct to laugh at the world as they found it, to *find* things to laugh at, to know where to look. Excitement at nothing and at everything, inextinguishable. Inexplicable under the circumstances.

Amusement *with* the circumstances.

He'd seen it in the village, in his siblings, or in one: his youngest sister, dead at eleven of treatable TB. As a younger man himself, he'd mistaken it for silliness, the blitheness of the youngest, a kind of blindness to things. To be that happy, that often, in that village, in the fifties, one would've *had* to have been blind or dumb, he'd thought, but he was wrong. His sister saw as much as he, he'd come to see the night she died, when the one village doctor (a maker of coffins) had done all he could before dinner. His mother had gone to the fetish priest with a white baby goat (a fair trade: kid for kid), leaving the four elder siblings in their usual clump outside the hut, the two youngest inside it. Ekua his sister had lain coughing on her side on a raffia mat in a tangle of limbs, as jutting-out thin as a pyre of twigs, and laughing. "What are you doing?"

He was kneeling beside her and touching her neck, wondering how all this blood could just up and run dry, in mere moments, as predicted, just halt its hot flow. It seemed worse than implausible. A cruel joke, a lie. "You're not going to die," he'd said, feeling her pulse, with his fingers, his chest, throbbing ache in his lungs. Ekua was his ally, just thirteen months younger, born on Wednesday like him, with the same restless mind. And a glint in her eye and a gap in her teeth (as he'd find between Fola's five years up ahead). "You are not going to die." With conviction now, believing, in the spectacular mystery of the pumping of blood above the failure-prone prayers of the villagers outside or the slaughtering of goats or the prognoses of hacks. He'd touched her face, whispering, "You're *not* going to die."

She'd whispered back, smiling, eyes glinting, "I am."

And had, with a smile on her hollowed-out face, with her hand in her brother's, his hand on her neck, wide eyes laughing, growing wider and colder as he'd stared at them, seeing that she'd *seen* through them. Laughing at death. (Later in America he'd see them again, in the emergency room mostly, where eleven-year-olds die: the calm eyes of a child who has lived and died destitute and knows it, both accepting and defying the fact. Not with formal education, his preferred mode of defiance. Not with blindness, as he'd imagined of his sister until then.

But with precisely the same heedlessness the world had shown her, and him, all dirt-poor children. The same disregard.) Her eyes were still laughing. Disregarding of everything: tuberculosis, destitution, hack doctors, early death. Looking back at a world that considered her irrelevant with a look that said she considered the world irrelevant, too. She'd seen everything he had—all the indignities of their poverty; the seeming unimportance of their being to and in the wider world; the maddening smallness of an existence that didn't extend past a beach they could walk the whole length of in half of a day—without seeing herself undignified, unimportant, or small.

That brand of cheerfulness.

It broke Kweku's heart.

This was the third of his heartbreaks, the cleanest, though he couldn't have possibly known it was that. The girl approached gripping the wrist of her brother who smiled with his eyes, a small gap in his teeth. Not quite clear why she held him as if he would bolt when he seemed so delighted, so willing, to come. But like this. Kweku saw them and thought of his sister, her wide laughing eyes. Felt a knot in his chest. But not sadness, as the victim of a third-degree burn, a very small one, will feel nothing of the infection beneath. The same reason: severe nerve damage. Loss of sensation. The eschar cemented black over that part of his past.

He could see them all, the images—village doctor, elder siblings, braying kid, setting sun—playing mute in his head, but they were like scenes from a movie with a long-dead child star shot in grainy black and white before his cameraman was born. They inspired no emotion. Or no emotion he could identify. Just the sudden bout of wheezing he attributed to the heat. Not to hurt. He never "hurt" when remembering his childhood, which was rarely, even then, at forty-nine, having returned. He was circling in closer—toward the center, toward the starting point, same points—by then, Jamestown, an hour from home. But didn't feel it. Was in his mind still moving "forward," getting "farther," his whole life a straight line stretching out from the start.

So if ever the odd memory returned to him, caught up to him, billowing forward from behind him like tumbleweed in wind, he would feel only distance, the uncoverable distance, deeply comforting distance, and with it a calm. A calm understanding of how loss worked in the world, of what happened to whom, in what quantities. Never hurt. He didn't add it all up—loss of sister, later mother, absent father, scourge of colonialism, birth into poverty and all that—and lament that he'd had a sad life, an unfair one, shake his fists at the heavens, asking why. Never rage. He very simply considered it, where he came from, what he'd come through, who he was, and concluded that it was forgettable, all. He had no *need* for remembering, as if the details were remarkable, as if anyone would forget it all happened if he did. It would happen to someone else, a million and one someone elses: the same senseless losses, the same tearless hurts. This was one perk of growing up poor in the tropics.

No one ever needed the details.

There was the one basic storyline, which everyone knew, with the few custom endings to choose now and again. Basic: humming grandmas and polycentric dancing and drinks made from tree sap and patriarchy. Custom: boy-child Gets Out, good at science or soccer, dies young, becomes priest, child-soldier or similar. Nothing remarkable and so nothing to remember.

Nothing to remember and so nothing to grieve.

Just the knot in his chest, which he tried to laugh off, at the sight of those eyes on the face of that boy. The boy started laughing, too, quietly, delightedly, unaware that such laughter could break a grown man.

"Sa, are you fine?" he asked. His sister tugged his hand. The boy tried to stop smiling but couldn't. He stopped trying.

"I'm fine." Kweku smiled, straightened up, cleared his throat. He glanced at the old woman, who was glowering, bored. He looked at the girl, who was mopping her brow. He looked at the boy, who smiled hopefully back. And sighed. Could now see where this whole thing was headed. Asked, "You, what's your name?" though he already knew.

Kofi, the houseboy he'd sketched on the napkin.

"Kofi, sa," the boy said, holding out his free hand.

The woman sucked her teeth again, impatient with the pleasantries. "Take him to the carpenter," she said, and waddled off.

Mr. Lamptey.

The yogi.

Who "slept by the ocean" as advertised, a treehouse some thirteen feet high. Here, he served tea, a bitter brew of moringa he had harvested during Harmattan, he said. Lit a joint. "That's very old!" objected Kweku, reaching protectively for the napkin Mr. Lamptey was scanning intently mere inches from the joint. "So am I," quipped Mr. Lamptey, not lowering the napkin. In Ga: "That doesn't mean I'm going to go up in smoke."

Kofi laughed. Kweku didn't. Mr. Lamptey returned to the blueprint. A gentle breeze wafted in smelling of salt. They were sitting on the floor on braided raffia mats, the only seats in the large, airy cabin-like space. Decor notwithstanding, it was phenomenally well done: in lieu of walls slatted shutters, floorboards sanded down to silk. Kweku sipped his tea, mute, admiring the workmanship. After a moment ran his palm across the floor by his mat. Smooth. This was why he wanted to find a Ghanaian to build his dreamhouse. No one in the world did better woodwork (when they tried).

When he looked up Mr. Lamptey was watching him, smiling. "When did you build this?"

"It hasn't been built."

Mr. Lamptey chuckled softly. "But it has," he said firmly. Kweku waited for him to continue. He didn't. He puffed his joint.

"What do you mean, 'built'? You've seen a house like this in Ghana?"

"No," said Mr. Lamptey. "But *you* have, have you not?"

"Seen it where?" Kweku chuckled, not following the logic. But the answer drifted toward him: *in one instant, all there*. Mr. Lamptey tapped his forehead and pointed at Kweku. Kweku grew uncomfortable and shifted on his mat. "If you mean 'where did I design it,' I designed it in med school."

"In med school?"

"Yes. Medical school."

"But why would you do that?"

"Design a house?"

"Go to medical school."

"To become a doctor." Kweku laughed.

Mr. Lamptey laughed harder. "But why would you do that?"

Kweku stopped laughing. "Do what?"

"Become a doctor. You're an artist."

"You're very kind."

"I'm very old." The man winked. He held up Kweku's napkin. "And these? All of these rooms? They're for all of your children?"

"No."

"Patients?"

"Just me."

"Hmm." He turned over the napkin as if looking for a better answer.

Kweku said quickly, defensive, "There's nothing else."

"Just you." Another puff. Mr. Lamptey pointed to Kofi. "And him." Held up the napkin. "And this. 'Nothing else.'"

Kweku got up. "I'm not sure what you're getting at . . ." Mr. Lamptey exhaled a curling little tendril of smoke. But said nothing. "But I'm looking for a builder, not a Buddha."

"And have you found one?"

Kweku faltered. He said nothing. He had not.

This was his eighth such encounter and counting. The plot had been vacant for over a year. He looked at the carpenter, the "old man," this Mr. Lamptey, there cross-legged and cloth-clad, the six-pack contracted, the cataracts glowing bluish like the bellies of candle flames. He looked like some bizarre sort of African Gandhi. With ganja. Nonviolent. Nonplussing. Triumphant. Kweku wiped his face, took a breath as to speak. But for the first time since arriving noticed the *shhh* of the waves. So fell quiet. And stood there, feeling foolish now for standing, his head a few inches from the thatch roof above.

He considered the thatch pattern, which was vaguely familiar (though the memory was too heavy to catch up from behind: rounded hut in Kokrobité not an hour from this treehouse, its roof, also thatch, much, much higher than this one, conceived of by an eccentric not so different from Mr. Lamptey, absent father, wheezing sister: heavy memory, too slow).

A second breeze, smelling of a pyre of twigs.

Someone burning something somewhere.

Kweku suddenly felt tired. "If you can build it, by all means the project is yours."

Mr. Lamptey said simply, "I can and I will."

And did, in two years, arriving each morning at four, not a moment before or after, while the sky was still dark, to do sun salutations on the then-empty plot, sixty minutes more or less, until sunrise.

Kweku—afraid that his materials would be stolen, by appointment if he got a watchman, by yard boys if not (and they were costly materials, imported marble, slabs of slate; it wasn't cheap establishing order in overgrown grass)—slept in a tent in those days, the one Olu had forgotten, wiry Kofi keeping guard with their adopted stray dog. Around a quarter past five they'd be woken by the racket song, hammer banging nail, handsaw moving through wood, both more swiftly than a seventy-year-old should have been able to manage, and more elegantly than any blade he'd managed himself. Indeed, six months in he took to shadowing Mr. Lamptey once a week for an hour, sipping coffee, hanging back. Mr. Lamptey, who sang, but never spoke, while he was carpentering, consented to be watched but refused to be helped. So Kweku loitered, attentive, with his Thermos, in his glasses, not helping, merely observing with mounting jealousy and awe, trying to learn what he could of the eyes-half-closed *calm* with which the man made incisions. "You should've been a surgeon," he'd say.

Mr. Lamptey would suck his teeth, spit, answer opaquely, not pausing his sawing to puff on his joint. "I should have been what I was destined to be. I should be what I am," and on. But he built the house perfectly, i.e., precisely as instructed, an unprecedented occurrence for Kweku in Ghana. He had never hired a Ghanaian to do anything (or anything aesthetic) without that Ghanaian reinterpreting his instructions somehow. "No starch on my shirts, please," and the launderer would starch them, insisting, unrepentant, "It's better this way." Or "paint the doors white," and Kofi painted them blue. "Sa, is nice, oh, too nice," with the indefatigable smile. Mr. Lamptey made no changes, mounted no objections, offered no suggestions, cut no corners whatsoever.

Until his last week of work.

The issue was the landscaping, such as it was, there being less than a quarter-acre of land left to "scape." Most of the plot had been cleared for the house, with a remnant patch of jungle off the sunroom.

Mr. Lamptey considered the stick figures. "Hmm. What kind of trees are these?"

"Never mind that," Kweku muttered, considering the size of the plot. The pool would have to be smaller than he'd drawn it at the hospital, but there were four fewer swimmers to use it, so fair enough. They'd just need to chop down the mango, or uproot it. The thing was looming verdant in the middle of the view.

Mr. Lamptey laughed uproariously. He would do nothing of the sort. Had the mango ever harmed them, done them wrong in any way? To kill it would be like slitting his grandmother's throat. "A bit rich," Kweku said.

"I will not harm this tree."

"For chrissake, you're a carpenter. You *work* with harmed trees—"

"Jesus was a carpenter—"

"That's quite beside the point."

"You're the one who brought up Christ—"

"For fuck's sake, man, enough! *Enough!*"

Mr. Lamptey stared at Kweku, surprised by the outburst. Kweku stared back at him, surprised by himself. But determined, he imagined, to assert some authority. In fact, he felt his vision slipping slowly from his grasp. No children sleeping peacefully, no Fola swimming glistening, and if the mango remained standing, no beach of bleached white. The tree had to go. "I'll just hire someone else."

"You will not." Mr. Lamptey sat, saying no more.

Cross-legged and cloth-clad at the base of the mango for three days, two nights, smoking hash, keeping guard, rising at dawn for the yoga, otherwise immobile, and smug, Kofi smuggling him coconuts for water. He didn't eat anything for the duration of the sit-in but the mangoes that dropped to his side, perfectly ripe, and the soft wet white meat of the young hard green coconuts.

Scooping out the jellied flesh with relish.

. . .

"You can't sit here forever," Kweku sneered through clenched teeth, coming to stand in front of Lamptey on the second day of protest. Mr. Lamptey puffed his joint, closed his eyes, saying nothing. Kweku sucked his teeth, storming off. On the third day he threatened to call the police to have the carpenter removed from the property for trespassing. But looking at the man—seventy-two now, half-naked, wearing a necklace of red string with a bell on it—he couldn't. He imagined his cameraman filming the scene: Ghanaian sadhu dragged off by armed, bribe-fattened cops while grim Landowner smiles from the mouth of his tent. "This is *silly*," he said finally, unzipping his door, suddenly missing the sound of the hammer and saw. The Master Wing had been suitable for occupation for months, but he preferred Olu's tent, the plastic skylight. "You're almost done, man. Let's just finish what we started."

"With the tree," said Mr. Lamptey.

"Come on then."

Mr. Lamptey found a stick, began drawing in earth.

His vision for the view from the sunroom.

A garden.

Everything lush, soft, too verdant, nothing orderly or sterile, jagged love grass and fan palms the size of a child and scattered-around banana plants like palm trees without trunks and hibiscus on bushes and gloriosa in flames and those magenta-pink blossoms (Kweku can never remember their names) flowering wildly on crawlers overgrowing the gate. A commotion of color. Rebel uprising of *green*. "And a fountain here," Mr. Lamptey concluded.

"Whatever for?"

Some long, baffling answer about the layout of a sacred space, the necessity of water, appropriate proportions, blue, green. Kweku followed none of it. He rubbed his brow, sighing, "Bah! I can't maintain this."

"I can and I will."

"You're a carpenter. Not a gardener."

"I'm an artist. Like you—"

"Never mind. Plant your garden—"

"*Your* garden."

"Whichever."

Mr. Lamptey waited for Kweku to continue. Kweku looked away, kicked a rock, a white pebble. When he looked up Mr. Lamptey was walking, a touch naughty, in the direction of the half-finished sunroom. Kweku watched, thinking they should scrap the big windows (keep down the cost of A/C, what was the point with no pool). He pulled out the blueprint and looked at it, rueful.

Stick figures on napkin.

One: waving, dripping wet.

And the other: every Monday coming to sit in this little sunroom, scanning the *Graphic* until distracted, somehow happening to glance up, always shocked to find a human being standing in his garden, always forgetting that it's Monday, Mulching Monday, spilling coffee. Then their dance: the man's eyes on him waiting for acknowledgment while he dabs at his pants leg, the petulant delay, until he gives up and looks up, sighs, forces a smile. Little wave of the napkin, in salutation and defeat.

There in his swami clothes and gardening gloves is Mr. Lamptey. Smiling, clipping hedges, waving back.

7.

But to look at the mango in the middle of the garden now, gravid, in bloom, bushy head held up high, he cannot for the life of him imagine it gone—though he might have said the same of himself years ago. Then, when he held Sadie in the bowl of his fingertips, her whole being trembling with the effort to *be*, he'd imagined himself irremovable, a fixture in the landscape. Intrinsic to the picture. The center, somehow. Then, for the life of him, he couldn't have conceived of it, his absence from the life he was fighting to save. Of the landscape without him. An alternative view. Pulled up by his roots and replaced by a hole.

Still, he thinks of it now and it startles him, as earlier, when Taiwo dissolved silently outside the Living Wing door: with a pang, significantly sharper, so that he starts to fall forward and clutches the edge of the doorframe for balance. He shakes his head lightly, to knock the thought loose, but though it rocks back and forth, it doesn't tumble, doesn't fall. So he searches for another thought to bowl this one over, something duller, with more weight than his absence. He thinks:

what are you doing out here staring at a garden?

It works. The spell breaks. The pang ebbs. He snaps back. Short of breath. "Grab a hold of yourself," he mumbles aloud, partly coughing, partly chuckling to ensure that his cameraman knows that he, too, finds these musings absurd, that he's not going crazy, was just lost in thought; indeed men lose their way in their thoughts all the time. Some oxygen is all, merry jaunt in the blossoms, make peace with the mango, smell roses, all that. He pushes the sliding door the rest of the way open.

He steps off the ledge to the garden and gasps.

. . .

Dewdrops on grass.

On the soles of his feet:

sudden, wet, unexpected, so shocking they hurt.

Only now does he notice that he's not wearing slippers, with the sting of the cool on his bare-bottomed feet. How long has it been since he's gone outside barefoot, gone *anywhere* barefoot, felt wet on his feet? Can't recall. (Decades prior, in the darkness before daybreak with the ocean beside, moon above, long ago.) He jerks himself back as if jumping off coals, fully conscious. Thinks: where are my slippers?

8.

For many years after, when Taiwo thinks of her father, she'll picture him here in the garden like this, with his feet in the grass and the dew on his feet, and she'll ask herself: *where were his slippers?* It is the least of all questions unasked and unanswered, the least of what's wrong with the picture—man down, perhaps poisoned by an illiterate (Olu's secret belief) or just dead in the tradition of people who just die (Mom's) or punished by God for his various sins (Sadie's) or exhausted by them (Kehinde's)—but Taiwo will ask. *Where were his slippers?* When she thinks of her father, when she lets the thought form or it slips in disguised through a crack in the wall she and Kehinde erected those first lonely midnights in Lagos.

It was a game in the beginning, as everything became there, a game between the two of them to keep them both sane somehow: never being allowed to say "father" or "dad" and having to pay if you slipped, a penalty the other twin chose (usually sneaking into the kitchen to steal milk biscuits for the both of them, three-packs wrapped in plastic, perfect for hiding for later use).

That was how they built the base.

Next they rewrote the stories.

This was a game they played mostly at night in that sticky second bedroom with the overhead fan and two creaky twin beds, the only room in the house that wasn't furnished with a working A/C. Taiwo would go first, telling some story from Boston, like the time he woke them up in the middle of the night and made them put on their snowsuits and piled them in the Volvo and drove them to Lars Andersen Park.

It was two in the morning and the snow had just fallen, the whole vista white, a dog barking somewhere. He pulled five plastic sleds from the trunk of the car while they gawked at him, wide-eyed, Mom sucking her teeth. "Kweku, no," she hissed softly, just now cottoning on, clapping her fingers together. Woolen mittens. "We'll get arrested."

Sadie wasn't born yet.

The snow fresh and perfect.

The park dark and empty.

Stars winked their consent.

They didn't get arrested. They sledded until dawn, even Mom, whispering, laughing, delirious with joy, with the mischief of it, ashy-skinned, an improbable picture: an African family playing alone in the snow.

But the way she retold it, their father wasn't in it. It was Mom's plan, night-sledding; there were four sleds, not five. Then Kehinde would tell one. And so on and so forth, short stories of snow, until they both fell asleep. Until the man was erased—from their stories and so their childhoods (which only existed *as* stories, Taiwo knew this, still knows). Not dead. Never dead. They never wished the man dead or pretended he was dead. Just deleted, walled off. Denied existence, present only in absence and silence. Reduced to a notion. No more than a thought. And a thought, which in itself was an arrangement of words, i.e., words they didn't use—so, a thought they didn't think.

Time passed and this wall grew higher.

Time passed and this wall grew weak.

Until, without warning, a thought. *Where were his slippers?* And again a week later. The crack in the wall. It was the one thing they forgot to erase from their stories, the disease-carrying mosquito on the evacuation plane: not a moment or a memory, a remembered detail in an anecdote, but a detail in *every* anecdote, omnipresent, the ground. So they missed them, didn't delete them, let them stay where they were, where they've remained, present, latent, fomenting the past.

The slippers.

Battered slip-ons, brown, worn to the soles. Like leather pets with separation issues, loyal, his dogs. And his religion, what he believed in, the very basis of his morality: mash-up cosmopolitan asceticism, ritual, clean lines. *The slipper.* So simple in composition, so silent on wood, bringing clean, peace and quiet to God's people the world over, every class and every culture, affordable for all, a unique form of protection against the dangers of home, e.g., splinters and bacteria and harm caused to wood, i.e., hand-scraped oak floorboards, fifty dollars per square foot. He'd visit other houses and take notice first and foremost of whether the family "practiced" slippers, all other judgments from there. And if anyone came to visit—God forbid, Taiwo's friends, the teeming hordes of high-pitched classmates who had crushes on her twin—there he'd be, at the ready, in the doorway, "Do come in!" Gesturing grandly to the basket that he kept by the door.

Like a bin of rental ice skates.

Every style of slipper. Thick quilted-cotton slippers from fancy hotels, brilliant white with padded insoles and beige rubber treads; shiny polyester slippers bought in Chinatown in bulk, electric blue and hot pink, embroidered dragons on the toes; stiff, Flintstones-looking flip-flops from the airport in Ghana (whence the crazy MC Hammer pants in *gye nyame* print). Kehinde's blushing stalkers almost always chose the dragons, glancing encouragingly at one another as they kicked off their Keds, pledging silent solidarity as they bravely marched in to this strange new world smelling of ginger and oil.

"Omigod, Taiwo, your dad's so *adorable!*" one would giggle, reaching into her uppermost register for *adorable*.

"Omigod, Taylor, you're so *artificial*," she'd be mocking when Kehinde appeared at her back. Materializing out of nowhere as only he could, without sound, entering the foyer in Moroccan babouches.

"Hello," he would greet them, sounding shy, speaking quietly. Not really shy, Taiwo knew. Not really interested was all.

Hi was a three-syllable word in their mouths. *Hi-i-i*. As they caught sight of Kehinde, and blushed. Taiwo would observe this in Westin Hotel slippers. Four blond ponytails bowed in reverence before her brother's babouches. Jealousy and bemusement would tangle, a knot. When the girls looked up Kehinde was gone.

Ninja slippers.

A religion or a fetish, like a form of podophilia—or so it suddenly seemed to Taiwo, encountering the word in eighth-grade Classics. Rather, *auto-podophilia*. She wrote this neatly in her notebook, shading the *o*'s in with her pencil while someone asked, "Then what's a pedophile?"

The teacher's nervous laughter was a distant sound in Taiwo's head, the shading of the *o*'s her more immediate concern. She was thinking of her father and the lavish care he gave his feet: the salt scrubs and the peppermint oils and the vitamin E before bed. *Love of feet*. But later they'll return to her, this laughter and its nervousness, the tension in the teacher's face, the classroom air, the titters, every movement, sound, and image, every instant of that moment, plain: precisely the kind of moment one never knows for what it is.

An end.

A warning shot.

A boundary mark. Between "the way things were" and "when everything changed," a moment within which one notices nothing, about which one remembers all. Which is the point. The difference between Taiwo's life at twelve, before everything changed, and the life that came next is this: not noticing. Not having to notice, not knowing to notice. That she never looked out. Not "innocent" as such—she's never thought herself innocent, not as Kehinde was innocent, of judgment, distrust—but *insular*, contented in the world in her head, a whole life taking rise from her dreams, her own thoughts.

She was thinking just then of her father's "love of feet," of his love of *his* feet, when someone asked about pedophiles and, half paying attention, she wrote the word down. A person who loves children. Who loves his own children.

Pedophile.

Auto-pedophile.

Auto-podophile.

And then. That familiar tingling in the pit of her stomach, the butterflies she felt when she knew she was right. Excitement and comfort and satisfaction mixed together with a touch of something heavier, more sinister: relief. Relief that she *knew*, that she'd gotten it right, tinged with terror at what might happen were she one day to be wrong. This is what she remembers most clearly ever after and laughs at most cruelly, her self-satisfaction that day: that she'd answered correctly, as she might have at a spelling bee, the question of who was her father?

One who loved his own feet and who loved his own children.

Misunderstanding the Greek *phile*, the connotation of "love." And misunderstanding her father, who would abandon his children and who hated his feet, as she discovered that night.

Rather, morning.

Four A.M., the house frozen in silence, Taiwo staring at the ceiling, her hands on her ribs. Suffering "middle insomnia," as yet undiagnosed. She got up and went to the kitchen.

Generally, when she couldn't sleep, she'd sneak in to Kehinde through the little trap door at the back of her closet. There she'd stand silently at the foot of his bed looking down at his face, watercolored by moon, and marvel how *serious* he looked fast asleep; he could only look serious, only frowned, when he slept. Awake, he looked like Kehinde. Like her, but with a secret, his gold-brown eyes hiding a smile from his lips. She'd smile at his frown until he, without waking, smiled back at her, eyes closed, a smile in his sleep. Just the one. A small smile, fifteen seconds and not longer, his eyelids still restive with Technicolor dreams. Then she'd blow him a kiss and return through the closet to her bed, where she always fell promptly asleep.

Instead, she went down the back stairs to the kitchen, one of several secret passageways lacing that house. This was the Colonial she hated, in Brookline, which the man had bought proudly after Sadie was born (and though Mom had wanted a townhouse, South End, pregentrification; better value for money, she'd said, and was right). It was perfectly lovely. Red brick with black shutters, white trim, gable roof, ample yard in the back. But comparing it to the massive Tudor mansions of their neighbors, Taiwo found the house lacking. Anemic somehow. (She'd laugh to herself that first evening in Lagos, in the car passing streets that made Brookline look broke.)

She went into the kitchen and opened a cupboard.

Then opened another.

Then reopened the first.

Olu had just started at Milton Academy and was insistent upon eating what prep school kids ate. The cupboards were now stocked with mysteriously named products like Mi-Del Organic Lemon Snaps. She closed the cupboard. Opened the fridge.

There was a remnant Capri Sun behind the Apple & Eve apple juice. She stabbed in the straw, drank the juice in one sip. Then threw out the carton and glanced out the window, clamping her hand against her mouth to stop the scream.

There, gazing back at her, alarming in moonlight, was the statue of the mother with the hand-carved stone twins. It looked like a child between the silhouetted fir trees, a four-foot-tall alien-child, glowing pale gray. She hated that thing. They all hated that thing. Even Mom sort of secretly hated that thing. She'd unwrapped it on Christmas, said, "I love it, Kweku! *Thank* you," and stood it after dinner by itself in the snow.

Taiwo laughed softly, her heart pounding loudly. She decided she should check all the locks on the doors. Just in case some little alien-child was roaming around Brookline trolling for lemon snaps. The back door was locked. She tiptoed through the dining room, which no one ever dined in, to the cold, empty foyer to check the front door. She almost didn't notice the figure huddled in the sitting room, which no one ever sat in (except important, slippered guests), to the left, off the foyer through the grand Moorish arch with the two sets of couches and red Turkmen rug.

Almost.

She was slipping through the darkness to the doorway when she turned her head a half-inch to the left and there he was.

. . .

Slumped on the couch, his feet propped on a footrest, his head tipped down, leaden, his lips hanging slack. He was still in blue scrubs, lightly spattered with red, as if he'd left the OR and gone straight to the car. His white coat was pooled on the floor where he'd dropped it. Both slippers had slipped from his feet to the rug. The moon from the window behind him fell brightly on the bottle of liquor still clutched in his palm.

She froze in the foyer. Her heart resumed pounding. She glanced at the stairs, trying to think, walk or run? She knew she'd get in trouble if he woke up and saw her, not for sneaking, for not sleeping, but for seeing him like this. Collapsed on the couch with his mouth hanging open, his coat on the floor, his head slumped to his chest. She'd never seen her father so—*loose*. Without tension. He was always so rigid, so upright, strung taut. Now he looked like a marionette abandoned by its manipulator, puddled in a jumble of wood, limbs and string. She knew he'd be furious to know he'd been seen so. She knew she should tiptoe-sprint back up the stairs.

But couldn't. Or didn't want to. She wanted to disturb him. She wanted to revive him, make him wake up, *sit* up. So, she went and stood in front of him as if he were Kehinde, at the edge of the footstool in front of his feet, then recoiled, hand to mouth again to keep herself from crying out with shock at all the bruises on the bottom of his feet.

How she'd never seen them was beyond her, is beyond her now, to think she'd only ever seen the one side of his feet, the smooth. The soles, by sharp contrast, were chafed, calloused, raw, the skin black in some places, puffed up at the toes. It was as if he'd quite literally crossed burning sands barefoot (in fact, had gone shoeless for most of his youth). Taiwo pursed her lips shut to mute her revulsion, but what she felt next had no shape and no sound:

an odd emptiness, weightlessness, as if she were floating, as if for a moment she'd ceased to exist: some new odd sort of sadness, part grief, part compassion, a helium sadness, too airless to bear. In the future, in adulthood, when she feels this same airlessness, when she feels her very being rushing out of her like breath, she'll long to touch and be touched, to make contact (and will, with an assortment of consequences). This longing, like most things, was innocent at birth, taking root in her hands and her fluttering heart: the urge to touch, to kiss his feet, to kiss-and-make-them better. Put her father back together. But she didn't know how. She didn't have the answer. She didn't know this father. She knelt. Began to cry.

She was frightened for reasons she couldn't explain, by a sense beyond reason but clear all the same: that something was about to go horribly wrong if it hadn't already, that something had changed. Most of this was her inexplicably keen intuition (along with middle insomnia, undiagnosed at age twelve). But it came without thought, a feeling completely without narrative. An opening up.

Something had opened somewhere.

The fact of her father here slumped in the moonlight meant something was possible that she hadn't perceived: that he was vulnerable. And that if *he* was—their solid wooden father—then that she was, they all were, and worse, might not know. He had hidden the soles of his feet her whole life, for twelve years; he could hide (anyone could hide) anything else. And finally, that he'd tried, that he had a thing to hide, meant her father felt shame. Which was unbearable somehow.

She rested her head on the stool by his feet. Whispered, "Daddy," touched him lightly. He continued to snore. "Wake up," she persisted. "Wake *up*." But he didn't. She noticed the slippers by her knees on the rug.

As gently as possible and as silently as she could, she slipped one of the slippers onto one of his feet. It dangled like a shoe on a shoe tree. Then the other. At the very least the bruises were hidden from view.

"No," he said, barely.

Taiwo leapt up in panic, taking a single bound back from the window and moon into the depth of the dark where, concealed by the shadow, she closed her eyes, waiting for yelling. It didn't come. He made another noise, a wet, fast-asleep noise, murmured "no" again, softly, then silence. Then snoring. She opened her eyes and stepped forward, still fearful. His head was now upright. He was talking in his sleep.

"It was too late," he said, just as perfectly clearly as if he knew she was standing there watching him speak. But didn't smile in his sleep as Kehinde would have at this juncture. His head slumped back over.

She ran for the stairs.

For all the years after, when Taiwo thinks of her father, when the thought slips in slyly through that crack in the wall—and the picture of him dead in a garden slips with it, his soles purpled, naked, for anyone to see—she'll ask herself hopelessly, "Where were his slippers?" and as she did when she was twelve, she'll start to cry.

9.

Where are his slippers?

In the bedroom.

He considers.

His second wife Ama is asleep in that room, plum-brown lips slipped apart, the plump inside-pink showing, and he doesn't want to wake her. A wonder the change.

Quite apart from the performances for himself and his cameraman, there is this new and genuine desire to accommodate his wife. It's as if he's a different (kinder) man in this marriage, which that Other Woman would argue is not his second but his third. That Other Woman is lying and the both of them know it: they were never close to married (though she'd lived in his house. He'd been desperate for warmth, for the weight of a body, the smell of perfume, even cheap Jean Naté. The thing had gone bust when she'd broken her promise to leave the apartment that morning in May, so as not to see Olu, who'd come for his birthday at last and who left at the first sight of June). With Ama, whom he married in a simple village ceremony, her incredulous extended-family members watching, mouths agape, he is gentle in a way that he wasn't with Fola. Not that he was brutish with Fola. But this is different.

For instance.

If he raises his voice and Ama flinches, he stops shouting. Without pause. Like a light switch. She flinches, he stops. Or if she passes by his study door and coughs, he looks up; no matter what he's doing, what he's reading, Ama coughs, he stops. His children used to do the same, intentionally, just to test him, to weigh his devotion to his profession against his devotion to them. By then he'd moved the sextet to that massive house in Brookline, a veritable palace, although his study door, an original, didn't close. They'd loiter in the hall outside the half-open door, giggling softly, whispering loudly to attract his attention, then peer in to see if he'd look up from reading his peer-reviewed journal, which he wouldn't, to teach them. It was a logically flawed experiment. He'd have told them if they'd asked. His devotion to his profession kept a roof over their heads. It wasn't comparative, a contest, either/or, job v. family. That was specious American logic, dramatic, "married to a job." How? The hours he worked were an *expression* of his affection, in direct proportion to his commitment to keeping them well: well educated, well traveled, well regarded by other adults. Well fed. What he wanted, and what he wasn't, as a child.

When Ama loiters noisily—and she is testing him also, Kweku knows—he marks his sentence and lowers his book. He gestures that she enter and asks if she's all right. She always says yes. She is always all right. And if they're riding in the Land Cruiser and she shivers even a little, he orders Kofi, who's started driving, to turn off the A/C (though he can't stand the humidity, never could, even in the village; they used to mock him, call him *obroni*, albeit for other reasons, too). And if he's watching CNN when she comes padding into the Living Wing in pink furry slippers, pink sponge rollers in her hair, he switches the channel instantly to the mind-numbing cacophony of the Nolly-wood movies that he hates and she loves.

And so forth: attends church (though he can't stand the hoopla), buys scented Fa soap (though he can't stand the smell), instructs Kofi to make the stew to her exact specifications (though he can't stand the heat, weeps to eat it that hot). He wants her to be satisfied. He wants this because she can be. She is a woman who can be satisfied.

She is like no woman he's known.

Or like no woman he's loved.

He isn't sure he ever knew them, or could, that a man *can* know a woman in the end. So, the women he's loved. Who knew nothing of satisfaction. Who having gotten what they wanted always promptly wanted more. Not greedy. Never greedy. He'd never call his mother greedy, neither Fola nor his daughters (at least not Taiwo, at least not then). They were doers and thinkers and lovers and seekers and givers, but dreamers, most dangerously of all.

They were dreamer-women.

Very dangerous women.

Who looked at the world through their wide dreamer-eyes and saw it not as it was, "brutal, senseless," etc., but worse, as it might be or might yet become.

So, insatiable women.

Un-pleasable women.

Who wanted above all things what could not be had. Not what *they* could not have—no such thing for such women—but what wasn't there to be had in the first place. And worst: who looked at him and saw what he might yet become. More beautiful than he believes he could possibly be.

Ama doesn't have that problem.

Or he doesn't have that problem with Ama.

First of all, she isn't as smart as the others. Which isn't to say that she's stupid. Far from. He knows that people talk, that people call the girl "simple," and he knows it's cliché, surgeon shacks up with nurse. But he also knows now that his wife is a genius, of a completely differ-ent sort than her predecessors were. She has her own form of genius, a sort of animal genius, the animal's unwavering devotion to getting what it wants. To getting what it *needs*, without disrupting the envi-ronment. Without tearing down the jungle. Without causing itself harm. He wouldn't have guessed this a talent at all, but for those smarter women's gifts of self-flogging, self-doubt.

Ama doesn't hurt herself. It doesn't occur to her. To question her-self. To exact from her psyche some small payment of sorrow for all worldly pleasure, though the world demands none. But she isn't a *thinker*. Isn't incessantly *thinking*—about what could be better, about what to do next, about what she's done wrong, about who may have wronged her, about what *he* is thinking or feeling but not saying—so her thoughts don't perpetually bump into his, causing all kinds of friction and firestorms, explosions, inadvertently, collisions here and there around the house. Her thoughts are not dangerous substances. The thoughts of the dreamers were landmines, free radicals. With them breakfast chat could devolve into war. Ama isn't a fighter. She comes to breakfast without weapons and to bed in the evening undressed and unarmed. She has no vested interest in changing his mind. Her natural state is contented, not curious. And so second of all, she isn't unhappy.

This was a complete revelation.

To live in a house with a woman who is happy, who is consistently happy, in her resting state—happy? And who is happy *with him*, not as an event or a reaction, not in response to one thing that he did and must keep doing if he wants her to remain happy, churning the crank, ever winding the music box, *dance, monkey, dance!*—but whom he makes happy, has made happy, and who's miraculously *stayed* happy? Who has the *capacity* to stay happy, with him, over time?

Never.

He didn't know this was humanly possible, or womanly possible, until fifty-three years old, when he packed up his tent and decamped to the Master Wing but finding it too quiet one day considered his nurse, and the rise of her buttocks, and the chime of her laugh, and the odd way she tittered and blushed when he approached, and asked if she might like to join him for dinner?

This is why (he believes) he loves Ama.

Because she said, "Thank you, I would, please," and the same thing again when he asked her to marry him (she always says yes) and is loyal and simple and supple and young. Because her thoughts don't explode over breakfast. He believes he loves Ama because of the symmetry between them, between his capacity for provision and her prerequisites for joy. Because he finds all symmetry elegant and *this* symmetry quiet: an elegant kind of quiet, here and there, around the house. He believes he loves Ama—although he once thought he didn't, thought he cared for and was grateful for but didn't "really love" her, and in the beginning he didn't, before he recognized her genius—because he knows something, now, about women. He has come to understand his basic relationship to women, the very crux of it, the need to be finally sufficient. To know he's enough, once and for all, now and forever.

This is why (he believes) he loves Ama.

He is wrong.

In fact, it is because as she sleeps at night, with a thin film of sweat above her ripe plum-brown lip and her breath sounding sweetly and loudly beside him, she looks so uncannily like Taiwo. Like Taiwo when she wasn't yet five years old and when he was a resident, postcall, staggering home, too tired to sleep, too sleepy to stand, too worked up to sit—and so pacing.

He'd pace to and fro about the narrow apartment (the best he could afford on his resident's pay, the dim, skinnier half of a two-family duplex on Huntington Ave where the ghetto began, beneath the overpass that separates Boston from Brookline, the wealth from the want) in his scrubs, in the dark. Down the hallway, through the kitchen, to the first room, the boys', with its rickety wooden bunk bed, Kehinde's drawings on the walls. To the little windowed closet, from which he'd watch some minor drug trade. To the bathroom, where he'd wash his face.

Press a towel to it.

Hold.

But finally to the front room and to Taiwo on the pullout couch, with no bedroom of her own as he so wanted her to have, his first daughter, a complete mystery despite the resemblance to the brother. A girl-child. A new thing. More precious somehow.

With a thin film of sweat above her lip care of the "project heat."

Which he'd wipe away, thinking *it's the least I can do.*

For a girl with no bedroom and conch-shell-pink lips.

Where he'd fall asleep upright, sitting next to her.

. . .

In fact, he loves Ama because, asleep, she looks like Taiwo when his daughter wasn't five and slept sweating on the couch, and because when she snores she sounds just like his mother, when *he* wasn't five and slept sweating on the floor. In that same thatch-roofed hut where his sister would die, on a mat beside his siblings' by the one wooden bed, where their mother snored sweetly and loudly, dreaming wildly, as her son listened carefully to the places she went (to the operas and jazz riffs and snare drums and war chants, to the fifties as they sounded in faraway lands, beyond the beach), dreaming aloud of on-the-radio-places that he'd never seen and that she'd never see. And this sight and this sound, these two senses—of his daughter, (a), a modern thing entirely and a product of *there*, North America, snow, cow products, thoughts of the future, of his mother, (b), an ancient thing, a product of *here*, hut, heat, raffia, West Africa, the perpetual past—wouldn't otherwise touch but for Ama.

A bridge.

Loyal and simple and supple young Ama who came from Kokrobité still stinking of salt (and of palm oil, Pink Oil, evaporated Carnation) to sleep by his side in suburban Accra. Ama, whose sweat and whose snores when she's sleeping close miles of sorrow and ocean and sky, whose soft body is a bridge on which he walks between worlds.

The very bridge he'd been looking for, for thirty-one years.

He thought when he left that he knew how to build one: by returning home triumphant with a degree and a son, laying the American-born baby before the Ghana-bound grandma like a wreath at a shrine, "See, I told you I'd return." And with a boy-child on top of it, a luckier-Moses. A father and a doctor. As promised. A success. He imagined this moment every day in Pennsylvania, how his cameraman would film it, panning up to her face. Cue strings. Tears in mother's eyes.

Wonder, joy, amazement. The awe of the siblings. The jubilation. Cue drums. Then the dancing and feasting, fish grilled, a goat slaughtered, red sparks from the fire leaping for joy in the sky, a black sky thick with star, the ocean roaring contentedly. The reunion a bridge, her fulfillment the brick.

This is how he planned it.

But this isn't how it happened.

By the time he returned she was gone.

10.

Heartbreaking winter, 1975.

A one-bedroom hovel.

A wife of one year.

Who was sitting at a table in the "kitchen," i.e., a corner where a stove and sink were shoved against a wall with a tub. He entered in an overcoat. He hated this particular overcoat. A bulk of dull beige from the Goodwill downtown. She'd insisted that he buy it and now demanded that he wear it. It was the warmest thing he owned, but it made him look poor.

He came into the apartment, looking poor. She looked gorgeous. She always looked gorgeous, even angry, to him. She wore bell-bottom jeans and a wraparound sweater, both care of the Goodwill, a scarf in her hair.

No, not a scarf, he saw, looking more closely. A gold-flecked *asooke*, the Nigerian cloth. Nigerians were far more artful than Ghanaians with their head wraps. "More flamboyant, more ostentatious," they Ghanaians liked to chide. But at that moment he saw otherwise: more insistent upon beauty. At all times, in all things, insistent upon flair. Even here, in this hovel, wearing secondhand clothing, at a table by a tub, she insisted on flair. Had found this gold cloth, no doubt expensive, from her father, to sort of wind around her Afro puff, true to her name. "Wealth confers my crown." *Folasadé*. She looked gorgeous.

He came into the apartment and froze at the door.

Her hands were folded neatly on the red plastic tablecloth, the kind that you buy for a picnic, then bin. They'd snuck it home, embarrassed, from his orientation barbecue. She thought it cheered things up a bit. Flowers, too. Of course. Everything looked as it always looked. The bed was made. The baby was sleeping. And breathing, he checked quickly.

Because something was wrong.

He stopped at the door knowing something was wrong.

He didn't see the letter lying flat on the table. Only Fola as she turned her head, neck taut with fear. She didn't speak. He didn't move. His cameraman slipped in the window. In this scene: a Young Man receives Horrible News. He set down his bag now. To free both his hands up. For whatever he might have do with them, given whatever she had to say.

She said, "Your mother is ill, love." She held up the letter. "Your cousin got our address from the college and wrote."

These were too many words to make sense of at once. *Mother. Ill. Cousin. Address. College. And wrote.* Which of his cousins even knew how to write? This mean, specious question somehow washed to shore first. "My cousins are illiterates! They know nothing!" he bellowed, not knowing why he was shouting, or at Fola. "It's a lie!"

She just watched him, with that expression, with her brows knit together and her mouth folded over, an upside-down smile. Only yesterday he'd noticed that she made this face with Olu, too, whenever he was wailing to communicate complaint. The brows knit together, the head slightly sideways. "*Okunrin mi*," she'd say. My son. "I know, I know, I know. It hurts."

And she did. In the literal sense could "feel others' pain." A proper empath, a thing he hadn't believed existed when they met. His questions were endless. Where in her body did she feel it? How did she know it was his pain, not hers? (In her chest, on the left, a purely physical sensation, of foreign origin, now familiar, proper empathy.) That face.

"Darling," she said.

"It's a lie," he repeated. But quietly. And was glad now to find his hands free. He grabbed his head, spinning, his gloves to his forehead, a futile attempt, keep the brain in one piece. "She's never been ill for a day in her life. How? What are they saying?" He went to her side.

She handed him the letter, touching his free hand with hers. It was that cheap air mail paper no one uses anymore, flimsy pastel-blue sheets that, folded up, became envelopes.

All caps, slanting upward.

Unsteady black pen.

The letter didn't say that his mother was ill. It said she was dying and would be dead in a month. It was two weeks old yesterday. He dropped it to the table. His hands began to tremble (other parts of him, too). Fola jumped up and wrapped her arms around his shoulders. For the first time since he bought it, he loved this beige coat. Its thickness put some distance between her chest and his trembling, his wife and his weakness, his quivering limbs. (And his cameraman in position across the room by the window couldn't shoot the crumbling hero for his dull protective coat.)

"We'll go to Ghana," she said.

"With what money?" he mumbled. "We don't have the money."

"We'll ask for it—"

"*No.*" And carried on, desperate, "They're overreacting . . . it's an infection, not cancer . . . she's not even fifty. She'll be better by New Year . . . I'll have the money by New Year . . ."

"We'll ask for it, Kweku. We have to."

They did.

Rather *she* did: that day spent the last of her cash on a ticket to Lagos to visit a louse, younger half-brother Femi, whose prostitute mother had taken her dead lover's money and run.

Then Ghana, and the smell of Ghana, a contradiction, a cracked clay pot: the smell of dryness, wetness, both, the damp of earth and dry of dust. The airport. Bodies pushing, pulling, shouting, begging, touching, breathing. He'd forgotten the bodies. The proximity of bodies. In America the bodies were distant. The warmth of it. Pushing through the jostling throng, warm bodies, clutching Fola's arm while Fola clutched the baby, leading his squadron on to the taxi rank. "Your purse!" he called over his shoulder. "Be careful! This is Ghana."

"It *is?!*"

But when he looked she was laughing. "My friend, I'm from Lagos. Never mind your small Ghana." She winked. "I'm okay. We're okay."

And then home.

They rode into the village in a ramshackle taxi, a red and yellow jalopy expelling black smoke, bumping awkwardly up the dark red dirt road, no one speaking, even Olu sitting silently, as if in his baby-heart he knew. This wasn't how he'd envisioned the triumphant return, political hysteria on the radio sans John Williams strings, but this driver was the only one working the rank who both accepted his price and knew the way to his town.

An hour outside of the city: the ocean.

Unannounced, without fanfare.

Just suddenly *there*.

From town they'd braved the then-unpaved road to the junction, where they'd turned up the dry empty hill to Kokrobité. The hill brought them down to the coast, blocked from view by the mounds of grass lining the left of the road. Then, abruptly, a clearing: cowed grass lying low before sand, sea, sky, endless. The dramatic reveal. The thing that was there all along, less surprising than startling, the scope, how it changed things. The air.

It was seven in the morning, he could tell without checking, by the men seated tugging in nets from the night: at least ten of them, eleven, in a vertical line along the end of a rope that stretched far out to sea. *Heave-ho.* Forward, backward, a perfected synchronization, hauling, all, with one movement like rowers on sand in once-bright colored T-shirts (much like the T-shirts sold at Goodwill), all the palm trees leaning with them. Fronds fluttering in the breeze.

He must have made some sound as he stared out the window because Fola laid a hand very lightly on his. As she did. Never taking, never "holding" his hand, just lightly laying hers on top. A choice. To hold or be held. He held her hand absently, not turning from the window. Unable to, glued there, transfixed by the view, with the first few tears forming now, loosely, like cumulus, clouding his eyes, too unripe yet to fall. The effect was to soften the edges, a filter, the beach sparkling gray in celestially blurred light, like a scene from those soaps all the nurses loved watching: irresistibly gripping if you only knew the plot. (And he did. Basic storyline. Dancing, sap, grandmas.) He stared like the nurses, through unfalling tears.

Why had he hated this view? Of this beach, of the backs of these fishermen, glistening brown, of the long wooden boats, evangelical names in bright tricolor paint on their splintering sides, *Black Star Jesus*, *Jah Reign*, *Christ the Fisher of Men*, in the red, yellow, green of the national flag and the national spirit of open-source ethos, this mixing of Anglican, Rastafarian, Ghanaian? What was there to hate in this? There was only openness. As far as he could see. A cheerful openness. An innocence. An innocent beach on the road to Kokrobité at seven A.M., November 1975, little country lurching, cheerful, unaware, to revolution. Little taxi lurching, blasting revolution, to grief.

And then her.

Not a bridge, her fulfillment the brick.

No jubilation, no drumming, no goats, and no fish.

Fola stayed waiting with his half-sisters Shormeh and Naa, their eyes filed with old hate and new grief. A crowd had gathered excitedly as they'd alighted the taxi and lingered now watching as he entered the hut. No one needed details (irresistibly gripping). His cameraman, among, didn't follow him in.

He ducked as he entered, forgetting his height. Or its size, this small shanty, his childhood home. He carried his son, half asleep, six months old then, the American-born boy-child, to her.

The one bed.

She was lying on her back with her arms at her side, with the mats on the floor, the same mats he remembered. Dark, and so cool with the dome overhead. It was a well-structured hut, however minimal. Rounded clay walls with the massive thatch roof sixteen feet at its peak, a triangular dome. His father had built it. An artist, they told him, a Fante, a wanderer, a "genius like him." (He'd been jailed after punching a drunk English sergeant who'd hassled his wife, jailed, then publicly flogged. There by the tree in the middle of the "compound," this cluster of huts. Stripped to shorts at midday. "He left," said the villagers simply. Thereafter. Just packed up his things, walked away, as he'd come. Others, now dead, claim he walked into the ocean in a sparkling white *bubu*, to his waist, then his head, without stopping. Further, forward, under, *into* the ocean. Like Jesus. With weights. Under moon. Into black.)

His brother looked surprised as he entered but said nothing. "Leave me," he said to his brother. His brother left.

She could have been sleeping from the way she was lying there. He'd heard families say this and chuckled before. "We thought she was napping," of beloved old Grandma, rushed putrefied to hospital days after death. *Idiots*, he'd think. Now he understood the confusion. She looked like she was sleeping. But was making no noise. Wasn't dreaming of the places that she'd never been to.

She was dead, in the village, the only place she'd ever go.

His heart broke in one place. The first break. He didn't feel it. Olu giggled, soft, the only sound in the room. Kweku looked at Olu, suddenly remembering that he was holding him. Olu looked, awestruck, at the butterfly on her toe.

Black and blue (swordtail), just coming to rest, an almost neon shade of turquoise, black markings, white dots. It fluttered around his mother's foot, a lazy lap, then lifted off, flapping blithely toward the triangular dome and out the little window. Gone.

"This is your grandmother." Changed the tense. "*Was.*" Olu looked at Kweku, not recognizing the voice. And he at his mother. "I told you," he mustered. "I told you I'd return—" but couldn't manage the rest.

So he sat on the floor, on a raffia mat. In the heat and the smell of it, the stench of new death. He rubbed Olu's back until the child fell asleep (fifteen minutes, not more, such a well-behaved boy). Then stayed in semidarkness, who knows for how long, maybe hours, with the sunlight changing, shifting, on the wall.

He didn't think what he thought he'd think. That he shouldn't have left. Without saying good-bye. That the last time he saw her—when they'd had that horrid argument about whether he should accept the full scholarship or not, when she'd said that he was needed *here*, not "Pencil-wherever"—he shouldn't have said what he said.

That she was "jealous."

Of course she was jealous. She was thirty-eight years old. She had never left Ghana. Her youngest daughter was dead. Her genius-husband had absconded with the tide in the moonlight (or abandoned her, more likely, unable to face her for shame). Now here was her son—her genius-son, sixteen, shoeless—trying to abscond with American missionaries to the president's alma mater (motto: "if the son shall make you free, ye shall be free indeed." Indeed. And if the son shall win a scholarship?). In her mother-heart she knew.

That he would *not* "go and come," that there was nothing to come back to, that he would learn—as she had wanted, a gifted youngster herself, plucked from school at age seven to fetch firewood and water—and leave. As she wanted.

It didn't need to be said.

Those thoughts came later. (And for many years after, when he'd try to unsmell the damp stench of new death.) What he thought as he sat was: how different the quiet. It had never been this quiet in this hut, growing up. And that he might have rather liked it if he only could have *sat* in it, like this, alone and quiet. And that she must have felt the same. This is why she'd made them all wake up so early and leave the hut, all of them, five A.M., *out!*, not for "idle hands" or "early birds," or whatever else the mission had Ghanaian mothers hawking to their *pikin* in those days. It was so she could lie on her back on her mattress in silence and solitude, arms at her side. Just looking at the reeds arching in toward the center high above her. Clever structure: on your back it felt huge. Clever lover: hoping, praying, that he'd one day make the widow "wife"—the one with the little black transistor radio that she carried with her everywhere she went like a pet—had designed his mud hut so a girl on his bed would look up and feel distance, expansiveness, height. She'd sent them away so she could: feel some distance. Some quiet. Just lie there. Five, ten minutes max. Soon they'd be back from the well and their washing, six children (then five), two boys, four skinny girls. Soon the whole hut would be full of their motion, then so full of moisture, they'd all go outside.

Now, five A.M., she could lie, still, in silence, the waves nearby making what wasn't quite noise. Perhaps admiring the genius of her runaway husband? At peace for a moment with the cards she'd been dealt? A woman, born in Gold Coast, in 1941, with the whole world at war with itself. But not here. Here at the edge of the world, the frayed edges. Here frozen in time pounding yam into paste. Fetching firewood and water. Watching boats push off, wistful. Above all things wanting to *go*.

Finally, Fola, from outside the hut.

"Darling," very gently. "Are you in there?"

He wasn't. He was nowhere, he was missing, he was outside of himself. "I'm here."

"Is the baby . . . ?"

"The baby's asleep."

But he knew what she meant: that it was wrong in some way to have new life so long in the presence of death. He lifted up the baby and handed him out to his mother, leaning in, her head tipped to the side.

"Just another minute." As if he were in a bathroom.

He stayed until midnight, the tears too unripe.

11.

His second wife Ama is asleep in that bedroom as he loves her most: dreaming, a bridge made of flesh. So he won't get his slippers. He'll go make the coffee. It can't be past four A.M.—what woke him up?—now he doesn't remember—what day is it? Sunday. Kofi's day off. No more banging of nails. Just the silence and stillness. Aloneness and quiet. He thinks, *I rather like it*, this odd sense of pause. Of the morning suspended between darkness and daybreak, and him suspended with it, adrift in the gray. Too late to resume sleeping, too early to get going. On pause for the moment. The coffee, he thinks.

And is turning to go in to decamp to the kitchen when he sees the thing, barely, from the corner of his eye. There is no way of knowing what would have happened to him otherwise, had he not seen, remembered, and thought of her face. Had he continued out of the sunroom through the door into the Dining Wing, through the dining room, to the kitchen, to make mocha and toast. Most likely he'd have noticed the constriction in the chest and the shortness of breath and known instantly: *go*. Would have tracked down the heparin in the medicine closet—unrushed, hyperfocused—then tracked down a phone. Would have called his friend Benson, another Ghanaian from Hopkins who now runs a high-end private hospital in Accra (and who just yesterday rang and left a very strange voicemail, something about having seen Fola here in Ghana; couldn't be). Would have gotten hold of Benson, agreed to meet him at the hospital. Would have found his sneakers waiting by the door for his run. Would have tried to think back, as he laced up his laces, to the first of the chest pangs (*too beautiful sometimes*). Would have glanced at the clock. Thirty minutes. Easy peasy.

Would have driven to the hospital, leaving Ama who can't drive. And so forth.

Would have noticed.

And so known.

And so gone.

But he sees the thing, barely, bright turquoise and black.

Just coming to rest on a blossom, bright pink. When it comes to him suddenly: the name, by her face.

"Bougainvillaea," he hears her saying.

"It sounds like a disease. The patient presented with bougainvillaea."

"You be quiet." She sucked her teeth.

But when he looked she was laughing. At the sink, hands in blooms, small, magnificent, magenta. "Absolutely beautiful," he said.

"Yes. Aren't they?"

"No. You are."

She laughed again, blushing. "You be quiet," but quietly. A smile taking shape. The sun from the window behind her a backlight. He thought to go hold her. Beheld her instead.

Why did I ever leave you? he thinks without warning, and the pang sends him reeling off the ledge to the grass. Once again his bare soles—which for years have known nothing but slipper leather, sock cotton, shower stall—object. The coldness, the wetness, the sharpness of grass blades. He takes these in, trying to unthink it, to breathe. But the words don't relent, nor the shortness of breath. Just the *why did I ever leave you*, a song on repeat (with the bridge yet inaudible in the distance, *too soon*) as he buckles now, gasping, brought low by the pain. "I don't know," he says aloud and to no one, but he's lying. He closes his eyes; in the dark sees her face. Her brows knit together. Her mouth folded over. The voice of a woman. *I know, I know, I know.*

So it's come to this, has it? Here barefoot and breathless, alone in his garden, no strength left to shout? Not that it would matter. He is here in the garden; she is there in the bedroom unplugged from the world. The houseboy at home with his sister in Jamestown. The carpenter-*cum*-gardener-*cum*-mystic comes tomorrow. Who would hear him shouting? Stray dogs or the beggar. And what would he shout? That it's finally cracked? No. Somehow he knows that there's no turning back now.

The last time he felt this was with Kehinde.

12.

A hospital again, 1993.

Late afternoon, early autumn.

The lobby.

Fola down the street in her bustling shop, having moved from the stall at the Brigham last year. A natural entrepreneur, a Nigerian's Nigerian, she'd started her own business when he was in school, peddling flowers on a corner before obtaining a permit for a stand in the hospital (carnations, baby's breath). When he'd graduated from medical school and moved them to Boston, she'd started all over from the sidewalk again: by the lunch cart (falafel) in the punishing cold, then the lobby of the Brigham, now the stand-alone shop.

Sadie, almost four, in white tights and pink slippers, doing demi-pliés in her class at Paulette's.

Olu, high school senior and shoo-in at Yale, attempting doggedly to break his own cross-country record.

Taiwo, thirteen, at the Steinway in the den attempting doggedly to play Rachmaninoff's *Prelude in C Sharp* while Shoshanna her instructor, a former Israeli soldier, barked instruction over the metronome. "Faster! *Da!* Fast!"

And Kehinde at the art class Fola insisted he take despite the exorbitant expense at the Museum of Fine Art three short train stops away on the Green Line, up Huntington, where Kweku was to meet him after work.

Except Kweku never went to work.

He left, calling "Bye!" as he did every morning: in his scrubs and white coat, at a quarter past seven, with Olu waiting for carpool, and the twins eating oatmeal at the breakfast nook table, and Fola braiding Sadie's hair, and Sadie eating Lucky Charms, and National Public Radio playing loudly as he left. "Bye!" they called back. Three contraltos, one bass, Sadie's soprano "I love yooou!" just a second delayed, breezing only just barely out the closing front door like a latecomer jumping on an almost-missed train.

He started the Volvo and backed down the driveway. He pushed in the cassette that was waiting in the player. *Kind of Blue.* He rode slowly down his street listening to Miles. The yellow-orange foliage a feast for the eyes. Pots of gold. In the rearview, a russet brick palace. The grandest thing he'd ever owned, soon to be sold.

He drove around Jamaica Pond.

He drove under the overpass.

He drove toward their old house on Huntington Ave. He slowed to look out at it. The old house looked back at him. A window cracked, bricks missing, stoop lightly littered. It looked like a face missing teeth and one eye. Mr. Charlie, former owner, would have turned in his grave. Such an attendant to detail. Kweku had liked him so much.

American, from the South, with a limp and a drawl. Had lost his wife Pearl over a year before they moved there but still kept her coat on a hook in the hall. He'd given them a 25 percent discount on rent because Fola tended Pearl's orphaned garden in spring, and because he, Kweku, doled out free medical advice (and free insulin), and because they were "good honest kids."

Kweku had always greeted him with the Ghanaian *Ey Chalé!* to which Mr. Charlie always responded, "Tell that story once more 'gain." (The story: in the forties the officers strewn around Ghana were known as Charlie, all, a suitably generic Caucasian male name. Ghanaian boys would mimic *Hey Charlie!* in greeting, which in time became *Ey Chalé*, or so Kweku had heard.) But no matter the man's insistence, they couldn't call him by his first name, so well steeped were he and Fola in African gerontocratic mores. Mr. Charlie would hear nothing of sir or Mr. Dyson. ("Mr. Dyson was my daddy, may the bastard rest in peace.") So "Mr. Charlie."

Mr. Chalé.

Had driven a bus. Prepared brunch for his sons every Sunday after church, then dispatched them to various DIY projects around the house: rehinging doors, replacing bricks, restoring wood, repainting trim. When he passed (diabetes), the sons inherited the house. The older one said unfortunately the discount was null, effective immediately, given the cost of the funeral next week, to which "Quaker" was invited with "Foola" and the kids. The younger one—the handsome one, his late father's favorite; a charmer and a drug dealer, unbeknownst to his father—took Kweku to the side at said funeral, a modest funeral, to say in a soft, almost soothing bass murmur, that given their respective lines of work—respectable work, not so different, his and Kweku's, they both sold "feeling better"—if Kweku could access any meaningful quantities of opiate, a new discount might be arranged.

Now the house was in ruins. *A ruin*, thought Kweku. Like a temple

on a roadside, cracked pillars, heaped trash. Less a lasting commemo-
ration of the efforts of the worshippers than a comment on the useless-
ness of effort itself. A face missing teeth among similar faces. A
falling-apart monument to Charlie's life's work: lover, husband, father,
bus driver turned homeowner, turned widower, turned statistic (dia-
betic, black, bested by brunch).

How did we live here? Kweku wondered. *All six?* And in back, where
even sunlight looked dirty somehow? He didn't know. A car honked.
He glanced back. Was blocking traffic. Glanced back at the house,
which seemed to say to him: *go*. He didn't want to go where he was
going, to go forward, but he couldn't stop moving or stay here or come
back. He nodded to the house and pulled out into traffic. In the rearview bricks missing. (He never saw it again.)

He drove to the Law Offices of Kleinman & Kleinman and parked
just a little ways down from the door. It was a free-standing building
with a massive front window, the windowsill crowded with overgrown
plants. The receptionist, in her sixties, sat facing this window peering
idly through the ferns at the road now and then. While still typing.
Always typing. She never stopped typing. Her varicosed fingers like
robots gone wild.

Kweku had noticed that when he parked outside the window she
would peer through the thicket and recognize his car. This gave her
just enough lead time to have at the ready that pitying look when he
walked through the door. He hated that look. Not the frown-smile of
sympathy nor the knit-brow of empathy but the eye-squint of pity. As
if by squinting she could make him appear a little less pathetic, soften
the edges, blur the details of his face and his fate. Biting her lip as with
worry—while still typing. Not that worried.

The pitter-patter rainfall of fingers on keys.

He walked up the sidewalk and entered the building. A bell jingled thinly as he opened the door. "Me again," he said, as she looked up and squinted.

"You again," she said with the bitten-lipped smile. "Marty's waiting to see you."

Kweku tried to breathe easy. Marty was never in early, liked to make people wait. If he was waiting for Kweku then something was wrong. The cameraman appeared and began setting up his shot. A Well-Respected Doctor receives Horrible News. "All right then."

"Very well then."

"So, I'll just . . . ?"

"Go in, yes."

"Of course." Stalling. "Thank you."

Still typing. "Good luck."

Marty didn't bother with pitying looks. "Listen to me, brother. We fought the good fight." Frazzled hippie turned attorney, one of the best in Massachusetts, six foot five, massive shoulders, massive belly, massive hair. Had hopped the Green Tortoise to Harvard Law from Humboldt County as the embers of the Movement went from glowing-orange to ashen-gray, etc. A lawyer's lawyer. Put his feet on the desk. Crossed his hands behind his head, his great shock of silver coils. "You've spent hundreds . . . of thousands . . . of dollars . . . trying to fight this. They're not backing down, man. It's eating you alive."

Kweku laughed mirthlessly. Not them, her, the family, but *it*, nameless, faceless. The monster.

The machine.

It was what he'd called the hospital when he first got to Hopkins, so awestruck had he been by how well the thing worked. By how shiny, how brilliant, how clean and well ordered, how white-and-bright-chrome, how machinelike it was. He loved it. Loved ironing his clothes in the mornings on a towel on the table by the tub, sink, and stove, his white coat, the short coat worn by students. Loved walking, still wide-eyed with wonder, into the belly of the beast.

He'd step off the elevator and stop for a moment to hear the machine-sounds: clicking, beeping, humming, hush. To breathe the machine-smells: pungent, metallic, disinfectant. To think machine-thoughts: clean, cut, find, pluck, sew, snip. He felt like an astronaut wearing astronaut-white landed recently and unexpectedly on an alien ship. Newly fluent in the language but still foreign to the locals. And later like a convert to the alien race.

Later, in Boston, when he'd finished his training, when he'd actually become a doctor, well regarded at that, he'd stride through the white and chrome halls at Beth Israel feeling part of the machine now and stronger for it. It was a feeling he never dared share with his colleagues, who'd take his pride in the hospital for lack of pride in himself: that he still felt so special, even superior, for being there. For being part of the machinery, when the machine was so strong. In control. The net effect of the show, the audiovisuals, the squeaky clean of the OR, nurse-slippers squeaking on floors, was to communicate control: over every form of messiness, over human emotion, human weakness, dirtiness, sickness, complications. It was the reason, he thought, they built churches so big and investment banks so impressive. To dazzle the faithful. Arrogance by association. The machine was in control. And so he was in control who belonged to it.

Then the machine turned against him, charged, swallowed him whole, mashed him up, and spat him out of some spout in the back.

"It was wrongful dismissal," he said without feeling, his thousandth time saying it.

And Marty's thousandth and first: "This we know," pitching a tent of his fingers on the hill of his belly. "We just can't *prove* it." Heavy sigh. "God knows that I want to. God knows that I've tried to. You're an incredible doctor, an incredible man." He tapped an unwieldy pile of files with his foot. "Have you actually read any of these character references?"

"I have not."

"You can practice wherever."

"I was wrongfully dismissed. I should be practicing *there*—" Kweku heard himself and stopped. He sounded like a teenager, a recently dumped girlfriend still desperate to be back in her tormentor's arms.

Marty cleared his throat. "Net net. They threw the kitchen sink at us. Shit. You were there. There was too much at stake. With the clout of the Cabots, they had to do something, so they let you go, right? But you took them to task. Then they couldn't just say, 'Yeah, okay, we fucked up, we threw you under the bus.' Though they did. 'Cause you're black. Right? 'Cause then it becomes: is Beth Israel racist? And this being Boston that question is . . . booooom!" A sound and a gesture to imply an explosion. "All these hospitals are connected. It'll be hard to work here. But it's a big fucking country. Move the kids to California . . ." and continued, but vaguely, halfhearted, by rote.

He'd said it all before. Kweku had heard it all before. Kweku had said what he'd say in reply all before. They were like a bickering couple headed for certain divorce who, too exhausted to concoct new accusations to hurl, nevertheless keep on slinging the same tired lines, afraid that even a moment of silence will mean an admission of defeat.

Marty fell silent.

Kweku felt nothing. Not panic, as he'd suspected, given the money he'd spent. Just numbness. Almost pleasant. He looked around the office. One of Boston's best lawyers, and the place looked like shit. A dim low-ceilinged unit behind a glorified strip mall with wall-to-wall

carpet and cheap plastic blinds. Kweku stared out the window behind
Marty, a mirror image of the window at the front of the building. No
plants. Gold two-story trophies for basketball and paperweights, those
rocks cracked in half to reveal gemstones inside. Crusted amethyst,
Fola's birthstone, refracting the light.

Kweku stared past the gems, at the trees.

Marty's view was the parking lot at the back of a strip mall that bor-
dered an incongruous little evergreen wood (or what was left: less a
wood than a band of survivors, five firs spared the chain saw). Kweku
stared at these trees. So at odds with the landscape. Which must have
been forest once, green not this gray, and once theirs, before concrete,
B.C., their native landscape. "The trees are native Americans." He didn't
at first realize he'd said this aloud. His eyes passed by Marty, who was
staring at him worriedly, as one regards a crazy who's finally snapped.

"The trees are native Americans?" Marty repeated. "Is that code?"

"This land is their land." Kweku pointed. "There, behind you—
never mind."

He fell silent.

Marty shifted: took his feet off the desk, stretched his arms,
rubbed his hair, slapped a hand on a file. "So whaddaya wanna do,
man? I'll do as you direct me. I mean, it's me you've paid these hundreds . . . of thousands . . . of dollars." Dry laugh. "But if you want my
professional opinion? This is the end of the road."

Kweku didn't want Marty's professional opinion. He wanted his land
back, his forest, his green. He got up without speaking and walked out of
the office. Into the anteroom, past the receptionist. The rainfall on keys.

"Dr. Sai!" she called after him. "Your invoice—" but Marty stopped
her, coming to lean against the doorframe of his office. "Let him go."

Kweku kept walking. Out of the building (a thin jingle), down the
sidewalk, to the Volvo where he'd parked in the shade. *Let him go, let*

him go, let him go, let him go. That's all these white people were good for was letting him go.

"I am afraid we have to let you go."

Silence, the length of the table.

So long.

An oval-shaped table with squat-rounded armchairs that looked like they spun, like the Cups ride at fairs. With half-circle armrests and leather upholstery, red with brass studs, and the hospital trustees. A room in the hospital he'd never before seen on the uppermost floors where the offices were, but familiar at once from a lifetime of interviews: med school, scholarship, residency, fellowship, mortgage, loan.

A Room of Judgment.

With the requisite, oppressive Room of Judgment decor: polished wood, Persian rug, unread books with red spines (maximum number, countless books, dark red books no one read), heavy drapes through which dribbled in bright, hopeless light, swirls of color, feasting colors, plums, mustards, and wines. And white faces. The odd woman. An Asian woman.

Who spoke.

"Having reviewed all the details of Mrs. Cabot's appendectomy and of the complaint that the Cabots lodged against you therewith, this body believes that, though a phenomenal surgeon, you failed . . ."

But Kweku couldn't hear her.

He could hear only Fola—at twenty-three years old, with her law school acceptance letter framed on the wall, with a full ride to Georgetown and Olu in utero—say, "One dream's enough for the both of us." She would follow him to Baltimore and postpone studying law and give birth to their baby with not a penny to their name and sell flowers on the sidewalk and take showers in a kitchen so that one of them could realize his dream. Twenty years exactly from that to this moment, the whole thing erected on the foundation of a dream: "general surgeon without equal," Ghanaian Carson and the rest of it, Boy-child, good at science, Makes Good—and he had. He had seen the thing through, the whole kit and caboodle: the accolades, the piano lessons, the sprawling brick house, the staggering prep school tuition, the calling "Bye!" every morning at a quarter past seven in scrubs and white coat. He had held up his end of the bargain: his success for her sacrifice, two words that they never said aloud. Never *success*, because what were its units of measurement (U.S. dollars? Framed diplomas?) and what quantity was enough? And never *sacrifice*, for it always sounded hostile when she said it and absurd when he attempted, like he didn't know the half. The whole thing was standing on the sand of this bargain, but they never dared broach it after "One dream's enough." When they fought they fought around it, about the diapers or the dishes or the dinner parties with colleagues (part of his job, waste of her time). But they knew. Or *he* knew: that her sacrifice was endless. And as the Sacrifice was endless, so must be the Success.

He would see the thing through—if he could, and he prayed so, he blushed to admit that it was what he wanted most, to be worthy of the Pan-Nigerian Princess as they'd called her, that sophisticated escapee from the '67 war with the bell-bottom jeans and the gap in her teeth, so much smarter and sexier than everyone else, even him, at little Lincoln, a princess among plebs—not by having succeeded but by *being* a success. To be worthy of Fola, to make it worth it for Fola, he had to keep being Successful.

. . .

So quite literally couldn't process the words that came next, if there *were* words that followed "you failed."

Then eleven months arguing that he hadn't, in court, hadn't failed, had been fired without cause. Which he had. She'd waited too long to be rushed to the hospital, where they'd taken too long to decide to proceed. Seventy-seven-year-old smoker with a ruptured appendix and a bloodstream infection, days old. Not a chance. Jane "Ginny" Cabot—patron of research sciences, socialite, wife, mother, grandmother, alcoholic, and friend—would be dead before morning, whether in a bed at Beth Israel or in bed on Beacon Hill, the higher thread count. The only reason Kweku had even attempted the appendectomy was because the Cabots had called the president of the hospital, a family friend, to suggest very politely that in light of their donation surely a last-ditch operation wasn't too much to ask? It wasn't. And they wanted the very best surgeon. The president found Kweku as he was leaving to go home.

The Cabots looked at Kweku, then back at the president. "A word," they said politely, then moved into the hall. Kip Cabot, losing his hearing, spoke too loudly for the acoustics. "But he's a—"

"Very fine surgeon. The finest we have."

The Cabot family physician, smug, a general practitioner (on retainer, a kept doctor, tanned, salt-and-pepper hair), stayed with Kweku in the office while Kip continued in the hallway. "And where did you do your 'training'?" Air quotes.

"In the jungle, on beasts," Kweku answered genteelly. "Chimpanzees taught. Great instructors. Who knew?"

The deliberators returned from the hall at that moment, everyone flushed to varied shades of unnatural pink—but resolute. Whatever else he was, Kweku was fit to operate. Someone thumped him on the shoulder. Kweku addressed himself to Kip. "In my professional opinion, sir, it's too late for surgery. But the longer I stand here the more useless I become."

The Cabots didn't want his professional opinion.

They wanted him to go and scrub in.

Hours, bloody business, trying to save the woman's life, with the president there observing from the gallery upstairs (apologetic, so embarrassed, "I gave my word to the Cabots"), but a masterful operation as per usual. His best. Clean, cut, find, pluck, sew, snip. Wipe blood from face. Until a weary nurse called it—time of death three A.M.—and he left, walked out, got into his car, let out his breath.

He still doesn't know how he drove himself home. The next thing he remembers is waking up, clothed, in the sitting room of all rooms with the Johnnie Walker Gold and his slippers sort of dangling from the tops of his toes and the smell of kiwi-strawberry inexplicably in the air and the sense that something somewhere had changed.

Then eleven months pretending that it hadn't.

That nothing had changed.

Getting out of bed every morning, leaving the house (scrubs, coat, briefcase) like the Singaporean protagonist in that movie he never saw but always discussed as if he'd seen it, having read all the reviews, it being fashionable among surgeons to see Asian-language films. According to the reviews, the man is fired from his bank but, too ashamed to tell his family, still pretends to go to work: getting up, suiting up, going to sit in local parks to scan job ads.

Like that.

But no parks.

He'd leave, drive to Kleinman & Kleinman for an update, long-term park, then cross the bridge to Harvard Law School on foot. Once there, he'd flash his plainly fraudulent alumni ID card—care of Marty's black classmate and doubles partner Aaron Falls—to the plainly underpaid Latino law library security guard whose accent produced the daily joke, "Good morning, Mr. False."

In the stacks until two o'clock researching cases: wrongful dismissal, discrimination, malpractice. Break for lunch. Then more reading, until evening, when he'd cross back to Boston, the river liquid gold in the gloaming.

❦

Now Marty, too, was letting him go.

He started the car.

But had nowhere to go.

He started to laugh. He had nowhere to go. He laughed harder. Had nowhere to *pretend* to be going. He was clean out of money. He was defeated. He was delirious. He was driving for some minutes before he realized he was driving. Driving, he discovered, as if these hands were not his, as if this foot were not his, to the hospital.

A word.

A word with Dr. Yuki, Dr. Michiko "Michelle" Yuki, who had patronized from her Mad Tea Party cup. "This body believes . . ." she the mouth of the body. Tiny mouth. Monotonic, multisyllable words. Former gymnast. Five foot zero with an asymmetric pageboy and the four-piece Harvard Box Set: B.A., M.D., Ph.D., M.B.A. He'd been to her house for a dinner in Cambridge. She was married to an attorney, a colleague of Marty's. The dinner was to celebrate her promotion to vice president. There were slippers in the foyer, he had noticed. Lovely home. The husband was a monstrosity, all curse words and bluster, piss drunk before the hors d'oeuvres had lapped the room once, but the room was so elegant, all woods and wind orchids, calligraphy scrolls cascading down the walls. Lacquer bowls.

A word with Dr. Yuki.

Or a question. Just the one. What he'd been wanting to ask and to ask to her face (or to half of her face: a good 50 percent was missing behind the shiny half-curtain of her asymmetric bob). Simply: how was she sleeping? Dr. Yuki the surgeon? Not the M.B.A., the administrator. The do-no-harm doctor. For the other one, the aspirant, the suit? Fair enough. Agent Yuki had her bottom line, her shareholders to please. One of Boston's richest families, one of the hospital's biggest donors, "the stakes were too high," as per Marty, not to act. The family had demanded that someone be held accountable. "These things sometimes happen" was not accounting enough. So in a back room over a weekend—a Room of Judgment but with cocktails—it was decided that the surgeon would be fired. Would that work? Would that appease the Cabots? Yes, thank you, it would, please. Fair enough, Agent Yuki.

But Dr. Yuki?

She knew.

She knew what it took, to scrub in, to say, "scalpel," to saw through the stomach with sharp sterile steel. *She* knew the great pride that he took in this terror, the joy—not just he but their whole prideful tribe. *She* knew that the procedure had been flawlessly executed. *She* knew, Dr. Yuki, and nevertheless when she spoke, it was to fire a good surgeon to appease a strong family, to say that he'd failed to "account for the risks."

Though no doctor (but one) would agree with her assessment. Though her boss, the hospital president, had watched the surgery himself, that final insult-added-to-injury that almost cost them the lawsuit and would have were the judge not Ginny's cousin.

Almost.

In the end it didn't matter. The machine was in motion. It ate all the letters, the petitions, the appeals, colleagues arguing his case, that he'd done all he could, that they couldn't have done better. To no avail. There was doubt. Dr. Putnam "Putty" Gardener—trusted Cabot family doctor, widowed Kip's DKE frater, Boston Brahmin, racist, golfer— was insistent that the surgeon had (a) failed to appreciate and (b) failed to communicate the risks.

And that was that.

Now the surgeon wanted a word with the hospital vice president, to ask her to her face was she sleeping through the night? And so found himself parking (at some remove, out of habit), walking casually through the lobby, just as calm as could be, the Jamaican security guard Ernie smiling warmly as he entered—always happy to see the doctor (one) who knew his first name, who said "Good morning, Mr. Ernie" on arriving every morning and "My best to the kids" on departing every night, instead of blowing by blindly without greeting, without *seeing* him, as if the guards were inanimate, were lobby decor—then riding up in the elevator, alone, to the offices, here pausing for a breath to hear the uppermost-hush—and onward, down the hallway in his scrubs and white coat, knocking once before barging in her door.

By the time they were dragging him back through the lobby, eyes bloodshot from shouting, a madman in scrubs, he'd forgotten entirely about the Museum of Fine Art class and Kehinde three train stops away.

So almost choked to find the child now appearing in the lobby having waited thirty minutes for his father to turn up before figuring that his father had gotten tied up in the surgery so he'd foot it to the hospital and wait there instead. Until this very moment Kweku would've bet money that her younger son couldn't have said where he worked—not the name of the hospital, one of several in the vicinity, nor the location of the entrance hall—but here Kehinde was: appearing calmly in the lobby at precisely the same moment two men dragged a madman across it.

"Get your hands off me!" he was shouting at the security guards.

And Ernie at his colleagues, "He's a doctor here! Stop!"

And Dr. Yuki at Ernie, "He's *not* a doctor here, excuse me! He was fired! Last year!"

Just as Kehinde appeared.

Just like that. Out of nowhere. As only he could, without sound, with leather art portfolio tucked underarm.

The guards, who were white, looked at Dr. Yuki, who was pink, little hands and mouth trembling with rage beyond words. She nodded to them once, a Hong Kong mobstress to her henchmen, and was smoothing down her skirt to go when Kehinde caught her eye. She drew back the curtain to squint at his eyes, as if drawn to some dangerous light source, too bright. Kehinde, squinting back at her, could feel what Dr. Yuki felt, the barrenness, so sad for her. He bit his lip with worry. Dr. Yuki saw his pity, and he felt her stomach fill with shame.

Spinning on her kitten heels, she click-click-clicked away.

The guards looked at Ernie with genuine regret and shoved Kweku, without, to the sidewalk outside. Kehinde sort of stumbled next—too stunned to speak—through the revolving door, surprised to find the world, too, revolving.

Late afternoon.

Orange sun.

They were still for one instant, Kweku catching his breath with his hands on his knees and his eyes on his knuckles, and Kehinde beside him, portfolio to chest like a float, eyes wide with silence. The very next instant a Brewster pulled up, all assaulting red lights and assaulting red noises, and true to its nature the machine sprang to life as if nothing had happened (nothing important). Paramedics poured out of the back of the ambulance, emergency department residents from the building, en masse, even Ernie had his function: clearing visitors out of the way to let the stretcher (screaming woman, crowning son) come rushing through. From the curb where he stood, Kweku made out Dr. Yuki waiting, stone-faced, by the elevator as the stretcher passed behind her, either deaf or indifferent to the cloud of pure chaos that blew past her back. Getting in, going up.

Out of habit, without looking, he took Kehinde's elbow. He did this—touched his family when there was chaos in their midst, just to feel them, feel their body warmth, to keep them close as best he could, as close as he came to physical affection—but the gesture felt preposterous now. He in his scrubs, beard unshaven, eyes wet, having been "fired last year!" and now forcibly removed: comforting Kehinde, so collected, spotless shirt tucked in neatly, pressed, always so impassive? Preposterous. He let go.

So many things Kweku wished in that moment: that he'd spent more time with Kehinde trying to learn to read his face, that the boy was watching *him* spring to life outside the hospital, saving lives and playing hero through the chaos in their midst, that he'd vetoed the art class (better yet, could afford it), that he'd parked a little closer to avoid this walk of shame. He was burning with the desire to say something brilliant, something wise and overriding, a burn behind the ears. But all he could think of was "I'm sorry you saw that."

"Sight is subjective. We learned that in class."

Kehinde looked at Kweku, his head slightly sideways, his brows knit together. An upside-down smile.

They got in the car.

Kind of Blue.

He turned this off.

He drove around the pond, the sun beginning its descent. He drove without looking, without needing to, from memory. Seeing instead of looking. He drove home by heart. Past the little public school, abandoned in the evening time, seen instead of looked at looking lonely somehow. Past the sprawling mansions—were they always this massive? Their house seeming suddenly so modest, compared. Past the teeming trees—were there always this many? Like ladies-in-waiting along the side of the road. Around the third of four rotaries (the pride of Brookline, gratuitous rotaries). Past a man and dog jogging. Past some point of no return.

The leaves on their street were ablaze in the sunset. He pulled into the driveway and turned off the car. He knew, though didn't think it, that he couldn't face Fola now (knowing, not knowledge), that he couldn't brook the sight. To see Fola's face on Kehinde's for that instant was sufficient. To see his failure on Fola's seemed too much to bear.

The light above the garage came on. All the lights in the house were on. Neither he nor Kehinde stirred nor spoke to acknowledge not moving. They sat as men do: side by side, facing forward, both silent and patient, waiting for something to say. "Do you want to see my painting?" Kehinde asked after a while. Kweku turned to him, embarrassed. He hadn't thought to ask.

"Thank you, I would, please."

Kehinde nodded. "One second." He unzipped his portfolio and pulled out the piece.

. . .

Even in bad light it was breathtakingly beautiful. Not that Kweku began to know how to judge a piece of art. But it didn't take an expert to see the achievement, the intelligence of the image, the simplicity of the forms. A boy and a woman, from the back, holding hands. Kweku pointed to the woman. "Who's that?" Though he knew.

"That's Mom," Kehinde answered.

"And that must be you."

"No, that's—"

"Olu?"

"Um, no."

"But it's a boy, right?"

"It's you."

"Me?!" Kweku laughed. A sudden sound in the quiet.

". . ." Stalling.

Still laughing. "But why am I so *small*?"

"Because Mom says she always has to be the bigger person."

Kweku laughed so hard now he started to cry. "Genius."

A small smile, fifteen seconds and not longer. "You like it?"

"I love it. Pure genius." He caught his breath. "She *does* say that, doesn't she?"

"With 'don't I' at the end of it. I always have to be the bigger person, *don't I*?"

Kweku laughed harder, tears streaming down his cheeks. "Right."

Kehinde giggled bashfully and glanced at the house. "It was supposed to be for Mom. But you can have it if you want it."

"I would love that. She won't mind?"

"Mom? No. She has loads."

"Right." It was he who didn't know that they had birthed a little Basquiat, not she. She was the parent. He was the provider. He stopped

GHANA MUST GO

laughing. "I'd l-l-love it." His voice breaking (other parts of him also). "How do I . . . take it?"

"I roll it. Like this."

"Wait. Don't you have to sign it first?"

"Only famous artists sign their paintings."

"Only foolish artists wait until they're famous. Do you have a pen?"

Kehinde was smiling too widely to speak. He reached for his back-pack. Kweku stopped him.

"Use this." He plucked the silver pen from his unused scrubs pocket (a graduation gift from Fola, for prescriptions, engraved). Kehinde took the pen and turned it over in his fingers.

"It's so nice. Where'd you get it?"

"From your mother. Of course."

Kehinde nodded, smiling. Another glance at the house. He laid the painting on the dashboard to consider where to mark. Kweku considered Kehinde with some wonder at the change in him: how at ease he became as his hand touched the paper, how his shoulders relaxed, breath released, standing down. *He* was the same with a body on a table, silver knife in lieu of silver pen. How had he missed it?

So often he'd confided in Fola at night that he just didn't "get" this slim good-looking boy; unlike Olu who reminded him so much of himself, Kehinde was a veritable black hole. Fola always said something vague in reply about the inscrutable nature of the second-born twin or recited again with great jingoistic pride the Yoruba myth of *ibeji*.

The myth:

ibeji (twins) are two halves of one spirit, a spirit too massive to fit in one body, and liminal beings, half human, half deity, to be honored, even worshipped accordingly. The second twin specifically—the changeling and the trickster, less fascinated by the affairs of the world

83

than the first—comes to earth with great reluctance and remains with greater effort, homesick for the spiritual realms. On the eve of their birth into physical bodies, this skeptical second twin says to the first, "Go out and see if the world is good. If it's good, stay there. If it's not, come back." The first twin Taiyewo (from the Yoruba *to aiye wo*, "to see and taste the world," shortened *Taiye* or *Taiwo*) obediently leaves the womb on his reconnaissance mission and likes the world enough to remain. Kehinde (from the Yoruba *kehin de*, "to arrive next"), on noting that his other half hasn't returned, sets out at his leisure to join his Taiyewo, deigning to assume human form. The Yoruba thus consider Kehinde the elder: born second, but wiser, so "older."

And so it was.

Kehinde wasn't lesser, less outgoing, less social, "in the shadow" of Taiwo, a shadow himself. He was something else. From somewhere else. Otherworldly like Ekua. An empath like Fola. And for whatever it was worth, Kweku saw now with awe, like his father (and *his* father before him).

Kehinde signed neatly in the lower right corner. Kweku touched his shoulder. "Why, thank you, Mr. Sai."

"You're welcome, Dr. Sai." Kehinde's smile quickly faded. The word *doctor* hung between them like an odor in the car. Dogs began a canon of cacophonous barking. Kehinde looked out at the house a little longer. The light went off in Taiwo's room. Then on, then off. Like a signal. Then on. Kehinde turned back to Kweku, turning back into a black hole. "Your pen."

"Yours."

"But it's—"

"Keep it."

"Are you sure?" Turning it over.

"I'd be honored for you to have it."

"Thank you, Dad." Another odor.

Kweku reached over and touched Kehinde's face, rubbing gently with one finger the space between his brows as he often did with Fola, trying to rub away her frown, though it never really worked and didn't now. "It must be time for dinner." Though it wasn't. Thirty minutes yet. "Your mother will want to hear all about class. You go ahead."

"You're not coming?"

"Just a second."

Kehinde nodded, not smiling. "Your painting," he said.

He rolled it up neatly and handed it to Kweku. The cameraman filmed: The Intelligent Parent Falls Dumb. Kweku gripped the painting as one does when one means *I'll treasure this always* but can't find the words. The words that he found were, "If you could maybe not mention—"

"Don't worry. I promise. I won't."

And then silence.

"Okay," said Kweku.

"Okay," said Kehinde. He waited for a moment then got out of the car.

"I love you," said Kweku, but the door closed on "I."

Kehinde didn't hear and went inside.

He waited one moment, then backed down the driveway. He didn't stop driving until Baltimore, seven hours, straight, I-95 stretching out like dark ocean. Flat. Driving without seeing, under moon, into black. He checked into a hotel near Hopkins Hospital, one he remembered. When he called home at last she was sobbing, but clear. "Kehinde won't tell me what happened, says he promised. You're scaring me. What happened? Where are you? What's wrong?"

He said very simply that he was sorry and he was leaving. That if she sold the house at value, she'd have enough to start again. That it was quite possible that he had never actually deserved her, not really. That he'd wiped them out trying to beat the odds.

"Beat the odds. What does that mean? Are you in danger? Have you been gambling? Are you in *physical* danger? Where are you?"

(He was nowhere.) He said it was for the best and that again he was sorry. That she'd be better off without him. "I'm letting you go."

"What does that mean?"

All his love to the children.

"When are you coming home?" she wept.

He wasn't.

13.

Sixteen years on he stands bent at the waist with his hands on his knees, his bare feet in the grass, partly wheezing, partly laughing at what's happened and how: the heartbreak he fled from has found him.

At last.

Of course when he left he assumed he'd return, to his life as he knew it, his family, his home—perhaps *sooner* than he did, in some days, not some weeks—but never once did he guess they'd be gone. Up in smoke. And could Fola be faulted? Was it *she* who overreacted, packing up as she did, shutting down in despair? Left to weep in that house, with its secret interconnections, its drafts and its shadows, original doors that wouldn't close, and four kids, a serious boy and two liminal beings and the baby—without him? Deserted. Alone. Not "helpless." Never helpless. She had never been helpless, not as a child even, pampered in V.I. before the war. She was a natural-born warrior, a take-no-shit Egba (or half of one, the Igbo mother dead giving birth), had faced feats far more fearsome than a mountain of debt not her making, than loneliness, than aloneness, despair. But not desertion, she would argue. Not deceit, disappointment. Not placing her trust in, then being let down.

Was it she, as he'd argued, perhaps knowing he was wrong, or rather knowing he had *lost*, that it could never be made right, and so right as one is when he's being done wrong by a person he's wronged: unable to believe in his righteousness? Was it she who betrayed him, having herself been betrayed? Who, having left a life twice, simply did it again? Or was it he, packing nothing, driving away in desperation, too exhausted to explain it, too exhausted to think: of other hospitals, of starting over, of finding work in another state, of being reasonable, of being responsible, of being a father, of being forgiven?

So going. With the whole of it down to an instant. Waiting, watching, for that moment (one) then backing down the drive. When if Fola had come to some window, seen the Volvo. When if Kehinde had made some small noise coming in. When if *he* had reconsidered, somehow come to his senses. Or considered in the first place. Gotten out, gone inside. In his scrubs, bowed and broken, but *in*, into the foyer, down the hall, into the kitchen smelling of ginger and oil. Instead of a question becoming a body there at sunrise, every morning, there to greet him with its weight and warmth, *what if*, when he opens his eyes. He thinks of it now and can scarcely comprehend it. That he lost her. That he left her. That she left him.

And how.

Days: in a stupor, barely sleeping, barely thinking, too afraid to call home, eating rice, drinking shame, back to the Goodwill on Broadway to buy a suit for a meeting at Hopkins (no positions), Johnnie Walker, *Kind of Blue*. Weeks: bled together. Six, eight weeks, then ten. Until one night, past midnight, simply driving back home. Snow beginning as snow begins in Boston, harmless, lazy, light, a blizzard by nightfall but flurries to start, pale fluttering flakes in the pink winter dawn. Fear in his fingertips, quivering belly, but certain he'd be able to argue his case, to confess and explain, beg his children's forgiveness, to earn back their trust, win her over again. Instead of: arriving at seven A.M. to a FOR SALE sign in front and the statue in back, which he took almost unthinkingly before speeding to the flower shop (shuttered), then the public school (children withdrawn). Racing, now sweating, to Milton in panic, looking desperately for the headmaster to ask for his son and somehow chancing upon Olu himself in that coat, the beige coat, with an L.L. Bean bag on his back. Before either could speak, a shrill bell ringing, steel, slicing clean through the distance from father to son, standing awkward and conspicuous in the sudden swirl of students issuing forth from brick buildings to cheer for the snow. Olu speaking clinically, describing a patient. "She cries every morning. She thinks I don't hear. She says you up and left us without a dime in the bank. The twins are in Lagos. The baby's still here."

"Where is your mother?"

"She doesn't want to see you."

"Look at me when you're speaking to me."

"I don't want to either." Olu looked down, gripped the straps of his bag. Kicked the ground. Another bell. "I have to go." Walked away.

The way it unraveled.

As things fall from cliffs. Like Irene, his first flatline, first patient he lost; admitted laughing at sunset, cold dead before dawn. The sheer speed of it. The mind-boggling speed of a death. (Or was it the other way around? Mind-boggling speed of a life?) He's a doctor, should have known, the body spoils, nothing lasts, not a life, why a love?, how loss works in the world and what happens to whom in what quantities, "the only constant is change . . ." and that business. Still, who would have thought? That she'd flee, refuse to see him, or to let him see them, or to tell him where they were when he got her on the phone? Weeks becoming months becoming seasons: unforgiven. An existence unraveled. Irreversible.

Open, shut.

How could he have known? That a life that had taken them years to put together would take weeks to break apart? A whole life, a whole world, *a whole world* of their making: dinners, dishes, diapers, deeds, degrees, unspoken agreements, outgoing answering machine messages, *You've reached the Sais, we're not here right now.* Beep. And won't be here ever again. *Leave a message.* Until nothing was left but the statue of the mother in the trunk of the Volvo and the painting, two forms. Oil on canvas. Kehinde Sai, 1993. Signed by the artist. *The Bigger Person.*

He laughs.

He takes a step forward and stumbles, and falls. He lands on his stomach, his face in the dew. *Why did I ever leave you?* The bridge on a loop per that tepid R&B to which Taiwo used to sulk. (To cure a broken heart, there was only Coltrane on vinyl. Coltrane would have cured her. He'd have told her if she'd asked.) But it's too soon to die. So he lifts up his face. *Not today,* he thinks, laughing. More "scoffing," short of breath. He has Coltrane, he has heparin, he has nothing to be concerned about. Jogging daily, Ama nightly. Never smoked. His heart is strong. But it isn't, and he knows it. It is broken in four places. Just the cracks in the beginning, left untreated now for years. His mother in Kokrobité, Olu in Boston, Kofi in Jamestown, Folasadé all over. That woman, all over him, deep in the fascia, in the muscle, in the tissue, in the matter, in the blood. He is dying of a broken heart. He cannot help but laugh at this. Or try to. Gripping the grass in pain, he rolls to his side. Lifts his head. Looks around. Is there something he can use to hoist himself up? The bougainvillaea, the butterfly, the mango.

And there she is.

Finally.

In the fountain.

A ridiculous place. Though not so surprising for a dreamer. Or for two. Standing (floating) in the fountain with white blossoms in their cotton hair, their bodies swathed in sparkling lace, white *bubas* flecked with diamonds, gold, with snow on their shoulders and gaps in their teeth, both, one with the radio, the other the camera. He peers at this, laughing. The invisible cameraman's? How did she wrest this away from his grasp? He gasps for breath, laughing. She is laughing now also. The radio playing softly. Sentimental mood, indeed.

She sets down the camera. It goes up in smoke.

"I love you," he says.

"I know, I know, I know."

"It hurts," he says.

His mother says, "Rest."

Fola says, "Yes."

So he lies in the grass. "Love grass" it's called, of all things. Bloody man.

He does not think what he thought he would think. That he never said bye or that it goes by so fast or that he should have chased Olu down the stairs when he came or seen Sadie grow up or not driven away. He thinks that he was wrong. About the whole thing being forgettable. Not that *he* won't be forgotten—he will, has been already—but about the details being unremarkable. What it amounts to in the balance. There is one detail worth remembering.

That he found her in the end.

Folasadé Savage on the run from a war. Kweku Sai fleeing a peace that could kill. Two boats lost at sea, washed to shore in Pennsylvania ("Pencil-wherever") of all places, freezing to death, alive, in love. Orphans, escapees, at large in world history, both hailing from countries last great in the eighteenth century—but prideful (braver, hopeful) and brimful and broke—so very desperately seeking home and adventure, finding both. Finding both in each other, being both *to* each other, the nights that they'd toast with warm Schweppes in cheap flutes or make love in the bathtub in moonlight or laugh until weeping: that he found what he hadn't dared seek. When it would have been enough to have found his way out, to have started where he started and to have ended up farther, a father and a doctor, whatever else he's become. To have *dared* to become. To escape would have sufficed. To be "free," if one wants swelling strings, to be "human." Beyond being "citizen," beyond being "poor." It was all he was after in the end, a human story, a way to be Kweku beyond being poor. To have somehow unhooked his little story from the larger ones, the stories of Country and of Poverty and of War that had swallowed up the stories of the people around him and spat them up faceless, nameless Villagers, cogs; to have fled, thus unhooked, on the small SS *Sai* for the vastness and smallness of life free of want: the petty triumphs and defeats of the Self (profession, family) versus those of the State (grinding work, civil war)— *yes, this would have been quite enough*, Kweku thinks. Born in dust, dead in grass. Progress. Distant shore reached.

That still farther, past "free," there lay "loved," in her laughter, lay "home" in her touch, in the soft of her Afro? He almost can't fathom it. Had never dared dream of it, believing such endings unavailable to him, or to them, who walked shoeless, who smiled in their deaths and who sang in their dreams and who didn't much matter. That he found her and loved her and made their love flesh four times over—it matters, if only to him. A point to the story. That girl-child met boy-child. And loved him.

Even if he lost her.

So he starts to rise up, to go kiss her in the fountain, not to behold or to be held by but to hold her. Or tries. He makes it as far as a sort of a push-up position before his valves lose the plot.

And so to death.

He lies here facedown with a smile on his face. Now the butterfly alights, finished drinking. A spectacular contrast, the turquoise against pink. But unconcerned with this, with beauty, with contrast, with loss. It flitters around the garden, coming to hover by his foot. Fluttering its wings against his soles as if to soothe them. Open, shut. The dog smells new death and barks, startling the butterfly. It flaps its wings once, flies away.

Silence.

Part II

GOING

1.

Fola wakes breathless that Sunday at sunrise, hot, dreaming of drowning, a roaring like waves. Dark. Curtains drawn, humid, the wet bed an ocean: half sleeping still, eyes closed, she sits up, cries out. But her "Kweku!" is silent, two bubbles in water that now, her lips parted, run in down her throat, where they find, being water, more water within her, her belly, below that, her thighs, dripping wet—the once-white satin nightdress soaked, wet from the inside, and outside, a second skin, now brown with sweat—and, becoming a tide, turn, return up the middle, thighs, belly, heart, higher, then burst through her chest.

The sob is so loud that it rouses her fully. She opens her eyes and the water pours out. She is sobbing uncontrollably when the tide subsides abruptly, leaving no trace whatsoever of the dream as it does (much as waves erase sand-script, washing in without warning, wiping the writings of children and of lovers away). Only fear remains vaguely, come unhooked from its storyline, left on damp sand like a thin sparkling foam. And the roaring: sharp racket in dull humid darkness, the A/C as noisy as one that still works.

Sparkling fear-foam, and roaring.

She sits up, disoriented, unable to see for the drawn mustard drapes so just sitting there, baffled, unclear what's just happened, or why she was crying, or why she's just stopped. With the usual questions: what time is it? where is she? *In Ghana*, something answers, the bulbul outside, so-called "pepper birds" bemusedly joining the racket in ode to oblivion to things that don't work. So not nighttime, then: pepper birds, the morning in Ghana, the place that she's moved to, or fled to.

Again.

Without fanfare or forethought, as flocks move, or soldiers, on instinct, without luggage, setting off at first light:

found the letter on a Monday, in the morning, in Boston, sorting mail at the counter (coffee, WBUR, "a member station supported by listeners like her"), bills for school fees, utilities. One dropped to the floor. Rather, floated to: pastel blue, flimsy, a feather, slipping silently from the catalogs of Monday's thick mail. A proper letter. And lay there. In the white light of winter, that cheap "air mail" paper no one uses anymore.

She opened it. Read it. Twice. Set it on the countertop. Left for the flower shop, leaving it there. Came home in the dark to the emptiness, retrieved it. Read again that Sena Wosornu, surrogate father, was dead. Was dead and had left her, "Miss" Folasadé Savage, a three-bedroom house in West Airport, Accra. Stood, stunned, in her coat in the kitchen and silence, soft silver-black darkness, tiles iced by the moon. Monday evening. Left Friday. JFK to Kotoka. Nonstop. Without fanfare. Just packed up and left.

Now she squints at the darkness and makes out the bedroom, unfamiliar entirely after only six weeks. Unfamiliar shapes, shadows, and the space here beside her, unfamiliar entirely after sixteen years, still.

She touches her nightdress, alarmed at the wetness. She peels the drenched satin away from her skin. She touches her stomach as she does when this happens, when fear hovers shyly, not showing its face yet, when something is wrong but she doesn't know what or with which of the offspring that sprang from this spot. And the stomach answers always (the "womb" maybe, more, but the word sounds absurd to her, *womb*, always has. A *womb*. Something cavernous, mysterious, a basement. A word with a shadow, a draft. Rhymes with *tomb*). She touches her stomach in the four different places, the quadrants of her torso between waist and chest: first the upper right (Olu) beneath her right breast, then the lower right (Taiwo) where she has the small scar, then the lower left (Kehinde) adjacent to Taiwo, then the upper left (Sadie), the baby, her heart. Stopping briefly at each to observe the sensation, the movement or stillness beneath the one palm. Sensing:

Olu—all quiet. The sadness as usual, as soft and persistent as the sound of a fan. Taiwo—the tension. Light tugging sensation. But no sense of danger, no cause for alarm. Kehinde—the absence, the echoing absence made bearable by the certainty that *if*, she would know (as she knew when it happened, as she knew the very instant, cutting pastel-blue hydrangea at the counter in the shop, suddenly feeling a sort of seizure, lower left, crying, "Kehinde!" with the knife slipping sideways and slicing her hand. Dripping blood on the counter, on the stems and the blossoms, on the phone as she dialed, already knowing which it was; getting voicemail, "This is Keh—" call waiting, clicking over, frantic sobbing, "Mom, it's Taiwo. Something happened." "I know." She knew as did Taiwo the very instant that it happened, as the blade made its way through the skin, the first wrist. So that now, a year later—more, nearly two years later—having neither seen nor heard from him, she knows. That she'd know). Last, Sadie—fluttering, butterflies, a new thing this restlessness, this looking for something, not finding it.

Fine.

Sadness, tension, absence, angst—but *fine*, as she birthed them, alive if not well, in the world, fish in water, in the condition she delivered them (breathing and struggling) and this is enough. Perhaps not for others, Fola thinks, other mothers who pray for great fortune and fame for their young, epic romance and joy (better mothers quite likely; small, bright-smiling, hard-driving, minivan-mothers), but for her who would kill, maim, and die for each child but who knows that the willingness to die has its limits.

That death is indifferent.

Not *she* (though she seems), but her age-old opponent, her enemy, *theirs,* the common enemy of all mothers—death, harm to the child—which will defeat her, she knows.

But not today.

The fear recedes. The roaring persists. The rough snuffling slosh of the broken machine. The heat grows assertive, as if feeing ignored. The bedsheet and nightgown go suddenly cold.

She gets out of bed, knocking her knee as she does, quietly cursing the house, its deficient A/C. The night watchman Mr. Ghartey was meant to have fixed it, or meant to have had his electrician-cousin come fix it, or meant to have called the white man who installed it to come fix it—the plan remains largely unclear. "He is coming" is the answer whenever she asks. "I beg, he is coming." For weeks now, hot air. But the relationship is young, between her and her staff, and she knows to go slow, to tread lightly. She is a woman, first; unmarried, worse; a Nigerian, worst; and fair-skinned. As suspicious persons go in Ghana, she might as well be a known terrorist. The staff, whom she inherited along with the house and its 1970s orange-wool-upholstered wooden furniture, sort of tiptoes around her poorly masking their shock. That she moved here alone. To sell *flowers.*

Worse: that she arrived on that Saturday, from the airport, in the morning, in the white linen outfit and open-toe shoes and, alighting the cab, said, "How *are* you?" incomprehensibly, with British *a* and American *r*. Worst: that no man alighted the taxi thereafter.

That she shook their hands, seeking their eyes.

That, leaving her suitcases (three? were there more? was this all? a whole life in America?) by the cab, she proceeded directly to the wall to put her face in the crawlers. "Bougainv*iiii*llea!" Still incomprehensible.

That she greets them in the morning with this same odd "How *are* you?" and thanks them as bizarrely for doing their jobs. "*Thank* you" to the houseboy when he washes her clothing. "*Thank* you" to the cook when he sets out her meals. "*Thank* you" to the gatekeeper when he opens the gate and again as he closes it.

That she smokes.

That she wears shorts.

That she wanders around the garden in these shorts and a sun hat with cigarettes and clippers, snipping this, snipping that, hauling her catch into the kitchen, where she stands at the counter, not pounding yam, not shelling beans, but arranging *flowers*. It amuses her, always has, this disregard of Africans for flowers, the indifference of the abundantly blessed (or psychologically battered—the chronic self-loather who can't accept, even with evidence, that anything native to him, occurring in abundance, in excess, without effort, has value). They watch as research scientists observe a new species, a hybrid, herbivorous, likely harmless, maybe not. Masked, feeding her, washing for her, examining her clothing when they think she's not looking, whispering, watching her eat. She hasn't yet told them that she once lived in Ghana, that she speaks and understands all they say in hushed Twi about her flowers, flowered nightdresses, distressing eating habits like pulling out and eating the weeds (lemongrass). She learned this from her father, who spoke the major Nigerian languages plus French,

Swahili, Arabic, and snatches of Twi. "Always learn the local language. Never let on to the locals," he'd say, a cigar at the end of its life on his lips, giving birth to a laugh—

upper left.

There it is.

The movement she was feeling for.

Left upper quadrant, in the vicinity of Sadie but closer to the heart, not a tugging or a tightening or a throbbing of dread but an echo, an emptiness, an emptying out. A familiar sensation. Not the one she was feeling for, fearful of (auguring harm done the child) but remembered, unmistakable, from four decades prior, a memory she forgot she still has.

She sits back down absently, abandoning her mission, whatever it was, a word with Mr. Ghartey perhaps, or a smack to the side of the wall-mounted machine, or a fresh set of bedsheets, a postnightmare drink. And thinks: *odd,* to be returned to the death of her father, which she thinks of so rarely, as one recounts dreams, out of focus, diluted, not the event but the emotion, a sadness that's faded, dried, curled, lost its color. The *event* she can see clear as day even now: Lagos, July 1966, the short chain of events:

first the waking up gasping, cold, thirteen years old, all her posters of the Beatles stuck with tacks to the walls, sitting alarmed in the dark with that space in her chest, unfamiliar with the feeling (same odd emptiness as now). Second: making her way from her room down the hall, to her father's room, forgetting that he'd traveled to the North, gone to see about his in-laws, her "grandparents," the Nwaneris, whom she'd never actually met and never would. No one said it. Never him, her kind, broad-shouldered, woolly-haired father, who wept for the loss of his bride every night, kneeling down by his bed beneath the portrait above it, Somayina Nwaneri, fair, gold-eyed. A ghost.

Twenty-seven.

Fairy ghostmother.

Had bled out in labor.

A stranger to Fola, no more than a face, so unusually pale that she looked in her portrait as if she'd been born without blood, cut from ice. Still so pretty. Stuff of legend. Local celebrity in Kaduna, Igbo father as famous for his post in the North as for plucking one rose from the grounds of the mission and marrying her, a Scotswoman, auburn-haired Maud. And the rest of it: shame, stillborn son, successive miscarriages, the shaking of heads and the wagging of tongues, *see, the Scotswoman can't bear the Igbo man's child,* then the one white-skinned daughter, the magic mulatto. Little princess of Kaduna. Colonial Administrator's daughter. Won a bursary to study nursing in London after the war, promptly met and immediately married Kayo Savage, Fola's father, lawyer, late of the Royal Air Force. Felled in childbirth, etc. No one said it. No one mentioned that they never came to see her, Rt. Hon. John and Maud. Nwaneri, never called nor sent a gift, but she could guess it: that they blamed her for their only daughter's early death, as she would come to hate them for his.

But not yet.

First: waking at midnight with space in her chest. Second: slipping down the hallway to her father's bedroom, vacant. Third: ascending to his empty bed, still warm with scent (rum, soap, Russian Leather) and covering her face with his thick kente blanket, then lying, unmoving, eyes open, heart racing. Still as a corpse, swathed in cotton and sweating, with the A/C not on, with her father not there, gone to Kaduna that morning, having heard from some friends that the Igbos in the North were in trouble again.

"*Again?*" she'd sighed, sulking, loudly slurping her breakfast (*gari*, sugar water, ice), already knowing he was going by his having prepared this. "A bush girl's breakfast" as he called it, mocking. Powdered yam in ice water, her favorite. If this grandfather of hers was as rich as they said, with his Cyclone CJ and his split-level ranch, then why must her father go "check on him" always, she'd asked, crunching ice, but she knew. He had to go, always, to appease them, to redeem himself, to beg again forgiveness for the death of Somayina (which was, technically speaking, not *his* fault but hers, infant Fola's, the doctor's at least, or the womb's).

"They're always in trouble, these Igbos. *Na wow o.*"

"Your mother was an Igbo."

"*Half.*"

"That's quite enough." But when she looked he was laughing, coming to kiss her head, leaving. "I'll be back before Sunday. I love you."

"*Mo n mo.*"

There was no equivalent expression for *I love you* in Yoruba. "If you love someone, you show them," her father liked to say. But said it nevertheless in English, to which she'd answer in Yoruba, "I know," *mo n mo.*

Out the door.

Just like that.

Stood, set down his coffee cup, kissed her on the forehead once, hand each on her Afro puffs, walked out the door. Gone. Woolly hair and woolen suit and broad and buoyant shoulders bobbing, bobbing, bobbing out of view. The swinging door swung open, shut.

Fourth: fourteen hours later in his bed beneath the blanket, sliding down beneath the kente into darkness, absence, scent and heat, a still and silent ocean. And remaining. In the quiet. Lying ramrod straight, not moving, knowing.

That something had been removed.

That a thing that had been in the world had just left it, as surely and simply as people leave rooms or the dust of dead dandelion lifts into wind, silent, leaving behind it this empty space, openness. Incredible, unbearable, interminable openness appearing now around her, above her, beyond her, a gaping, inside her, a hole, or a mouth: unfamiliar, wet, hollow and hungry. Un-appeasable.

The details came later—such as details ever come, such as one can know the details of a death besides one's own, how it went, how long or calming, cold or terrifying, lonely—but the thing happened there in the bedroom. The loss. Later, if ever alone, she'll consider it, the uncanny similarity between that and this moment: alone in the dark in the sweltering heat in a room not her own in a bed far too big. Mirror endings. The last of a life as she'd known it, that midnight in Lagos, never suspecting what had happened (it simply wouldn't have occurred to her, that evil existed, that death was indifferent), yet *knowing* somehow. This was the event for her, the loss in the concrete, the hours in which she crossed between knowing and knowledge and onward to "loss" in the abstract, to sadness. Six, seven hours of openness slowly hardening into loneliness.

The details came later—how a truckload of soldiers, Hausas, high on cheap heroin and hatred, had killed them, setting fire to the mansion, piling rocks at the exits—but the details never hardened into pictures in her head. So she never really believed it, not really, couldn't *see* it, never settled on a sight that would have made the thing stick, put some meat on the words (roaring fire, burning wood), put a face on the corpses. The words remained bones. They were no one, the "soldiers." They were shadow-things, not human beings. The "Nwaneris" were what they'd always been: a portrait on the wall, a name. A pallid cast of characters. Not even characters, but categories: civilian, soldier, Hausa, Igbo, villain, victim. Too vague to be true.

And not him.

It was him. He was there without question (though they never could confirm it, his bones turned to ashes, in REM, dreaming, his "Fola!" two bubbles), as rampant anti-Igbo pogroms kicked off the war. But she simply couldn't see him, not her father as she knew him, as she'd seen him from the table, bobbing, bobbing out of view. It was someone else they'd killed that night, these "soldiers" whom she couldn't see, this "victim" whom they didn't know, anonymous as are all victims.

The indifference of it.

This was the problem and would be ever after, the block on which she sometimes feels her whole being stumbled: that he (and so she) became so unspecific. In an instant. That the details didn't matter in the end. Her life until that moment had seemed so original, a richly spun tale with a bright cast of characters—she: motherless princess of vertical palace, their four-story apartment on Victoria Island; they: passionate, glamorous friends of her father's, staff; he: widowed king of the castle. Had he died a death germane to this life as she'd known it—in a car crash, for example, in his beloved Deux Chevaux, or from liver cancer, lung, to the end puffing Caos, swilling rum—she could have abided the loss. Would have mourned. Would have found herself an orphan in a four-story apartment, having lost both her parents at thirteen years old, but would have been, thus bereaved, a thing she recognized (tragic) instead of what she became: a part of history (generic).

She sensed the change immediately, in the tone people took when they learned that her father had been murdered by soldiers; in the way that they'd nod as if, yes, *all makes sense, the beginning of the Nigerian civil war, but of course.* Never mind that the Hausas were targeting Igbos, and her father was a Yoruba, and her grandmother Scottish, and the house staff Fulani, some Indian even. Ten dead, one an Igbo, minor details, no matter. She felt it in America when she got to Pennsylvania (having been taken first to Ghana by the kindly Sena Wosornu), that her classmates and professors, white or black, it didn't matter, somehow believed that it was natural, however tragic, what had happened. That she'd stopped being Folasadé Somayina Savage and had become instead the native of a generic War-Torn Nation. Without specifics. Without the smell of rum or posters of the Beatles or a kente blanket tossed across a king-size bed or portraits. Just some war-torn nation, hopeless and inhuman and as humid as a war-torn nation anywhere, all war-torn nations everywhere. "I'm sorry," they'd say, nodding yes in agreement, as one says *I'm sorry* when the elderly die, "that's too bad" (but not *that* bad, more "how these things go" in this world), in their eyes not a hint of surprise. Surely, broad-shouldered, woolly-haired fathers of natives of hot war-torn countries got killed all the time?

How had this happened?

It wasn't Lagos she longed for, the splendor, the sensational, the sense of being wealthy—but the sense of self surrendered to the senselessness of history, the narrowness and naïveté of her former individuality. After that, she simply ceased to bother with the details, with the notion that existence took its form from its specifics. Whether this house or that one, this passport or that, whether Baltimore or Lagos or Boston or Accra, whether expensive clothes or hand-me-downs or florist or lawyer or life or death—didn't much matter in the end. If one could die identityless, estranged from all context, then one could live estranged from all context as well.

This is what she's thinking as she sits here, wet, empty, a newly wrecked ship on a shore in the dark: that the details are different but the space is unchanging, unending, the absence as present, absolute. He is gone now, her father, has been gone for so long that his goneness has replaced his existence in full. It didn't happen over time but in an instant, in his bedroom: he was removed, and she remained, and that was that.

That is that.

One pepper bird, pluckier than its bickering playmates, pecks at the glass at the back of the drapes. "Kookoo, kookoo, kookoo," it cries, and she is reminded for a moment of what she said as she woke. What was it? She can't remember. A nightmare. It was nothing. "*Koo*-koo," insists the bulbul, but the A/C cuts in.

"Tat-tat-tat-tat-tat." A death rattle. It dies, and the bedroom falls silent.

Fola waits a minute, then laughs at her waiting. Waiting for what? *There is nothing*, she thinks. He is gone, she remains, that is that, *tat-tat-tat*. She changes and goes back to sleep.

❧

But doesn't sleep deeply.

The telephone rings.

At first she thinks: *no, I'm still dreaming.* Ignores it. But then wonders how, if she's dreaming, she's thinking. So opens one eye. Hears the ringing. Picks up. "Hello?" she murmurs.

"Fola," he answers.

A man. But who has this number? Not him. Not Olu. Not Kehinde. The voice is too deep. "Who is this?"

"It's Benson," he says.

"Benson, hi. What time is it?" she asks, looking around for a clock.

"I'm sorry to call you so early . . ."

No clock. "What time is it?" she repeats.

"Just, you gave me this number last Thursday . . ."

A man who is stalling.

She perceives this in an instant and sits up now, worried. "What is it?" A very brief silence ensues. "I'm sorry," he begins—so she runs through the quadrants: alive if not well, fish in water, they're fine. She knows that he's crying though doesn't know how. She hears nothing. She comforts, on instinct, "Don't cry. The children are fine."

Which he thinks is a question. "Yes," he says quickly. "I'm sure they're all fine." A cough, one soft sniffle, and then there is nothing.

"Benson?"

"I don't know how to say this. I'm sorry."

Now she knows what and knows who and is silent.

"Fola?"

She wonders how she missed it. Not the child. "Where are you?" she asks.

"At the house," Benson answers. "His wife—" then stops short. "I'm so sorry."

Not the father. The roaring returns without warning and, rising, the tide from the middle. "Not him," Fola breathes.

"She called me at home and I came straightaway, but the heart had—he—it was too late."

Benson continues in his sonorous voice, a dead ringer for Luther Vandross. Among the various disjointed things she now thinks, Fola remembers meeting Benson at Hopkins that day. Twenty-three years old in the hospital lobby with Olu tucked into her *wrappa*, asleep. Benson in scrubs with his skin of burnt umber, the taller of the handsome Ghanaians.

The other one.

"Kookoo!" the bulbul cries.

"*Please . . .*" Fola whispers. "Not yet please no Kweku-*no*."

2.

Olu walks in no particular hurry out of the hospital, puts down his coffee, puts down his phone and starts to cry. Five quick sobs, drumbeats—*your-fa-ther-is-dead*—then he wipes his face, closes his eyes. Snowflakes fall, land on his nose and his lips. It is one A.M., zero degrees Celsius.

"So sorry."

He opens his eyes to find an elderly woman, not five feet tall, fur coat, below him. She has just made her way through the handicapped exit and stopped by his side on the sidewalk outside. In the peculiar silence that invariably accompanies the opening act of a storm in the nighttime, they stand there together and watch the snow swirl through the black then the bright of the hospital sign.

She gestures to the lobby through the glass doors behind them, then touches him, winking. She says in a rush, "I know I should have stayed with the kids. Well. The *kids*. Jesus. Forty years old is our youngest, *my* youngest. Two boys. Brett and Junior. Bruce Junior, like my husband. He's always had impeccable timing, my Bruce. Twelve twenty-one A.M., December twenty-first, time of death. How's that for good timing? Yes, sir. I love it at night when it just starts to snow. It just goes by so quickly, though. Who did you lose?"

"—a doctor," he says, his voice cracking on *I'm*. "I'm a doctor."

"I could tell by your outfit," she says. "But I assumed you weren't standing here mourning a patient." After a moment she laughs and he joins, clouds of breath. She pulls out a Cohiba Esplendido in a handkerchief. A small silver lighter. Sparks, loses the flame. Olu cups his hand around the lighter, fingers trembling. "Your fingers are shaking," she says.

"Sure is cold." He says foolish things like this whenever he's nervous, short sentences that start with *sure is* and *how 'bout*.

"Dressed in those," touching him, "cotton pajamas? You know we're in a blizzard here, darling. Yes, sir. Doesn't look like much now, never does to begin with, but wait until sunrise. Not here. Don't wait here. You'll catch a death of a cold—oh dear me. Did I say that? Not what one says at such times. Here, take this."

"No. I'm a—"

"Doctor. You said."

"I don't—"

"Take it. I promised my Bruce that I'd smoke it for him. If he died, *when* he died. Like he did when our children were born, our two boys. Pack of three. But I'm old." She laughs again, takes one good drag with her eyes closed, then puts the cigar—"*That's* a dear"—in his mouth. A nurse inserting a thermometer. He bends to receive it. With his face there before her, she touches his cheek. "You're crying." A statement. She holds his chin, gently, and wipes off his cheek with her handkerchief. "There." She pats his cheek, smiling, and adds before leaving, "The cold always makes me cry, too."

Olu walks, smoking, up Huntington Ave. Streetlamps drip gold into puddles of light. The snow gathers strength as he makes his way home, leaning forward, lips chapping, arms naked. No coat. Saturday-night revelers stumble and shout. A few cars pass slowly, no traction, in fear. No one seems to notice someone walking in the street itself. Nude arms, blue scrubs, and the drumbeat.

Ling is asleep with her back to the door. He stands in the doorway and watches her sleep. The light cuts her body in two on an angle, her hair on the pillow an oil spill. Slick black. The bedroom is white, all white, everything white. She thinks it excessive, a sham wouldn't hurt. She's left her red shirt on the floor, a suggestion. He picks this up, making no noise. Looks around. He goes to the Eames chair (white), clutching the shirt as a child would a blanket or bear, for the smell of it. Chanel No. 5, Jergens lotion, cherry-almond. He tries to say her name, wants to hear it. Says, "L—." But hears instead Fola, her voice flat and distant, the shoddy connection, "Your father is dead," and the few things she told him, the pause that came after, that hush between heard and received, before hurt.

He asked every question and heard every detail—"on his face," "in the grass," "Benson found him like that," "seems he walked outside, fell down, and couldn't get up," "six A.M."—but she didn't have answers. She wept. He set down his stirrer, dripping soymilk on the tabletop. He looked around the house staff lounge, packed at this hour. Emergency department interns, coked, Red Bulled, and coffeed, their eyes dim and bloodshot with fear and fatigue. Days before Christmas, wee hours, Sunday morning, the sorrows of the Saturday left at their door: desperate barroom brawls, suicide attempts, crashes presnowstorm, hypothermia among the homeless. He didn't want to go home. This is what he misses in his second year of ortho now, buzzing through shifts high on sports drink and drive. Orthopedic surgery is intensity by appointment: fallen grandpas, fallen quarterbacks, procedural, well paid. He chose it for these reasons, the procedures above others, the physicality, the precision, nostalgia for track. But he misses the rush of ED, the desperation, the prospect and hovering presence of death.

Fola. "Are you there?"

"Yes."

"Please call your siblings? To tell them that . . . ?"

"Yes."

"You don't mind? You're okay?"

"Yes."

"I just need to rest for a moment. Long morning. I love you, my darling. You know that."

"I know."

He sits in his scrubs with the shirt in the dark, with the moon making ice of the floor and the walls, and thinks maybe she's right, all this white is oppressive, apathetic; a bedroom shouldn't be an OR. In the sunlight it's gorgeous, hard angles and harder the light crashing brilliantly against its own shade, to an eerie effect, white on white, like an echo, the sun staring at its reflection. Not now. Now it is lonely and cold in the darkness that isn't quite darkness, a cold and dark light. With the snow falling onto itself out the window as noiseless as hopelessness, more white on white.

He watches her chest as it rises and falls. She stirs in her sleep, shifting here, shifting there, as she's wont, tossing, turning. He tries again, "L—," with the *ing* getting stuck in his throat, thick with shame. Of all things. Not with sorrow or grief, thick with tears, but a shame he feels spreading like warmth down his throat and below to his chest, to his stomach, his groin, where it stops, gathers strength, and spreads out to his knees. Of all places. *Warm knees* as he sits in not-darkness, her T-shirt pressed up to his mouth like a mute. And why this? Why this candle-wax-melting sensation that renders him too weak to stand or to speak and now turns into burning, a fierce, violent burning so caustic he bends at the waist, crying "H—!"?

The T-shirt reverses the outpour, red cotton ball pressed to his lips muting fury and shame, so back *in* goes the outburst, down, back down his throat to his stomach and lands there with one breathless "—ow."

How is the question (does an exceptional surgeon just die in a garden of cardiac arrest?). *How*, when his whole life he's sought to be like him, has forgiven the sins in the name of the gift, has admired the brilliance and told of the prowess, general surgeon without equal, remembered even now. "Sai, you say? I knew a Sai once. Ghanaian. A knife-wielding artist. You know who I mean?" "Yes. That's my father." "Your father! How *is* he? Oh my, it's been *years* . . ." "Sixteen years, yes."

He's dead.

Dead in a garden of cardiac arrest, basic coronary thrombosis, easy peasy, act fast, Kweku Sai, prodigal prodigy, a phenom, a failure.

A doctor who failed to prevent his own death.

How is the shame Olu holds in his stomach, bent over, while Ling in her sleep turns away. *How* can he wake up this woman and tell her the father he's told of died this kind of death? *How*, when he's promised for years, fourteen years now, that one day he'll take her to meet him at last and she'll love him, he knows it, a doctor like they are, a mind such as they have, for everything else. Ling, whom he's loved since they touched pouring punch at the Asian American Cultural Center Open House at Yale. ("I'm sorry," said the greeter, embarrassed, to Olu. "We thought *Sai* was Asian. You're welcome to stay.") Ling who, not looking, reached out for the ladle the moment that he did, soft skin finding skin. Ling, whom he's loved since, still touching, now flushing, she frowned. "You're not Asian. Wait. Why are you here? Do you play a stringed instrument? Excel in mathematics? Attend a kind of cult-like Korean-American Christian church?"

Laughing, still touching, "Piano. And science. A Catholic church, no, but the priest is from Laos."

"Then what am I saying? Stupid me. You *are* Asian."

"I'm Olu."

"I'm Ling."

And the rest on from there: making flash cards and kissing in CCL cubicles, eating ramen over o-chem, then Harvard, four years, they both matching in Boston (he ortho, she obstetrics), the "golden couple," nicknamed, wherever they went. Ling-and-Olu, tall, tiny, a study in contrasts, their photos like print ads for Benetton clothes: Ling-and-Olu in Guam building homes for the homeless, Ling-and-Olu in Kenya digging wells for the waterless, Ling-and-Olu in Rio giving vaccinations to vagrants, Ling-and-Olu at Pepe's, enlarged, black-and-whites. "The love of his life," though he finds the term cloying, "the independent variable" rather more to the point, across time and place always held constant, his confidante, the only to whom he tells all.

But not this.

How, when he sat there and looked at her father and said in despair and defense of his own, "He's a surgeon like I am, the best in his field," with Ling listening from the bathroom the day he proposed?

October: a little congress, a glass box apartment, Dr. Wei on the slipper chair, Ling on the couch, holding Olu by the elbow, via vise grip, an announcement, the ring-bearing hand on her self-bouncing knee. Dr. Wei sipped his tea, looking calmly at Olu, who looked him right back as he'd learned at Beth Israel. ("Always look a patient in the eye," said Dr. Soto. "No matter what you have to tell him. Look your patient in the eye.") What Olu had to tell him was he'd come to ask to marry Ling, but all the patient Dr. Wei replied was, "Well. I see."

They'd met once before, at the medical school commencement, both smiling politely as if at a child. Mrs. Wei was there, healthy, with Ling's older sister, who goes by Lee-Ann, née Lihúa, and her husband. Olu brought Fola to meet them at last (he had skipped Yale commencement). "Fola Savage. My mother."

"Mrs. Savage. Pleased to meet you." Mrs. Wei nodded, smiling.

"Likewise," said Fola. "*Ms.* Savage is fine."

"Ms. *Savage?*" Dr. Wei said. "Did I hear you correctly?"

"Rather unfortunate," laughed Fola. "But what can you do?"

The husband, whose name Olu can never remember (standard-issue Caucasian, like Brian or Tim, a Californian, beige hair and beige skin and beige trousers), erupted in laughter. "Of what provenance?" he asked.

"Empire," said Fola, still chuckling. "The British."

Brian/Tim laughed, as did Ling and Lee-Ann. Mrs. and Dr. Wei tensed, as did Olu. He peered at the sky. Early June. "Sure is warm."

Twice all these years he'd met both of Ling's parents, though they'd raised her in Newton, a T ride away. Dr. Wei lived in Cambridge now, facing the river, in faculty housing (engineering, MIT). He was slender like Ling, with the same narrow frame, less so fragile than streamlined. From concentrate. Compact. Sixty years old with the same slick-black hair streaked with silver, worn long, to his ears. Rimless frames. At regular intervals he smoothed down his hair with his hand, without need, on the right, near his neck, one calm movement so slow that the casual observer might not recognize it as a nervous tic. In repose he wore trousers, a button-down shirt, and a blue V-neck sweater with slippers, Olu saw. Olu wore socks, there being a shortage of slippers, there being a shortage of guests since "the Loss," Ling explained. A photo of the Lost hung behind her thin widower, the only thing mounted on the one nonglass wall, the other three making a fish tank of the living room, the river view heightening the piscine effect.

A huge Ru ware vase standing guard in one corner, a piano in the other as upright and stern, yellow books at its feet familiar instantly to Olu, *Schirmer's Library of Musical Classics*, in piles.

Jingdezhen tea set.

Mozart playing softly. "Lacrimosa" from *Requiem*.

Ling gripped his arm.

．．．

"你要发言," she said finally in Mandarin.

"Speak English, my dear. There's a guest in our house."

"*Our* house," said Ling, "is on Huntington Avenue."

"Well," said her father, and said nothing else.

Olu shifted positions, wishing Ling would let go, feeling incarcerated rather than claimed by her grip. "Ling was against it," he spoke up politely. "But I thought it only right that we ask, that I ask."

"For my 'daughter's hand in marriage,'" Dr. Wei said bemusedly. "Which one?"

"Of your daughters?" Olu frowned.

"Of her hands. The one with the ring would appear to be taken—"

"I knew you would do this! I *knew* it," Ling seethed. "And it's not your decision! I've already said yes. I *told* you." She turned to face Olu. Let go.

Olu, ungripped, felt his stomach turn over. Dr. Wei smoothed his hair down and said, "Well. I see." Ling stood abruptly and left the room, crying, her small shoulders shaking. A door slammed somewhere.

Then Dr. Wei laughed—rather shockingly, warmly, a rich and deep sound in the space Ling had left. He took off his glasses and wiped them off, tearing. More rumbles of laughter then, smiling, he spoke. "I'm laughing at myself. I should have known this was coming. Ling's mother always said you were friends. 'They're just friends.' For fifteen years? No, I didn't think so." Another rumble. "So often one knows, without seeing, the truth." He put on his glasses, looking closely at Olu. Smoothed down his hair again. "Olu, yes?"

"Yes."

"I knew an Olu. Oluwalekun Abayomi." He pronounced the name perfectly. "Nigerian. As you'd know. Top of our class at UPitt by a long shot. It's not that I'm racist. Far from it."

"Sir—"

"Please." He nodded, as if agreeing with himself to continue and crossed his legs, crossing his hands on his knees. "It is true that you don't have my blessing. And won't have. But not for the reasons that you may suspect. Certainly not the reasons that she does. That Ling does." He glanced at the hallway down which she had stormed. Olu shifted, too, but to settle in, listening, lulled by the cadence, the professorial tone. Odd how this happened, even now in his thirties, this defaulting to Student at the first sign of Teacher. "When I was in grad school in Pittsburgh—fine city—I befriended a fair number of Africans. Men. All of them men, unsurprisingly. Engineering. Just grown-up boys playing with toys." Sipped his tea. "They'd come from all over, some wealthy, some destitute, but all of them brilliant, pure genius, those five. The hardest-working men in our cohort, I tell you. All bafflingly good at the math." Smoothed his hair. "Americans call Asians the 'model minority.' At one point this may have been true. Recent past. But now it's the Africans. I see it in the classroom. Asians are through. We got fat—no, don't laugh. You never saw overweight Asians, not young ones, not back when we came, when the girls were still young. I see them all over now, Koreans, Chinese, on the train, on the campus. It's the beginning of the end. A fat Asian child can win a spelling bee maybe, but a science fair? No. It's the Africans now. I'm serious. You're laughing."

But Olu couldn't help it.

Dr. Wei started also, his deep, bossed gong laugh. "I say this to say that I admire the culture, your culture, its respect for education above all. Every African man I have *ever* encountered in an academic setting excelled, barring none. I haven't met a single lazy African student, or a fat one for that matter, in forty years here. I know it sounds crazy, we laugh, but believe me. I teach undergraduates. I see it every day. African immigrants are the future of the academy. And the Indians." He paused here to finish his tea.

While Olu sat, smiling, an odder thing still: to be enjoying Dr. Wei's conversation. Ling had always reviled him as arrogant, unyielding, charming to a point and indifferent beyond. She'd never gone home for vacation in college, finding overseas community service work to do instead. She'd skipped her sister's wedding so as not to see her father, and ignored the man's calls when they came, twice a year, the one—September second—for an off-key "Happy Birthday," the other Chinese New Year for "Kung Hei Fat Choy." Olu knew better than to probe, and he didn't, for fifteen years almost had never once asked: *honey, why don't we drive out to Newton to see them?* or *what did he do to you?* Never once asked. And Ling didn't either: what had happened to his father, why they'd never been to Ghana (they'd been everywhere else), why he'd balked only recently at an e-mail from Fola inviting them for dinner on Christmas? Instead, they hung there between them, in Allston, New Haven, now a ten-minute walk from where Olu once lived: all the questions and heartbreaks, unanswered, untreated, just left there to dry in the silence and sun.

So Olu was shocked now to find himself smiling, at ease with this man whom Ling hated so much. There was something even appealing about Dr. Wei's manner, the efforts of the fastidious mathematician to make friends. As smug as he seemed, the hair smoothing betrayed him: Dr. Wei was self-conscious, of what was unclear. Perhaps of the accent that coated his consonants, a threat to the facile delivery, the *r*'s? Perhaps of the slightness of build, further slighted by nearness to Olu's own wide-chested frame? Perhaps of the sadness alive in his pupils, as present as laugh lines around his bright eyes? Or of something else, dark, Olu couldn't see what, but could sense that this man was no stranger to shame. And was opening his mouth to say "Interesting" or suchlike when Dr. Wei smoothed down his hair and went on.

"You know, I never understood the dysfunctions of Africa. The greed of the leaders, disease, civil war. Still dying of *malaria* in the twenty-first century, still hacking and raping, cutting genitals off? Young children and nuns slitting throats with machetes, those girls in the Congo, this thing in Sudan? As a young man in China, I assumed it was ignorance. Intellectual incapacity, inferiority perhaps. Needless to say I was wrong, as I've noted. When I came here I saw I was wrong. Fair enough. But the backwardness persists even now, and why is that? When African men are so bright? as we've said. And the women, too, don't get me wrong, I'm not sexist. But why is that place still so backward? I ask. And you know what I think? No respect for the family. The fathers don't honor their children or wives. The Olu I knew, Oluwalekun Abayomi? Had two bastard children plus three by the wife. A brain without equal but no moral backbone. *That's* why you have the child soldier, the rape. How can you value another man's daughter, or son, when you don't even value your own?"

Olu was silent, too startled to speak.

"You can't." Dr. Wei opened his hands: QED. "Your mother, for example. *Ms.* Savage. Not *Mrs.* With a different last name than yours. Sai. Is that right? I'm *assuming*—and it is just an assumption, I acknowledge—that your father left your mother to raise you alone?"

Olu sat, frozen, too angry to move.

"Exactly. And there's your example. Your father. The father is always the example." He paused. "Now you may say, 'No, no, I'm not like my father—'"

"No," Olu mumbled.

"And that's what you *think*, but—"

"I'm just like my father. I'm *proud* to be like him." Just barely a whisper through Olu's clenched teeth. Dr. Wei, caught off guard, tipped his head and looked at Olu—who, hands and chest trembling, looked steadily back. Said, "He's a surgeon like I am, the best in his field," and the rest in an outpour, one soft seething rush: "The problem isn't Ling wants to marry an African. It's not that she's marrying *me*, and she will. No, the problem is *you*, Dr. Wei. *Your* example. *You're* the example of what they don't want. Both of them, Ling and Lee-Ann, and why is that? Why aren't there pictures of them in your place? What was it, 'the father is always the example'? Both of your daughters prefer something else."

Ling appeared now in her coat, holding Olu's.

Aaaaaaa-men. "Lacrimosa," the choral climax.

Dr. Wei cleared his throat, but before he could speak Ling grabbed Olu and left. Out the door, just like that.

Then laughing together, a flute and a cello, the car windows open to birds and a breeze.

"You were there the whole time?"

"I was listening from the bathroom. Lee-Ann was on speaker. I love you so much." She was crying. "Let's get married. Tonight. Go to Vegas."

"Right now?"

"It's been fourteen years, fuck it, why not? Have we ever been to Nevada? Wait, where's the Grand Canyon?"

"Arizona."

"Go to Logan," she said, and he did.

Then the Little White Wedding Chapel six hours later.

Ling-and-Olu in Vegas.

Of all places.

Now she wakes herself up with her tossing and turning. "Hey," she says groggily, rubbing her eyes. She peers at him sitting in scrubs in the chair and assumes that he's sliding his shoes off, or on. "Coming or going?"

Caught. "Going," he lies. He puts down her T-shirt, embarrassed, and stands. He goes to the bedside and kisses her softly. Says, "Go back to sleep," and she does.

He goes to the bathroom and closes the door. He sits on the toilet seat, taut from the lie. The mirror in front of him shows him a face, raw and ashen, eyes red from the thing, and the cold, and a phone peeking out from his little scrubs pocket. He pulls this out, sighing, and dials.

3.

And what was it this time that bade her from bed to the closet, the coat and the short coat-length dress, to the street, to the gray of the soon-coming snow, to the cab, to the Village, and (back) to his bed?

What was it this time? Insomnia? A nightmare?

Was midnight already uptown when she left: just the man and his pug hurrying home saw her go, turned their heads as she passed in the thigh-length fur coat. (She does this, has always done this since Everything Changed, these little scenes from the movie she shoots in her head: frazzled lead enters frame, looking right, looking left, spots the taxi, leaps in, and zips off in the night.) She didn't zip. She rode slowly through Saturday traffic, the streets of New York clogged with seekers of love, to the old stately home of her old stately lover where Taiwo got out, paused to look at the snow. Downward it danced through the black and the quiet, the yellow-gold lamplight, and onto the ground where some stuck and some melted, a funny thing, really, that something so soft could remain, could endure.

And pausing looked down the short block at the windows—some

black and some gold, after midnight downtown—as she'd done as a child driving home in the Volvo, her hands pressed against the cold glass in the back. Those houses had seemed so impressive, imposing, set back from the road on low slopes or with gates, Brookline brick with black shutters or Tudors with turrets, ten bedrooms at least as compared to their five. But it wasn't this grandeur that dazzled her mute. What bewitched her was all those warm windows. The glow. All those warm, wealthy people she peered at inside, with their dining rooms yellowed by chandelier light or their bedrooms turned amber against the night darkness, against the outsideness. The families implied. For though they, too, lived there—*her* family, in Brookline, not five or ten minutes from where she now passed—she had never once felt what she saw in those windows, that warm-yellow-glowing-inside-ness of home.

Even in the beginning, before things went pear-shaped (before Kehinde came in from the car without sound, up the stairs, down the hall, to her room where she'd been watching, where she was waiting in the windowsill, sat down, and wept), there was the sense in her house of an ongoing effort, of an upswing midmotion, a thing being built: *A Successful Family*, with the six of them involved in the effort, all, striving for the common goal, as yet unreached. They were unfinished, in rehearsal, a production in progress, each performing his role with an affected aplomb, and with the stress of performance ever-present for all as a soft sort of sound in the background. A hum.

There was "him," straining daily to perform the Provider, and Fola's star turn as Suburban Housewife, and Olu's as fastidious-cum-favored First Son; the Artist, gifted, awkward; and the Baby. Then she. Determined to deliver a flawless performance, to fly from the stage chased by thunderous applause, Darling Daughter of champions, elementary school standout, the brightest of pupils in bright-eyed class pictures. No one asked her to do this. Not him, never Fola. No one mapped their joint progress toward the one goal—were they there yet? had they made it? had they *become* a Successful Family—but she knew to keep going, to keep striving, by the hum.

The families in the windows were Successful Families already, had finished the heavy lifting generations ago, were not building or straining or making an effort; the goal had been reached. They could rest now, calm down. At night, through their windows, she saw them there, finished, with silence between them in place of the hum, placid familyness captured in paint above mantels, with feet up on cushions, at rest and at home.

But how could she answer when Fola would ask her, about to start laughing, perpetually amused, "What are you always staring at back there, my darling?"

"The houses."

"The houses? You have a house of your own."

But not a home was the difference she saw even then, peering in from the car, from outside, as they passed—and saw now as she paused on the sidewalk outside. Lighting a cigarette. The cliché. *But not a home.*

"Is it you?"

He had cracked the door open at the top of the stoop to look down at the sidewalk. At first she didn't turn. She stared down his block at his neighbors' lit windows, thinking partially of how she looked to him. Short white fur coat. "For God's sake, it's freezing out. What are you looking at?" He followed her gaze down the block. Now she turned.

And there he was, lovely and solid and ruffled in sweatpants and sweater, an incongruous scarf.

"It is I," she said, blowing out smoke with a flourish. "Did you miss me?"

With aching. "Come here."

And she went.

. . .

What was it this time, at midnight, near sleeping, that bade her to rise, to get dressed, and to go? When she *knows*, she thinks now, that to go is to start the thing over right back where they ended it last?

She rides in the cab with her head on the window, her coat rather flattened for its hours on the floor, looking out at the Hudson, New Jersey in lights, feeling light-headed, empty, an odd sort of calm. And remembers now: midnight, alone in her room, having gone to sleep early, the rare weekend off, bolting up in the bed in the dark barely breathing, then crying for no reason at all.

She forgot.

It happened so quickly—this moment on waking, the tears which began without cause and then stopped—that she didn't remember, not two minutes later, and not until now, what had woken her up. It wasn't the insomnia, her lifelong companion, nor the "feelings of emptiness," as Dr. Hass says (a misnomer, says Taiwo: there is just the one feeling, only one way to *be* empty, only one way to feel it). It was something entirely different, what she felt before going and remembers (too late) as she makes her way home, those forgotten few seconds of some bizarre sorrow, intense beyond reason, a force field of grief. Yes. This is what woke her. A force field of sorrow. But how can she answer Dr. Hass, who will sigh, "So we saw him . . . ," Monday morning on Central Park West, with the trees out the window all dressed up in snow, bare brown branches like legs in a short white fur coat, with the gesture, ceremonial, that goes with the sigh: the raising of the glasses (which may well be fake, Taiwo thinks, fashion glasses, a therapist prop) from the tip of her nose to the top of her head. "Did he call you?"

"No."

"But you saw him."

"Yes."

"It was you who called him."

"I didn't call. I just went."

Further sighing. Furious scribbling. "Spent the night."

"Early morning."

"Let's start with our decision. Do we know why we went?"

And what can she say to this? Why did "we" see him? *We felt our very being rushing out of us like breath and longed to touch and be touched, to make contact, and did.*

We missed our father.

"You said?"

The cab driver peers through his rear view at Taiwo, who stirs, caught off guard, lifts her head off the glass. "I'm sorry?"

"You said something." The driver is Ghanaian. She can tell by his accent. "'I missed my father,' you said."

"I did?" Taiwo flushes. The driver nods, smiles. Their eyes meet in the mirror, and she sees him react: looking quickly away and then back, at her eyes, as one caught doing something he should but can't stop.

"W-where are y-you from?" he stammers shyly. "What are you?" But means what they all mean. What are your eyes?

"I don't know."

"You sound English."

"I studied in England."

"Me, I'm from—"

"Ghana. I know. I could tell."

"*Ey!* How did you know that?"

"My mother's Nigerian."

"*Bella naija!*" He beams. "And this father you missed?"

"Did I say that?"

"You must have been thinking out loud."

"Did I think that?" She's smiling. Her BlackBerry rings.

"It's your father!" He's laughing, glancing back through the mirror.

She fumbles for the phone in the bag at her feet. It stops ringing. She finds it. "It's my brother." She's frowning. She puts down the phone and leans back and is quiet. The radio plays softly, Wagadu-Gu, "Sweet Mother," the merry Sierra Leonean Afro-pop hit. The driver stops laughing now, focused on the road again, knowing as cab drivers do when to stop, when the moment is over, how to exit a scene: keep one's eyes on the road, turn the radio up.

Taiwo rests her head on the glass, out of habit, the phone in her fingers, "O. Sai" on the screen. She is glad that she missed him, she thinks (donning armor), does not need a lecture this time of the night, Olu's five-minute speech about Sai family glory, what Others Must Think of Them, *oh the shame.*

No.

What would he know about shame, Perfect Olu, as clean cut and taut as the other once was, with his cold little life in cold Boston, his girlfriend, their cold-white apartment, white smiles on the walls, *Ling-and-Olu do good in warm weather,* two robots, degree-getting, grant-winning, good-doing androids, a picture of perfection, New Immigrant Perfection, of cowardice rewarded, she thinks (readied bow), an old habit, this, bad one, to attack her attackers or whomever she perceives to be planning attack, right or wrong, noting all of their flaws in her mind, in this manner discrediting them). What would he know?

Yes.

If one had just stayed on that carousel, amassing gold rings, seated, smiling, and safe, going round and round, living the same four years over, at Milton, Yale, med school, a life on repeat—(1) compete for acceptance to elite institution, (2) get accepted, (3) work hard, (4) do well, then start back at (1) four years later—then *yes,* one might lecture on "shame." Might call her a "failure" for withdrawing from law school, condemn her as "reckless," "disappointment to Mom," the final blow to the production, *Successful Family* in shambles, curtains closed, theater shuttered forever. But how? How can *he* know what it is to be stared at and talked about; worse, not to care, to give in to it? He who knows nothing of hot things, of wrong things, of loss, failure, passion, lust, sorrow, or love? When even she can't explain it, to Dr. Hass, to herself, doesn't know where it comes from, the ravenous urge to be swallowed, digested, to pass through a body only to drag oneself back to the mouth of the beast?

Olu can't.

So he lies there, mute, riddled with arrowheads, the fastidious-*cum*-favored-*cum*-fallen First Son, as she leans her head back on the cab seat, defended and spent by the act of resenting her brother.

It brings her no comfort, this felling of Olu. Instead, as she draws her mind closer to look, she sees *her* face, not Olu's, her body, not his, pierced with sharp flint-knapped stone, bleeding out in the snow.

"No?" says the driver.

"I'm sorry?" says Taiwo.

The driver frowns, worried. "You just told me, 'No!'"

"I meant no, don't take 96th," Taiwo lies quickly, dismayed by this new habit of thinking aloud. "If you exit at 125th it'll be faster. Just go up to Amsterdam, right, and we're there."

"You got it," says the driver. He glances at Taiwo.

She stares out the window, at blood in the snow.

And how had *this* happened?

The death of Darling Daughter. The brightest of pupils, who never looked out, who had spent half her life with her head in a book, learning Latin roots, spewing right answers. Alone. She had never been close to a man, not since Kehinde; her efforts to make or keep friends came to naught: there was always the issue of beauty between them, as envy in women, desire in men, indistinguishable in the end, lust and envy, co-original, the flower and leaf of the same twisted root. Regardless, when the press learned, they made it sound natural: a tale old as time, beauty, power, and sex, dean of law school in love tryst with editor of *Law Review*, BEAUTY AND THE DEAN! in "Page Six," and the rest. And it was, in a way; it *was* natural, that it happened, that Girl in a city that adulates blondes should find Boy (fifty-two, former blond turned to silver-and-gold) in a city that adulates youth. The press didn't say this. They said that Dean Rudd, born Rudinsky, the fund-raising whiz kid uptown, charming lawyer-turned-scholar with old money wife (noted *New York Times* food critic Lexi Choate-Rudd), one-time Marshall scholar, White House fellow, intern to Carter, special assistant to Clinton, the crown Prince of Gifts, had at last lost his titular Golden Boy glow and would step down at once, move downtown.

Curtains closed.

Dr. Hass, the psychotherapist appointed by the school to calm hypercompetitive postteens on the eve of exams, found it natural, too, albeit a good deal more interesting than the eating and anxiety disorders *du jour*. This is why, Taiwo has long since suspected, Dr. Hass had insisted they continue pro bono after the scandal erupted and Taiwo withdrew, with her Columbia Student Medical Insurance Plan abruptly canceled—and continues still now over a year and a half later, insistent that they finish, that they "see the work through." With the thinly veiled references to quitting and abandoning. A valiant exemplar of how not to do both, Clara Hass, with her buzz cut and tortoiseshell frames and the voice of a DJ of late-night soft rock. Further tales: "father hunger," "Electra Complex," perfectly natural.

But nary a word about nature.

As if the thing could be accounted for by psychology, sociology, but not biology, given the different age and race, not by nature. By the *basics* of nature, senseless baseness of nature, instant-basic attraction, lust, visceral reactions, the thing that simply happens at times between humans as between animals crossing paths in the forest (or jungle): the one sees the other or catches its scent and is drawn as by magnet to mount it, to mate. The press didn't consider this. Dr. Hass doesn't believe this. That Taiwo, with no history whatsoever with older men, simply entered a room and saw *this* older man, this Dean Rudd, and he her, and it simply began.

"Dean, this is Taiwo."

The assistant, Marissa.

The interview, March, winter dying outside, with the trees on the quad sprouting shy pinkish blossoms despite the loud protest of sharp, howling wind: female lead enters frame and stops short at the door at the edge of a carpet of mustards and wines—so much different then, younger, determined, believing, just back to New York after three years at Oxford, the god of Approval still fat on its altar—and stands, looking in from the threshold.

Feels tension.

In blue velvet blazer and dress-cum-dashiki, the tongue-in-cheek dress code, half devil-may-care, quarter Yoruba priestess, quarter prim British schoolgirl, her upsweep of locks dripping tendrils, high heels, with that feeling of conquest she still sometimes gets before entering rooms in which points must be won, in which men must be smiled at and women impressed, prey and predator both, stretching forelegs and jaw. Stopping short, with Marissa, both jarred by the tension, the male lead's expression, the way he just stares.

He didn't stop staring. Marissa was blushing, the nature of the reaction plain even to her. "Well, I'll leave you two to it," she said without irony.

One caught doing something he should but can't stop. "M-Miss Sai," he said, coughing. "Come in. Please. Excuse me." He cleared his throat twice. "Marissa, thank you."

Marissa left.

Taiwo entered.

Walking slowly across the carpet between the doorway and the armchair, red leather, across from his desk. Repelled and drawn, both, as if pulled by a current, resisting a current, undone by his stare, azure blue in the shadow of inky-black lashes, a see-through stare, seeing through. Seen through, she sat.

"It's a pleasure to meet you," he said, sitting also. They didn't shake hands, as if knowing *not yet*. "I was hoping to see you in person, to meet you. After reading your essay." He held up her file. "I can't remember the last time I read something like this." He shook his head, laughed. "You write too well to be a lawyer."

Unsure where to look—at his eyes, at his smile, at his finger on the folder, at the light in his hair, making silver-gold glitter—she looked at her hands. She said, "Thank you."

"Don't be silly. Thank *you*." How he laughed. "The only thing I wanted to ask at this meeting is whether you're certain that law school's for you? Not Columbia Law. We'd be honored to have you. But law school in general. I know what you wrote. About your mother's decision to give up on law school, to sacrifice all for the sake of her children."

"It wasn't as bad as all that. Did I write that?"

"In glorious prose, yes, you did, Taiwo Sai." With the light from the window behind him between them. "May I ask where it comes from, your last name?"

"You may." With the light in her eyes, in his laughter. "From Ghana."

"Your parents are from Ghana?"

"My father was, yes."

"I'm sorry," he said. Hearing *was*, thinking death. "And your mother?"

"Less sorry than you are, I think."

And began. Out of nowhere: this ease and this banter, as if they were peers, friends for years and now more: how they laughed and then stopped, half-smiles staining their lips from the laughing, then blushed at each other, and knew. They spoke for an hour politely, pro forma (the usual thing, her unusual past, the twin brother the artist in London, how impressive, a Rhodes, how outstanding, the Latin and Greek), and she spun the tale lightly and loosely as always, a story told well about somebody else, without detail or heat, "I did this," "I did that," with great flair but no feeling, no truth past the facts—and he listened intently, the azure eyes burning with knowing that nothing was being revealed, that the facts were a coat with the truth there beneath it, bare skin to be accessed at some other time.

Some other time.

Raining, November, on Barrow.

Both bashful, the fact of it baffling somehow, what the dean of the school and a student had *done* quite apart from the blushing and knowing they would.

They'd come from a function at his townhouse on Park, where he'd asked her and three other students along, 1L standouts already in early November, to explain to alumni why they'd chosen the school. After, he'd taken them all down to dinner at Indochine, the five of them squeezed in a booth, with the three others babbling on eagerly and ably, well pleased with their spring rolls and litchi martinis, and Taiwo squeezed next to him watching him charm with his arm on the banquette behind her. Cologne. It wasn't that she found him so physically attractive—though he was, in his way, for his weight class so to speak, with the lean sort of body of a middle-aged runner, all the tautness intact in the arms and the legs, less the torso, not tall, five foot ten at the outside, a very good frame for a very good suit, with a nose sloping down to a cup of a mouth, a hook nose, pointy chin, heart-shaped mouth, narrow cheeks. Rather, she found him magnetic. A presence. He'd pass in Greene Hall, and she'd feel him go by in a rippling of air. A light tugging sensation. Eyes tugged, she'd turn, see him. "Miss Sai," he'd say, smile.

After the dinner the others went clubbing, with cold rain just starting and she begging off, "I'm too tired, maybe next time," and he saying quietly, "At least let me hail you a cab," but no cabs. They walked some, together, moving closer and closer, as two people do when it's starting to rain, halfway looking for cabs, halfway looking for excuses. Down Lafayette, over to Washington Square Park.

"I lived here," she said as they passed Hayden Hall.

"So did I."

Taiwo objected, "You never went to NYU. It was Yale, then Yale Law School, then the Marshall, then the White House."

"All that from Wikipedia?"

"Your intro tonight."

"Of course." He was blushing. "I grew up in the Village. When the Village was the Village still, Jewish and black." He reached for her hand, less a pass than punctuation. Without looking.

"The band's back together." She laughed. She held up their hands, interlocked, and let go. The rain picking up as they crossed through the park. "From the Village to the Upper East Side, *non é male*."

"My parents-in-law gave us that house after school. A wedding gift." He chuckled. "I hate it."

"Your house?"

"Well, my wife's house more precisely; my house is still here. Little two-bed on Barrow. My mother never sold it. A consummate pothead, never held down a job more than three or four months, waiting tables in diners, but bought the apartment, may God bless her soul. Grew her own grass, smoked it three times a day. It was calm in that house. Kissed my first girl just there." He pointed to a bench. "Lena Freeman."

"Nice Jewish girl?"

"Member of the Black Panther Party in fact. We met at a protest right here by the fountain."

"Your first kiss was a black girl?"

"A woman. Twenty-eight."

"How old were you?"

"Sixteen."

"You're lying."

"I was, yes. Pretended I was a student at Columbia Law School."

"Look at you now, kid!" She hit his arm, playful. "It's a bit past your bedtime, no, speaking of home?"

He didn't stop laughing. "Yes. Lexi's in Napa. I should call you a car service. Let's get inside."

Whereon they ran the short distance to Barrow Street, up the three flights to the silence and darkness where feeling for light switch and shaking off jacket, they shifted positions and bumped, chest to chest.

Presently, they were kissing as one does in darkness in foyers still dripping from running through rain: with one's hands and the other's removing wet clothes with an urgent choreography learned without words. Postfinale they lay in his mother's old bedroom, the downpour a soundtrack, both nude, on their backs, and he took her arm, steel brown in moonlight, and kissed it. "I love how you smell."

"Like Lena Freeman?" And laughed.

He propped himself up now. "I know what you're thinking."

"Now, *that* would impress me."

"For the first time tonight?" Feigning shock. "You mean to tell me that my speech didn't impress you? 'The Gift Is the Giving'? My outfit? Okay. The bow tie was rich. Another gift from the in-laws."

"A bow for the house?"

Laughing harder, "*Touché*." He leaned on his elbow to face her more squarely. With sadness, "You're thinking I lost it somewhere. That I once had a freedom, a vision, had Lena, a Black Panther girlfriend, a Jew-fro, a fire, had this sense of the world and myself, burning in it, this burning desire to change things somehow, that I went off to school and met Lexi, got married, cashed in, married up, lost the heat, lost the fire, that I'm looking for something, a spark, inspiration, that you're Lena incarnate, you think. But you're wrong. I've never met anyone like you, not Lena, not anyone, anywhere."

"Impressive," she said.

"Besides, there's your hair. Hers was"—gesturing—"bigger. A cloud. A constellation."

"An Afro."

"A world. Yours isn't"—touching her dreadlocks—"horizontal."

"You don't like my white-girl hair?"

"Don't like your *what*?"

"My dreadlocks. My white-girl hair."

Laughing, always laughing, "Aren't dreadlocks Jamaican? Afrocentric at least? Do people still say that? Afrocentric?"

"Yes. White people."

"I adore you."

"You don't know me."

"Then help me," he said. "I want to. I want to know you."

"You can't. I'm a student. You're married."

He was quiet. After a moment, "I know." He lay down beside her, to face her less squarely. For minutes neither spoke. "What are you thinking?" he asked.

Taiwo was thinking—for the first time in hours, not reacting but *thinking*—that there had been some mistake, that if casting young women to play the puss/pupil to a professor whose wife was away tasting wine, one should look for a student better suited to scandal (or to the Village or Napa or the Upper East Side), one of the very pretty pill addicts with whom she'd gone to high school, for example, hair tussled, black eyeliner smeared, and not her, an overachiever only playing at temptress, an ex-goody-two-shoes in bad girl footwear. It was a show, the vintage dresses and American Spirits, the rapid-fire wit and implied sex appeal, with learned lines and sharp costumes and dull supporting actors; she was playing at sex but knew nothing of love. There was the Thing That Had Happened in Lagos, and after, the countless encounters with lustful male friends, but not this, never passion (moreover, admiration), the show come to life, manifest, turned to flesh. But what could she say? *I don't know what I'm doing?* And how could she answer Dean Rudd when he turned, touched her cheek, found it wet, and said, "Taiwo, don't cry," and assorted sweet nothings along the same lines?

She left the bed abruptly and went to the bathroom. She didn't turn the light on. She stood at the mirror. And here she was: naked and seeking approval, the doer of homework and earner of praise ever desperate to win back her erstwhile Darlingness dazzling the judges, whoever they were. With the body, as always, a stranger post-coitus, the long, lanky limbs and congenital tone, *a good body*, she'd heard, though she didn't believe it, or couldn't quite see it, not least after sex. Now it looked functional, a thing, instrumental. A means to an end, though she didn't know which. She thought of her sister, who longed for this body. Half laughed at the irony, at how these things worked: that she, Taiwo, had inherited and maintained with no effort the model-esque figure that Sadie so craved—and from Fola, who, frightened by the baby's low birth weight, had overfed Sadie and babied her sick. (The disorder. Unmentioned. Though all of them saw it. If only she could, she'd have said, "Sadie, here, take my body, I don't want it. I never even liked it. It's not like I asked for it.") Luck of the draw. A cow born in India or Gary, Indiana. Who was to be faulted? The deified cow? And yet she was. Faulted. Was wanted, and faulted, or felt so, and still went on seeking the want. She thought of Dr. Hass in hemp scarf, chunky turquoise. "You don't have to impress me," she'd recently said, leaning back in the armchair to lift up the glasses and stare at her client, a strange gentle stare.

"Of course I don't," Taiwo had quipped, laughing hoarsely, the sound of the laughter false even to her, in her ears, as she'd shifted, unnerved by the comment, eyes trained out the window. "I already have. You treat me for free, no?"

"I do," Dr. Hass said. "And why would I do such a thing, do we think? Your unique family background? Your remarkable accomplishments? Your formidable intelligence? Your stunning good looks?"

Taiwo laughed again, but it hurt her to do so. She shrugged, rubbed her elbow. "You got me," she said. She looked at the clock, built-in bookshelf, O'Keeffe print. *Cup of Silver Ginger.* Out the window again. A word was taking shape on the tip of her tongue but the tears got there first and she swallowed them both. "Time is up." Stood.

"I care." Remained seated.

"I know," she said, leaving, and meant it.

A fraud.

The word came, belated, and floated before her, a shape in the mirror, a tint to the light. She reached out a finger to touch her reflection, her eyes glowing back at her, strange in the dark (an inheritance, the color, from the Scottish great-grandmother), tracing her lips, conchshell pink, on the glass. "Taiwo, don't cry," she said, softly, in mimicry. She laughed at the sound of it, dropping her hand. What was there to cry about? The same thing as always. The crushing disbelief in the truth of their love.

She returned to the bedroom and stood in the doorway (in armor) and looked at him, noting the flaws. The torso less taut than the arms and the legs with a thinning of hair near the crown of his head. A better cast woman would have asked at this juncture if the man found it strange to be here in this house, in his mother's old room (albeit remodeled completely, a childhood apartment turned bachelor pad), but it didn't occur to her, was vaguely familiar, a son in the bed of his mother. Instead, she found her damp purse by the bed where she'd dropped it and went to the windowsill, steel brown, and sat. "Do you mind if I smoke?"

"Do you mind if I watch?"

She was laughing now, changing the subject, blowing O's. "Think about it. Barring Rastafarians, the real ones, religious ones, what kind of black girl grows locks? Black girls who go to predominantly white colleges, that's who. Dreadlocks are black white-girl hair. A Black Power solution to a Bluest Eye problem: the desire to have long, swinging, ponytail hair. The braids take too long after a while, the extensions. But you still need a hairstyle for running in rain. Forget the secret benefit from affirmative action; this is the white woman's privilege. Wet hair. Not to give a *shit* about rain on your blowout. I'm *serious*."

"You're gorgeous."

"You think so?"

"Come here."

"Your baby is crying," says the driver to Taiwo, the Ghanaian way of saying *your cell phone is ringing*. They've turned off the highway and onto the street's unplowed snow. She says, "Thank you," and, sighing, picks up. "And to what might I owe this anomaly?"

"It's Olu."

"Yes, Olu, I know. I have caller ID."

He ignores this, saying softly, "You sound like you're crying."

She notices her tears and his voice. "So do you."

"What's wrong?" they say in unison, then laugh as do siblings suddenly reminded of their siblingness after a fight. "You first," she says, using the old line, "You're the oldest." She hears him laugh harder, a choked sort of sound.

He says, "Remember when we used to have something to tell him, and we'd stand by his study, too afraid to go in, and we'd fight over who should go first, when we entered, and I'd say that you should because you were the girl, and you'd say that I should because I was the oldest, and Kehinde would always just go, while we fought?"

She loses her breath for a moment. "W-what are you saying?" But it isn't her brother. She knows that she'd know. "Olu, what happened?"

"He died today, Taiwo."

"Who did?"

The drumbeat.

A force field of grief. "How do you know that?"

"Mom called me to tell me."

Inexplicably, anger. "She couldn't call me herself?"

"Taiwo."

She doesn't answer. She looks out the window. Remembers night sledding, Lars Andersen Park, stars. "How?"

"Of a heart attack." Here, Olu's voice catches. "I don't have Kehinde's number in London, do you?"

"No."

"Taiwo."

"What?"

"You haven't spoken?"

"No."

"In two years?"

"It's been one and a half."

"He's your twin—"

"I'm aware of that. Do *you* have his number? He's also your brother. It's not only me."

"Taiwo."

"*What?!* Stop saying my name like that." Now she is crying.

"Don't cry," Olu says.

"Why do people say that? 'Don't cry'?" She is trembling. "I'm sorry."

"I'll find his number. Don't worry. It's okay."

"You already called Sadie?"

"I'm calling her next."

"I should do it." She wipes off her face. "I'm the girl."

Olu laughs gently, sniffling softly. They are quiet. After a very long silence he asks, "Are you okay?"

"I'm not sure yet. Are you?"

"Sure."

She looks out the window. "Well, I'm at my apartment."

"I should hope so," he says. "It's two in the morning."

She ignores this, counting money. "I'll call you when I've spoken to Sadie."

"Okay."

The driver peers back through the mirror, engine idling. She hands him the cash, shoulder to ear to hold the phone.

"Are you there?" Olu asks.

"Yes, I'm sorry."

"Okay, listen. She needs to come down to New York for the flight. I'll try to find something out of JFK tomorrow night."

"Tomorrow?"

"For the funeral. We should go straightaway."

He continues in his Olu voice, logistics, administration, their duty to be there for their mother, the weather. Finally, a silence. He says, "We'll talk later."

"I love you," in unison, and Taiwo hangs up.

She sits for a moment, looking out at her building, the Christmas wreaths bleeding red droplets of light. The driver knows better than to ask, and he doesn't; just sits there in silence until she gets out. She is thinking to ask him to drive and keep driving, to wherever, not here, not this house-not-a-home, but to where? There is nothing. There is the lover who is married. There is the job waiting tables at Indochine, a joke, a private joke with herself, the middle finger to Approval; there is her family, all over, in shambles, down one. Where would she go? There is nowhere. She is laughing. No man and his pug see her step from the cab, fancy heels sinking down in the snow on the curbside, enduring and soft, bare legs trembling with cold. It occurs to her suddenly how stupid she must look to this driver from Ghana in his sensible coat as he watches her, waiting to see that she gets from his cab to her building and safely inside. She teeters up the stoop in the platform stilettos and turns to look back at the driver, the snow.

Downward it dances and lands on her shoulders and nose and his windshield, the hush of a storm, with the street emptied out of all seekers of warmth and a wind blowing gently. She holds up a hand.

They are angels in a snow globe, both silent and smiling, two African strangers alone in the snow: kindly man in a cab in a bulky beige coat waving back as he pulls from the curb and honks once and a girl on her steps in a short white fur coat crying quietly watching him go.

4.

Someone is banging on the bathroom door. "SADIE!"

She is kneeling at the toilet bowl, fingers down throat. Out comes the alcohol, followed by the birthday cake, followed by a thimble of thin, burning bile. She pulls off some toilet roll, wipes off her mouth with this. She listens for a moment. The someone walks off. Elsewhere in the suite swell the sounds of the party, overlapping, boys' laughter, girls' squealing, from a distance, as heard by a child at the bottom of a swimming pool, lying down, looking up, pretending to have drowned. She peers in the toilet as she does at such moments, the patient turned doctor, inspecting the food. It is fascinating, however disgusting, the vomit. How it emerges, with a logic, in the order received. With a touch of the ceremonial, she thinks, in the action, the kneeling and performing the same gruesome rite, the repetition and silence, always this moment of silence just after. A sacrifice. Ribbons of blood. She examines her fingernails, religiously short and still stinking of vomit—

the smell interrupts.

A pin in the bubble, an end to the silence, return to awareness: she's on a cold floor. And not in an act of enlightened purification but throwing up birthday cake (hers). She stands up. The doctor turned criminal. Disposing of the evidence. She rifles through her tote for the usual tools. Handi Wipes, sanitizer, Scope, travel toothbrush. She cleans off the tiles with the wipes as she's learned. (Sometimes the person who uses the bathroom next notices, if she doesn't attend to the floor.) She washes her hands and face, flushes the toilet twice, brushes her teeth, and again. Gargles Scope. Out of habit, without looking, she opens the cabinet. She knows this bathroom cabinet and its contents by heart. On the bottom row Adderall and Zoloft and Ativan; middle: Kiehl's face washes, Molton Brown lotions; top: sweet perfumes and Trish McEvoy makeup and Vera Bradley pouch with the papers and pot. She taps out an Ativan and swallows without water. The phone again. "SADIE!"

"I'm coming!"

She's not.

.   .   .

She learned this at Milton, to hide in a bathroom, a perfect place really, a cocoon, a world away. The peculiar insularity of bathrooms, a comfort. The sameness of bathrooms, pale yellows, blues, greens. And the *things* in a bathroom, a woman's especially: not the eyes but the toiletries the window to the soul. She would go to their homes after school, or on vacations, to their summer houses—always invited, every year, dearly beloved of mothers, a Good Influence on daughters, with good grades and good manners, what a peach, *so polite!*—and she'd slip off at some point, upstairs, to a bathroom, the friend's, or the mother's, more fascinating still.

The bathroom of a mother.

A world of concealment.

A chamber of secrets, insecurities, scents, crystal bottles with spray pumps and baby blue boxes, an undue proportion of labels in French. She would twist off the tops, smelling this, smelling that, creamy lotions, perfumes, and the small shell-shaped soaps. She would wash off her fingers with hand soap (a revelation: at home they used black soap for all body parts), then dry them on the monogrammed hand towel provided or, better still, the towel on the back of the door.

She'd always use the towel on the back of the door if there was one, which smelled of defenselessness, skin, of a person in a vulnerable, sweet-smelling state, of a girl in the morning, false tropical fruit. Sometimes she'd press up her face to these towels, overwhelmed by the smell, suddenly wanting to cry. Always, she'd peer in the tote bins, the cabinets, the makeup bags, Kaboodles, and take something with: a kind of clumsy kleptomania, not as professional as the bulimia, not as clinically executed, and nothing of note. A scrunchie or eyedrops or squashed tubes of lip gloss or sample-sized hand creams brought back from the spa or, the one time, an earring, uncharacteristically, a diamond. Until someone called "Sadie!" or knocked on the door.

"Did you get lost in the bathroom?" they'd ask her, eyes smiling, all waiting to hear what smart thing she would say, Clever Sadie, so bright, and so nice, and so *cute*, like a member of the family. "I locked myself in." Always this lie. Inexplicable, really, that anyone believed it, but everyone did.

Then other times she would just sit in the silence or lie in the bathtub, alone, in her clothes, looking up at the ceiling or ducks on the wallpaper, exhausted from making an effort.

As now.

She sits on the toilet seat, feet up beneath her and hugging both shins with her chin on her kneecaps. Again the phone rings, with the shrill "SADIE! PHONE!" from a distance, but no one comes knocking. She counts.

1, 2, 3, 4, 5, 6, 7, 8.

A game that she plays with herself, or against. Goal: guess how many seconds it will take them to notice that someone's gone missing, that Sadie's not there? She made up the game in that first house, in Brookline, with its funny little stairways and secret trap doorways. She'd hide in the bedroom just next to her parents' (when her parents existed as such, in the plural) and hear them all talking in the kitchen below her, their voices a rumble, a hum through the floor: her father and brother, his voice newly deepened, the twins in eighth grade with their one husky tone, and her mother always laughing, steady rainfall of laughter, pitter patter, like crying, a laugh full of tears.

1, 2, 3, 4, 5, 6, 7, 8.

Which of them would notice that Sadie was gone? It was Olu, usually Olu, a bass in the distance, "Where's Sadie?" floating up through the floorboards, a flare, but she always somehow hoped that her sister would notice, would come up to look for her. Taiwo never did.

9, 10, 11, 12, 13, 14, 15, 16.

Sitting in the bathroom she shares with her roommate, waiting for Philae to notice she's gone.

. . .

Philae. "Like a sister" to Sadie. As skinny. The light of her life and the thorn in her side, Philae Frick Negroponte, former darling of Milton, a sophomore-year transfer from Spence in New York, now the darling of Yale, with her Greek magnate father and American mother of Henry Clay fame. Philae, whose smile and gray eyes and blond hair and tan skin and long legs Sadie loves as her own, who had walked into homeroom that day in September knowing no one at Milton and sat next to *her*. Of all people. Of all miracles.

"Do you mind if I sit here?"

"Of course not, no."

"Thank you." In black leather pants, the first leather pants Sadie had ever seen in person. "Is it me, or is everyone looking at you?"

"You. And I wouldn't say looking. More staring, or gawking."

She was laughing. "I'm Philae."

She was smitten. "I'm Sadie."

"Philae and Sadie," proclaimed Philae, smiling brightly. "I like it. I like you." And the rest on from there: movies, sleepovers, vacations, matching BFF necklaces with *BFF* in Arabic (gift from Philae from Dubai), applying early to Yale, where Philae's mother and uncles and grandfather and great-grandfather and Sadie's brother had gone. Philae and Sadie: the inseparable, the invincible, Miss Popularity in partnership with Most Likely to Succeed, a high school match made in heaven relocated to New Haven as Campus Celebrity and Most Valuable Friend. The loyal, the indispensible, the wing beneath, etc. A role Sadie plays as if made for the part: the Nick to Philae's Gatsby, the Charles to her Sebastian, the Gene to her Finny: there is always the Friend, Sadie knows, any freshman who's done all her reading knows the narrator of the story is always the Friend.

Still, Taiwo is wrong when she mocks her for speaking like Philae—overusing *whatever* and *like*, or for dressing like Philae, monthly stipend permitting—by saying she, Sadie, secretly wants to be white. It isn't a matter of "white," though it's true that she's never had many African American friends, neither at Milton nor at Yale where they all seem to find her inappropriately suburban, nor a "secret" as such. For all of the hoopla about race, authentic blackness (which, as far as she's concerned, confuses identity and musical preference), it is obvious to Sadie that *all* of them carry this patina of whiteness, or WASP-ness more so: be they Black, Latin, Asian, they're Ivy League strivers, they all start their comments with overdrawn *um*s, and they'll all end up working in law firms or hospitals or consultancies or banks having majored in art. They are ethnically heterogeneous and culturally homogenous, per force of exposure, osmosis, adolescence. She accepts this without anguish as the price of admission. She doesn't want to be Caucasian.

She wants to be Philae.

Rather, part of Philae's family, of the Frick Negropontes, of their pictures on the wall along their stairs on the Cape, mother Sibby, sister Calli, Philae, father Andreas, of their photos on the Internet, Fashion Weeks, galas. They are larger than life—at least larger than hers, Sadie's family, spread out as it is, light, diffuse. Philae's family is *heavy*, a solid thing, weighted, perhaps by the money, an anchor of sorts? It holds them together, the wealth, Sadie sees this, it makes them invested in one solid thing and so *keeps* them together, first Andreas and Sibby, then the Fricks and Negropontes, a gravitational pull. It isn't only that her family is poorer by contrast that makes Sadie cling to the Negropontes as she does. It is that they are weightless, the Sais, scattered fivesome, a family without gravity, completely unbound. With nothing as heavy as money beneath them, all pulling them down to the same piece of earth, a vertical axis, nor roots spreading out underneath them, with no living grandparent, no history, a horizontal—they've floated, have scattered, drifting outward, or inward, barely noticing when someone has slipped off the grid.

17, 18, 19, 20, 21, 22, 23, 24.

It was Philae's idea to throw this party for her birthday. Sadie abhors birthday parties—they always make her feel sick, the crushing pressure to be *happy!*, to be having a *happy birthday!* such as she can't remember having had once in her life—but Philae insisted, and Sadie relented, and now their dorm suite is a mess of drunk friends. They'd gathered at midnight to belt "Happy Birthday!" and cut a massive chocolate cake shipped from Payard, very festive and dramatic, very Philae, who'd hugged her, and kissed her on the lips to the delight of the crowd. In a way she'd been waiting six years for this moment, for Philae to grab her and kiss her like this (perhaps minus the eighty-odd onlookers whooping, lacrosse players shouting with glee, "Girl on girl!"), but just after, as Philae was shouting, "Are you one?! Are you two?! Are you three?!" Sadie wanted to cry.

She looked at her friends (Philae's friends more precisely) now shouting "Are you seventeen?!" in orangeish light, with the birthday candles twinkling and reflected in the window. She looked out the window. It was starting to snow.

"Are you eighteen?!"

"It's snowing," she said, but too softly; the friends kept on shouting.

"Are you nineteen?!"

"I'm twenty."

She sits in the bathroom and thinks of it. Twenty. She doesn't *feel* twenty. She still feels four. With the tears surging up from her stomach, someone banging. "I'm coming," she mumbles as she sets her feet down.

And here she is, gorgeous, inebriated Philae, her face flushed a pale shade of pink, and the smile, sticking her head in the door without waiting, entitled and smelling of Flower by Kenzo and beer. "Your sister keeps calling."

"My sister?"

"Yes, Taiwo. She called, like, four times on the phone to the house. You're missing your party. Wait, why are you crying?"

"I don't know," Sadie says.

"You don't *know*?" Philae beams. "Is my little girl becoming a woman? Are you *rolling*?" She claps with delight. "It's about fucking time! Dare to do drugs, Sadie Sai! Dare to do them!" She grabs Sadie's shoulders and spins her around. Then hugs her, abruptly, too tightly. She whispers, slurred, "Love you, S. Never forget it." And leaves.

The landline is ringing again in the hallway. Sadie pushes out through the crowd and picks up. "Taiwo?"

"Where *are* you?"

"You called me at home."

"I've been calling for hours. What *is* that?"

"What's what?"

"The music."

"It's a party. For the end of exams." She doesn't remind her sister of her birthday.

". . . bad news."

Taiwo continues, but Sadie can't hear her. "It's kind of hard to hear. Can you call me on my cell? I can go to my bedroom." She thinks she hears, "Sure," and repairs to her room, doesn't switch on the light. Later, she'll count back the hours, back to midnight, the start of the snow in New Haven, the kiss, Philae's lips on her lips, and the tears in her stomach: five hours ahead of her sunrise in Ghana. Did she know? Did she feel it? The loss of her father, the death of a man she had almost not known, who was gone before she was in grade school, a stranger? How could she have? What could she claim to have lost?

A memory.

Someone else's.

The man in the photo, that one blurry photo of her and her dad in those dull shades of yellow and brown and burnt orange that all of their photos from the eighties seem to have: of him sitting in the rocking chair in the hospital nursery as seen by the nurse from the nursery doorway, she bundled up, newborn, her hand on his finger, he dressed in blue scrubs with an unshaven beard. The Man from the Story. Who barely resembles the man she *remembers*, the upright, precise, always leaving, clean-shaven and crisp, in the morning, breezing out the front door in a fresh-pressed white coat. But the man she *imagines* when she thinks of "her father," this frail, handsome figure with Olu's dark skin and the same eyes that she has, thin, narrow, and angled, the shape vaguely Asian, as soft as a cow's (not the eyes that she longs for, the eyes that the twins got, exotically hazel, but gentle dark brown), not so tall, maybe five foot ten, same height as Fola, but large as all heroes are, thirty-eight years old.

The Man from the Story.

How he valiantly saved her.

A memory of Fola's, of Olu's, not hers—and yet crying at midnight, undone by her sadness, a hurt without cause until Taiwo calls back. "Our father is dead." But not now. There is nothing now, hearing the news. Not so much as surprise. She looks out the window at the Davenport courtyard, remembering a poem she memorized once. *Whose woods these are I think I know, his house is in the village though.* "'Then he will not see me sitting here,'" she murmurs. Taiwo hasn't heard. Marches on, "I realize that you didn't really know him that well . . ." while Sadie's thoughts drift to the smaller of things, to the oldest of things, the most trivial, really: the sense that her sister doesn't like her.

Never has.

It started that summer when they came back from Lagos, when

Sadie was five, almost six, they fourteen. Olu had gone off to school the year prior, leaving Fola and her in that house with the twins, "little house on the highway" as Kehinde had called it, its back to Star Market, single story, no yard. Sadie was meant to share a bedroom with Taiwo but most nights her sister would slip down the hall to the boys' room (i.e., Kehinde's, with an air bed for Olu), hardly talking to Sadie, hardly talking at all. Kehinde spent the bulk of his time in his bedroom with Discman and old sheets for canvases, painting, Fola at work at the shop until late, and she, Sadie, on play dates with friends after school—but she never knew exactly what Taiwo was doing, where she went in the daytime, on the weekends, with whom. She never had boyfriends, at least none she spoke of. She had, but seemed bored with, her few female friends. She was prodigiously gifted at playing piano but hardly ever practiced and quit at sixteen. Fola found weed in the bathroom that one time and, dramatically and defensively, Taiwo confessed. But hiding in her bedroom with the window half open to the front stoop below it, just after the scene, Sadie heard Kehinde say, "Thank you, I'm sorry," and Taiwo, "Stop *saying* that. Stop saying sorry." Sadie peered down at them, backs bronzed by streetlamp. "Anyway, she wouldn't have believed it was yours."

So not getting high.

What had Taiwo been doing? Getting As, getting taller, getting attention, getting angry, picking fights with their mother or picking on Sadie or simply not speaking for days at a go. Kehinde assures her that their sister doesn't hate her, that Taiwo's "just like that" with everyone else, but Kehinde *would* say that, playing peacemaker always, and Sadie thinks Olu is telling the truth. "She resents you for getting to stay," he says plainly. "They got sent to Nigeria. You got to stay here." Maybe. Or maybe like Olu and Kehinde, who aren't exactly bosom buddies, they just don't *match*: mismatched siblings, the one dutiful, unrebellious, fair-to-middling if affable. The wind beneath. The other the bird.

. . .

A bird squawking. "Are you listening?"

"I'm listening."

"Make noise then. I thought you hung up."

"No, I'm here. I'm still here. I'm just . . . quiet when I listen."

"I know this is hard—"

"It's not hard. It's surprising. I'm listening. You said?"

Taiwo is saying, "I *said*, if you'd been listening, that we need to get our visas from the consulate at ten, so you need to take a train down to the city soon as possible," when Sadie thinks suddenly of Kehinde, of the card. "Have you spoken to Kehinde?"

"W-what? Not yet." Here, Taiwo's voice catches. "Did you hear what I said? You need to come down to the city."

"I . . . I can't. I have to submit an essay."

"You what now?"

"I have to submit it in person."

"Why?"

"It has to be signed for. To show, like, the date."

"Our father is dead."

"It's half of our grade." (Which touches the nerve.)

"Are you *joking* right now?"

Taiwo continues, the usual ramble about socialite values in her gravelly voice while Sadie sorts, frantic and silent, through the trash until she finds the FedEx envelope in which the card came. She hears a brief silence, then "again with the silence," lifts the phone to her lips. "No, I'm here. I'm still here. And you're right. I just thought of something. I can bring it to her apartment."

"Whose apartment?"

"My professor's."

"Okay, where?"

"In New York."

"Okay, *where* in New York?"

"I think somewhere in Brooklyn." (Scribbled on the FedEx form, a Greenpoint address.)

"Sadie, fine." Taiwo sighs. "Come. I'll take you to Brooklyn. How soon can you get here?"

"I'll take Metro-North. If I leave around seven, I'll be there around nine-ish?"

They exchange parting pleasantries.

Sadie hangs up.

Quiet. She sits in the darkness, repeats it, "Our father is dead." Not so much as surprise. Squeals, peals of laughter from the hallway, a sing-along, "'Under the bridge down-tooooown!'" The snow. "*Your* father is dead," she says, waiting for (willing) the sadness. Still nothing. She closes her eyes. She wants to feel something, some normal reaction, some sign that it matters that someone is gone, never mind it's her father now gone for so long that his gone-ness replaced his existence in full. She squeezes her eyes shut, envisioning him sitting at the center of the picture having just saved her life, but feels only the distance, the gathered-up absence like soft piles of snow in between then and now. "Your father is gone," she tries, squeezing—or hears it, remembered, a memory that rarely comes up, of an afternoon, wintertime, when she was in kindergarten, her mother in the kitchen, her eyes and voice flat.

"Your father is gone," announced Fola, then, softly. A weekend, it must have been; Olu was home. They were sitting at the table eating breakfast, the four of them, Fola at the counter chopping onion. There was snow. No one asked questions, at least none she remembers; she was marveling at the colors of her Lucky Charmed milk. She looked at their faces, her brothers and sister, one stern Oyo mask and the four amber sparks. Taiwo left the table, saying nothing. Fola nodded.

Kehinde left the table, saying, "Taiwo," giving chase. Olu walked over to their mother and hugged her. Fola said, "I love you," and Olu, "I know." Olu left the kitchen, kissing Sadie on the forehead. Fola looked at Sadie. "Just the two of us then."

Now comes the sadness, an upswell from silence. She opens her eyes and the sorrow pours out, not the one she was bidding at the loss of her father but longing for Fola. She misses her mother. The simplest of feelings, a low-throbbing longing, though a few minutes pass before she knows what it is, and a few minutes more before she catches her breath and lies back, crying, tired, on her old kente throw. (Rather, Fola's old throw—threadbare, faded and soft, with the blacks turned to grays and the reds turned to pinks—but her favorite thing, Sadie's, unearthed in the basement in Brookline playing dress-up with Fola's old things. She'd wrapped herself up in the kente, delighted, and marched to the kitchen, "I'm a Yoruba queeeen!" Fola had seen her and let out a breath, as if punched in the stomach. There were tears in her eyes. "You're a princess," she'd whispered, and hugged her, "a little princess," but never said more, never speaks of her past.) Sadie lies back with her knees to her chest and the tears rolling down to her ears on both sides, to the pillow. And thinks of it:

Fola, years later.

That look as if punched.

It didn't need to be said.

Another house, another kitchen, two months ago (barely, seven weeks, though it feels like two years, Sadie thinks). She was home for the weekend, Halloween, carving pumpkins, Fola's newest invention, a hit at the shop: scooped-out pumpkins full of foliage, Cottage Apricot chrysanthemums, African marigolds, gold rudbeckia, heather, cranberry branches, all the rage among Chestnut Hill housewives that season since appearing in the *Boston Globe*'s Sunday magazine. Mini pumpkins as flower pots. In every way Fola: the something-from-nothingness, the making of the best of it, an ode to Halloween, her most favorite of rites, what with spirits in costume and giving of gifts. "Like a Yoruba fetish ceremony, with candy," she'd delighted. Had hand-sewn their costumes, each year an *orisha*, half mocking as ever, never taking things seriously. Anything other than beauty. And sometimes her, Sadie.

The baby. "Baby Sadie," Fola calls her (or called her), the most like their mother and the closest in a sense, having remained in the house for ten years without siblings, just they, only child and single mother, BFF: used to talk every day at least once on the phone, spend two weekends together each month without fail, making stew, baking cobbler, unbraiding her braids, watching natural disaster movies, discount-shopping downtown. Taiwo says Fola treats Sadie like the favorite (to which Fola, "She's my favorite second daughter; you're my favorite first"), but Sadie says it's more that Taiwo doesn't *get* their mother who, for whatever reason, Sadie understands, accepts as is. The way Fola thinks, the funny ways Fola acts, with her vague, neutral answers and faraway laughter, the appearance of indifference and impenetrable silence—Sadie finds these things calming, relieving. What is more, Philae says she's jealous of how "chilled out" Sadie's mother is, and Sadie rather overflows with pride at Philae's envy. It's the only thing that Sadie has that Philae doesn't (she thinks). Her mother. Her loyal, indispensable, keeper of secrets, secretive, unflappable, beautiful mother.

Whom, nevertheless, as they stood in the kitchen disemboweling pumpkins not two months before—with the afternoon turning to evening unhurried, the leaves in the garden a gem show outside, with that odd film of quiet that settles between them, around them, now forming, as thick as the light—she suddenly begrudged her impenetrable silence. A knot in the stomach. She set down the knife. "So, Mom—" she started.

"Mmm?" said Fola, but distracted, not looking, wet seeds on her hands.

The theme song for *All Things Considered* began, giving texture to the quiet.

Sadie turned to look at the leaves in the sunset, the New England Spectacular, a modest backyard in a grid of small yards for these townhouse apartments (the third and last house to which Fola had moved when she'd started at Yale, up and moved in a week, put their bedrooms in boxes, the boxes in storage), still foreign, the view, after three years of weekends—then back at her mother, trying to gather the thought. What was it, she wonders now, there, out the window, in that firestorm of yellows and umbers and reds in the sun, like a postcard, idyllic Coolidge Corner, Indian summer running long this year, *wish you were here!*—that made her so lonely, so desperately lonely? Made her feel that their life, hers and Fola's, was a sham? That they *didn't* belong to this picture, in this postcard? That both were impostors? She still doesn't know. "I know what you wrote about Christmas vacation, but last year was Boston. This year is St. Barth's."

"I know that, my darling," said Fola without looking. "You can double up next year."

Sadie faltered. *What now?* She spent every other Christmas in St. Barth's with the Negropontes, always leaving on the twenty-third with Philae from JFK and always returning on the thirtieth for New Year's in Boston with Fola, their one family tradition. First Night festivities, then dinner at Uno's, spinoccoli pizza, then the harbor to count, with the twins never home, Olu always with Ling, just the two of them, huddled up, arms interlinked. Now, for whatever reason, her mother was insistent that Sadie be in Boston two years in a row and that *all* of them come, Olu, Taiwo, and Kehinde, at least for the event, Christmas day. In a wholly uncharacteristic display of emotion and even more uncharacteristic use of electronic communication, she had sent out a message three sentences long on the subject last week, a group e-mail. It read: "My darlings, I would like us to be together this Christmas, all of us. Please let me know. Love, your mother." A strange salutation, as she'd never once called herself mother, their mother. Sibby, yes: red-faced and sobbing and seething at the bottom of stairs with the shaking of fists, "I am your *mo*-ther, young *la*-dy," each syllable separate, "You'll do as I say!" Fola doesn't sob or seethe. She never raises her voice at them. Whenever one of them shouts at her she simply tips her head and waits. It's not exactly patience, nor dismissal, something in between, an interest in the shouter's plight, an empathy, with distance.

"That's not the point," Sadie said at last, at which Fola looked up, at which Sadie looked down. With the counter between them (and harder things also). "I want to spend Christmas with a *family*."

Fola smiled. "You have a family of your own."

"We're not a family," mumbled Sadie. Very quickly, very softly.

That face, as if punched.

"Whatever do you mean?" Fola carried on smiling. But tightly. "I can assure you, you all came from me."

"That's not what I meant."

"Then what *did* you mean, baby?"

To which Sadie, "I AM NOT A FUCKING BABY ANYMORE!"

Fola dropped her spoon with shock. Sadie burst into tears with shock. She'd never in her life sworn or shouted at Fola and couldn't seem to stop herself now. "My baby! Baby Sadie! Baby, baby—at nineteen *fucking* years old? I'm *not* a baby! I'm *not* a child! And I'm *not* your replacement husband! It's been, what, Mom, fifteen years, since you left Dad, or Dad left us? I mean, don't you think you should start to date, to have a life of your *own*? I'm nineteen—practically twenty—years old. I'm sick of having to *be here* with you. On the weekends. At Christmas. On the phone. It's too much. I want to live my *life*!"

Fola tipped her head to the side, her brows knit together, her lips folded down. But said nothing. She laughed, a sound like sobbing, turned, and left the kitchen.

Sadie waited a moment too long, then followed the sound of the footsteps on wood down the hall, past the room for the children (one bedroom) to the back, the master bedroom, but got there too late. The bathroom door was swinging shut. The clicking of a little lock. "Mom," she said. She knocked on the door.

"Go," said Fola. "Go live your life."

She knocked again. "Please, Mom, I'm sorry."

But Fola said nothing and didn't come out. Sadie sat by the door of her mother's locked bathroom, that chamber of secrets, and waited, an hour, maybe more, while the sun set outside, dripping orange, and the bedroom turned dark and then moonlit, pale gray. Finally she stood, knocked again, said, "I'm leaving," and waited for Fola to open the door. She didn't. "I love you." No reply. Knot in stomach. She went to the bedroom, expunged a late lunch. Then back to the kitchen, the scene of the crime, where she cleaned up the mess, called a Red Cab, and packed; took a cab to the station, the train back to school, still unsure what she'd meant by the things that she'd said.

Fola didn't call that night. Fola hasn't called her since. A few days later Olu called to say their mom was moving. "What do you mean, moving?"

"She's moving to Ghana."

"When?"

"She's leaving Friday."

"*What?*"

"That's all she said. And that you still haven't talked. You should call her."

"I know."

But she hasn't.

She wants to tell Fola that she loves her, that she's sorry, that she didn't for a moment mean to say those horrid things, and that however it appears from that apartment in Coolidge Corner, whatever Fola may think, that she isn't alone—but can't: for two of the four things aren't true, and she doesn't have Fola's new number.

Your mother is gone, she thinks, curled on the bed in her clothes on the blanket that smells of the past, of a time, very brief, when they lived in a house with the Man from the Story and they were still whole, and she cries very softly for all that *is* true, for the loss of that man and for missing her mother, how light things became and how lost she's become, how alone they all are, how apart, how diffuse. What she couldn't tell Fola is why she hates Christmas, why she longs to disappear for that week in St. Barth's: so as not to feel the distance, the heartbreaking difference, between what they've become and what a Family should be. At least in St. Barth's with the bronzed Negropontes she's spared the iconography: the commercials on TV and the vitrines at the mall and the carols and pronouncements that this is the most wonderful time of the year. At least in St. Barth's she can observe from the outside the fighting and laughter, the family at play, and a real one, a real family not pretending to be happy because it's Christmas but happy because it's St. Barth's. The beach and the sun and the boats smack of falseness, the truth in the open, that the whole thing's a sham, roasting chestnuts and sleigh bells, her greatest fear realized: she *doesn't* belong. But isn't meant to. Not here.

What she couldn't tell Fola is how much less hurtful it is not to belong to a family not her own than to sit there in Boston, just the two of them smiling, rehearsing all the reasons that no one comes home. Even if they do—Ling and Olu and Taiwo, and Kehinde from London— it won't be the same. Fola thinks she can change things, but Sadie knows better, knows all they will do, all they *can* do, is lie. And doesn't wish to brazen it out at the table in the apartment Fola moved to over a weekend on a whim, with her brother and the twins and their mother all lying with their laughter about feeling, each, utterly alone, either eating something Nigerian and delicious made by Fola but out of context somehow, given the tree and the snow, or some traditional Christmas fare even *further* out of context and not delicious for being bought at Boston Market. She weeps at the thought of it. The lot of them together, scattered fivesome (down one) eating Boston baked beans. And cries herself to sleep in this manner, with her clothing on, with no one coming to look for her, for hours, undisturbed.

Someone is tapping on the bedroom door. "Sadie?"

She is sleeping on the kente throw, still in her clothes. She opens her eyes to the shining gray dorm room and squints out the window: a blanket of snow. Sunrise, pale pinkness, the storm's grand finale of absolute silence, the whole world washed white. She peers at her iPhone clock. Seven in the morning. She rubs her eyes, swollen from crying and raw. And is thinking that she dreamed it—the phone call, the kiss—when the someone taps lightly, cracks open the door.

There she is. Gorgeous, inappropriately dressed Taiwo, her face flushed a ruddy shade of brown from the cold, peeking her head in the door with the snow on her dreadlocks and furry white coat smelling thickly of cologne. "You're here," she says, breathless. "Thank God you haven't left yet." And other things also, about having been wrong, having rushed to Grand Central when they finished their call for a train to New Haven, having seen her mistake: it wasn't *true* that there was nothing, no one, nowhere to go, there was Sadie turning twenty, Baby Sadie, at school . . . none of which Sadie follows for her deafening astonishment, the same two words blinking, on, off, in her head. Such that all the years after, when she thinks of this moment—of her sister on the threshold of her dorm room at Yale, covered in snow, in high heels, closing the door, falling silent, coming to lie at her side on the extra-long twin, wrapping her arms around Sadie like wings of white fur that smell strangely of father, someone Sadie doesn't know—she'll hear only her voice in her head in the quiet *she came she came she came she came she came*.

5.

They ride to the city, Sadie's head on Taiwo's shoulder, Taiwo's head against the window, both pretending they're asleep. When they get to the station Taiwo wonders whether Sadie shouldn't contact this professor, bring the essay over now? They're closer to Brooklyn, she explains, at Grand Central; they can take a cab there then the subway uptown. Sadie says it's awkward, like, to *call* a professor, that she'll simply leave the essay in the mailbox with a note. She produces a manila envelope, on the back of which, cursive, "Nº 79 Huron Street, Brooklyn, New York." A gruff Russian driver assents with some grumbling to take them, cash only, over the Queensboro Bridge, wondering what one could possibly want besides maybe kielbasa in Greenpoint on Sunday at ten? Taiwo peers out at the store signs in Polish, white fences, the brick, has never been here before. When they arrive at the building, she frowns out the window. The driver, equally dubious, "Seventy-nine. This is it." Number seventy-nine Huron looks more like a bunker, a little brick warehouse or garage, than a home, with its huge grid of windows with industrial casings too high to see into, a rusting front door. Taiwo asks Sadie if she's sure about the address; exactly what kind of professor lives in a two-car garage? Sadie says a professor of feminist theory at Yale and is opening the door on her side when Taiwo, feeling newly protective of her sister, tells the driver, "Run the meter," and gets out on hers. Sadie, suddenly anxious, hands the envelope to Taiwo. Taiwo, suddenly gallant, says, "Stay in the cab," and hobbles-slides across the heaps of snow hiding the sidewalk to get to the door of the strange warehouse-home, and is looking for a letter slot or mailbox in the doorway when, squinting, she sees it.

The name by the bell.

6.

Kehinde is listening to Saint-Saëns's *Danse Macabre*, the screaming of a kettle and the heat's steady whir. Though he'll remember hearing rustling sounds and going to investigate, he senses (not hears) that there is someone at the door. In his chest, on the left, a light tugging sensation. He abandons the painting, the kettle, the heat, coming calmly to the entrance, down the hallway to the doorway. Not the mailman on Sunday, he thinks, but who else? The only people who know that he's living in Brooklyn are his assistant in London and his dealer in Bern. (All the rest seem to think that he's holed up in Mali or, judging by his auction results, that he's dead.) He is holding a brush dripping blue on the floor, brilliant ultramarine mixed with white as per Fez. He is wearing what he always wears to work: spattered sweatpants, an NYU T-shirt, Moroccan babouches. He is thinking that he maybe should have turned off the kettle or put down the paintbrush before coming out, that the blue needs more white, that it's cold in this hallway, a scatter of thoughts, and the fixed one, of her, when he opens the door, scattered-thinking, not looking, so hearing (not seeing) his sister.

"Is it you?"

She is standing in his doorway, a taxi behind her, the passenger door opening and Sadie getting out. Her eyes, which are his eyes, are filling with tears, as are his. She is touching his cheek, jawbone, chin, the faint beard he's been wearing since summer (a new thing, the one thing that makes his slim face not *her* face, the one thing of all things that have come in between them in months of not speaking that they can both see), she is touching this, barely, her fingertips skimming, a pianist, a blind woman taking it in, this new difference between them, new distance between them, her eyes open wide as she touches him, just, as if pressing too firmly might cause him to vanish, might ruin the illusion, that they are here, now, after all that was said and unsaid came between them, that all that remains of this distance is fur—when her hands start to shake, *with the cold*, he might think were it not for the heat in his fingertips.

Shame.

Hers. Of foreign origin, now familiar, unmistakable. Her shame, which he feels as if it were *his* shame but is not, albeit born of the same place and time, much like they, separate shames at the same sudden thought. *We shouldn't be touching.* She thinking, he feeling, she dropping her hand and he dropping his eyes, saying, "Yes," then, "It's me," to his paint-splattered fingers, and she, disbelieving, "Is this where you *live*?"

It is: above the studio, a two-story workspace with massive brick walls painted white and skylights and nine half-finished portraits against the back wall that he hopes they won't see from their chairs by the door, painted blue, the original, a massive garage door that he kept when he purchased the building last year from the elderly Yugoslavian who lives at the corner, who used to fix cars here before he fell ill. Little foyer by the entrance, a "reception" for guests, should they come, with a rug, raw-log table, three chairs, Frank Lloyd Wright chairs, a gift from a now-dead admirer, a critic, in exchange for a portrait he'd done. Nothing else. Just the paints and the one work-in-progress stretched out on the concrete, some seven feet long, so-called mud-cloth, the new thing, a departure from the portraits he's made out of beadwork since going abroad.

At the top of the stairs, overlooking the studio, is a mezzanine with kitchen and bathroom and bed, like the top of a duplex with two white-brick walls and one floor-to-ceiling window that leads to a deck. This is where he lives. For a year now, just over, the doctors having decided it was safe for him to do, after six months of in-patient chit-chat and relaxants and rehashing all the reasons that he'd wanted to die (just the one) in a room overlooking a garden, very drizzly, very English, but calming somehow, underwater, all greens and grays, por-celain nurses and porcelain service for pain meds and tea, half a year sitting facing and painting that garden, the scars turning taupe and the gray branches green, until one day in August, "You're ready," Dr. Ship-man, his bushy white eyebrows uplifted, "to live."

This is where he came to. Left London in August, the flowers gone mad with the heat in the parks, asking Sangna to pack up his flat and to ship it, unable to face it, the scene of the act. As she's done. Saintly Sangna, the assistant-*cum*-accountant without whom he'd cease to exist in the world. In his mind, in his skin, sure, could go on without her, a spirit, just visiting, a dream, passing through—but the outside world? object world? art world? the body world? Not without Sangna. No. Not for a day. He'd drift, red balloon-like, away from his body and up through his art to the clouds, where he'd pop but for Sangna, the string twirling earthward below him, unfurling in air like a braid come undone. Sangna who, having been yanked out of RISD by her family and remanded to LSE for reform, had approached him at an opening: "Mr. Sai, I am Sangna. I have a degree in business management, and I can mix paint." He was twenty-six, young with the newness of money, the strangeness of money and fame and the world; she was thirty, looked twenty, the long braid and glasses, as skinny and browned as he'd been as a child, grounded, grounding, clipped accent, Gujurati, no nonsense: the dealers all feared her, which made them both laugh, on the floor of his flat where they often ate dinner, *aloo ghobi* and chapati homemade by her aunts. Sangna, who'd flown to New York for the week on a tip from a buyer, "there's a warehouse for sale," rode to Greenpoint with cash, spent an hour with Hristo, brought the price down by thousands and bought him a home—and who'd called, early morning, from London, October, "I found her," voice steady as ever, "New York," with an address for a place on Lafayette Street in Soho to which he's gone nightly, bang nine, ever since.

Just to see her.

Sixty seconds, never longer, often shorter, just to peer in from the sidewalk, just to glimpse her whizzing past, dyed-bronze dreadlocks in their upsweep bobbing, bobbing, past the window, just to know that she is near him. Peering in then going home. Miraculous that nobody has noticed nor harassed him, a black man at the window, with dreadlocks, no coat, although it's always been his magic trick to be there without being there, to muddy his form, not to need to be known. This is what he lives from. The art of not being there. With Sangna, who remains there, sending payments to Yale and attending openings and refusing interviews and generally sitting at the control board of the mother ship in Shoreditch (her loft apartment, formerly his), selling paintings for gazillions on the spreading speculation that he bled to death in bathwater, art world it-boy's tragic end, a kind of darkly comic comment on the nature of this art world, wherein nothing is so thrilling as an artist's dying young.

But how can he tell her—now standing before him, the blur at the window resolved into flesh, when she means: *have you been here, this close, without calling, this whole time, here in* Brooklyn, *just over a bridge?*—that he doesn't, doesn't "live" here, or lives without "living," by which he means hurting and causing to hurt; that it is all he has wanted and all he was seeking in etching thin T's into both of his wrists: a way out of the hurting, for her, who is life-full, who lives and has always lived fully on earth, in the world, in and of it, not grounded nor grounding but ground, in her person, the canvas itself?

"Is this where you live?" she says, peering behind him, then at him. He shakes his head. ". . . ," then, "come in."

Later, indoors, another congress of three blowing, all, on the tea he'd been brewing from leaves (and on other things, hot things, to cool down the anguish, as one soothes a baby, *shhhhh*)—Sadie explains. "I wanted to call you," she says to him, sheepish, "but I didn't have a number. I only had this." She holds up the card that he made for her birthday, on the one side a drawing in simple pastels, brown and violet and orange, her face vaguely, close up, the other his writing, *happy birthday, baby s*, which he'd sent to her wrapped in glycine via FedEx, having scribbled on the label the required return address. "So I made up that story about the paper, I mean, kind of, we *did* have to write one instead of an exam, and the professor said if we needed extra time after Friday, we could leave it with the doorman at her building in New York, but I mean, clearly, I lied," with a quick glance at Taiwo, "because I didn't think you'd come if I told you the truth," with a quick glance at Kehinde, "and you're, like, in *hiding* and no one can call you . . ." and more in this vein, not a word of which Kehinde can hear for the silence his mind sometimes lays on his tongue and his ears. Like a mother, protective, covering the ears of her infant as something too loud makes a sound in its space, or its eyes in the sunlight. Two soft hands of silence that rest on his mouth and his ears. ". . . Are you mad?" Sadie is frowning, at him, then at Taiwo. "What's wrong with him?"

"Nothing," says Taiwo, sipping tea.

"I'm not mad at you," he says in his head.

"Why aren't you talking?"

"I don't know why," he says in his head.

"He doesn't know." Taiwo nods to Sadie and gestures. "Keep going."

"We haven't even gotten to the *bad* part." Sadie sighs. She looks at him pityingly. She looks like their father. The tilting-up eyes set in valleys of bone. He has always rather envied her this, and his brother, that they bear such a resemblance to the people they come from, Olu a darker-skinned Fola, classically Yoruba, Sadie a lighter-skinned Kweku, classically Ga. "Aboriginal intransigent" he calls this kind of feature set, the marker of a people with a sticky set of genes or else the product of a process of refinement and reinforcement over century upon century of mass reproduction. Ethiopian eyes, Native American cheekbones, the black hair/blue eyes of the Welsh, Nordic skin: it's a record of something, he thinks, a visual record of the history of a People, capital *P*, in the world. That he can find, and finds familiar, the same squarish lip shape, the high-riding brow bone and regal hooked nose on his mother and brother as carved out of ivory by sixteenth century artisans on ritual masks, that the face keeps repeating, the one face, over and over, across ages and oceans and lovers and wars, like a printmaker's matrix, a good one, worth reusing—is wondrous to Kehinde. He envies them this. His siblings and their parents belong to a People, bear the stamp of belonging.

He and Taiwo do not. Their features are a record, yes, but not of a People, the art history of Peoplehood, constant and strong, but the shorter, very messy, lesser history of people, small *p*, two at least, who one day happened to make love. As children they'd decided they were aliens, or adopted, notwithstanding the funny photo of their mother in the hall (Fola massively pregnant with a smiling Mr. Chalé and the pink twinned tomato she'd grown in his yard). It wasn't until later, at thirteen, in Lagos, just arrived at Uncle Femi's, ushered into the lounge, that they'd see, from the threshold, standing frozen with wonder, the face that theirs came from, there, white, on the wall.

The woman behind them, Auntie Niké, pushed them forward, her ruby red talons digging into their skin. "What is it?" she asked—rather, spat: hostile *t* sounds, a thick Lagosian accent, matching accent-piece scowl. She'd been pushing and pulling since they got to the airport, both stunned into silence she assumed to be awe, pulling their suitcases, "This way, darrings," pushing them into the Mercedes, "don't touch the leather with your fingers, *ehn*, they're oily," as they drove.

Lagos, through the window, was not as he'd pictured, not luscious, the tropics, bright yellow and green. It was gray, urban-gray, the sky smoggy and muted and clogged with tall buildings, a dirty Hong Kong. The highway from the airport was packed with huge lorries and rusting *okadas* and shiny Mercedes, all honking, one long steady whine of annoyance, the whole city singing the same nasal dirge. The palm trees looked weary. The harbor was gray, the same shade as the sky, full of barges and yachts. As they'd crossed the bridge, leaving the island of Ikeja for the mainland, Lagos Island, he glimpsed a large sign: THIS IS LAGOS. Not *Welcome to Lagos, Lagos Welcomes You*, but simply THIS IS LAGOS.

"This is Lagos," Niké spat.

He found her grotesque, this never-heard-of Auntie Niké with her skin chemically bleached to a wan grayish-beige and a tawny-brown wig falling slick to her shoulders, red lipstick and blush bloodying cheekbones and lips. But the black eyes betrayed her—exposing some sorrow, collected and stagnant, rank puddles of grief—when she touched his cheek, pulling, "A pretty boy, ar't you?" and he wasn't afraid of her, not then, not yet.

They'd pulled into the gates of their uncle's apartment, which from the outside didn't look like much, four or five floors. It was not until they entered the foyer, then the elevator, that they understood the scale of things. The *building* was his. The whole building, four stories, belonged to the uncle who was waiting in the penthouse, they were told, going up. She pushed them off the elevator, "Leave your luggage for the houseboy," with the uncontainable joy of a child on Christmas morning, "To the left, *ehn*, he's waiting," down the double-width hall-way to doors standing open to opera, full blast.

Indeed, he was. Waiting. This heard-of Uncle Femi who had come, late in the action, out of nowhere, months before: winning solu-tion to the problem of Where the Twins Should Go to High School, what with their father having hoofed it and the prep school fees too high. Alternatives included the very tony public high school that their mother chanced to visit on an unfortunate afternoon, pulling her car into the lot just as a bus of Metco students was off-loading fighting freshmen screaming swears and throwing blows. The most odious of options was to ask (her word, "beg") that Olu's high school, Milton Academy, review their eligibility for financial aid, despite the compli-cating facts that they had paid the full tuition for the three years he had been there and that no one had, say, died. Then out of thin air appeared an uncle in Nigeria with whom they might live, attending international school and avoiding potential indoctrination into a "pathologically criminalized culture" while their mother found her sea legs as a working single parent.

Fola, who had never once mentioned a brother, nor any other fam-ily, nor any of her past, had sat them down simply, him and Taiwo, in the kitchen. "I can't manage at the moment," she had started, then stopped. She shook her head, closed her eyes, covered her mouth, as if willing the hurt to stay put in her throat. He could feel her tears rising, a tide, up the middle, but stared at her, frozen, unable to speak. He wanted to say, "He'll come back, Mom. Don't worry." He wanted to say, "Dr. Yuki threw him out in his scrubs." But had promised in the Volvo, *if you could maybe not mention—, don't worry, I won't,* so said nothing at all.

Fola wiped her eyes, took a breath, shook her head again. "Excuse me," she said.

Kehinde said, "It's okay."

Taiwo said, "*What* can't you manage?"

"The four of you." Her eyes and voice flat, "At least not for right now. My b-brother in Lagos, your Uncle Femi, has offered."

"Offered *what?*" Taiwo persisted.

"To take you. For now."

"Take us where?" Taiwo asked, her voice rising. "To Lagos? You've never even *mentioned* a brother before." Then, "You're sending us to live with a stranger." She was laughing. "Is Olu coming also, and Say, or just us?"

Fola shook her head. "He's a senior in high school."

"And Sadie?!" Taiwo shouted. "She's your favorite, is that it?"

Sadie had appeared at the door to the kitchen in pajamas, almost silent. Only Kehinde looked up. "No one came to find me," Sadie mumbled, softly, sweetly.

"It's okay," Kehinde whispered. "Come here. We're all here."

"We are *not* all here," Taiwo said, standing, voice trembling. "He left us with *her,* and she's kicking us out." She looked at their mother, who looked out the window. Kehinde followed her gaze to the edge of Route 9.

"He took it, he took the statue," Fola mumbled, distracted.

"He would have *never* let you do this!" Taiwo raged, and stormed out.

Kehinde looked at Sadie and smiled warmly. "Don't worry."

Fola looked at Kehinde and shrugged. "What do I do?"

"Don't worry," he repeated. "It's okay, Mom. Don't worry. That was kind of your brother. To offer, I mean."

He'd pictured this brother as a male form of Fola, so an older form of Olu. A Yoruba Daddy Warbucks. Instead, from his position on the fourth-floor parlor threshold, with eyes and feet frozen, refusing to move, he made out a figure, neither balding nor strapping, sprawled loosely on a leopard-skin waterbed, slim. The absurdity of the picture—of Femi there waiting as shahs await ladies-in-waiting with grapes ripe for peeling in an outfit befitting Fela Kuti at the height of the 1970s (it was 1994), in that room with its thicket of palm trees in vases and zebra-skin rugs on the white marble floor—was lost on him, Kehinde, for his shock at the portrait looming, gloomy, above the mantel, looking down on the bed.

He had never seen the subject—a woman, a young woman, a breathtaking woman—before in his life and quite literally could not take his eyes off her eyes, which were his eyes, and Taiwo's eyes. "Who . . . ? Who is that?" Taiwo was trembling, reaching instinctively for Kehinde. He squeezed her hand, feeling her shock and her fear. She took a step inward and pressed up against him. Neither stopped staring, nor moved to go in.

The figure was stirring, sitting up on the bed, twisting his torso to consider the portrait himself. A loud high-pitched laugh, without mirth, without warmth, broke the silence. He clapped with delight. "You don't *know*?" He spoke with an accent very much like their mother's (the strongest taste "England," faint notes of "equator") and softly, even gently, as one who has learned that in a land of shouters the soft-spoken man is king. "Niké, who is that?" He turned to his wife, who was clutching their shoulders like handlebars. "Mmm?" His eyes fell on Kehinde, who, feeling the shadow, extracted his own from the portrait and looked.

The uncle was watching him, standing up, smiling, his eyes hardened, blackened, at odds with the smile, to a hostile effect, as one luring a child left alone in a shopping mall, hard, sparkling black. Standing, he was striking, less attractive than eye-catching, lithe as a woman with long slender limbs, ramrod straight with lean muscle, at ease, like a dancer, but not at all beautiful, not in the face. The face was all angles and thick-lidded eyes too wide open and red-rimmed, a dull shade of brown, upturned nose, low-set mouth, the proportions the problem, thin cheeks far too narrow for features this wide. *Almost ugly,* thought Kehinde, though he used the word sparingly, and reverently, like *beautiful,* equally awed. It was a precious thing, ugliness, in humans, in nature; he noticed this, always, in airports, on trains: that for the most part most people looked fine (if unremarkable) with inoffensive features placed well, or well enough. He found he had to *look* to find ugliness, natural ugliness, no less than natural beauty, and trickier still, that no sooner had he found it and quietly thought a thing ugly than he found there in the ugliness a beauty of a kind. He'd stare at a face as at those Magic Eye stereograms where three-dimensional images emerge out of two-, and the beauty would rise out of nowhere, a distortion, after which he couldn't recognize the ugliness again. He stared at his uncle, then, squinting, trying to freeze it, the mismatch of features and wanness of skin, but it happened as it always did. The optical illusion. Jimmy Baldwin morphing into Miles Davis.

"And you. What are you staring at? You like it? My outfit?"

Kehinde, realizing he was staring, blinked twice.

"Don't you speak?" Auntie Niké, behind him, shook him roughly by the shoulder, but Femi was laughing, "*Ehn,* let the boy be." He walked toward Taiwo, ignoring Kehinde for the moment. "And this one, and this one," he repeated. "It's *her.*" He stopped in front of Taiwo and took her chin, gently, the touch less aggressive than the look in his eyes, fingers cold, almost freezing, Kehinde felt. Taiwo shivered. Femi laughed. "Look, she's frightened."

"Don't touch her," Kehinde said.

A very soft sound, equally surprising to all of them.

Niké dug her nails in and sucked her teeth, "*Ah-ah!* How dare you address an elder in that manner?! *Ki lo de ke*—" but again Femi stopped her, erupting with glee.

"Omokehindegbegbon speaks! That's your name. Omokehindegbegbon. Kehinde for short. Do you know what it means? 'The child that came last becomes the elder.'" To Niké, "God, look at them. They're perfect. She's perfect. She's *her.*"

At which all of them looked as on cue at the mantel, whence the woman in the portrait looked sullenly back.

Indeed, she was. Taiwo. A lighter-skinned Taiwo in ten, fifteen years, thinner lips, straighter hair. Femi aimed a silver remote at the face like a gun, whispered "Pow!" and the music went off. Kehinde half-expected the woman to fall, mortally wounded, slumping out from her frame to the floor. Or half-wished. As he stared at her, something else happened, the inverse illusion: an ugliness emerged. He found the woman ugly, overwhelmingly ugly; knew ugly things would happen on account of her face; and he hated her, her appearance, her milky-white pallor, he hated this woman, neither African nor white, who belonged to no People, no past he had heard of, who sat on the wall, cold with death, cut from ice, the only member of their family they had ever vaguely looked like, this pale, hateful beauty entrenched in wrought brass.

Femi said, presently, "That woman is your grandmother," pronouncing *that woman* with pointed distaste. "The wife of my father Kayo Savage, your grandfather. The mother of Fola, *your* mother, their child." He gestured to the painting, his voice growing softer and tighter, a raspy sound pushed through his teeth. "It was always in the bedroom just over his bed, always watching him fucking *my* mother, his whore. Somayina his wife. Folasadé his daughter. Babafemi his bastard. Olabimbo his whore." He spread his arms, beaming, eyes bloodshot and shining, and laughed. "There you have it. The Savage family tree."

Niké sucked her teeth. "Femi, *please*, oh—"

"Be quiet. I'm telling them a story. It's clear they don't know. One should know where one comes from, don't you think? It's important. They should know about our family, how we all came to be." He laughed again, loudly, looking sharply at Taiwo. "And now here you are," then at Kehinde, "my twins. You know what we Yoruba say about *ibeji*. You bring us good luck and great fortune, you twins. And you know what my name means, yes? Femi means 'love me.' I want you to love me, *ibeji*, you hear?" He bent down and kissed them now, slowly, on their foreheads, his hands and lips freezing. "I love you so much." He looked at his wife. "Woman, what are you looking at?" Niké sucked her teeth. "Show our twins to their rooms."

Would that he looked like his father, he's thinking, while Sadie frowns, pitying. The silence abates. His ears sort of pop, and he hears himself saying, "I love your face, Sadie."

"You can have it," she says.

"Did you like it? The card?" He is blushing, embarrassed, aware that she, Sadie, must think him insane.

But she giggles, flushing deeply. "I loved it, I really loved it. You made me so . . . pretty." She smiles, at her hands.

"I'm sorry. You were saying. About a bad part? What's the bad part? You're here, both my sisters. I'd call this part great." He shifts his chair studiously to the left to face Sadie, as one does when one means *now I'm listening; proceed.* He is aware of his sister, of Taiwo, beside him, to his right, but can't look at her, not quite, not yet. Sadie starts to say something, glancing at Taiwo. Eyes trained on Sadie, he doesn't look right. Instead, he follows Sadie's eyes following Taiwo, who's left her chair, mute, for the back of the room.

"No!" he gasps, standing to stop her, "Wait. Taiwo." Too late, and too softly. She reaches the wall. She stares at the paintings, her back to him, silent, her questions a hollow, a hole in his lungs. Loss of breath. "They're not done yet . . ." a weak exhalation. She doesn't stop staring, and Sadie stands up.

"*Now* what?" she calls down to Taiwo, who ignores her. Interest piqued, Sadie leaves her chair, goes to look.

He is watching himself springing into authoritative action, making comments and gestures that make them step back, turning the canvases over so the faces aren't showing—while standing, immobile, unable to move. He is telling them, "No! They're not done yet! They're nothing!"—while watching them, silent, unable to speak. The thing that he does, that he hates himself for doing, the mute-and-immobile act, locked off in space. Why does this happen? he'd asked Dr. Shipman. Can you stop it? Can you fix me? I'm a coward, I'm a punk. I stand in the chamber behind the glass walls, I can see all the people there passing me by, but can't *get* to them, can't speak to them, can't tell them I'm *in here;* I can't break the glass, and they can't hear me shout.

"Protection," said the doctor.

"Protection from what?"

"From your fear, from your hurt, from your anguish, your rage."

"I'm not angry," said Kehinde.

"You are, and you should be. Allow it, your anger. Permit it to be."

"But it's *not.* I'm not angry."

"You aren't? With your mother? Your father? Your uncle? Your sister? Yourself?"

"*Not my sister*," he'd say, but too sharply, too quickly.

The bushy white eyebrows uplifting, "You're not?" And after a moment, "Then why did you say it?" That same wretched question, again and again. Half a year facing and painting a garden, and still he can't answer it. Why the word *whore*?

He hadn't felt angry. He hadn't felt anguish. They were lying in comfort at the Bowery Hotel, he in town for his opening down the street at Sperone, she spending the weekend indoors, on the lam. Someone had seen her and the dean of her law school entwined in some kind of revealing embrace and had snapped a phone photo to send to the papers, specifically the paper at which the wife worked. Such that now, Taiwo said, she was stared at on campus; she'd stopped attending classes and intended to withdraw. Could she stay, for the weekend, eating popcorn in sweatpants and not seeing reporters wherever she went? Of course she could, longer, he'd pay for a hotel room; better yet, she could come back to London with him. *No, just the weekend,* she said. As per usual. She always said no to his money, his help. Of late he'd stopped offering, afraid that by pushing he'd seem to be bribing or buying her off. *Just the one weekend.* Alone with her brother. It was all that she needed, she said.

Here they were.

In night clothes. Near sleeping. New York out the window a low lilting chorus of laughter and cars horns, the suite looking incongruously (if comfortingly) like a room in a house on Nantucket: beige, florals and all. Friday night. Quiet. Then:

"K . . . ," she said faintly.

"Yes?" he said, turning to face her. She didn't turn. She was lying on her back with her feet by his pillow, his feet by her head (how they always shared beds). She was looking at the ceiling, not turning to face him. He wiggled his toe by her forehead. She laughed.

"I'm serious," she said.

"About what?" He was laughing. She still didn't look at him. "You only said *K*."

"But that's what I say when I'm about to be serious. You know what I'm asking. You still haven't said." Now he was quiet, his eyes on the ceiling. He could feel her peering down at him, over her toes. After a few seconds she set down her head, and they both lay in silence. "Just tell me," she said.

"What do you want me to *say*?" he said softly, but knew what, and knew that she knew that he knew. She wanted to know what he thought about the pictures, her name in the papers slipped under their door, his twin sister, his Taiwo, embroiled in a "scandal," embroiled in the World, and not the world in their heads but the real one, capital *W*, where people were ruthless, where stories were written *about* them, not by, where real men and real women had motives and bodies (and sex, which no longer existed in the world that they shared). He understood the question but didn't have an answer. The girl in the photos was not one he knew, not his sister, his Taiwo; she was someone else, older, and harder, than the girl he had left in New York. To answer her question he'd have to face *that* one, the question of why he had left after school, won the Fulbright to Mali, waited tables in Paris, started showing in London, and never came home. She, too, got a scholarship to study in England, two years she had lived there, in Oxford, not far, but he never suggested she visit in Mali, nor the next year in Paris, never said he was there. She left, started law school; he never came to see her. Two years in East London and rarely flew home. "You're busy becoming a world-famous artist," she'd tell him, "don't worry."

It was *his* line, not hers.

Kehinde worried.

About what she was doing at a law school to begin with, having never shown an interest in that kind of work, or in that kind of life (it was for Olu or Sadie, good grades and swish schools and top jobs and all that), and now this, with this man, who was handsome enough, but not—what was the word that he wanted? Not *him*. If Taiwo needed company or someone to talk to or someone to lean on, it should have been *him*, Kehinde thought, though he'd fled, and had run, and was running. He shouldn't have left her. It should have been him.

"I want you to say what you think," she said, weary.

"It should have been me," Kehinde said in his head. "What I think about what?" he heard, staring at the ceiling.

"What you think about *it*, K, what happened, about *me*." She sat up at her end of the bed to look down at him. Feeling odd lying down, he sat up, then stood up. Feeling odd standing up, he sat down in the armchair. He crossed his leg, tapping his foot on the air. Taiwo—who distrusted all silence, found it threatening—crossed her arms, frowning at, willing him to speak. "For example," she said finally. "'I think it's immoral. To sleep with someone's husband, to do what you've done. I think that you should have rebuffed his advances. I think that it's sad that you felt so alone.' For example. 'I think that you acted like,'"—gesturing—"'I think that you acted like . . . Bimbo . . . a—'"

"Whore."

The word slipped so quickly from his mind to his mouth, riding the outgoing breath like debris on a tide, that he didn't even know he had spoken at all until the silence subsided and the word was still there.

"A *whore*?" Taiwo whispered. "Is that what you said?" He didn't know what he'd said, why he'd said it, not yet. And was glad for the darkness, this chair in the corner, the shadow obscuring his form and his face. But not hers. He could see her, electric in moonlight, the hurt in her eyes like a light from within. "A whore," she repeated. She was standing, voice cracking, afraid of the silence. "Y-you called me a *whore*?"

"No," he said, barely. "Please, Taiwo—"

"How dare you?"

He stood, stepping forward. "Please—"

"*That's* what you think?" She was crying, but noiselessly, tears without respite, a thick, steady downpour. "Is *that* what you think?"

"It's not your fault, Taiwo. It's my fault. You know that—"

"Is that what you think? It's your fault I'm a whore?"

"No. I didn't say that."

"You did."

"I didn't mean that—" He reached out to touch her.

"DON'T TOUCH ME!" she screamed.

Not a human sound. Animal. Coming rumbling from under, a snarl in the darkness. She held out her hands. "Don't touch me, don't touch me, don't touch me, don't touch me." She was backing away from him, hands and arms out. "I hate you, don't touch me," she was sobbing, near choking.

He took a step forward. "Don't say that," he begged.

"Don't touch me, goddammit, I swear to God, Kehinde, I'll kill you, don't touch me, not this time," she wept. She took a step backward and into the nightstand. She started to fall, caught off guard, reeling back. He reached out and grabbed her to stop her from falling, afraid that she'd land on the back of her head, but she balked at the contact and flailed at him, manic, her nails digging into his skin. "LET ME GO!"

He didn't. Or couldn't. He couldn't let go of her. He held her, more tightly than he knew that he could. He knew he was strong (every morning the yoga, the scale of the artwork, the labor involved) but had never used strength as a means to an end, as against someone else with an opposite goal. He felt her surprise at this strength, and her anger, a physical, equal, and opposite force. She hit him and scratched him and bit him and kicked him, invested entirely in being let go (and the other thing, also, the fury, belated, some fourteen years on, at his touch, they both knew). In this way, they struggled, knocking lamps from the nightstands, Jacob wrestling with the angel, whichever she was.

She screamed until she lost her breath, sobbing, "Don't touch me."
He held her until someone knocked, once, on their door. "Are you
going to go to jail now?" she seethed, a hoarse whisper. "Is that what
you want? Another Sai in the news?" He was holding her arms against
the wall, pressed against her. For the first time in hours (or in years)
their eyes met. She looked at him, squinting, the tears streaming
mutely. "I am your *sister*," she said.

He let go.

She fled to the bathroom and slammed the door.

Knocking.

He opened the door, dripping sweat and some blood.

"Good evening, Mr. Sai," said the porter, unblinking. "Is everything all right in here?"

"Everything's fine."

"Your neighbors heard banging."

"I was watching a movie."

"May we ask that you turn down the volume?"

"It's off." He gestured to the television. "I'm sorry."

"No worries. First aid's in the minibar."

"Thank you."

"Good night."

Kehinde dropped down to the bed in stunned silence. His fingers
were trembling. The lights were still off. The shower was running in
the bathroom. He waited. Thirty minutes, then an hour, he sat in the
dark. At some point he rested his back on the bed with his feet on the
carpet, blood dried on his chin. When he opened his eyes there was
light at the window. The shower was running still. Taiwo was gone.

Now she is studiously examining his portraits, her back to him, there,
across all of this *space*, having refused all his phone calls and then
changed her number, having told him through their mother to leave

her alone, which he attempted to do in irreversible fashion, falling short of his goal by six liters of blood, *grâce à* Sangna (who, thinking he'd gone on vacation, popped round to ensure that he'd locked all his doors). Nine full-length portraits, the bodies unfinished, but clearly her face, slightly altered in each, with some object, a lyre or a hymn-book or a pencil to make the thing plain to nonreaders of Greek. On the floor by each canvas is an index card label. Sadie walks the line of these, reading aloud. "Euterpe, Polyhymnia, Terpsichore, Clio, Thalia, Erato, Urania, Melpomene, Calliope." She squeals. "Omigod! Calliope! That's Philae's little sister."

"You remembered," Taiwo says. "Eighth grade. The muses."

"Hey!" Sadie turns to Kehinde. "She gets nine paintings and I get a *card*?"

"They're not finished," he mumbles, hurrying over to the canvases. Beginning with Erato, he turns them around.

"Stop. What're you doing?" says Taiwo.

"They're not finished."

"*Stop*," she says quietly, touches his arm.

And leaves it, her hand on his forearm, turned upward. He looks at her, tensing, too startled to speak. "He's dead, K. He died. That's the bad part. In Ghana. A heart attack. Yesterday morning, I think." He is thinking of the question when she answers, "We're going. Olu bought tickets. Tomorrow at six." He looks at her hand on his arm. She squeezes harder. His shirt has slipped back from the scars on his wrist. He starts to pull back, but she holds even harder, stares harder, demanding his eyes with her gaze. He looks at his sister. She looks at his forearm. She drops her hand quickly now, seeing the scars. "I'm sorry," they say in such similar voices that neither is sure that the other one spoke.

7.

Ling is rapping gently on the bathroom door. "Olu?"

He has fallen asleep with his head on his knees. He opens his eyes and coughs roughly, disoriented. "Yes?"

"Are you in there? Can I come in?"

"Yes."

She opens the door and peers in. "Hello, sleepy. I thought you left."

"No."

"You were here all this time then?"

"Yes."

"You okay?"

"Yes." He stares at her blankly.

"You smell like smoke."

"I don't smoke."

"Yes, dear, I know."

"A woman at the hospital had just lost her husband," he says, and, as flatly, "My father is dead."

"Baby." She covers her mouth. "I'm so sorry." She enters the bathroom and kneels on the floor. She places her hands on his kneecaps and rubs them. She hugs his legs, resting her head in his lap. "I'm so sorry. What happened?" She looks at him. "Tell me."

"A heart attack."

"When?"

"Their time, morning. I guess." He speaks in a monotone, entirely without feeling. He shakes his head, squinting, trying to break from the fog. Still, there is nothing but dull, heavy numbness. He stares down at Ling, trying to *see* her, to feel. "We're going to Ghana. Tomorrow. My family."

"Then I'm coming with you."

Too quickly, "You can't."

Both of them start, at the clip of this answer. Ling stands up, tensing. He straightens his back. As in *fire at will*. "Meaning what?" she shoots quickly. He shakes his head, presses his palms to his eyes. "I have the week off. I'll come with you."

"I know that. And thank you for thinking to offer to come."

"*Offer* to come? You're my husband, remember? It's kind of a thing a wife *offers* to do."

"Don't, Ling. Don't do that."

"Do what, please?" Reloading.

"We said nothing changes. No name change, no rings." He rubs his head, frowning. Has not meant to say this, and tries to explain it, "We're still who we were. You said 'you're my husband'—"

"You are."

"No, I know that. But we said it wouldn't matter, wouldn't change things with us. Those words, *husband, wife,* they're just words, they're not mandates—" He stops, grabs his head. "I don't know what I mean."

"I think you do, Olu." She shakes her head quickly. "I won't come to Ghana."

He looks at her, pained. "I should go with my family."

"I thought *I* was your family."

"No," he says, desperate, "you're better than that." He squeezes his eyes shut to bid back the tearfall. He feels her small hands on the sides of his face. Her lips on his lips, then the taste of her toothpaste. The smell of her, Jergens, Chanel No. 5. "Ling," he says, breaking. He still does not touch her. She holds his head gently and he doesn't resist. "I don't *want* to be a family," he says to her, anguished, as a child says, exhausted, *I don't* want *to go to bed*. "I don't believe in family. I didn't want a family. I wanted us to be something better than that."

The phone in his scrubs pocket rings now, abruptly. For a moment he ignores it, not wanting to move. He wishes to stay here forever, in this posture, his head on her breastbone, her hands on his cheeks, in a space very small and contained, like a bathroom.

"Should you answer," she says gently. Without the question mark.

He pulls out the phone without looking and answers. "Hello, this is Olu."

"It's Kehinde."

". . ." with shock.

"Kehinde. Your brother."

"I know who you are." He is smiling. He is lying. He doesn't, never has. Has never known Kehinde, never really comprehended how he moves through things so loosely, never straining. That he's somehow in this manner become a remarkably successful artist only confuses Olu further. Still, he's smiling. "There you are." The sound of his brother's soft voice and soft laughter, the same as their mother's, is soothing somehow. "Where are you?"

"In Brooklyn. With Sadie and Taiwo."

". . ." More shock.

"Can you hear me?"

"I hear you," Olu says. He blinks, trying to process. "You said you're all there, right?"

Here, Kehinde's voice catches. After a moment, "We're all here."

"So, tomorrow," says Olu. "We'll meet you at the consulate. We'll get our rush visas, eat lunch, and go straight."

"Who's we?"

"Ling and I. We're both coming," he says, as she kisses his forehead, her tears on his face.

"I'm glad."

"I'll call Mom, let her know we're all coming."

"Great. Thank you."

"No problem."

"'Til tomorrow."

"Take care."

8.

Fola sits smoking at the edge of the lawn in a beach chair she's lodged by a palm in the shade. She knows that she shouldn't—she was married to a doctor and raised one; she knows that it's foolish at best—but she puffs with great relish, as an act of defiance, or acceptance, complicit with the riddle of death. To do or not do this or that to live longer, as if longevity might be purchased with exemplary health, *this* is foolish, she thinks. Surely vegan nonsmokers get struck by stray bullets and cars all the time?

The house staff is working, pretending to ignore her, Mr. Ghartey at his post by the thick metal gate and the housegirl Amina washing clothes in a bucket, the houseboy little Mustafah, the car in the drive. When she arrived there was a driver, a Brother Joshua, very awkward, a Christian fanatic with a thing for the brake, who had ferried her about in sudden violent lurches forward, blasting Ghanaian gospel music without respite. He is gone. When she ran into Benson at MaxMart last Thursday she mentioned the need and he said he would help, but she rather enjoys getting lost, driving, aimless, windows down, zipping along the ocean. Alone. She'll coast down La-Teshie Road past the black targets, the training site, gallows of Ghana's last coup, with the maudlin Atlantic lapping languidly at the seaweed and plastic debris on the poorly kept beach. It could be quite scenic if anyone cleaned it, if anyone cared that an ocean was there. It could be as gorgeous as Togo, Cap Skiring. Instead, it is Ghana, indifferent and blessed.

But seen from her beach chair, the house has some promise: a bungalow built on a half-acre lot, quite a rare thing to find here, she's told, a full parcel; now developers pack cookie-cutter homes on such plots. The problem is the light flow. There aren't enough windows, and the windows aren't big enough and face the wrong way. Instead of a view of the garden, for instance, the den boasts a view of the barbed border wall; the windows in the bedroom are long, skinny rectangles with views of the shrubs at the side of the house. The whole thing looks huddled up against its surroundings, making do, hunkered down, with its eyes tightly shut, as if dreaming of its natural habitat (Aspen), some mountainside wood and not luscious Accra.

Still, the bones are redeemable, she thinks, dragging slowly and squinting her eyes as she blows out the smoke. If she knocked down some walls and inserted some windows, big sliding-door windows, the place might just sing. *Kweku would love it*, she thinks, without warning, and sits up, alarmed by the visceral pain. *He is gone now* comes next, with another tsunami, subsuming, washing over and rising within. A bit like contractions. A thing that comes, passes. She bends at the waist, waiting, closing her eyes.

"Madame, are you fine?" Mr. Ghartey is calling.

Amina rushes over with suds on her hands. "Madame, can we help?"

Fola looks at the woman, much prettier than she'd realized when seen this close up. Amina peers down at her, genuinely worried. Fola feels the worry and smiles, nodding, "Yes. Would you mix me a drink in the kitchen, Amina? One quarter cup of vodka from the freezer, not the bar. Three quarter cups of tonic water, four solid ice cubes. A single slice of lemon, no seeds in. All right?"

Amina nods. "Yes, Madame."

"*Thank* you, Amina."

Amina frowns. "Yes, Madame." Hurries inside.

Fola leans back with her hand on her pelvis. A newly found "quadrant," the lower-down fifth. A strange and deep longing here, throbbing, almost sexual—in fact, *only* sexual, she notes with some shock. *And why on earth not?* she thinks, laughing, now crying, when he was her lover for all of those years, and damn good, if she's honest, it was that which convinced her, the sheer desperation with which he made love, as if all that he wanted for all of those hours (and hours: he was careful, and thorough, and slow) was to get to the bottom of it, all of the longing and wanting and striving through which they had lived, was to plunge to the depths of it, all the way *into* it, naked and sweating, afloat in the void.

She still couldn't say if he ever touched the bottom, ever felt his big toe bump against the pool floor, but he'd drift down all night and she'd hold him, go with him, go find him if ever he stayed down too long. As the one night, in Boston, in the small house, Mr. Chalé's, when she found him by the pull-out watching Taiwo asleep. She had touched him very gently, but startled him badly. He was still breathing heavily when they went back to bed. When he pulled her, not roughly, toward him, from behind her, and lifted her nightdress with one fluid move, and then entered, heart throbbing, her back to his stomach, his hand on her face, then her breast, then her thigh. His chest was still heaving against her, an hour, two hours. Moving slowly, and deeply, a dive. Downward and downward, until she was aching. "Enough," she said softly. He came, then he wept.

This was a man, she had felt, one could *live* with, build a life with, whatever "a life" might yet mean: who gave all to the living, with deep, trembling breathing, his life to protecting the living from death. Though he knew it was futile. The way he made love, as if now were forever, gone deaf to the rest, as if breathing were music and hovels were ballrooms and all that they needed to do was to dance. It was this that convinced her despite his low wages for nearly two decades and everything else, that her husband made love like a man who loved life. That he put up a fight where she conceded defeat.

Now she is laughing and crying in her beach chair. Mr. Ghartey is watching, alarmed, from his perch. Mustafah abandons the car and just stares with his mouth hanging open, the hose on the loose. Amina hurries back with an earthenware tray, with the glass and the drink in a measuring jug. Fola laughs harder, says, "*Thank* you, Amina," and swigs from the jug.

Amina stares at her, shocked. "Madame, but, the glass."

"This is perfect," says Fola. She takes off her sunglasses, wipes off her eyes. "*Thank* you, Amina." The telephone is ringing. Amina goes to get it, comes back, still aghast.

"The telephone, Madame."

"Who is it, Amina?" She takes another swig from the measuring jug.

"A sir, Madame."

"Is it? A sir with a name?"

"No, Madame."

"Very well. To the sir with no name." She gets up, still laughing, and crosses the garden. Through the doors, to the foyer. She picks up the phone. "Benson," she says.

"Mom, it's Olu."

She straightens. "Olu, my darling, how *are* you?"

"We're fine. We're coming tomorrow. The five of us."

"Lovely." For a moment it doesn't strike her that the number is off. The five of them. Olu and Taiwo and Kehinde and Sadie. And Kweku. She bends at the waist. Another wave passes. She whispers, "*Four*, darling. The four of you."

"Ling's coming also."

"Of course." She wipes her eyes quickly. "I'll make up the guest rooms. I fired my driver so I'll be there myself."

"Of course." Olu laughs. "It's the Delta."

"I know it." They laugh again, together, and, presently, hang up.

She stands at the table in the mountainside foyer with her hand on the telephone, catching her breath. Olu and Taiwo and Kehinde and Sadie. All four, her whole oeuvre, her body of work. All here, in this house, with its retro wood furniture. And Ling, she thinks, smiling; at last he brings Ling. Her tall, guarded son who feels, more than the rest of them, frightened of loving, uncertain of love. And her baby, whom she hasn't called once since October, since that day in the kitchen, that horrid exchange. She'd heard Sadie sitting just outside of the bathroom, had heard her "I'm leaving," but couldn't reply. Had just sat, staring blankly at the trees out the window, the light in the leaves at that hour like oil, like the light on that evening in the autumn in Brookline when Kehinde came in and she knew one was gone. And they. Her *ibeji*, whom she hasn't seen in decades, since watching them walk to their gate in their coats, airline escort beside them, Kehinde turning to face her, to wave and to smile, Taiwo not, marching on. The children who returned to Logan Airport, months later, now fourteen years old with their skin tanned to clay and their eyes—her mother's eyes, which she'd found so disturbing—were not the same children. Not children at all. All of them. Coming. Together. Tomorrow. She wants to tell someone, to shout of her joy. But looks at her hand on the old Slimline phone and thinks, letting it go, *There is no one to call.* "Amina!" she calls. "Let's go make up the bedrooms."

Amina comes running. "Yes, Madame."

Part III

GO

1.

Mr. Lamptey sleeps balanced at the edge of the ocean, a foot from the foam line, legs crossed and eyes closed, palms on kneecaps, back upright, the stray waiting, patient, its eyes on the water, its chin on its paws. The ocean moves, lazily, forward and backward, advancing to a point near the paws and then not, a few inches, no more, of net movement, indecisive, redrawing its borders then rolling them back. Does the water not wish to come further, in conquest, own more beachfront property? Subdue more damp sand? Apparently not. Forward, backward, net change a few inches, while bored with this, watching, the clouds start to yawn.

In trickles light, weakly, drab, without color, its single distinction not being the darkness. A star, blinking slowly, vivacious by contrast, alerts the dog, waiting, that this is the dawn. The dog leaps up, legs out in *adho mukha svanasana*, then licks its wake up to the sleeping man's soles.

The garden is empty of all but its shadows. He hears but can't see for the eyes going off. The issue is the cataracts, he knows, without minding. The surgeon minds terribly and offers to help. (A friend, an operation, no cost to Mr. Lamptey. The surgeon is foolish, if determined and kind. An unusual combination, determination and kindness. An unusual individual, the surgeon.)

The birds.

They are clustered in the fountain, all but covering the statue. They coo very softly and flutter their wings. Ten of them, twenty, or thirty. A conference. He enters the garden and hears first, then sees.

"Good morning," he says to the birds, bows politely. They coo very softly and flutter their wings. "Really?" he says, with some shock, and great sorrow.

The dog whimpers sadly and sits by his feet.

A light flickers on in the house-with-a-hole-in. A shape through the window, slow moving and round. The woman, young, plumpish, her face like a cushion with buttons for features, as pleasant and soft. He likes her, this woman. There is nothing not to like in her. Usually he likes to have something to dislike, finds the likable dull, but he's not the right age for it, too old for effort, too young for ennui. At ninety he'll dislike her. He'll mock her bad English and semiautonomous buttocks that move one at a time; he'll say that the country will never move forward so long as the common man moves in this way. Without line. Unambitious thighs and shoulders rolling over, all round edges, like amoeba, like an early form of life. Like the ocean. He watches her move through the shadow and feels for her something as soft as her shape.

She walks to the kitchen where she turns another light on. She stands for a moment, a cloud at the glass. She comes to the door to the sunroom and pauses, then opens the door and comes out with a drink, Milk and Milo. She is crying, he can see by the moonlight, the breasts trembling lightly against the sateen, but she doesn't seem to notice all the birds in the fountain nor the man by the mango, bare feet, saffron cloth. She goes back inside, turning each of the lights off, the kitchen, the bedroom, a shadow of light.

He rolls out his mat by the base of the mango and sits. *Padma asana.*

Five after four.

ii

They fly into Ghana, Taiwo's head on Kehinde's shoulder, Kehinde's head on Taiwo's head, before they wake and detach. Olu sits upright, his arms on the armrests, his leg bouncing lightly, Ling's hand on his thigh. Sadie, behind them, with no one beside her, her head on the window, legs tucked on her seat, gazes listlessly out at the clouds, also listless, the sunrise a flatline, bright red in the black.

iii

Fola hauls her catch in, from garden to kitchen, still dark: couldn't sleep, went to snip this and that, spongy earth, damp with dawn, dripping blossoms and dirt, sets the boughs on the countertop, wipes off her hands. She fills four small vases with just enough water, stands six boughs in each and sets two in each room. On each nightstand, just so. And is turning to go when it hits her: *There aren't enough rooms anymore.*

There are just these two small ones apart from the master, a shortage she hadn't perceived until now, always thinking (rather dreaming) if they all came to visit, the girls would take the queen bed, the boys the two twins. Now that there's Ling, there's the question of etiquette. She knows that they're grown, frankly couldn't care less, would quite like that they seek some small respite from sorrow in dancing together to breath after hours, but he's always so *scrupulous,* Olu, so proper, saying grace before eating, Sunday service and that (not that *she* is a heathen, good friend of hers Jesus, but one that she speaks to as such, as a friend, a wise, good-natured friend with an air of detachment, not

Olu's stern Jesus with long face and hair) and she doesn't want to make him feel awkward, self-conscious, not least as he's never brought Ling to the house. Olu would do better in the bedroom with Kehinde, less blushing and bumbling at bedtime, less suffering, but that leaves the question of where to put Ling as she can't very well put a guest on the couch. To put her with Taiwo would border on callous as Taiwo tends not to treat other girls well (not that *she* fares much better with the gender, in general: they all seem to find her aloof or too proud, insufficiently histrionic while she tires of their tragedies, cosmetic, romantic, long faces, long hair), and she wishes for Ling to feel part of the family, whatever "the family" in their case might mean. Better in the bedroom with the queen bed with Sadie—a lover of girls skinny, pretty, like Ling; of things girlish, shared soap and told secrets—but Taiwo, left bedless, would think she was being left out. And mightn't then Sadie feel awkward, self-conscious, to share the one bed with a woman like that, when she's taken to acting like Olu, puritanical, and hasn't done the stating of the obvious yet? Not that she minds in the least whom they love—*where* they love for that matter, be it guest bed or couch—just as long as they're happy or not too unhappy, in the condition she delivered them, etc., no worse. If the baby likes girls or this one girl, this Philae (who seems to be cheerful and clueless enough not to break a heart badly), then so be it, bully, but what does it mean for the rooming? she asks. Can the baby double up with a woman in comfort? Or might she take this as a comment on what Fola knows. Rather, what Fola thinks. Perhaps she *doesn't* know Sadie, not really, and not the baby, mustn't call her daughter "baby." She is twenty years old, as she said, as of—

"Yesterday." She breathes this aloud, with a twinge, upper left.

Yesterday was her birthday.

She forgot Sadie's birthday.

She covers her mouth, shakes her head. Of all days. She laughs for not knowing what else she can do, leaves the room, and goes back to the kitchen.

Never mind. Sadie can share the big bed in her bedroom; let Olu get over his issues with sex. She starts to call Amina, then remembers, *too early*. She takes down the flour for a cake.

iv

"Why did your mother move to Ghana?" Ling asks him. "I thought she was Nigerian."

Olu thought she was asleep. He smiles at her, shifting positions. "Something different."

Behind them, Sadie, listening, sotto voce, "Because of me."

Taiwo, in the aisle seat, peers out the window. "You haven't been back," Kehinde says, looking, too.

"Did I say that aloud?" she asks quickly, snapping backward. He hasn't meant to bother her. He shakes his head no. "I do that now," she mumbles, frowning, rubbing her forehead.

"I can hear what you're thinking," he says in his head.

"No, you can't read my thoughts," she adds, leaning back over to pull down the window shade, closing her eyes.

v

A plane overhead.

2.

Fola stops at MaxMart to pick up the candles. The cashier smiles blandly. "Yes, ma. Right this way." She looks at the candles and laughs. "No, not this kind. The small ones, for a birthday cake."

"This is all we have."

She drives to the airport, unnerved by the silence. She turns on the radio. It appears not to work. Then blasting through static comes Joshua's gospel, off-key and forlorn, like a shrill cry for help. She switches the station. Evangelical Mormons. She switches again. BBC, all bad news. She turns off the radio and peers at the traffic. The usual crush on the new Spintex Road. She rolls down the window and peers at the junction where a policeman appears to be making things worse, shouting, "*Bra, bra, bra,* stop," with conflicting gesticulations, the newly installed stoplight not working (no power). She rolls up the window and hums, without thinking of it, "Great Is Thy Faithfulness," two bars of it, stops. *Where did that come from?* she thinks, frowning, honking. That hymn, which he always used to sing before work, perfect pitch, though if ever she mentioned it, his singing voice, he'd shake his head, laughing, "Just sound waves," and stop.

Arrivals is teeming with Christmas returnees deplaning in coats with freight tons of checked luggage. She pushes her way to the front of those waiting, not roughly, but firmly, in the Nigerian tradition. And stands. She is early, she knows, thirty minutes, but couldn't brook waiting alone in the house with the cake on the countertop sitting there, done, with the look of one waiting for something as well. Better here: closeness, the throng, humans being, aunties wailing as prodigals appear half-asleep, pushing forth from the crowd to grab, hug, sob, and welcome, the tearful theatrics of old women's happiness. Better here, sweating, surrounded by talking, the low steady throbbing of heartbeats in wait, hundreds, all of them waiting in collective anticipation of some beloved somebody's coming back home. Bodies. Familiar. She never told him *how* familiar, she is thinking, thoughts drifting as thoughts will in heat as one waits standing still with still time all around one, a space into which enters Past, seeing room. Some motion, slight movement, away from the moment, and off one goes, drifting, from this day to that:

to the airport, same airport:

"Be careful, this is Ghana!"

"My friend, I'm from Lagos."

And I've been here before.

Why didn't she tell him? It wasn't a secret. He knew that she'd fled at the start of the war, that she'd somehow left Lagos to finish her studies and showed up at Lincoln in bell-bottom denim, but he never asked *how*, how she got to Pennsylvania, as if her life had begun where their shared life began, and she never proffered answers at night in the dark after he had gone diving and held to her, wet. Then, it seemed normal to lie there beside him alive in the present and dead to the past with the man in her bed, in her heart, in her body but not in her memory and she not in his. It was almost as if they had taken some oath— not just they, their whole circle at Lincoln those years, clever grandsons of servants, bright fugitive immigrants—an oath to uphold their shared right to stay silent (so *not* to stay the prior selves, the broken, battered, embarrassed selves who lived in stories and died in silence). An oath between sufferers. *But also between lovers?*

She doesn't know. Maybe. So much she never asked him. So much she never told him. The aching for example. "Enough," she would say, which he took to mean "stop," and he would: floating gently to the surface, coming up, thinking *she* was exhausted when in fact it was the opposite: she feared his exhaustion. She was aching for more. More, always more of it, more of him, all: having opened, having been opened, wanting only to be filled: but never saying it, just holding him, lying, in silence, he sleeping beside her, he fulfilled, she unfilled. *Why didn't she tell him?* And other things also. Why she never said yes when he asked her to come to those parties in Cambridge with colleagues in khakis and cheese cubes on toothpicks and immigrant maids and the requisite child trotted out after drinks to rend "Für Elise" proficiently before trotting to bed. Yes, they were boring. But the more it was heartbreaking, to watch him seek approval from far lesser men in his own fresh-pressed khakis, small eyes wide with hope that he, too, might soon be so at home in the world. *Why didn't she tell him?* "You don't have to impress them," she might have said, "your excellence speaks for itself." Instead of "the dishes" or "Sadie has a recital" or "Olu needs help with his science fair booth." Instead of the silence, protective, destructive, like mites on a daylily nibbling away undetected for decades. And the biggest thing. The precedent. How she got to Pennsylvania.

How she packed up and left.

How: she had lain in that bedroom, in Lagos, unable to move or to think or to breathe with her head under covers, her hands on her ribcage, her chest emptied out, until nightfall. The housegirl returned as she did every Sunday and let herself in through the door at the back. She'd prepared the whole dinner and laid out the table before she thought strange that the house was so quiet. "Master!" she called, up the stairs, down the corridor. "Master, are you home? Miss Folasadé? Ah-*ah*." Only then had Fola left his bed covered in sweat to ride, trembling, to the second-floor kitchen. "I'm here."

The housegirl Mariama grabbed her forehead when she saw her. "A fever, you have a fever, where's your father?" she cried.

Fola shrugged, groggy. "He went to Kaduna."

"No!" cried Mariama, slumping promptly to the floor.

How: they'd just sat there, neither speaking nor eating, at a dining table set for two, built for fourteen. The Nwaneris from their portrait watched them sitting, black John seated, too, white Maud beside him standing, hand on husband's epaulette. The food was set out, Fola's favorite, *egusi*, but neither of them touched it; after an hour it was cold. After two her father's partner at the law firm, Sena Wosornu, leaned frantically on the doorbell. Fola looked at Mariama. The housegirl was trembling, rocking, clutching her elbows and shaking her head, noiselessly mouthing some prayer. Fola took the shaking of the head to mean "don't get the door" and stayed seated. Mariama lost her nerve. She stumbled to the entry, from which Fola heard whispers, then loud sudden sobbing, then Sena's high voice. "The baby will hear you," he scolded. *The baby*. What her father always called her, even then, and his friends.

Later that evening Sena came to her bedroom. He knocked on the door, came to sit on her bed. She was lying on her back with her feet on the wall on a poster of Lennon, her head hanging off.

"Fola," he said. "I have something to tell you."

She didn't lift her head up. "I know, I know, I know." Sena was upside down, bending to face her.

"Your father—"

"Don't say it," she said, and sat up.

He said she should pack. They would leave in the morning. His parents lived in Ghana. She'd be safer with them. *If anything ever happens, take the baby to Ghana. Don't leave her in Nigeria*, her father had said. She packed a gold *aso-oke*, a birthday gift, records, his thick kente blanket and bell-bottom jeans. She didn't pack photos or dresses or teddy bears. The details came later. They left before dawn.

How: at this airport, much smaller, as crowded, they landed, midsummer, July 1966, all the colors so different from Lagos, more yellows, the smell like the smell of a broken clay pot. A man with an Afro gone gray came to greet them, all bushy white beard, laughing eyes, wings of wrinkles. "You must be Fola!" He shook her hand. She shook her head. She didn't know who she must be anymore. "People call me 'Reverend.' Reverend Mawuli Wosornu. Sena's father," he said, though he looked far too young.

The house was on a tree-lined street, wide with white houses for friends of the British, the odd Lebanese. They took her to a bedroom painted pink, a funny shade of pink she'd find decades later while shopping for mulch. (Home Depot. She was passing through the paint aisle when she saw it, from a distance, just the color swatch, familiar at once. She read the name. *Innocence*. Laughed out loud, bought it. Four gallons for the nursery for the child who follows twins.) She stood in the doorway and looked at the bedroom. Reverend Wosornu, behind her, "And this is your room." She walked in and sat on the narrow twin bed, the stiff mattress; she stared at the candy pink walls. She looked at the man in the doorway. Said, "Thank you," then lay down and slept, without eating, three days. On the fourth day the wife Vera Wosornu came to see her. Mrs. Wosornu looked older, looked *old* (fifty-four). A fat woman, haggard, no light in her pupils. She wore a black wig that slipped back, showing grays. "It's time to get up," she said. "Come eat your breakfast." When Fola rolled over the woman was gone.

Breakfast was cocoa bread, pawpaw, eggs, coffee. Mrs. Wosornu ate noisily. Thick, buttered lips. Reverend Wosornu sipped his coffee, listening attentively to the radio. *Pogroms in Nigeria ongoing.* He switched this off. "Sir Charles Arden Clarke is a friend of the parish. Do you know who that is?"

Fola shook her head no.

"Eat," said Mrs. Wosornu.

"Former governor of Gold Coast. And the founder of the Gold Coast International School."

"It's *Ghana* International School now," snapped Mrs. Wosornu. "Eat," she snapped at Fola.

Fola picked up her fork. The woman's commands were so tactlessly forceful; it was almost a relief to be told what to do. She put a piece of pawpaw in her mouth but couldn't chew it. She moved it around until it dissolved on her tongue.

"They've agreed to accept you," said Reverend Wosornu, excited. "In ten years they've built quite a fine little school."

"You'll take your GCEs, then go to college in America."

"Yes, ma'am."

"Call me Mother."

"Yes, Mother," Fola said. The word sounded strange to her. Empty.

"That's better."

"Me, I'm just 'Reverend.' Not Father, not yet."

"Speaking of fathers, yours was kind to our Sena."

"*Vera*," sighed the reverend, but his wife forged ahead.

"He can't have any children, our Sena. Such a pity. Only son. And you know what the villagers say." Fola didn't know what the villagers said. The proverb was recited with mouth full of egg, "'The woman who has one child only, has no child.'"

The reverend kept smiling. "Infant mortality," he explained.

How: she finished high school, seldom speaking, barely eating. When the war came next summer, she didn't much care. She skimmed the local papers, saw the pictures, heard the rumors (slaughtered civilians, starving children, German mercenaries, Welsh) but this "Nigeria" they spoke of was nowhere she knew of, not home, not a place she could *see*, so not real. She lost too much weight and excelled in her studies, having done it all in Lagos with her erstwhile private tutor.

Her classmates took to calling her "Biafran," but jealously. They envied her hair, glowing marks, tragic glamour. She allowed herself to be fondled by one out of boredom. He lived up the road in East Cantonments. Yaw. He was actually quite handsome, an athlete, later soldier, but modest in ambition (how: Kweku was her first). She sat her exams and came first in the year. She cut off her hair, tired of brushing. A scholarship was arranged by more friends of the parish at Lincoln University, where Nkrumah had gone. She'd wanted to go to Kings College as her father had, but didn't object.

To the airport again.

How: she crossed the tarmac to the aircraft with the smell of dripping evening in her nostrils thick with soon-arriving rain. She didn't turn to smile or wave or look back at the terminal at the reverend, whom she'd rather liked, or Vera, whom she'd hated. So almost didn't see him coming running in his three-piece suit. The passenger behind her had to tap her on the shoulder. "Miss?"

And there was chubby Sena, jacket flapping out behind him like a broken magic mantle. "Fola, stop!" Fola stopped. He was wheezing when he reached her. "Thank goodness I caught you. How are you?"

She shrugged.

"I've been meaning to come. The firm is still operating, if you can believe it, in Lagos."

She shrugged.

"But I should have come sooner, I know." He hugged her now, pressing an object against her. An envelope. "He left this. Don't open it yet. I was afraid that my mother would steal it so I waited." He hugged until she had it, then he backed away. "*Go*."

How: when she got there she opened the envelope. United States dollars in crisp bounded stacks. Enough to start over, to remain in America, enough not to have to watch fat women eat or take handouts or need them or ever go hungry or go back to that airport in Ghana again.

.   .   .

A passenger behind her is tapping her shoulder. "Miss?"

She turns, startled. The passenger points.

And there they are, all of them, watching her, waiting, here, back at this airport in Ghana again.

ii

"She doesn't look happy to see us," says Sadie.

"I'm sure she's still shocked," Kehinde tells her. "Don't worry." But pulls down his sweatshirt sleeves, covering his wrists with them, worried that Fola has noticed the scars.

"You remember my mother," Olu murmurs to Ling, thinking how much this airport has changed since he came.

Ling whispers, awestruck, "She's *beautiful*, Jesus."

Taiwo feels inexplicably angry.

All of them slow to a stop and stand staring. *Someone should do something*, everyone thinks. Kehinde steps forward to hug her but Fola, thrown, cradles his face, rather thwarting the hug. "A beard," she says, laughing.

"Don't cry," he says gently.

"Oh, am I?" Still laughing, she wipes off her cheeks.

The others come forward now, forming a huddle, and taking their turns with their hugs and hellos. "Ling," breathes out Fola. "I'm *so* glad you made it," while Sadie waits, watching them, trying not to scowl.

She knows this moment. This welcoming smile. This weightless expression of genuine warmth such as only exists for like-a-member of the family. *Actual* members get heavier welcomes. "And Sadie," says Fola, her two hands extended, her mouth folded over, head tipped to the side. Sadie shuffles forward, suddenly nervous at the audience, intending a calm, very grown-up embrace, a stiff "Mom. Good to see you," but the smell is overwhelming, and she feels herself crumbling, sobbing desperately instead.

The smell of her mother—so instantaneously familiar, the smell of baked goods and Dax Indian Hemp, Fola's twenty-year-old hair product, green with brown speckles like something she uses for gardening, too—and the *feel* of her mother, so impossibly yielding, the skin on her arms and her hands like a child's, are a welcome too warm, undiluted, wide open for Sadie to bear it, to feel she deserves it. She buries her face in her mother's soft shoulder and grips her waist tightly. "I'm sorry," she slurs.

Fola laughs softly, stroking Sadie's braids lightly. Olu watches, wishing that they'd do this at home. At least without Ling looking awkwardly at her sandals, remnant smile from "you made it" gone stiff with surprise. Fola lifts her chin up to peer over Sadie and gestures that the rest of them join in the hug. Olu looks at Taiwo, who looks inexplicably angry, and worries that she won't accept Fola's soft "Come." By way of good example, he takes a step forward and wraps a long arm around Fola's tall frame. Kehinde moves also to stand behind Sadie, pressing gently between her shoulder blades, calming her down. Ling touches Olu, too, maintaining some distance, reaching quickly for his elbow, squeezing once, letting go. Taiwo watches, thinking that she wants to go forward, for once in her life to feel *part* of the thing, however loose and misshapen the form of the huddle to feel somehow inside it. But she can't.

iii

There isn't enough room in the Mercedes for all of them. Taiwo and Kehinde follow behind in a cab.

iv

She is sitting with her face to the window, her back to Kehinde, remembering seeing Lagos for the first time: the grayness, the haze and the chaos, the road from Ikeja, the hawkers with trinkets and live death-row chickens, the way Femi clapped when they reached the apartment, his cocaine-cold lips on her browbone, his laugh, how her brother looked standing there colder and harder than she'd ever before seen him except when he slept—

when the memory jump-cuts to Barrow Street, November, nude, sitting in the windowsill, blowing out O's—

and then onward to the end of it, sunrise, late summer, the wife in Apuglia in search of wet cheese, little inn on the oceanfront ideal for endings, the paper between them, the silence a knell.

It was always the ocean they came to on weekends. He called her his "water girl," appropriately so: she was happiest the closest she was to the water, the ocean foremost, though the Hudson would do. (A matter of astrology, he says, she's a water sign. Nonsense, says Taiwo, just doesn't make sense. The scorpion is terrestrial, but Scorpio a water sign? And Aquarius an air sign? The logic is flawed.) A wind from the water washed over the porch where they sat, and she drew in a breath of the salt.

"I'll withdraw," she exhaled.

"No. I can't let you do that."

"I don't want to be a lawyer," she said, with some bite. She ran her middle finger along the incriminating headline. *Allegations of Infidelity Mire Elite Law School Dean.* "You didn't even think I should be a law student."

"Two years ago, Taiwo. You're at the top of your class."

"I'm always at the top of my class," she snapped quickly. "Has it ever occurred to you it's bullshit, the 'class'? What is this 'class'? Just the same group of cowards seeking solace in schoolwork. How smart can we be?"

Helpless laughter. "You're relentless."

"I'm honest."

"No difference. I can't let you quit."

"Well you can't make me stay." She stood in demonstration and walked down the porch steps. "Taiwo!" he called, but he didn't give chase. She walked and then jogged and then ran to the beachfront, and sat looking out at the Atlantic alone. How wonderful it would be to walk in, she was thinking, just follow the path of the sunrise on waves, pinkish-gold, in her flip-flops and lover's wool cardigan, to walk and keep walking, onward, under, away. Instead she just sat there, an hour, maybe longer, just long enough to hurt him, to ensure he felt pain. She wasn't particularly angry—at least not with her lover; she'd been angry with her lot now for fifteen odd years—but she wanted him to suffer, and not from disgrace, but from a sense of having failed her. Of having caused her to fail.

Why did she want this?

He never deceived her. Neither chased the other, nor clung, nor insisted. They'd simply fallen into it, both, in an instant. Succumbed to the sucking-down feeling, and drowned. Now there were whispers and photos and rumors, a manner of discourse she'd never before known, as if some well-trained robot were spitting out stories involving some facts from her life but not *her*. This wasn't his doing. He was clumsy and lovestruck with modest amounts of what one might call power; had been able to entertain her where no one could see them but unable to resist his own need to be seen. Two years of sex in a room in the Village and sweet beachfront inns up and down the East Coast, and he'd started to long for an audience to applaud him, to *see* his great conquest, to know his great joy. A dinner did them in. There were friends of his wife's there and friends of his enemies from government days. In less than a month there was scandal in the offing. University president and board were apprised. In the middle of August they repaired to Cape May to negotiate the terms of surrender. End scene.

They were allies still, lovers. There was no cause for anger. She'd never asked nor wanted that he tell or leave his wife. She had no particular interest in being a wife, for rather obvious reasons, and none in being his. But she wanted that he *suffer*. To know that he'd failed her. She was determined to withdraw so that he'd know that she'd failed; so that all of them, seeing her failure, would puzzle, would ask in hushed tones how this girl, this *success*—summa cum laude, NYU! PPE, Magdalen College! summer associate, Wachtell!—came to fall on her sword, whereon the answer would come, if not to them who were asking, then to him:

Because he let her.

And not him alone.

There was the other one, the first one, the one they'd deleted, the one who had backed down a sunset-lit drive while she watched from the window obscured by the darkness, having played with the lights to bid Kehinde inside: first off, then on, then off, then on: just sufficiently dark now to see in the car, the man's face through the windshield, soft, narrow eyes narrower, fighting: then filling with, tears—but resolute.

He would know, too, she thought, sitting there silent as one sits on beaches: with knees to the chest, and the chin on the knees, and the breeze in the hair, and the taste of one's tears bearing salt from the breeze. She would find him and tell him. He was somewhere in Ghana (according to Olu); she'd go there and wait. She'd be seated on his stoop when he came home from work, in a Volvo as she saw it, the sunset full swing. He'd see her from the driveway and slow to a stop with that look on his face per that scene in such films when a man on the run returns home before dark and the hit man is waiting, at ease, in plain sight, with his boots on the railing, a gun in one boot where the man in the driveway can see it. Like that. He'd stop, kill the engine, and stare from the car with his eyes meeting hers, hers unblinking, his wet, for he'd see in her face that a light had gone out and would know without words that his daughter was dead, that the girl he had left on a street in North America was not the one sitting on this stoop in West Africa, with boots propped on railing and pistol in boots, that she'd died because no one would save her. Indeed. She would drop out of law school and earn waiting tables the thousand-odd dollars to fly to Accra (against prior beliefs about the injustice of such pricing, an insult to immigrants the cost to fly east) so that he, too, would know, and would suffer from knowing, that he'd been too weak to protect her.

Or rather: this is how she planned it.

She should have come sooner.

She laughs, looking out at the streets of Accra. Two years imagining the look on his face, she is here and her father is gone.

v

He is sitting with his face to the window, his back to Taiwo, looking out at the road from the airport, at Accra, somehow different than he expected, not like Mali or Lagos, less glamour, more order. A suburb. With dust. There are the standard things, African things, the hawkers on the roadside, the color of the buildings the same faded beige as the air and the foliage, the bright printed fabrics, the never-finished construction sites (condos, hotels) giving the whole thing the feel of a home being remodeled in perpetuity, midproject, the men gone to lunch, the new paint already chipping and fading in the sunshine as if it never really mattered what color it was, stacked-up concrete blocks soldiers awaiting their orders, steel, sleeping machinery interrupting the green. This is familiar.

What strikes him is the movement, neither lethargic nor frenetic, an in-the-middle kind of pace, none of the ancientness of Mali nor the ambitiousness of Nigeria, just a steady-on movement toward what he can't tell. There are the same big green highway signs seen the world over, proof positive of "development" as he's heard the word used, as if developing a country means refashioning it as California: supermarkets, SUVs, palms, smog, and all. Children in T-shirts with rap stars' huge faces run up to the taxi to peddle their wares: imported apples in columns, PK chewing gum, bananas, daily papers, deconstructed exfoliation sponge, matches. The wares beckon cheerfully in primary colors, imported from China, South Africa, all plastic, all manner of plastic and cellophane and packaging as if the poor love nothing more than kitsch wrapped up like gifts. A man without legs has a boy without shoes wheel him carefully through the traffic in the middle of the road to the cab, where he knocks on the passenger window and holds up a hand missing fingers for coins.

"Go, go, go," shoos the driver, suddenly agitated. He rolls down his window to shout in coarse Twi.

Kehinde peers down, sees the man, is embarrassed. He rifles through his sweatshirt for five single bills. "Don't shout at them, please, sir," he says to the driver. The driver looks back at him, sweating and stunned. Kehinde rolls his window down and holds out the dollars. "Here," he says. "Take it." The driver sucks his teeth. The boy without shoes takes just one of the dollars. The man without legs smiles, a smile without teeth. "Take the rest," Kehinde says, but the boy doesn't hear, and the taxi starts moving as the stoplight turns green.

"They're thieves," says the driver. "They come from Mauritania. They steal from the tourists."

"We're not tourists," Kehinde says.

The driver starts laughing, one golden tooth glinting, as if to say *only tourists give beggars U.S. dollars*, but quickly recovers and rolls up his window, asking casually, "So where are you from?"

Kehinde looks at Taiwo, who is paying no attention, then back at the driver, not much older than they. He can sense in the man a very particular form of aggression, mounting, familiar from Lagos and London and New York, to do with the fact that they're both brown-skinned males unequally yoked by the side effects. He'd rather be ferrying some tense blond-haired couple in his taxi than them—brown, well dressed, the same age—whom he takes for American and assumes to be rich, at least richer than he by some cruel twist of fate. "Have you ever been to Africa?" he adds proprietarily.

"Nigeria and Mali."

"But not Ghana," he insists.

Kehinde shakes his head, and the driver looks satisfied. Kehinde feels the need to add, "Our father's from here." The instant he says it he wishes he hadn't, for now comes the surge he's been keeping at bay in the form of a headache, a sudden searing something in the space between his eyebrows so sharp he gasps, "*Was.*"

The driver doesn't hear this. "Where's 'here'?" he asks, challenging.

"Ghana," mumbles Kehinde. It sounds like a lie.

"Oh yeah? Where in Ghana?" The driver is smirking.

"I don't know where," says Kehinde, now closing his eyes.

"You don't know where he's from, your own father," says the driver. He sucks his teeth, glancing at Taiwo, still mute. "Why don't you ask him?"

As it finally hits him, "He died," Kehinde answers and starts, at the laugh.

He can't quite imagine what his sister finds funny, but she appears to be laughing, outright, her back turned. "Taiwo," he whispers, thinking maybe she's crying, but she turns to him dry-eyed.

"He's gone." She shakes her head. She doesn't stop laughing.

The driver looks incredulous. "Father na' dead and she laugh for," he scoffs. But says nothing further, just turns on the radio (inconsolate gospel) and looks straight ahead.

3.

Both the taxi and Mercedes pull into the drive where the house staff stands waiting at attention, in a line. Sadie has been sleeping for the twenty-minute ride and now opening her eyes says, "Where are we?" Olu and Ling side by side in the back, neither moving nor speaking, peer out at the house. Fola peers also with hands on the wheel as if considering whether this is the right place or not. One breath, then she stirs, pulling the key from the ignition and her sunglasses from her forehead. "We're home, I suppose."

The staff comes forward as the car doors open. Everyone alights and stands looking at the house (except Kehinde who—much to the annoyance of Taiwo and the disturbance of Olu—stands looking at Ling). There is the usual combination of disorder and determination that occasions the arrival of a group at a residence: half of the bodies moving busily, lugging suitcases, half of the bodies looking awkward, out of place, trying to help, to be of use but not to get in the way of the bodies who know where to go, what to do. With the lightly frantic energy of awkward introductions, with no one quite knowing what to say or to whom, smiling at no one, shifting positions, making lax observations. *Where's the bathroom?* Longing suddenly to be on one's own.

Fola holds shoulders, steers bodies down hallways. "This is the room where you two boys will sleep." She pushes in Olu and Kehinde and continues, "The girls in here," pushing in Taiwo and Ling. "The baby—" she stops herself. "Sadie's with me. I'd suggest a good nap now. We'll eat at half six." Any questions? No questions. "Good. Welcome to Ghana." She takes Sadie to her bedroom, and leaves them to sleep.

ii

Sadie stares up at the wood-paneled ceiling, alone in this room down the hall from the rest.

"The bloody A/C died this morning—" said Fola, then bent as if nauseous and didn't go on.

"Mom, are you sick?" Sadie asked, stepping forward, but Fola stood straight, waved a hand, shook her head. "Comes and goes. Going" was her cryptic nonanswer. She turned on the fan, left the room, closed the door.

Sadie stares up at the blades in the shadow, like bats on the ceiling, too hot all the same. Through the thin bedroom walls she can hear other voices but can't extract words from the soft throbbing din. Olu, maybe Kehinde. A phone in the hallway. The pretty girl, Amelia or something like that. "Please, Madame. Telephone." The rustling of footsteps, then Fola's voice, gravelly, the words indistinct. Someone's laughter. Her mother's, she realizes after a moment. But higher than normal, a burst of it, false.

She rolls to her side, where she glimpses a photo in light slipping in from the stiff wooden blinds. Just barely she makes out the faces, the location, and suddenly remembers: why Greenpoint seemed familiar: this strange-looking warehouse on Oak Street in Newton, the famed home of Paulette's Ballet Studio. Winter. Her family stands bundled in coats close together on the sidewalk outside, the recital just over. The

Man from the Story holds her up on his shoulders; she is still in her costume, red lips, pink tulle tutu, her four-year-old potbelly pushing unabashedly against the pink skin of the leotard, laughing. Taiwo and Kehinde wear matching red earmuffs, neither looking at the camera, Fola looking at her. Olu looks dwarfed by a massive brown coat. A stranger, another parent, must have taken the picture.

She wonders why Fola has this, of all photos, here framed on the nightstand, the frame the wrong size so the photo slips sideways, the shot out of focus, some Christmas performance of no real consequence. She abandoned ballet sophomore year, first semester, despite great potential and greater "commitment." Had seen it: could lift her big toe to her forehead, demanded a split of her muscular legs, had defied her flat arches to bend into pointe shoes, could do all the steps in her sleep, no mistakes, but had stood at the bar in a line that September and noticed the palette, the pinks and the whites, light brown hair, light brown wood, clean-straight lines in the sunlight, and noticed herself, neither long, straight, nor light, and had seen in an instant what was meant by commitment: she was great at ballet but was no ballerina. (Philae had suggested that she take up Team Management to meet her requirement for after-school sports, and indeed she had found a perverse kind of pleasure in watching her light-brown-haired classmates in skirts—yellow mouth-guards bared, snarling, browned legs churning earth, drawing blood from bare shins with their field hockey sticks, later ice hockey, lacrosse sticks, so bafflingly violent, "Blood makes the grass grow!"—while she ticked off stats.)

She rolls the other way but feels the photo-faces watching her. She turns the photo over so it's lying facedown. The position has promise. Unseen and unseeing. She rolls to her stomach and lies there facedown. At first she finds comfort: the intensified silence, the absolute darkness befitting the occasion. She isn't quite sure what she's meant to be feeling, but this here would seem the appropriate pose, sort of prostrate with grief (that won't come) for her father and guilt at the thing with her mother, what's left. If she embarrassed them all with that scene at the airport, she unburdened a bit of the anguish at least. Maybe they'll talk a bit more a bit later. Probably not. It is not Fola's thing, "talking out." More likely they'll act as if the thing never happened, not least as there's now this more solid despair that her siblings won't mention, not once at the airport, not once in the car, as if it's not really true, as if they're all here in Ghana—where no one has been except Olu, someone mentioned, when he was just born—just by chance, here for Christmas, a family vacation, and not for their father, unmentioned and gone.

The comfort becomes panic, with her face in the pillow, unable to breathe for the cloth and the heat, and now, rolling back over, she finds that she's crying for nothing more epic than feeling left out. There they are, the lot of them, somewhere else, talking, their voices drowned out by the overhead fan while she's here on her own, the one not like the others, feeling inferior as she always does whenever they're home. With one of them (two max, the twins for example), she can generally rise above it but not with all three, so much older and taller, inexplicably *taller*, and surer, more spectacular, more *shiny* than she.

Her siblings are shiny. Olu, Taiwo, and Kehinde. They shine into rooms with their confident strides, their impressive achievements, and she with her beauty; they glow with their talent, their stuffed bag of tricks. There is Olu's calm brilliance, his mastery of science, his deep steady voice sure with knowledge of facts. There is Taiwo's dark genius, her hoarse luring whisper aglow with long words and the odd phrase in French; all her life she has had it, since Sadie can remember, this thick air of mystery, of effortless grace, as have only those women whose beauty is given, not open to interpretation by beholder, a fact. There is Kehinde's pure talent, the gift of the image, that quiet assurance with which he looks out as if all of the world were overlaid with some pattern indescribably beautiful and meaningful, a grid, and if only you could see it as clearly as he could, then you too would take to blank easel with brush just as simply as one watches movies, the news, without commitment, simply seeing and understanding the seen. And there's she. Baby Sadie. A good decade tardy, arriving in winter, a cheerful mistake, with her grab bag of competencies—photographic memory, *battement développé,* making lanyards—but lacking entirely in gifts.

Fola is convinced that the thing is there latent; for years now she's said, "Just you wait. It will out." Nothing has outed. She has done all her homework and studied with diligence so done well in school, not like Olu or Taiwo, more so eighty-fifth percentile; has made it to Yale (off the wait list but still); has settled in comfortably to a life of B-pluses and management positions on teams and class councils; has basked in the attention refracted by Philae of tow-headed frat boys endeared by her braids—but has yet to unearth any particular gift that might place her in league with her siblings at last.

Panic. Rising gently from the place in her stomach such panic lies waiting for moments like this. She runs from the bed to the adjoining master bathroom and kneels by the toilet to let the thing out. Up come the peanuts and Coke and six bread rolls she ate on the plane behind Olu and Ling, tearing the bread into pieces more appropriate for pigeons before scarfing them down when the rest fell asleep.

iii

Taiwo and Ling in the one-bedded bedroom.

Awkwardly pretending to begin to unpack.

Ling sees the vase on the nightstand and thinks of it. "Your mother's so gorgeous."

"Mmm-hmm," Taiwo says. She is crouching on the floor by the

bed with her suitcase, looking vaguely for a shirt for the household-wide nap. She can feel Ling behind her trying to strike up conversation as if they were roommates, day one at the dorm, by turns nervous and excited at the distinct possibility that this stranger might well be a life-long best friend. They've met on other occasions—Olu's various cele-brations, mostly birthdays, when the family would drive down to Yale in the little blue hatchback, a mess from the flowers, Baby Sadie in grade school, and they just returned—but those were the years that she, Taiwo, spent mute, when she'd sit there in silence at Sally's, and eat, so it wasn't until later, circa med school graduation, that she spoke to Ling really, got to know the girl some.

It was then she discovered that Ling, much like Olu, is dead set on things going well at all times and so cannot sit still: flutters, flits, laugh-ing constantly as if trying to keep a beach ball from touching the ground. The problem, to boot, is the lack of a filter. She says what she's thinking, then laughs at her thoughts to an endearing effect (if exhausting, ado-lescent). If she weren't pretty, she'd be annoying. Instead she is cute.

This more than anything is what disturbs Taiwo, how *cute* is Ling, barely five feet off the ground, with her skinny black ponytail bobbing along as she bobs beside Olu double-step to keep stride. She doesn't find cute women trustworthy, not grown-ups. A cute girl is one thing, cute adult another. Such women always seem to have something to hide, to be playing at helplessness, masking desire. Invariably, she sees in their sweet long-lashed eyes the same smoldering want that burns blatant in hers, if not more of it, cunning, more clarity of purpose, obscured by the girlishness, false to its core. They are *women* in the truest sense, ripe with soft power, yet pretending not to know what they want, *that* they want—as if want were unbecoming, a flaw clev-erly masked by the appearance of being both needy and content.

As invariably, it is *she* who seems flawed in their presence, who feels herself strangely too present, exposed, somehow pungent, almost threatening, too much of a woman, exposed for a woman, a dark thing, black swan. While Ling laughs and flits from one thought to the next like some erudite Tinker Bell with ADHD (and with forceps), she Taiwo looms solid and livid, unyielding compared, a thing fallen to earth. She wants now that Ling feel this same sense of weightiness, awkwardness at failing to get her to chat—so abandons the search for a T-shirt to sleep in and lies on her back on her side of the bed fully dressed, yawning loudly and covering her face with her forearm to mean that she's moments from sleep.

Ling doesn't notice, her back turned to Taiwo, unfolding small clothes at the foot of the bed. "I don't think your brother likes me." She laughs, after a moment.

"Olu's just like that," Taiwo mumbles. But smiles. Does this mean that Olu has abandoned the pretense of being in love with his college best friend? Fair enough, only fools rush, but this is excessive: some fifteen years in and no wedding in sight. Her brother never kisses the woman in public nor touches her unthinkingly when putting on coats; all but left her there standing in the driveway on arrival; displays nothing of the clinging that passion begets. Taiwo has long since suspected a cover-up (asexuality, abortion in college, that sort) and imagines that, compelled by the tragedy upon them, the two of them might be at last coming clean.

Instead, Ling says, "Kehinde. He looks at me strangely."

At the name Taiwo tenses, the age-old reflex, as if *her* name were spoken and not her twin brother's. She peels off her forearm to glower at Ling. "What do you mean, strangely?" Without waiting for an answer, "It's a difficult time for our family—"

"Of course."

"So if Kehinde looks *strange*," as if the words were not English, "it isn't because he is . . . *looking at* . . . you."

"I didn't mean to suggest . . ."

The suggestions float there between them.

"I'm tired," says Taiwo, as if this were Ling's fault. She turns to the window, heart racing from lying, from the surge of aggression that still coats her throat, an old feeling resurfacing: thick, visceral, inexplicable, *unnatural* that she should feel jealous.

iv

While Olu and Kehinde lie looking at the ceiling.

"Sure is strange," Olu says, "sleeping like this."

"Like the old days," says Kehinde, to say something. Silence. They agree, by soft laughter, to leave it untouched.

Olu folds his hands on his stomach, eyes open. He is thinking that the smell is familiar, though strange, the thick/sweet combination of sap and humidity and burning and sweat and dark reddish-brown oil. He knew it the moment he alighted the Mercedes and stood in the pebbled drive breathing it in and was seconds from placing it (1997, Accra) when he noticed that Kehinde was staring at Ling.

Staring, not looking, unaware he was staring so squinting, lips pursed as if finding the word, until Olu said, "Shall we," and picked up a suitcase and, leaving Ling standing there, marched for the door. He'd never seen his brother interact with a woman and had always kind of vaguely thought Kehinde was gay, less so interested in men than uninterested in women, almost womanly himself, like a dancer, the hair. It startled him therefore to find himself threatened, offended, by Kehinde's reaction to Ling. The feeling, like the smell, was both strange and familiar, an old one, gone rusty and loud with disuse. The last time he felt this they would have been children, he fourteen or fifteen, his brother not ten, when some friend of their parents, more careless than callous, said, "One got the beauty, the other the brains."

It wasn't the first time he'd noticed the difference between the reaction of others to Kehinde and to him. They were extraordinarily good-looking, his two younger siblings, and *twins*; there were two, more extraordinary still. It was perfectly logical the way people ogled, a matter of science, of cause and effect. Causes: the infrequent occurrence in nature of greenish-gold eyes against deeply brown skin and the incidence in America of dizygotic multiples (as opposed to, say, Nigeria where twins were the norm). Effect: thrill of shock, like the trick to a punch line, the eyes zooming in on the sight, unprepared. If anything, he felt that he had to protect them, not least on account of their relative size. To him they seemed frail, not just younger but weaker, thin-wristed and -waisted, his brother the more. Compared to his body, athletic and solid, his brother looked fragile. The opposite of threat.

Then Sadie was born, and the thing sort of shifted. Their father disappeared for four, almost five days. Olu knew where he was—down the street at the Brigham—but couldn't shake the fear that his father was *gone*, gone away, called away to some faraway battle, with mothers and children left to fend for themselves. It would have been one thing if Fola were present. He was close to his mother, unusually so. In those days they went every Friday for ice cream, Carvel, on Route 9, just the two of them alone eating Rocky Road sprinkled with fine cookie crumbles, he prattling away on the short ride back home. On weekends, if his father had parties with colleagues, she'd take him for dinner at the Chestnut Hill Mall, leaving Taiwo and Kehinde with the kind Mr. Chalé while they ate clam chowder at Legal's. He took a quiet pride in their physical resemblance; almost everybody noticed, and she smiled when they did. Furthermore, his father looked awed when he looked at her, and Olu thought he saw a sparkling residue of awe when his father turned to look at *him*, now and then, a hint of it, in the hospital for instance, when the baby was born.

But Fola was absent. Distraught and distracted. She sat in the nursery for most of the day staring out the one window in a torn wicker rocking chair reclaimed from the porch when the seasons had turned. With heat blasting mercilessly. She didn't make breakfast. She didn't prevent them from watching cartoons. She didn't make dinner. She didn't make phone calls. Just sat looking out at the slow-falling snow.

Olu served breakfast to himself and his siblings. They looked at him expectantly, nibbling their toast. Four amber eyes throwing sparks at his forehead. They seemed newly strange to him, frightening almost.

"What's wrong with Mom?" Taiwo asked him.

"I don't know yet."

"Are you going to know soon?"

Olu frowned. "I don't know. She's scared about the baby."

"But Dad's with the baby."

"I know." Olu stood but didn't know where to go. He went to the sink and washed his hands, which weren't dirty.

"Don't worry," said Kehinde. "He'll save her."

"I *know*. That isn't the question." They waited for the question. He dried his hands, feeling his eyes well with tears. He used the scratchy dishrag for his face, too, surreptitiously, then hurried from the kitchen, down the hall, out the door.

He stood in the yard in his Brookline High jacket, where the air was too cold for the tears to re-form, watching station wagons headed for the underpass, slowly—the street slick with ice under grayish-brown sludge—but determined, it seemed, to leave Boston for Brookline (where he, too, was bused in for school) up the road. There were less than two miles to that ENTERING BROOKLINE sign, white with black letters in definitive font, and it still seemed like "distance" from this to that zip code: more trees, Carvel Ice Cream, lights hung by the town. Their corner seemed particularly ugly that morning, the trees and the houses alike drained of life with a thin coat of filth overlaying the snow banks, a lone pit bull barking, a bass line somewhere. The odd plastic Santa and halfhearted Christmas lights flung across branches like strings of paste gems only made matters worse. They were futile. It was useless. The grayness defeated all semblance of cheer.

Why do we live here, he wondered, suddenly angry, *in grayness*, like shadows, like things made of ash, with their frail dreams of wealth overwhelmed by faint dread that the whole thing might one day just up and collapse? Was there something about them that kept them in limbo despite their intelligence and all their hard work? And if so, could they not just accept their position and settle in here among the dignified poor? He thought of his classmates, the rich ones in Brookline, the poor ones in Metco, and he in between, somehow stuck in the middle with none of the comforts of in-group belonging, ashamed and afraid. He knew, though they hid it, that his parents had suffered, perhaps were still suffering in some unseen way; that it lightened their burden to think that their children would not have to suffer—and yet here he was. Top of his class: at a high school he hated foremost for the school bus that ferried him in, like an immigrant, a foreigner, a native to brilliance but stranger to privilege, bused in, then sent home. Formidable athlete: who loathed competition, was nauseated with dread before taking the field, though he hid it, the panic, the sheer desperation that launched him to victory still breathless with fear. Having learned that his father was saving for prep school, he'd determined to perform at the height of his gifts (for if only he lived where he learned, as a boarder, as a *permanent resident*, surrounded by green, he could shake off the grayness that clung to his corner, his place in the shadowy gap between worlds).

He was thinking of shadows when he looked up and saw her at the window of the nursery, a shadow herself. It seemed she couldn't see him. Or saw but saw *through* him, as if he were part of the grayness, a ghost. He wanted her to smile or to call from the window to admonish him for wearing such a featherweight jacket, but Fola just stared, rocking backward and forward. He went back inside, to the nursery (née closet).

"Mom?" he said softly.

She didn't stop rocking. She drew on her cigarette. "Come in, love," she blew. He went to the chair and stood awkwardly beside her, unsure he should touch her. They looked at the snow. "Do you like it? The color?" she asked after a moment.

"The gray?"

"Here. The pink."

He considered the walls. "Seems good for a girl."

"For a girl." She was laughing. "Yes. I had a room with the same color walls." Then abruptly, disjointed, "You can't just keep losing and accepting the losses, or else what's the point? I don't know. That's the question. If they just keep on dying—my *baba*, my baby—then why love at all?" She looked at him blankly. "Do you know what I mean?"

He didn't have the slightest idea what she meant.

"Look at you. You're trembling," she said. "Is the heat on?"

The closet was sweltering, the heat on full blast. "I'll check," he lied, eager to make a swift exit. "Do you need anything?" he asked her.

"My daughter. Alive."

His father returned, and his mother recovered, but something was different, still hard to say what. Fola was enraptured by "Sadé" the newborn, Kweku by buying a five-bedroom house, newly finished with training, now paid as a surgeon; the new house was massive, a cavity. Hollow. The center of gravity had shifted for the family, though no one seemed to notice the movement but him: instead of Kweku and Fola at the center, together, a twosome talking softly, laughing softly, present, home, there was now the small open space left by their absence, she lost to the baby, he lost to the work. Into this space slipped their Dreams for the Future, a vision of home a good decade ahead in which both of their projects had come to fruition (grown-up babies, private practice) and they could re-merge. This became the nucleus, of nuclear family fame—Future—with rings fanning out from the core, a new order, decentralized, disaggregated efforts to climb up the mountain each man for himself. Gone was his place between twosomes, the Eldest, a broker midway between parents and children; he no longer seemed special to Kweku or Fola, their firstborn, the prize horse, nor close to the twins.

With the center dissolved, they'd closed ranks, turning inward. An autonomous unit, they stopped seeming fragile. They whispered and chuckled, conspiring with glances. They didn't need protecting. They didn't need their brother.

And perhaps because this brother was fourteen years old and had just had a growth spurt and lost his old voice and was stranded in the anteroom of Awkward before Handsome, ejected from boyhood with one graceless thrust, he noticed very suddenly that he was not beautiful, at least not like they, not a beautiful boy. The privilege was Kehinde's, both beauty and boyhood, two states he had never quite noticed before but missed desperately now that he knew what he wasn't. Around this time someone said, meeting them both, "One got the beauty, the other the brains," with a >, not a =, there implied in the equation, by the reaction (patted shoulders, forced laughter, changed subject) while Olu stood smiling, gone red with the ache, *so it was true, he was lesser than* . . . Jealous of Kehinde.

Some twenty years later the feeling returns: the same clamoring ache as they stood in the drive and he followed the feeling of being observed to his brother observing his girlfriend, lips pursed. *Ling would choose Kehinde* was what he thought next, promptly losing the scent of the past of the smell of the sap and humidity and burning and sweat and dark reddish-brown oil, as he reddened himself. If ever it came to it, Ling would choose Kehinde; any woman in her right mind would make the same choice. He was glamorous and famous and wealthy, an artist, whereas Olu was a resident. Cause and effect. Though he couldn't quite bear it, *to lose her*, he thinks, with his hands on the ache and his eyes on the fan and his brother beside him as silent as threat is. Or more to the point, *to lose her, too*.

v

Kehinde can sense that his brother's not sleeping, perhaps that his eyes are still open (and filling) but lies there unspeaking, unnerved by the feeling he's had since they got to the house and got out. "He died," he said, hurting, she laughing, choir bellowing ("no shadow of turning")—and then they were here: at the front of a house that brought to mind Colorado, a houseboy appearing with cash for the taxi. A very pretty housegirl was fussing with Fola, the others climbing out of the dusty Mercedes, the houseboy lifting cases from the trunk of the taxi, the rusty door grating as Taiwo alighted. He opened his door and stepped out, blinking slowly, assailed by the light and the sting of her laugh and the thought, *she was right*, though she'd said it to hurt him, though he used to be able:

he can't read her thoughts.

For years he had. Read—or more accurately *heard*—them. As if they were words in her voice in his head, only snippets but clear ones, and clearer the feelings that went with the thoughts; he could feel what she felt.

He still doesn't know when he lost good reception. It wasn't in Nigeria, for all of the horror. After college or the last time he saw her or earlier? He doesn't trust his memory when he tries to think back. The wrist-slitting scrambled his memories, rearranged them. The archives remain but are all out of order. He can't tell what age he was when such-and-such happened; couldn't say in which country he was in which year. He knows that at some point the line filled with static, then little by little went properly dead. He senses his sister—still experiences her presence like the space between magnets to a finger passing through—but can't hear, so doesn't know, her now.

Radio silence.

"He's gone" made her laugh, and he couldn't hear why.

He was blinking with sadness when he stepped from the taxi and stood for a moment to steady himself with the sun slanting down at an angle toward him, his eyes blurring slightly against the rich light, and was bringing a hand to his eyes for some shadow when, shifting, he caught that quick glimpse of Ling's face. They bear no resemblance. It was just a distortion—the angle, the sunlight, the sadness, the shadow—but there beside Olu she looked in that moment exactly like one Dr. Yuki.

vi

Fola pauses briefly in the hall between bedrooms to listen for voices behind the closed doors. Even in silence she senses the bodies, their presence as strange as their absence once was. She remembers the first time she felt it, one morning, unremarkable among mornings when she thinks of it now (though it goes that way always, it seems, with revelations, the banality of the context as striking as the content):

the odd Monday morning in Boston in April, that strangely named month, so misleading somehow, the very sound of it, *April,* all open, pastel, telling none of the truth of relentless gray rains. Her husband had called from a Baltimore pay phone to say he was gone and was not coming home (late October); she'd lain in their bedroom that evening and remembered him leaving the kitchen that day. She'd been standing at the counter fixing breakfast for the children and had glimpsed him only briefly as he floated from the room, but had heard him calling

"'Bye!" from the foyer, then "I love you!" She'd answered in Yoruba, *I know,* *"Mo n mo."* His phone call at midnight came so unexpectedly, so thoroughly out of nowhere, that she couldn't quite think. Couldn't listen, couldn't reason, could only lie sobbing, remembering the morning, his voice from the door. By the time she woke up that next morning, eyes swollen, her tear ducts were dry and her grief had gone cold. Gone, he was gone, *very well, getting on with it,* one could mourn only so much in one life; they were broke, she discovered, so sold the house (winter), moved the children to a rental at the edge of a lot overlooking Route 9 but at least the same school district, two little bedrooms, her "bed" on the couch; settled debts, found a lawyer, got divorced (early spring); brought the twins to the airport and Olu to Yale (end of summer); blurry autumn, then Christmas, she and Sadie, then New Year, then snow warming slowly to rain . . .

until one day in April, an unremarkable morning, she was heading to the kitchen to make herself tea, having dropped off the baby at the bus stop in wellies, the radio playing softly, and softer the rain—when she paused in the hall in between the two bedrooms and noticed the silence. And that she was alone. *Gone, they were gone,* all the voices, the bodies, one lover, four children, their heartbeats, the hum, heat and motion and murmur, the rush and the babble, a river gone dry while she'd wept. She remained. She stood there, a remnant, as conspicuously alone as a thing left behind on a beach in the night, suddenly aware of the silence, its newness and strangeness, the *sound* of her solitude, clear, absolute.

As strange was that silence, their absence that morning, is what she feels now: that she isn't alone. She stands in the hall in between the two bedrooms and feels them there, silent if not yet asleep. She chuckles at the feeling. She doesn't quite trust it. She returns to the kitchen. Is there something she forgot? She turns off the radio so as not to wake Sadie; the walls are so thin in that bedroom. Something else? The phone call from Benson, who is coming for dinner. Amina to prepare the *egusi* at four.

Nothing needs doing.

She is stuck with the thinking.

She returns to the chair in the garden to smoke.

It is foolish, she knows, at her age to address it, to let the thing in as a fully formed thought, but it forms itself anyway; she thinks *I've been lonely* and laughs with surprise at the tears that spring up. It should not perhaps come as so shocking a revelation, seems obvious now that she's met the truth's eye, but it hurts all the same: a dull aching, like hunger, a hunger for a taste that she almost forgot.

Almost, but didn't.

She closes her eyes, hugs her waist with one arm as she blows out the smoke, with the taste of companionship mingling with nicotine, hurting with happiness to have them all home.

4.

Dinner. They are scooting their chairs to the table—a change in the air, each one sensing the weight, with the Reason They're Here dawning jointly on all of them now that they're formally gathered like this: a collective: beholden to collective desperation, to meanings that flourish in long-lasting silences, in down-turning glances, in moments of awkwardness masked as politeness—when someone turns up.

The bell, out of nowhere; a sound out of context; even Fola forgets she's expecting a guest. They hover, midscoot, with their hands on the chair legs and wait for some seconds for someone to speak.

"Madame," says Amina, from the dining-room entrance, three steps leading down to the den. "Please, a guest."

"Who is it?" says Fola.

"A sir please."

"Where is he?"

"Outside please."

"For God's sake, at least show him in." But she hasn't had company since arriving in Ghana and knows that the staff has no protocol yet. She's still rather shocked by their efforts this morning, all springing to action with newborn aplomb from the moment they appeared in the driveway, five strangers and she (still the strangest one), no questions asked. Perhaps they prefer it, a house full of people instead of just Fola with clippers in shorts? "Come," she adds gently, and accompanies Amina. She finds Benson waiting outside the front door.

With a bottle and flowers. "I'm sorry," he murmurs, stepping forward to embrace her.

For a moment she recoils. The velvet bass voice and the smell of black soap and cologne mixed together too strong, too familiar: a wave rises, passes. She clutches the doorframe, then waves her hand, laughing, "I'm fine, really, fine. Please. *Thank you*, and welcome." She reaches for the flowers to waylay a second attempt at embrace. "We're just getting started."

"I'm not interrupting? In Ghana it's rude to be early."

"Thank God. Six is an uncivilized hour for dinner, I know, but with—"

"Jetlag—"

"Exactly."

"Of course." He swallows hard, nodding. "And the children?"

"Hardly children." She laughs. "They're all here, we're all here, through the den." He follows behind her to where they're all standing, their hands on the table now, eyes on his face. "My darlings, this is

Benson. A friend of your f . . . of the f-family's," she stumbles. "From Hopkins."

"Hello." He holds up the bottle and smiles at them sadly. "It's a pleasure to meet you. I'm sorry for your loss."

They stare at him blankly, the expression before *coldly*, even Ling, as if *he* were the cause of this loss, being the first one to mention it here in this pause with the facing of facts on the tips of their tongues. Sensing this, Benson adds softly, to Fola, "You all must be shell-shocked. God knows that I am."

Fola, with a feeling that she hasn't had in decades, concern that every stranger think her children well behaved, holds up the flowers. "Aren't they glorious? Gardenias." She smiles with such force that they all smile back. She places the arrangement, intended for a mantel, in the middle of the table; it doesn't quite fit. The decorative fern fronds dangle into the rice pot, the height of the blossoms obscuring the view. When everyone sits—as they do now, instructed—they can't see the person across, for the vase.

Benson takes the empty seat, smiling at Olu. "I knew you looked familiar," he says, scooting in. The voice is too bass for the others to hear it, and Olu too dark for his blushing to show, but he shakes his head stiffly, left, right, just once, quickly, and Benson nods once—up, down, up—in reply (having somehow understood to abandon the subject as men sometimes do with the slightest of hints: a quick nod, a quick frown, the dark arts of the eyebrows, *poof!* subjects are changed without changes in tone). "The last time I saw you two, you were in diapers." He smiles at the twins, faces blocked by the flowers. "My last year of residency. Now you're what, thirty?"

"Twenty-nine," they say in unison, the same husky tone.

"October," offers Kehinde. "We'll be thirty next October."

"And you." He turns to Sadie, next to Kehinde, less obscured. "*You* . . . were just a glimmer in—"

"My ovary," says Fola. Preempting. "More precisely."

"That's obscene," Sadie says. This is the part she dreads most: when the stranger starts asking their ages, what each of them does. She senses it coming just as sure as a key change the moment a pop song approaches its bridge and looks ruefully at the man at the head of the table, wondering why he is here but not minding too much. At least with a guest, there's a guise for the dolor that hovered above them in silence before, doubly massive for being unnamed, unacknowledged, the size of itself *and* its shadow, a blob. Now they can pin, each, their anguish to Benson, who took the seat no one else wanted to take and who said the thing no else wanted to say and who cut the grim picture in half with his flowers. *He* is the reason they all sit so upright, speak softly, smile politely, *because there's a Guest*, as ensconced in the drama that attends family dinners (even absent a death in the family) as they, but a visitor, an innocent, in need of protection. They must ensure, all, that the Guest is okay. She smiles at him wanly. "Right. I was born later. I'm Sadie."

Ling contributes her finger bell laugh. "Ovaries aren't 'obscene.'"

Turning quickly to Benson, "She's an ob-gyn. I'm in ortho," Olu says.

"Two doctors!" exclaims Benson. "So it runs in the family. I didn't get your first name." Ling tells him. "Well, Ling. Ghana is wanting for excellent doctors, foremost in obstetrics and maternal and child health. I opened a little hospital in town seven years ago. We *still* have a wait list for consults." He laughs. "We could also use surgeons," with a gesture to Olu, "and knowing your father, I know that you're good." He pauses. They all do. To see where he's going, to see if the Guest is now stuck in the weeds, but he laughs again softly and presses on strongly, "The top of our class at Johns Hopkins, bar none. No one could touch him. And I don't mean the Africans. *No one* was better. No one even came close. I remember when he got there I thought, who's this bumpkin? From this Lincoln University? Never heard of it before. I *should* have, I know it. God. Kwame Nkrumah. But I'd been in Poland, of all places, for school. Funny times, those. Cold war scholarships for Africans. You could study in Warsaw and not pay a dime. I arrived in East Baltimore with an Eastern Bloc accent. I think they all thought I was deaf for a while." Another laugh. "But we managed. We banded together. Everybody wanted to be friends with your dad. And Kweku was . . ." He pauses, smiling, turning to Fola. Seeing her face, he turns back. "He was shy. A geek, if we're honest. But handsome, so meticulous. All the girls loved him. But he only loved one."

Fola says, "Really. I don't think—"

"Keep going," says Sadie, not loudly. "He only loved one?"

Benson looks at Fola, who tips her head, sighing. He looks back at Sadie, returns the sad smile. "There were four of us. Africans—well, five counting Trevor. Jamaican—"

"Trinidadian," Fola corrects.

"Ah, right. Trinidadian. Five of us brethren," says Benson. "Prodigious, but desperately poor. We got stipends with our scholarships but blew them on airfare so no one had much; we shared all that we had. We used to eat dinner together, in rotation, so Monday to Friday a different one cooked. Wednesday was Kweku. He always cooked *banku*. We hated his *banku;* it tasted like glue. But we'd all get there early to talk to your mother. Or stare at her. No one could work up the nerve. And we'd look at your father, this shy guy from Ghana, not strapping like Trevor, or tall, not like me, with these shirts buttoned up to the uppermost button like a Ghanaian Lumumba, with glasses—with her."

A silence has settled on all of them, thickly. They stare at the flowers as if at a hearse. No one quite knows what the other is thinking or whether to speak and reveal the wrong thought.

Finally, Fola. "For goodness sake, Benson." She laughs with such sadness, they start to laugh, too. "That isn't what happened—"

"It's true—"

"No, it isn't. He also made bacon and eggs. Which were worse." She stands up to pick out a fern from the rice pot. "The food's getting cold," she says. "Eat," and they do.

Joloff, egusi. They muddle through bravely, evading fraught silence with pleasant requests: *pass the wine please, what time is it, do you have enough space there, more wine please, what's in this, should we open another bottle?* When Fola observes that the questions are waning, she stands, disappears, and returns with the cake. "I am not to be forgiven," she says, "for not writing or calling on time, but I didn't forget." She sings the first notes, then the rest join in, smiling, while Sadie sits blushing and chewing her lip. On the last long "to yooou . . . !" Fola settles the cake on the tabletop, bending over Sadie to do so and pausing, so stationed, to kiss her and say, "You were right," and that's that, the thing finished, "talked out." Taiwo and Kehinde say "The wish!," again in unison, which makes them both frown and which makes Benson laugh. "So they really *are* twins!" That daft oft-repeated comment, which makes Olu tense. He recovers and chuckles. Sadie laughs, too, suddenly noticing the candle: one big white utility candle dripping thick wax. She starts to ask why, glancing back at her mother, who shrugs, laughing also, then changes her mind. *The sturdier the candle,* she thinks, leaning forward, *the better for bearing such wishes.*

ii

Taiwo retreats to the den after dinner, three shallow steps down from the dining room table. She sits on the love seat's strange orange plaid wool with a copy of *Ghana Ovation.* Behind her Fola, at the table with Benson, is discussing the tradition of fantasy coffins; she hears them there, faintly, conferring in whispers like grown-ups evading the hearing of children. They felt like that, *children,* she thinks, during dinner,

as watchful and rule-bound as Catholic school pupils—and wonders
why all of them do this, still now, even now, the African Filial Piety
act? Lowered eyes, lowered voices, feigned shyness, bent shoulders, the
curse of their culture, exaltation of deference, that beaten-in impulse
to show oneself obedient and worthy of praise for one's reverence of
Order (never mind that the Order is crumbling, corrupted, departed,
dysfunctional; respect must be shown it). She loathes them for doing it,
herself and her siblings, the house staff, her African classmates. Quite
simply, she isn't convinced that "respect" is the basis, not for them the
respectful nor for them the respected. She suspects that it's laziness, a
defaulting to the familiar, or cowardice in the former and power in the
latter. Most African parents, she'd guess, grew up powerless, with no one
on whom to impose their own will, and so bully their children, through
beatings and screaming, to lighten the load of postcolonial angst . . .

or assorted observations along the same lines, when she flips to a
page and is yanked back from thought. By the name first. The caption,
fine print amid faces (weddings, polo matches, funerals, glossy chaos
of society photos), "Femi and Niké Savage at . . . ," and then by the
photograph:
the shoes
and suit
and shirt
and neck
and smile
and nose
and eyes.
Those eyes.
Black, thick-lidded eyes gazing back at her, red-rimmed, the wild
sort of gaze of a man on a drug, matching smile (hard, unfocused), the
wife there beside him gone ashen with age, the new wig a blond bob.

She hurls the magazine across the room, gut reaction. It lands with the splatter of pages on wood. Fola and Benson look up from the table. "Darling?" says Fola, but Taiwo can't speak. "What is it? What happened?"

"A bug," breathes out Taiwo. She points to the magazine splayed on the floor. "I was k-killing a bug."

"Ah, yes. Welcome to Ghana." Benson doesn't notice her tremulous voice. "That reminds me. Are you all on antimalarial medication? The mosquitoes can be killer. I've got Aralen in the car." Taiwo shakes her head. "I'll go grab it. No worries. I might just have enough to get you started for now." He glances at Fola as he stands from the table.

Fola nods, distracted. "Great, thanks," as he goes.

iii

Fola stands also and stares at her daughter, aware of a heartbeat too fast and too loud, throbbing ache, lower right, where she has the small scar from the day she went tumbling down the stairs with the girl. Almost hard to believe she was just twenty-eight, half a lifetime away, with three children (first girl: a complete mystery to her mother next to Olu and Kehinde, a new thing entirely, more perilous somehow). Already at one she was beautiful, Taiwo. They both were. Wherever they went, they were stopped. Strangers always thought they were both baby girls and would gush in high voices, "How bea*uuu*tiful." They were. But it made Fola nervous. To handle such children. Too precious, too perfect, the girl in particular, like a very expensive gift made of breakable material that one should just look at and try not to touch. Kehinde was easy, like Olu, even easier, but Taiwo would cry whenever Fola put her down and would wail without pause until Fola returned—only Fola, never Kweku—to pick her back up. It was this that confused her: how much Fola *liked* this, the thrill she'd receive when she picked up the girl, and she'd immediately stop crying to smile at her mother, to cling to her, burying her face in her neck. The neediness touched her, overwhelmed her, unhinged her; she worried about favoring or spoiling the child, or confusing her, leading her to believe that the world was less patently apathetic than it actually was.

On the occasion of note she was washing the babies in the bathtub upstairs when the front doorbell rang. It was Olu, then five, driven home by a teacher who lived down the street and now honked, pulling off. The door was at the bottom of those two narrow staircases, too long a trip down with the twins unattended. She picked them up, dripping suds, one in each arm, and went rushing down the stairs to get Olu. And slipped. She can remember the feeling still now, that pure panic that flooded her lungs as her slipper flew out and her back hit the stairs and she tumbled down clinging to babies' wet skin slick with sweet-smelling suds. When she came to a stop she was holding Kehinde only, having somehow nicked her ribcage on the stair edge, and bleeding. Taiwo had landed, by some act of mercy, at the bottom of the staircase completely unharmed. She was sitting there staring as Fola rose, bleeding, her arms around Kehinde. Not crying, just staring. But the look in the eyes was more piercing than screaming. The eyes seemed to say *you let go, you let me go.* Those eyes—which she'd found so unnerving, in the beginning, having only ever seen them in a painting, unblinking—now stared at her, heartbroken, heartbreaking, accusing: a dead woman's eyes on a baby girl's face.

Olu pressed the doorbell, and Taiwo started crying. At his sister's distress Kehinde promptly started wailing. Fola started screaming in her head; crying silently, she opened the door to stunned Olu. "Hold your brother." Olu took Kehinde, and Fola grabbed Taiwo, ushering them all up the stairs and away from the cold. But the girl kept on crying, a very tired cry, untiringly, for hours, until evening when her father came home.

Fola looks at Taiwo and can feel the girl's heaving, her wide eyes unyielding, dry, heartbroken, seething. This is the thing that has come in between them, this rage, Fola knows, since the twins went to Lagos—but neither will tell her what happened with Femi, and Sena, who found them, alleged not to know. There was just the one phone call at sunrise in summer ten months from the day that she left them at Logan: Uncle Sena, last seen on a tarmac in Ghana, now calling from Nigeria at five in the morning. "I knew they were yours from the moment I saw them. Those are Somayina's grandkids, I said to myself," Sena blubbered while Fola sat fumbling for a light switch, still sleeping on the couch. "From the beginning. Start again."

His story was confusing—the more for the static, and how Sena told it, both rushing and halting, conflicted, determined to help, hiding something—but Fola got the gist of it. The first bit she knew:

when her father was murdered his mistress decided his house was now hers and moved in with their son. The two lived together as queen and little prince running a brothel for soldiers through the end of Biafra. In this way young Femi began his career as a dealer of women, small arms, and cocaine, striking out on his own as an underworld wunderkid when Bimbo OD'd at the end of the war. This Fola learned on her last trip to Lagos, in 1975, to beg Femi for help, having heard from a Nigerian in Baltimore by chance that her brother was knee deep in naira. Reunion. They'd never been close. He was four years her junior. He'd come to the house now and then with his mother, this Bimbo, a tall, hard, and wiry woman who in another life may well have modeled, not whored. Her father had never sought to hide them from Fola ("her mother was dead and a man had his needs"), and she knew that the boy who would wait in the kitchen while Bimbo went upstairs was her *aburo*.

But didn't care. Had never even thought the names Bimbo and Femi—they were extras, unnamed in the cast of her youth, without lines, manly woman and womanly boy—until then, when she learned of the money. Too late. Femi alleged that he thought she had died with their father that night in the fire in Kaduna; otherwise, he claimed, he would never have excluded her entirely from their father's inheritance. Alas. Too late now to redistribute the monies but Fola need only but ask for his help; they were siblings after all, you could see the resemblance, never mind that their father never claimed him as a son. Fola left Lagos with the money she needed to get to Accra to see Kweku's ill mum, but vowed never again to give Femi the pleasure of offering help. She broke this vow for the twins.

This time her brother refused to send cash but proposed a small trade as an alternative solution: if Fola would send her *ibeji* to him, he would pay all their school fees plus college tuition. At some point he'd wed the only daughter of a general turned oil entrepreneur; he was tricked, she was barren. Having *ibeji* in the household might "cure" this wife Niké, he explained, as *ibeji* were magic. A deal. Fola sent the twins to Nigeria in August and forty weeks later Sena sent them back home.

From what she can gather, her twisted half-brother had hosted some bacchanal that Sena attended (the details, to do with drugs, prostitutes, orgy, have always been largely unclear). Sena had his own tragic tale to unburden: of expulsion from Lagos under "Ghana Must Go," winter 1983, with the Nigerian government's summarily deporting two million Ghanaians; of return to East Cantonments, impecunious and affronted, to build up a practice from scratch in Accra, only two fragile years past a barbarous coup in his homeland, no longer his home; death of parents. One hard decade on—his first week back in Lagos, having arrived at a house party driven by friends, unaware that the house was Kayo Savage's townhouse, unaware that the party was Femi's—he found them. Just saw them there huddled up, children among adults, and knew who they were and that something was wrong; they were both wearing makeup and spoke as if drugged, in a monotone, clutching their elbows, eyes down. He took them at once in the clothes they were wearing, got a taxi to the Sheraton in Ikeja where he was staying, called at midnight in a panic to explain he was sending them back on the first thing moving. End of story.

She drove in the dirty blue hatchback, four hours, got to JFK early, and sat there and waited, not moving, not eating, just clutching her stomach, asking Jesus her friend to go easy this time. They appeared in arrivals in thin summer clothing, the lipstick rubbed off to a blood-stain, dark orange, their hands clasped together, their eyes still turned downward, too skinny, not speaking, not Kehinde, not Taiwo. How many times did she ask them to tell her? "Just tell me what happened," "Please tell me," "I'm begging." She telephoned Femi; she screamed, wept, and threatened. "How *dare* you take my darlings away?" Femi sneered. And hung up. They were shadows. They slept in the daytime and whispered at night in the bedroom they shared in that house that she loathed, with no yard to grow flowers. She couldn't afford therapy but begged for financial aid. The prep school assented on the basis of Olu's spectacular performance the four years before. They started in autumn as freshmen, repeating the year they'd just done at interna-tional school, Kehinde quiet and sullen, Taiwo restless and furious, the both of them mute on the subject of *why.*

She still doesn't know.

She looks at Taiwo unknowingly, so longing to hold her, to squeeze out this *why*—and the sorrow and fury and shadow out with it, to hold her so tightly it all rushes forth, leaving breath bubbling out as when Taiwo was one and still longed to be held, and by *her.* But she can't. She imagines that baby—slick-wet and defenseless, in every sense, naked and mute where she'd dropped her—and seizes with guilt, a ghost, half a life later. She wants to but can't take the three steps between them.

"What happened . . . ?" she asks weakly from the dining room table, but Taiwo doesn't hear and walks away.

iv

Kehinde finds Sadie in the garden in a beach chair, her feet on the palm trunk, eyes closed, tilting back. The distance from the house to the edge of the garden is such that no light source illumines this spot. There is only the starlight, a thin coat of silver that muddies the blackness a dark opaque gray. He hesitates for a moment in the shadow behind her, not sure if she's sleeping. "May I join you?" he asks. She hasn't heard the footsteps and starts, veering forward.

"You scared me," she gasps. "It's so dark. You're so *quiet.*"

He whispers, embarrassed, "I'm sorry."

"No, don't be."

"What were you doing?"

"I was counting," she says. (They both speak in hushed tones as if they were hiding or planning a break and in spite of themselves, overcome by the context, the dark of the garden, the confessional implications of chitchat in moonlight.) "Sit," she adds, rising.

"No, stay there," he murmurs. He positions himself neatly on the ground by the tree. They are silent, slightly awkward. The shadow a comfort. Sadie speaks presently, unnerved by the lull.

"Don't you think it's weird? That she *lives* here? In Ghana?" She slaps at a mosquito.

"Is it? I don't know. Maybe."

"She didn't even tell me she was moving."

"Me either." He shrugs. "But she's like that."

"I know, but it's *Ghana.*" She rubs her arm, scowling as if particularly offended by having been bitten by an insect from *Ghana.* "If she wanted to do that whole thing, back to Africa, then why not Nigeria? At least she's from there."

"It's quieter," says Kehinde, not saying as he thinks it that he'd never return to Nigeria, even if Fola moved there permanently. "The same thing in Mali, the house where I stayed in Douentza, the quiet. You could *see* it. You could think."

"Did you like it there? Mali? Oh, wait. Are you thinking? Am I talking too much?"

"I like talking to you." He smiles at the smile he can feel in the darkness. "I never get to talk to you."

"You mean you never call." But she's laughing. "And thank you."

"For what?"

"The tuition. Mom told me last year that you're helping her out. And that you told her not to tell me. But she kind of tells me everything. Except that she's moving to *Ghana.*"

He laughs. "You're welcome."

"So, you're famous?"

Laughs harder. "Not really, no."

"Yeah you are, Kehinde, I see you online. My best friend, her family's super into the art thing. They bought one, I think. Of your new ones."

"That right?"

"I like them. The mud cloths."

"You do?"

"They're enormous, though. How do you make them?"

"With mud. And big cloths."

They laugh again together. She kicks his shin. "Jesus. I've never been to Africa, I know, but come on."

"How is that possible? That you've never been to Africa?"

"Shocking but true."

Kehinde senses the frown. "It's nothing to be ashamed of," he says to her quickly. "Our parents never brought us when we were kids."

"Why?"

"They were hurt. . . . Their countries hurt them."

"But *you* came. The rest of you."

"Well, Olu was a baby. And we were fourteen." He feels his voice catch, clears his throat. "It was different. It's not like we asked to be sent—" Now he stops. A light has come on above the door to the house, a faint puddle of yellow into which enters Benson. He strides toward the driveway, a man with a purpose. Kehinde and Sadie stop whispering to watch him. Benson doesn't see them. A driver appears suddenly from the side of the house where the staff takes their dinner. Benson says something that Kehinde can't hear, then the *beep-beep* of car doors unlocked, blinking lights. The driver lifts open the SUV trunk, pulls a box out. The two men confer, not in English. Benson takes the box, briskly marches back inside with it. The light above the door goes off. The driver disappears.

Kehinde finds a stick, begins drawing in earth, an old habit. "Reminds me of our first house." A face. "They used to sell drugs there. The son of our landlord. Right there out our window, me and Olu's room—"

"Wait. You and Olu shared a room?"

He notes that this is what shocks her. "Until you were born, yes."

"Of course," Sadie says. With a hint of aggression.

"Why of course?" He has heard it.

"Until I was born. It's what all of you say. Like you all lived this whole other lifetime before that, like I was an afterthought. Like I messed it all up."

"Sadie—"

"Don't say it. Don't say I'm being sensitive. Don't say that it's just that I'm younger or whatever. I'm *different* from the rest of you, an idiot can see that, shit, strangers *do* see it, it's not in my head. I know what I'm feeling," she whispers, insistent, to which Kehinde replies with a smile, "So do I." She hears that he's smiling and, thinking he's mocking, says, "Thank you for laughing—"

"I know what you feel." He *does* laugh now, quietly, to remember the feeling so plainly, to see his own face in her words, that small face, a girl's face, as had troubled him deeply for ages, the teasing for being so pretty. "I used to feel the same about our family. That I was different. That I didn't belong—"

"Didn't *belong*? You had Taiwo." She whispers this passionately, with no trace of sympathy, overcome by the possessiveness one feels for one's suffering, the aggressive insistence on the suffering's uniqueness, in nature and depth and endurance over time.

"I did. I had Taiwo," he says, and considers it. "Back then. I had Taiwo. But she was the girl. *I* was the one who shared the bedroom with Olu. I was supposed to be the doctor, the boy, the other son. That was the dream, Sai and Sons, family business. Except for . . . I hated them."

"Who?"

"Math and science." He laughs again, retracing a line in his drawing, then murmurs the rest, less to her than himself: "See, I know they didn't mean to, but I hated how they *looked* at me, like I was the break in the chain, Dad and Olu, like I was a stranger, which maybe I was to them, maybe I was to myself, I don't know. I just wonder, you know. Being here, seeing Olu, I ask myself, what if it was him in the car? Instead of me, that night with Dad. Would this whole thing be different? If it happened like that, with the good son, you know?"

Sadie doesn't. "What car? If it was Olu in what car?"

"I'm just rambling," Kehinde says, tracing over the face.

"No, tell me. What car?" she persists.

Kehinde falters. "I . . ."

"No one tells me anything," she mumbles. "Never mind."

He can feel that heavy silence taking form now around him, the familiar film of silence that shields, locks him in—but his sister would appear to be in it here with him, beside him, locked also, her breath, and her heart. He hears her thin breathing, the sound before crying.

He feels her aloneness, a space in his throat. A space, opened up. Through which trickles, unbidden, as thin and uncertain, the sound of his voice. Which tells her, very simply, how he went to meet their father, how he walked into the lobby, saw the guards and Dr. Yuki, how they drove home in the Volvo, parked and sat there in the driveway, how he signed his art class painting with a pen that he still has. He pulls this from his pocket and hands it to Sadie.

"What does it say?" She can't see in the dark.

"I think Mom engraved it. It's Yoruba. Keep it."

"Really?"

"Sure."

"Thank you. And for telling me that." She thumbs the pen carefully. "I would have been happy. That it happened with you and not anyone else. I bet he was happy."

"You think so?"

"I know so."

"*E se,*" he says, though it hurts him to do. The music of the language makes him think of Nigeria. His sister. He stands. "We should get back inside."

"Really?"

"Mosquitoes."

"But our *family's* inside," she says, laughing.

"I know it." He kisses her head.

Fola and Benson come out of the house now, Amina behind them with Tupperware containers. "You're really too kind," he is saying.

"Please. Take it. It's just some *egusi* and *joloff* for later."

"I have a small staff—"

"But your cook is Ashanti. He can't make *egusi,* at least not like mine." They are smiling, glancing downward, when Fola, feeling butterflies (lower left, bafflement), squints at the garden. There by the tree she can make out the beach chair, a figure beside it, tall. "K, is that you?"

v

Taiwo comes in and finds Olu there reading, the other bed empty. "Do you mind if we switch?"

Olu looks up from his book, sees she's crying. "Are you . . . ?" he begins, but it's clear that she's not. He stands, slightly awkward, unsure what to do with his body, embrace her? He takes a step forward. Taiwo steps backward, a kneejerk reaction that doesn't offend him.

"The rooms. Can we switch?"

Unnerved by the crying, he leaves without question. She closes the door and he goes down the hall.

vi

This bedroom is larger, a queen bed, small window, the smell of Ling's lotion, faint sound from the garden. He thinks to go join them, hears Fola, "Where's Olu?" his brother, "Nice to meet you," but doesn't go out. It doesn't make sense to distrust this man Benson, to duck him. He'll be back again, tomorrow it sounds like: was talk of a drive in his car to the village, preparations, picking coffins, greeting family, logistics—which are similar, thinks Olu, to the logistics of a hospital, these logistics of a funeral, clinical, procedural, managerial, *what to do with the body* the general question, a series of actions sucked dry of emotion—but strange to him, still, to be bothering with the answers, to be carrying out the actions when the body is dead. He doesn't fear Benson will tell them, not really, but why he can't tell them himself he doesn't know.

He shouldn't have waited. He should have just told them, or her, told his mother at least at the time, senior year, when he'd gotten that ticket to Ghana, the same airline ticket that came every spring. To the

College. Wrong address: they all had a box at the New Haven post office for personal use, but the Temple Street address of Timothy Dwight College was all that his father could find from Accra. These, the last days before mass use of e-mail. Every year on his birthday, the twenty-sixth of May, came an envelope for Fola (which he'd send back unopened), a letter for him, and a ticket to Ghana. Thin hard-copy ticket in fading red ink with the three carbon copies of tickets of old, dated 26 May every year for four years until 26 May 1997, when he went.

He's never really asked himself why, or why then, why he skipped graduation, didn't want to attend. He'd always been frightened that Kweku would surprise them, showing up in New Haven unannounced and uninvited on a day that he knew that they'd all be together, but it was obvious that his father wasn't thinking of this. Or wasn't thinking. Not a stranger to American education, he would have known that graduations happened every four years, and that sometime in spring-time in 1997 there would be two commencements (twins from high school, his from college); nevertheless sent the letters and ticket as always, same desperate entreaty that Olu come for his birthday, that he stay for a week, that he hear Kweku out, with no mention at all of the conflict of dates.

It was just a coincidence that the two graduations happened to fall on one day and his birthday at that, but he sat with the tickets—Milton commencement, Yale commencement, Ghana Airways—and wept for the first time in years. That his father had forgotten that his children were graduating, three of the four, somehow drove the point home: that he wasn't a part of their lives any longer, their schedules, their rhythms, their world; he'd dropped out. It wasn't that Olu hadn't ever considered this (he had, once a day, since the Volvo drove off), but despair was dulled first by the sheer numbing shock, which in time became denial, which in time became hope.

Only now does it dawn on him, here at the window where Fola's deep laughter outside through the screen is a rumble of thunder before rushing rain, that perhaps he went *seeking* some final betrayal? It seemed obvious enough at the time why he left, with the lie about a poorly timed volunteer trip, "Doctors Without Borders," he said, producing a pamphlet for Ling, saying that Fola should be with the twins, he didn't mind: not to face the thing squarely, his father's indifference. His greatest achievement, and Kweku forgot. He wept in his dorm room, alone, thirty minutes, then typed out a letter to say he would come, wiped his face, slapped his cheek, clenched his teeth in the mirror, silent vow *no more crying, man,* left the next week. Metro-North to the city, crowded subway to the airport, little shuttle to the terminal space reserved for Ghana Airways (now defunct), a funky alcove on some back lot at the airport where the circus act of check-in was just getting under way, ticketed passengers bumped at random off the flight protesting loudly, louder check-in agents shouting "There is no reason to shout!," entire families pleading mercy for their overweight baggage with tearing of sackcloth and gnashing of teeth, bags unpacked and repacked on the floor around Olu (gifts, foodstuffs, cans, clothing, toys strewn at his feet), up the stairs to the aircraft, then ten hours later down the stairs to Accra.

To forget the occasion.

But there was something else also, apart from the horror at imagining himself on a stage in the sun with no family there cheering, neither parents nor siblings. For proper cauterization, still more was required. To scorch away hope—as he must have intended, he thinks, must have wanted—he *needed* what happened: a thing still more searing than being forgotten, the burn one knows only at being betrayed.

His father looked younger, or smaller, than he remembered. He'd always been short, as per Benson, "not tall," maybe five foot ten, same height as Fola, and sturdy, with strong arms and shoulders, a runner's lean legs—but looked *small* in the crowd that was gathered there waiting, a density of primary color and sound, men and women, the men rather short, Olu noticed, all strong-armed and smooth-skinned and, shockingly, brown.

For all of his life when he'd looked for his father, like this, scanning quickly to spot Kweku's face in the bleachers at meets or the seats at recitals, he'd scanned for the contrast, first and foremost for brown. A bluish color brown appropriately likened to chocolate and coffee, the complexion that he had himself—and that no one else had, no other father in Boston. He could always pick out Kweku in an instant by the color. Here at the airport his eyes, as conditioned, scanned quickly for contrast and blinked at the shock: they were *all* the same color, more or less, all the fathers, his own blended in, indiscrete, of a piece. When his eyes at last settled at the edge of the gathering on a man in pressed khakis, a crisply white shirt, squarish glasses, brown shoes, with his hands in his pockets, so much smaller than remembered, his feet set apart, Olu saw with some awe that his father stood out like the proverbial thumb from the men in the crowd. Though their skin and their height and their builds were the same, more or less, his own father was different.

He paused at the door between baggage claim and exit hall (the old airport exit, before renovation) and stared through the glass at the throng of brown men, shifting his bag on his shoulders but not stepping out. Not quite recognizing his father, or overwhelmed by recognition, as if seeing the man clearly for the first time in his life, suddenly seeing him singular, without the benefit of contrast, without the backdrop (on white) and *still* different (on brown). This is what stopped him and held him there staring, the way Kweku looked, like a man on his own, small and strong and apart, the one not like the others; all the familiar peculiarities more peculiar somehow: how his trousers were creased down the front, tightly belted, his cuffs rolled back once, thinning hair neatly cut, those same wire-frame glasses, scientist-immigrant glasses, the same ones as wore his professors at Yale (as if all nonwhite postgrads in America in the seventies had arrived from their homelands and received the same pair). Kweku. Not a father, a surgeon, a Ghanaian, a hero, a monster, just one Kweku Sai, just a man in a crowd with an odd sort of bearing, a stranger in Accra as in Boston. Alone. He couldn't see Olu concealed by the doorframe so stood like a child told to wait without fuss, with his hands in his pocket, his eyes on the exit, his shoulders relaxed as if all things were well, the single visible sign of his mounting distress the rote up-and-down bounce of his foot on the ground.

Someone clipped Olu on the calf with a luggage cart. "Excuse me," said the person, Luther Vandross it seemed. Olu turned around and saw Benson (a stranger). "Didn't realize you were stopping there . . ."

"Sorry. You're right." Olu stepped aside to let the stranger wheel his luggage through the doorway, but he didn't. He was smiling, pausing, too.

"Were you on the flight from New York?"

"Yes, I was."

"Yes, I thought so. I saw you. God, this may sound strange, but I thought—just, you look like a woman I knew once. The wife of a friend." Olu shook his head no. The stranger looked embarrassed. "Well. Welcome to Ghana." He left with his cart, disappeared in the crowd.

Feeling somehow discovered—as the coward at the door, if not the son of Fola Savage—Olu looked at his dad. *What is a man who cannot face his father?* he thought. As a shame or a threat or a lark, as a small thing, too small in his lone peculiarity, or a large thing, too large per the shadows he cast: the root angst didn't matter, the thing was the facing, and here he was hiding, afraid to step out. "Go," he mumbled softly, rearranging his backpack (the one he always traveled with, the one Taiwo mocked, further proof of the "white boy" who lived inside Olu, guzzling water from Nalgenes, wearing Tevas in snow). He stepped into view, gripped the straps at his chest as if preparing to skydive. Called, "Dad."

They drove into town from the airport without speaking, Kweku clutching the wheel, Olu clutching his backpack, the three years of silence a solid between them unsoftened by presence, proximity, flesh. Olu gazed intently out the passenger window, trying to work out the color of what he was seeing: the roads were lined thickly with wild shrubs and palm trees, but somehow the vista read brown and not green. It reminded him of Delhi (without the auto-rickshaws), the small honking taxis, good cheer, dusty haze, well-planned roads somehow wanting for order, retail signboards with hand-painted faces—but something was new. *The color*, he thought, it was back to the color, the newness of majority, seeming familiar to oneself, chancing to catch his reflection in the window of a passing car and thinking for a moment he was looking at the driver.

When they stopped at the junction between Liberia Road and Independence Avenue, Kweku cleared his throat. "T-this is our N-national Theatre," he began haltingly. He gestured through his window at the structure. Modern, white. "We have a National Symphony Orchestra and the National Theatre Players. They built it five years ago. A gift from the Chinese."

"Interesting," Olu said politely. "Five years ago." Back when his father was part of their world.

Kweku rubbed his brow, sensing his error, falling silent. The stoplight turned green and he tried a new tack. "It's changing, this city, not quickly, but changing. I think you might like it."

"Seems nice," Olu said.

"You wouldn't remember your first trip to Ghana."

"I don't."

"No, of course. But the place has transformed. The change is remarkable."

Olu nodded, saying nothing, unsure if Kweku's subject was his country or himself.

They turned into a side street off Independence Avenue and wound their way slowly through a maze of small streets to a clump of large houses set back from the road with chipped white stucco walls overgrown with dry blossoms. Stray dogs milled here and there nosing indifferently the small heaps of trash. Fruit skins, black plastic bags. A woman near the end of the road in a *lappa* and incongruous red Pop Warner Football T-shirt was turning meat on a grill like the black one they'd had at the first house in Boston, a half of a globe. Behind her the road stopped in overgrown weeds, a huge plot of dry grass with a lone mango tree.

Kweku stopped the car by the woman, engine idling. "I know you must be tired." He leaned forward, looking out. "I just wanted you to see this before we go back to the house—to my house—to the place where I live."

Olu peered out at the woman. "Who is she?"

"The land. I'd like to buy it. To build us a house." He took off his glasses and wiped them off carefully as Olu sat frowning at the sound of this *us*. His father continued shyly, "It's just for perspective. We'll go now. I just thought we'd make that quick stop. The place that I'm living in now is quite humble. I've never believed, as you've noticed, in rent. I'd rather rent a modest place—some might say an ugly place—until I can purchase on the scale that I want. My father never rented, see, designed his own property. Quite striking—" He caught himself rambling and stopped.

But Olu turned, interest piqued, surprised at the mention of this father, whom Kweku had never discussed. Both of his parents were famously tight-lipped on the subject of who their own parents had been. "Died a long time ago," was the general impression, to which Fola added only, "My mother died giving birth." They didn't have photos, such as Olu found lining the stairs of the homes of his classmates in school, faded, framed and important, generations of *family*, at which he'd stand staring until someone inquired, "You like our family pictures, ey?" Usually the father, who'd thump him on the shoulder blade, offer a tour (the fathers of friends rather loved to be near him, loved to thump him on the shoulder blade, eyes bright with awe, as if nothing in the world were more wondrous than Olu, a prodigiously intelligent athlete in dark chocolate skin). He'd tour their homes aching with longing, for *lineage*, for a sense of having descended from faces in frames. That his family was thin in the backbench was troubling; it seemed to suggest they were faking it, false. A legitimate family would have photos on the staircase. At the very least grandparents whose first names he knew. "What did he do?" Olu asked, suddenly hopeful.

But Kweku answered vaguely, "He did the same thing as me." He put on his glasses and started the engine. "Come on then. Enough. You must be tired, and starved." He bought them four pieces of char-grilled plantain wrapped in newsprint and served with small bags of smoked nuts, then drove back, past the junction, and parked by a row of low beige concrete buildings, most missing their doors.

"Is this where you live?" Olu asked as they entered, unable to mask his dismay at the stench: two parts deep-frying fish, four parts urine and mothballs intended to neutralize the smell of the urine.

"When one rents in Ghana, one has to pay twelve months upfront," Kweku said, "and I'm saving for land. As you saw. It's not much, but the rent is near nothing and no one disturbs me or knows that I'm here."

Olu didn't ask him whether this was a good thing, to live without anybody knowing where you were, thinking, *later, they'd get to the heart of it later*, never suspecting that ten minutes later he'd leave. They climbed up the three flights of stairs to the flat, which was unexpectedly large, the whole uppermost floor. And clean, if monastic, bereft of decoration: a table, two chairs, velvet loveseat, the statue. He didn't bother asking how his father had shipped it, just swallowed his laughter at seeing her here, this stone thing that they'd hated but could never get rid of. Like everything hated, she never disappeared.

He sat at the table and opened his backpack. He was rifling for his toothbrush at the bottom of the bag when he found the small tent he had squashed there last summer when hiking with Ling in New Hampshire. "My tent."

"I thought we could share the one bed in the bedroom," said Kweku, glancing over.

"No, I brought it by mistake." Now Olu *did* laugh, and his father did also, a strange sound, much sadder than shouting or crying. He reached in again, found a gray Yale sweatshirt. "It's graduation." As he remembered it. "It's graduation today."

Kweku was running water into the kettle in the kitchenette. "You said?" He turned the tap off. "Couldn't hear you. It's what?"

"It's Yale graduation. Today's my graduation."

The clatter of the metal kettle dropped in the sink.

Kweku turned, heaving. A realization, not a question. "I forgot your graduation."

"Yes, you did," Olu said.

"Why did you—how did you—how could you miss it?" He took off his glasses. "Why—why aren't you there? Why are you *here*?" Wiped his eyes. "Graduation."

"It doesn't really matter."

"How can you say that?"

Olu shrugged. "It didn't seem worth it."

"What do you mean?!" Kweku persisted. "You should be *there* in New Haven, not *here*—"

"So should you."

Kweku fell silent. He started several answers with "I—" "You—" "We're not—" and then settled on, "Look. They're two separate issues and you know it, Olukayodé." Olu frowned, recoiling at the use of the name. No one ever called him by his full name but Fola and only when angry, so practically never. "You can't *do* that . . ." his father said, weakly now, faltering. "Give up when you're hurt. Please. You get that from me. That's what I do, what I've done. But you're different. You're *different* from me, son—"

"I'm *just* like—"

"You're better."

What was the thing that arose out of nowhere now? Pity? Shame? Longing to see the man whole, not to see him here standing in a barebones apartment, his trousers still ironed as if he were home, but *not* home, in this hellhole, a prison of his making, in exile, cut off from the family and worse: with this look on his face of a man without honor, at least of a man who feels *this is my lot*? He still couldn't say what he thought he would find when he touched down in Ghana, but this wasn't it, this hot, half-finished apartment, the half man here in it, now backing up, sitting down, too shamed to stand. How had his father come to wear this expression: defeated, and willing to accept the defeat, not resisting, not objecting, as if somewhere inside him lived someone who felt quite at home in this place, in these halls, dirty windows, bare bulbs, stink of urine, the concrete, chipped paint, never mind the pressed pants? It was *he* Olu hated, this man inside Kweku, with whom he felt anger, at whom he now shouted, "It's *you* who is better, goddammit, not me, I'm no different. It's *you*. You are better than this."

To which Kweku, very softly, "This? This is what I come from."

As if this were all that there was to be said.

As if twenty-two years, the whole kit and caboodle, were just a short stop on the way back to this; as if all one could hope for was closing the circle, was ending right back in the gray, in the ash.

"Not good enough, Olu!" shouted Olu. "Not good enough! *That's what you said when my answers were wrong. That's not good enough, Olu! Lazy thinking! Think smarter!* Not good enough, Kweku—" and would have gone on were it not for the sound of a door down the hall creaking open and footsteps approaching. High heels. Hard to say now where the pep talk was heading, or if it had worked where his father might be, whether Olu could really have spurred him to action, convinced him to come back to Boston. Who knows? There she was, suddenly, a shape in the doorway, some slim Other Woman with long tiny braids, rather sharp in her pantsuit—and that was that, really, his second trip to Ghana concluded.

"Halloo!" A dense local accent very carefully strained through the sieve of affected inflections. "How *ah* you?" She stepped toward Olu. "*Akwaaba*. You *ah* welcome."

"J-June," stuttered Kweku. "I didn't know you were home."

Olu stood blinking, unable to see her, to take in her features, to move or to speak. The woman said something in Ga to his father, then blew them both kisses and breezed out the door. Kweku tried "I—" "You—" "We're not—" before choosing, "It isn't what it looks like. But I should have let you know."

"Let me know what? That you live with this woman?"

"For now," answered Kweku. "It's only for now. She's helping me set up a practice in Ghana. It's hard to break into this market. Are you listening?"

Olu wasn't listening. He was shouldering the backpack and marching, straps gripped, to the still-open door. Kweku reached out to detain him. "Don't touch me!" he shouted, and left.

Down the stairs.

Into sun.

Then back to the airport, on foot to the junction, where the backpack made him look like a hitchhiking teen; an old jeep full of students, mostly German, stopped to get him, dropped him kindly on the airport road covered in dust; to the check-in desk, pleading to change his departure to fly out on standby that night. Back to Yale. The day after commencement, the campus half-dressed like a debutante stumbling back home from a ball.

To think of the smell (Jean Naté, fainter: mothball) fills Olu still now with the need for fresh air. He is attempting to yank up the window when someone caresses his back and "Don't touch me!" bursts out.

"I'm sorry," says Ling, taken aback, stepping backward. He turns to her, embarrassed, wipes his face with one hand. She frowns at him, worried, reaching up to embrace him, and he feels himself move, ever so slightly, away. "Why do you do that?" she asks. "When I touch you? You flinch when I touch you." She crosses her arms. "It's okay if you're crying—"

"I'm not. I'm not crying."

"Of course. You never cry." She sits down on the bed.

He sighs. He can see that he needs to say something to fill in the distance he's opened between them. "I switched with my sister," he tells her. "With Taiwo. She's sharing with Kehinde and I'm here with you." He sits down beside her and touches her shoulder. She leans in against him, her arms at his waist. He kisses her head but, his own arms gone leaden, he can't hold her back in the way that she'd like.

vii

Kehinde comes in and sees Olu there sleeping, then sees that the form is too small to be him. He gets into bed and lies waiting for something, a crack in the silence.

"I saw him," they both say.

Kehinde turns over. He was going to tell Taiwo what he just shared with Sadie. Instead he says, "Who?"

"Uncle Femi," she whispers, not turning to face him. "In *Ovation* magazine. There was one in the den."

The name slices through, a clean line through his center. His lungs spit up air, split in half. "In this house?"

"In a picture with Niké . . . ," she begins. "Just forget it."

"I can't 'just forget it,'" he says.

"Yeah, well, try."

"I *have* tried," he says.

"Yeah, well, try a little harder."

"Taiwo," he says.

"What do you want me to say?"

Kehinde doesn't know what he wants her to say. Has never known.

"Forget it," she says. "We should sleep."

He hears her readjusting her position in bed and is reminded of that other little bedroom they'd shared, of their first night in Lagos; can see them there, dumbstruck; can hear their sick uncle, "Show our twins to their rooms." Can see Auntie Niké saying, "This one's for Taiwo," and pushing in his sister, her face as she turned, a wild pleading in her eyes as she looked at her brother with a look that seemed to say *don't leave me in here alone.* But Auntie Niké pushed him forward, down the hall, to the next room, a much smaller bedroom with two little beds. "This is yours," she said coldly. There was a crib in the corner. Auntie Niké saw him noticing. "We'll have that removed." He entered the room while she watched from the doorway. "Someone will bring up your things, *ehn?* Just wait. Sleep if you want to. We'll call you for dinner."

"Thank you," he mumbled.

"Thank you, *Auntie.*" She left.

He sat for some moments looking around the little bedroom, the veined marble floor, barred-in windows, large crib. He looked out the window at the back of the building, a large well-kept garden and huge swimming pool. A gardener was working here, trimming the hedges. Reminded of Fola, he turned back around. A houseboy was standing at the door with his suitcase.

"Good evening, sa," the boy said.

"I'm Kehinde," he replied.

"Kehinde, sa," the boy said. Bowed slightly. "Your suitcase." Before Kehinde could respond, he walked quickly away. The apartment was like that: people appearing in doorways, bowing slightly with their eyes down, then hurrying away, a huge staff, twenty people at least, for the four of them: chefs, gardeners, houseboys, guards, all of them male. All of them dressed in white pants and white shirts, without shoes, slender boys, without names, in their teens, the one blurring into the other, slipping in and out of doorways bearing food and drink and whatever else, then hurrying away.

He lies, stiff, unspeaking, and thinks of his sister a shape in the doorway that first endless night, appearing suddenly in moonlight, her voice like a lifeboat. "Can I sleep here, Kehinde?" He should have said no. "It's too cold in my bedroom," she said. "I can't sleep." "Yeah, me either," he said, and she climbed into bed. The other, by the doorway, too far from the window, too hot in the night with the broken A/C. He'd wake one week later to find that she'd slipped in with him in his bed, with her feet by his pillow: a girl and a boy in thin Disney World nightclothes, a version of themselves that he hasn't seen since.

viii

Fola lies staring through the darkness at Sadie, who snores as if sighing across the huge bed with her hands in small fists as they are when she's sleeping, a habit she's had since the day she was born. *Alive if not well*, Fola thinks, with a frown, suddenly wondering whether this is enough after all? One of six dead, the five left all unwell? For she feels this, she *sees* it, she knows they're not well.

A single sensation overwhelms her, a new one, not dissimilar to panic, or the feeling of drowning, as if she'd been floating in flat luke-warm water—her face to the sky, and her arms and legs out—and abruptly began sinking, unexpectedly, irreversibly, too weary to stop herself, drifting down, down.

She sits up, alarmed, trying to steady her breathing, trying not to wake Sadie, but can't catch her breath. She slips from the bed, rushing quietly to the bathroom, where she doesn't turn the light on. Just stands, until calm. She turns on the tap, a little trickle of water to splash on her face, dabs her cheeks with a towel. As she lowers this, she glimpses her reflection in the mirror in the moonlight, and stops, lean-ing forward to look.

At her face.

Rather shocked by the large, chiseled features, somehow foreign after years of not looking in the mirror—merely rubbing rose lipstick across as she leaves in the morning or patting her hair down, top, back. How long has it been since she's looked at these features, the angular shapes of the mouth and the nose, the fair skin, still unwrinkled, the wide eyes familiar—yet different. She leans in to peer at her eyes.

The shade and the shape are the same as her father's (and Olu's), but something has changed over time; they are *more* like her father's than she's previously noticed, or more like her father's than they previ-ously were. She thinks of him less frequently than she looks in the mirror, so rarely has occasion to remember his face, to compare it to hers, as she does in this moment. His eyes on her face, where her own used to be. *His* eyes, with their faint sheen of grief and their laugh lines, the soft brown made softer by sorrow, by aching: these are the eyes Fola finds in the mirror. She stares, disbelieving. She touches the glass. Her father's eyes glisten in the light from the window behind her, aglow with the gathering tears. One slides down her cheek and she touches the droplet, as one lifts a finger to just-starting rain.

She returns to the bed from the bathroom on tiptoe. She slips back the cover and lies on her back. She touches her stomach but doesn't feel movement. She weeps until dawn without making a sound.

5.

They pile into Benson's SUV after breakfast, each shut in the silent glass box of his thoughts, seven boxes, locked, soundproof and shatter-resistant; the eighth man, the driver, hums, present, alone. The day has dawned coolish, deceptively clement, sun covered by clouds, a thick coat of pale gray with bright whiteness behind it, a threat or a promise, breeze running its fingers through leaves, not yet noon. In thirty or so minutes the clouds will start parting, the leaves will stop moving, the air will stand still; the sun will stop playing demure and come forward; the day will turn muggy, unbearably hot. The weather in December is like this in Ghana: an in taken breath held until the world spins, trail of tears to the New Year through sopping humidity, the worst of the heat, then the respite of rain.

ii

An hour outside of the city: the ocean.

Unannounced, unambitious.

Just suddenly *there*.

They've flown up the freshly paved road to the junction, where they turn up a hill lined on both sides by homes. The main road is bustling with noonday commotion, plump women bearing water and goods on their heads, thin children in uniform, dark brown and light orange, trotting briskly down the road to catch a *tro-tro* to lunch. The men are less visible. A few stand in doorways in loose faded trousers and wifebeater shirts, peering out, partially squinting, partially frowning, undecided, as Benson's Benz truck rumbles past, stirring dust.

Benson is seated up front with the driver, in straw hat and Ray-Bans, a safari tour guide. Ling, between Fola and Olu, sits tensely. Sadie between Taiwo and Kehinde, behind.

"I remember this road," murmurs Fola.

"You've been here?" Benson turns to face Fola, and Olu shrinks back.

"Only once. And too late." She touches Olu on the shoulder blade. "You came too, darling." A twinge, upper right.

The car crests the hill and descends by the water, the road belted in from the beach by a field. They all turn to stare as one does when he hasn't seen ocean in months, shocked afresh by the scope. Even Sadie stops pretending to sleep on her brother, sits up, and leans over to stare out the glass.

A halfhearted wall made of mortar and concrete block starts and then stops like a six-year-old's smile, with huge gaps between bits of it exposing the goats grazing lazily on grass, in no rush, a large herd. To the right of the road the steep hill continues upward, red earth densely greened with tall grass and short trees; to the left a low field, a mile deep, flowering shrubs, knotted crawlers, wild grass thinning out into sand. Then the beach. It is farther than it seems from the car, where one thinks if he wanted he could simply leap out and make a beeline for the water like a toddler, peeling clothes off, kicking shoes off, screaming, joyous, for his freedom as he ran. In fact, it would take more than a little bit of effort to approach through the weeds at this point in the road; better access lies ahead at the edge of the village, where the fishermen have beaten out a trail through the grass.

Still, the water beckons, stretched flat to the horizon, the same moody shade as the clouds overhead, not the prettiest beach in the world but there's something, a calm getting on with it, calming to behold. Palms stretching forward at forty-five-degree angles appear to be shaking out their hair on the sand over long wooden boats in spectacular colors festooned with black seaweed, white, blue and green nets. Just visible in the distance, three women are walking with babies tucked into their *lappas*, bare feet, three abreast, with a touch of the patriotic to the *lappas*, one goldish, one red, one a bright emerald green.

Benson begins speaking to no one in particular, a rambling little speech in a tight, chipper voice. "I came here with Kweku when he first moved to Ghana to treat some young nephew who'd broken his leg, and so happened to meet the local maker of coffins, who was also the local physician, it seemed. Ga people believe that a coffin should be a reflection of the life of the person inside it. So a fisherman's coffin might be shaped like a fish or a carpenter's shaped like a hammer, I guess, or a woman who likes shoes, in the shape of a shoe. They can be quite elaborate."

Fola offers, "Indeed."

"What's this town called?" Olu asks. (Benson answers.) "Kokrobité," repeats Olu. "Sounds Japanese." Disappointed.

"Reminds me of Jamaica," Ling murmurs. "Ocho Rios."

Different palette, thinks Kehinde. *Less azure, more red.*

"Village," says Fola. "Less a town than a village."

"I didn't know he grew up by the ocean," Taiwo says.

"That's why we always had a house near the water. The harbor, the river, in Brookline the pond . . ." Fola trails off, seeing trees in the distance, the boats beached on sand.

They are silent again.

The road travels on past the first glimpse of ocean and into the village, where it loses the view—and the paving and straightness, becoming instead a dirt path winding, rock-strewn and rough, through the homes. They're single-room structures—of wood, brick, or concrete, some mud, with tin roofs, a few thatch, glassless windows, wooden shutters—in clusters, with clotheslines and open-air stoves and bath buckets and trees between clusters. Women bent over these buckets wash clothing and very young children, who wave as they pass. Chickens wander pecking at earth, as do goats, these much dirtier and skinnier than the ones by the beach. The elderly sit watching ancient TVs under shade trees, in a circle beneath the leaf cover. Barbershops mingle with braiding stalls, signboards, BLOOD ON THE CROSS CUT & SHAVE, CROWN OF THORNS BRAIDS, kiosks sell calling cards and top-up cards and aliment, with wares stacked in piles to the roof, blocks of color: yellow (Lipton, Maggi), green (Milo, Wrigley's), red (oil, tomato paste, corned beef, instant coffee).

The holes in the road make for truly rough going, which inevitably begins to feel like the fault of the driver. When he finally stops abruptly by a small walled-in compound, one tire in a groove, tilting off the main road, they glare at him, nauseous, unaware that he's parked and not simply run the car into a ditch by mistake. Benson turns to speak, stopping short at their faces. He manages a halting "Yes. Right. Okay. So."

The air has gone heavy with the stopping of the vehicle, the moment they've been waiting for appearing to have come. Fola touches Olu on the knee, which stops the bouncing. Ling observes the gesture, notes that Olu doesn't flinch. Kehinde mouths to Sadie *you okay?* She nods her head. He looks across at Taiwo, who is staring out the back. Benson tries again, removing Ray-Bans and sunhat, and forcing a slightly less chipper "We're here."

iii

"Here" is a compound at the edge of the village, a square of nine huts in a large patch of dust with a tree in the middle befitting the context, the same type of tree found in every such patch: massive, ancient, gray, twisted, thick trunk a small fortress, raised roots bursting up through the hardened red earth, knotted branches fanned out in imperial fashion, horizontal, dropping leaves on their way to the roofs. A behemoth. Beneath it are five wooden benches arranged in a circle, to a social effect. Around it, six huts form a three-sided square with their doors standing open to dark, bed-less rooms; behind these two more, and behind that the biggest, or tallest, a mud hut with massive thatch roof.

The driver has stopped in the groove by an entrance marked off by a wall made of crumbling red brick. They get out in silence, first Benson, then Olu, then the rest of them, shading their eyes with their hands. A heavyset woman is waiting to meet them in a traditional outfit of simple black cloth. She's fashioned a swath of this cloth as a head wrap with bow tie in front, short gray hair tucked inside. Her skin is so smooth that she could be much younger, but she stands like a woman of seventy hard years: with her elbow on the wall and her head on her fist and her hip pushing out, other hand on that hip, as if seeking to rest the full weight of her past on this crumbling brick wall for these one or two breaths.

Fola steps forward, arms extended, ever gracious. "Shormeh," she says.

"I am Naa." The woman sighs.

"Naa, excuse me. Of course." Fola laughs. "It's been ages. God."

Naa doesn't laugh. "You are welcome in Ghana." She straightens up slowly, taking her head off her fist and her elbow off the wall and her eyes off of Fola, a shift in position that draws her attention to Sadie at the edge of the circle.

iv

Sadie feels the gaze on her face, with the humidity, a pressure or a magnet: it tugs at her eyes, though her chin, out of habit, resists the ascension and sinks to her chest while her eyes travel up. She rarely looks people in the eye when she meets them, preferring their mouths or her hands as an audience—anything to throw off the would-be observer, to avoid being looked at too closely, too long. She's doing it now, standing slightly behind Taiwo in the broken-doll position she perfected in high school, with shoulders hunched forward and flip-flops turned inward, an arrangement of limbs that conveys such unease that the onlooker invariably feels uneasy himself and after one or two seconds looks away. Undaunted, indifferent, or accustomed to uneasiness, Naa gazes on, drawing Sadie's eyes upward—and holding them put: Sadie can't look back down, for her shock at the striking resemblance.

She could be her mother, this heavyset Naa, with the same angled eyes ("half-Chinesey," per Philae), same stature, short, sturdy, same negligible eyebrows, round face, rounded nose, like a button for coins. The joke of genetics. That of all of his children it should have been she who inherited this appearance, the one who would spend the least time with their father and come to so loathe his particular features. They worked out just fine on *his* face: he was handsome in the way that a man can be, without being pretty, with the skin like this Naa's or like Olu's, so flawless. A tidy face. Elegant.

Not so her own.

Philae likes to call her "a natural beauty," while Fola uses phrases like "you'll come into your own" (in a tone reminiscent of "we'll find your hidden talent"), but Sadie knows better. She isn't pretty. End of story. Her eyes are too small and her nose is too round and she hasn't got cheekbones like Taiwo or Philae, nor long slender limbs nor a clean chiseled jaw nor a dipping-in waist nor a jutting-out clavicle. She's five foot four, solid, not fat per se, stocky, pale milky-tea skin, number-four-colored hair, neither tall nor petite, with no edges, no angles; she looks like a doll, one she wouldn't have wanted. It isn't worth trying to explain this to Philae, nor to Fola for that matter. They wouldn't understand it. They're *pretty*, a state of being they both take for granted, through no fault of theirs (through the joke of genetics). Their empathy is bound within the limits of their reality, Sadie knows. They can't imagine it, *not* being pretty. A bit like, say, a woman might imagine being a man—can merely close her eyes and picture it, whatever "being a man" may mean to her—but can't in fact picture *not* being a woman, would have nothing to draw on, however she tried. So the pretty woman's imagination is limited, absent reference for the experience of not being seen. Most of the time she *herself* can't be bothered to sort through the reasons the world doesn't see her. It all seems a bit too cliché, melodramatic, for a girl with her sarcasm and level of education. She accepts that the media are to blame for her bulimia, her quiet, abiding desire to be reborn a blond waif; vigorously castigates Photoshop as a public health threat; has examined and condemned her childhood taste for white Barbies; and so on. Isn't stupid. Can see the thing clearly. But the fact remains: she is invisible. Unpretty.

The sense of being looked at is new and alarming. "H-h-hello," Sadie stutters, flushing, offering a hand.

Naa takes the hand, frowning deeply, squeezing tightly. "Ekua," she says.

"Um, I'm Sadie." Sadie smiles. "My name is Sadie. Nice to meet you."

But Naa is insistent. "Ekua," she repeats. "Sister Ekua. It's you."

Sadie laughs nervously, not following. "I'm Sadie. That's my middle name. Ekua."

Naa nods. "Welcome back."

Sadie thinks to clarify that she's never been to Ghana, but Naa moves on to Olu, and on down the line. A second heavy woman in the simple black muslin with head tie appears with a large plastic tray piled with bottles of Coke, Fanta, Malta, Bitter Lemon.

Fola tries again. "Hello, Shormeh."

Correct.

The soft drinks are distributed with hardened eyes, pleasantries, introductions made briefly, condolences exchanged. "We have prepared a small welcome," says Shormeh. "Please be seated." She gestures to the benches in a circle in the shade.

The sun has stopped playing demure and come forward, the air pressing down on their arms like a hand. They sit on the benches with their sodas, sweating lightly. A small crowd has gathered to observe the affair. They are children mostly, appearing from inside the modest houses dressed in faded American clothing, wearing cautious, watchful smiles. *Girls*, Sadie notices after trying to place the feeling that there's something here she's missing. All the children are girls.

"Where are the boys?" she asks Fola beside her.

Fola chuckles wryly. "They're at school."

Case in point, a small troupe of girls dressed in indigo batik lines up neatly in the space between the houses and the benches. Three teenage boys with large drums, dressed in tunics take up position to the side of these girls in the shade. Naa takes a plastic chair, sipping a Malta. Shormeh remains standing, a hand on Naa's chair. The girls—there are six of them, ranging in age from the smallest, maybe eight, to the oldest, chubby, twelve—look dutifully at Shormeh, who nods to them curtly. With no introduction, the drumming begins.

Ling finds her phone in her purse, takes a picture. Sadie sits up straight, rather bracing herself. But the sound of the drums is unexpectedly calming, as relaxed and at ease in this space as she isn't. She's never been particularly drawn to this music, to African drumming, though she wonders why not: the reaction is visceral, she feels her heart slow, or succumb to this new form of beating, more ordered. Only now does it occur to her that her heart has been pounding, quite literally throbbing, since they left Fola's house, such that now she is sore, bodily sore, physically exhausted, as if she's been exercising, running for miles. This pounding becomes harder but also calmer with the drumming, her breath breaking off from the pace of her thoughts, following instead the mounting rhythm as it builds in its complexities. A surrogate heartbeat. Harder, calmer, and surer. *Why don't I listen to this music?* she thinks. *Or enjoy it?* It is wonderful. It drowns out all thoughts. As lulling as that sitar and flute they're always playing where she goes to do yoga with Philae. Transporting. She closes her eyes for a moment, feels dizzy. When she opens them the girls have come closer, gained speed.

They are moving in a circle, in perfect precision. Feet out, feet in. Hips out, hips in. The drummers change pace, and the girls change formation, from a line to a half-circle. The youngest comes forward. She dances a little solo, then returns to the circle. The next one comes forward. And on down the line. Others from the village have trickled into the compound to watch the performance; they clap for each girl. The last of the dancers, the eldest, short, chubby, shimmies forward, beaming brightly, to the delight of the crowd. *She doesn't have the look of a dancer*, thinks Sadie. She rather has the appearance of Sadie herself, or of Naa: of a substance, a thick sort of substance, less long dancer limbs, liquid-fluid, than land mass: thick arms, thighs, high buttocks, broad shoulders, small bosom, the same solid body that she has. And hates. It startles her to think this so clearly of another, so cruelly, of this dancer, but the thought comes again. *I hate this body*, she thinks as she stares at the girl, *I hate this body, it is ugly, I hate how it looks.*

There.

Very simply.

This body is ugly.

Never mind the more gentle "unpretty," the face; it's the body she hates, if she thinks of it, really. The body is the difference between her and the rest. How much easier to see it of this young chubby dancer, or to say it, thinks Sadie, than to say of herself what she saw in that mirror, sees here with her siblings. The body is the reason she cannot be seen. She considers the dancer with something like sadness, for both of them, a sadness made soft by acceptance. Preparing to watch this girl's solo, sympathetic, she crosses her arms with a pitying smile.

Funny how it happens.

How the girl begins moving. Almost awkward at first, sort of jerky. Stiff movements. The crowd begins clapping and Sadie laughs softly, suspicions confirmed. *An ugly body can't dance.* The girl is still beaming, her narrow eyes twinkling, maybe laughing at the joke of genetics as well. She rolls her hips once to the right, then the left. Looks directly at Sadie, waves a hand, and begins.

Incomprehensible, indescribable how this girl moves her body. Virtuosic, without effort, without edges, without angles: an infinity of tiny movements made with thighs, feet, and torso, and in time to syncopation that only she hears, and the drummers: a current, round body electric, the crowd cheering wildly as the hips whirl around, until the one drum goes *crack!* and she stops before Sadie, her right hand extended, one foot off the ground.

Sadie, who is staring, mouth open, breath suspended, doesn't at first process what the gesture implies. The drummers resume drumming, the girl resumes whirling, the crowd resumes clapping, then *crack!* She stops again. A hand out to Sadie.

Sadie turns to Fola. "I-i-is she asking for money?"

"She's asking you to dance."

"*Bra, bra, bra,*" says the girl, palms turned upward. "Please *sees-tah*, come. Come and dance, please, I beg." She takes Sadie's hand, takes a little step back, making Sadie lean forward, then rise off the bench. The assembled crowd claps with delight at this progress. Sadie flushes red, shakes her head, "No, I can't." She is seconds from weeping; she feels the thing building, the knot in her stomach, the accumulating bile. She takes a step back, but the girl pulls her forward, and she hasn't the heart to use force to break free. Her siblings are watching with what looks like a mixture of worry and encouragement, their eyes and smiles wide, as if watching a baby trying to learn how to walk, ready to spring to their feet when she falls.

She doesn't fall.

When they speak of it later they'll say that a girl came to Sadie and pulled her up off of their bench, gave a little demonstration of the base two-step footwork, which Sadie repeated a few times herself, that the drummers, encouraged, started drumming a little faster, that Sadie kept pace, to the delight of the crowd, and that before they all knew it, she was dancing in the clearing as if she'd been born doing traditional Ga dance. No one will know what it is in this moment that overwhelms Sadie, not even Sadie herself, as the insistent lead dancer catches hold of her elbow and repeats, tugging gently, "Please *sees*-tah, please come." She pulls Sadie forward, away from the benches. "Like so," she says, demonstrating the footwork: one, two. There are tears in Sadie's eyes that will fall if she doesn't, so she stares at the ground, at the girl's small bare feet. One two, one two, one two, one two. A surrogate heartbeat. Calmer and surer. She takes a few steps. Hears the onlookers cheering. Goes red with embarrassment. Too late to sit down. She stares at the ground, at her feet, willing movement. The feet obey, shockingly, and move, left to right. The girl cries, "*Ehn-hehn!*" with great pride in her pupil. Sadie glances up as she moves. "Yeah? Like this?" More movement. More cheering. Transporting, the drumbeat. Tension in the stomach. Which moves to the thighs. Then the knees, then the calves, then the shins, then the feet. Too embarrassed to stop, she keeps moving. Starts dancing. Slowly at first, with her eyes on the ground, on the feet of the girl, which she follows with ease—then a spark, something clicking, a logic inside her, a stranger inside her that knows what to do, knows this music, these movements, this footwork, this rhythm, the body relaxing, eyes trained on the feet, she is moving, not looking, afraid to stop moving, afraid to look up at the small cheering crowd, she is moving, she is sweating, she is crying (*I am dancing*, she thinks, disbelieving, unable to stop), stomach taut, thighs on fire, lids slack, hips in circles, shoulder up shoulder down, around, foot out foot in, she is outside her body or *in* it, inside it, unaware of the exterior, unaware of the skin, unaware of the eyes, unaware of the onlookers, aware of the pounding, aware of the drum.

Crack!

The drum stops. Sadie stops. Sweating, breathless. The small gathered crowd ceases clapping and stares. An instant of silence, then Olu: "Go, Sadie!" with all of the might of his baritone voice. The children resume clapping and cheering in Ga, the chubby dancer, "My *sees-tah!*" Pictures taken with phones. Fola leaps up from the bench to embrace her as if she has just run a footrace and won. "My God," she is laughing, clutching Sadie by the forehead. "My daughter's a dancer, *ehn?*" Kissing her braids. Sadie, overcome by belated self-consciousness now that she's stopped and can feel the warm eyes, lets her mother embrace her, her heart pounding wildly for, among other things, joy.

v

But to see Sadie now in her moment of triumph, enfolded by Fola as she was at the airport (all smiles-through-the-tears, face to breast, and the rest of it), Taiwo feels something rather startlingly like rage. She's been trying all morning to stick to the script, looking somber, sounding interested, dabbing sweat without complaining, an attempt at being civil that the rest take for sulking, accustomed as they are to her silence, her brooding. This is her preassigned part in the play, as it's Olu's to administrate or Kehinde's to peacekeep or Sadie's to cry at the drop of a hat or their mother's to turn a blind eye: Taiwo sulks. They expect it, await it, would miss it if she stopped it. No one worries or asks her what's wrong, did something happen? *That's just Taiwo,* they'll say with their eyes to each other when they think she can't see, eyebrows raised, shoulders shrugged.

Such that she, too, believes that she's always been like this, was a "difficult infant" and will always be difficult—*and that,* she thinks suddenly, watching Fola and Sadie, *if only I were easier, then I'd be hugged, too.* Her mother doesn't hug her, it occurs to her, jarringly. Doesn't rush to her side at the first sign of need, reserves this privilege for Sadie, who is sweeter and weepy and cute like a doll, like a thing that you hold. So it was yesterday at the dining room table when Fola just stared as she'd started to cry. Had it been Sadie, Taiwo knows, Fola would have embraced her, as now, instead of watching as her daughter walked away.

Rage, out of nowhere. She stares at her mother and feels this rage surging, both startling and embarrassing, that it should come *now,* with the rest of them laughing, putting grief aside momentarily to celebrate Sadie, small Sadie, sweet Sadie, clean Sadie, pure Sadie, as cute as a baby they can't help but hug. Out of nowhere, overwhelming, a rage beyond reason. Her body begins trembling, then moving, without bidding: first quivering, then burning, then standing, then walking: without thinking, without speaking, she is walking away. The others don't notice her go, taking pictures, the children still chattering, older women uninterested. Only Kehinde stands worriedly. "Where you going?" he murmurs. She answers, "To the bathroom," and he doesn't pursue.

She hasn't the foggiest idea where she's going. Just strides out the entrance to the compound, along the wall, sees the driver by the car, goes the other direction, away from the town, down the dark red dirt road. Rage bids her onward, a visceral seething that quickens her pace and inhibits her thinking so all she can see is her mother hugging Sadie and all she can think is the thought *but not me.* Rage and self-pity and shame at self-pity. A fire in the legs. Faster, onward, consumed—until, reaching the edge of the village, nearly jogging, she looks up and sees that she's reached a small clearing. Absent clustered structures obstructing the ocean, the sand beckons, open, like an answer.

The beach is almost empty, the sun near its height, just the four little boys playing soccer without shoes who smile pleasantly at Taiwo as she appears between palm trees but don't stop their passing or chitchat in Ga. She pulls off her flip-flops and walks down the sand, which is hard, whitish-gray, piping hot at this hour; feels the rage start to cool with the new, damper air, with the salt taste and sea breeze and sound of the waves; and keeps walking, away from the boys, from their laughter, not thinking, still heaving, now dripping with sweat.

A half mile ahead stands a colonial structure, what looks to have once been some grand beachfront house, complete with terraces and pillars, now abandoned to the sunshine. A few miles beyond another village begins. Somewhere in her mind is the idea of escaping, of making her way to the end of this beach, but the building distracts, looming darkly before her, the sand turning brown in its shadow ahead. It reminds her of that house that she hated, the sullenness, the ghosts of other families, strangers, long-dead Europeans, here plopped on a beach with the boats and the palm trees and few thatch-roofed huts someone's built in the shade. She stops to consider it: out of place in this picture, as they always felt, an African family in Brookline; as *she* always felt late at night in her bedroom, the ghosts more at home there than she was. And laughs.

The visual is laughable: this house on a beach in a village in Ghana, some white family home, with its paint stripped away and its eye sockets empty, but *here*, still assertive, imposing itself. She laughs at the thought of her father, in childhood, a child on this beach looking up at this house, thinking one day he'd have one as big, as assertive, thinking one day he'd conquer some land of his own. *Which he did*, she thinks, laughing—those acres in Brookline on which stood that equally joyless old home, i.e., "home" as conceived by the same pink-faced British who would have erected this thing on this beach, hulking, rock, a declaration—*but without the immovability*, the faint air of dominance, the confidence or the permanence. He conquered new land and he founded a house, but his shame was too great and his conquest was sold. Or sold *back*, very likely, to a sweet pink-faced family, the descendants of Pilgrims, more familiar with dominance. Retrieved from the new boy, returned to the natives, to Cabots or Gardeners, reclaimed from the Sais. *Poor little boy,* who had walked on this beach, who had dreamed of grand homes and new homelands, she thinks, with his feet cracking open, his soles turning black, never guessing his error (she'd have told him if he'd asked): that he'd never find a home, or a home that would last. That one never feels home who feels shame, never will. She laughs at the thought of that boy on this beach, and laughs harder at the thought of the house that he bought, and laughs hardest at the thought of herself in that house, twelve years old, still a girl, still believing in home.

The usual thing happens:

she laughs until she's crying with laughter, then crying without it, just crying. Then sitting. Where she is. Drops her bag, just stops walking, has nowhere to go, is a stranger here also. Had she any more energy she'd likely go anyway, start running, waiting (hoping) for some person (man) to follow her—but can't, is too tired, in her legs, in her body; something seeping out the center, some last stronghold giving in, within. So sits. In the sun, on the sand, sweating, crying. As one sits on beaches. But without the lover's cardigan.

She fumbles in the bag for her American Spirits, lights one, smokes it quickly; small, jittery motions. She clutches her knees to her chest, to feel closeness, overcome by a grief she can hardly make sense of. The last time she felt this was midnight in Boston, her father slumped over on the couch in his scrubs: that the world was too open, wide open, an ocean, their ship sinking slowly, weighed down by the shame. What she hadn't known then was that it would be Fola to cut off the ropes, set the lifeboats adrift. Or that it *could* be Fola. Not a father but a mother. What she hadn't known then is that mothers betray.

So then.

The thought that she hasn't been thinking.

Stepping at last into light after years at the edge of awareness, a shadow of consciousness, peeking then hiding when her mind turned its way. Dr. Hass has it wrong, as she's long since suspected: it isn't the father. Or not him alone. It was Fola who sent them to Femi that summer like two fatted calves to the altar. Not he. How has she missed this? The source of her anger. The rage without name: that she sent them away, that she shipped them to Lagos when she should have known better, when she *must* have known somehow what would happen, who he was, her own brother, her own family. For the cost of tuition. The thought in the open. That mothers betray. And what happens to daughters whose mothers betray them? *They don't become huggable like Sadie*, Taiwo thinks. They don't become giggly, adorable like Ling. They grow shells. Become hardened. They stop being girls. Though they look like girls and act like girls and flirt like girls and kiss like girls—really, they're generals, commandos at war, riding out at first light to preempt further strikes. With an army behind them, their talents their horsemen, their brilliance and beauty and anything else they may have at their disposal dispatched into battle to capture the castle, to bring back the Honor. Of course it doesn't work. For they burn down the village in search of the safety they lost, every time, Taiwo knows. They end lonely. Desired and admired and alone in their tents, where they weep through the night. In the morning they ride, and the boys see them coming. And think: my, what brilliant and beautiful girls. Hearts broken, blood spilled. Riding on, seeking vengeance. This a most curious twist in the plot: that the vengeance they seek is the love of another, a mother-like lover who will not betray. At the thought she laughs harder. To think of her lover, his scarf and his sweatpants, his motherly smile. And his wife and his children. Prepackaged betrayal. A foregone conclusion. "Marissa, thank you." *And . . . scene.*

She stares at the water, eyes blurry for seeing things clearly, unsure what to do or think next. (If she hears it the first time, her name doesn't register.) She lights another cigarette. She smokes this one slowly. The sun beating down on her shoulders and back is a comfort of sorts, a reminder of skin, a reminder of pain in a different dimension, outside of her body, outside of this grief. She lies on her back in the sand, which is damper than she realized sitting upright, a welcome surprise. She stretches her toes in the direction of the waves, but the tide doesn't wash in this high at this hour. And is lying there, smoking, her locks full of sand, when she hears it again.

Someone calling her name.

"Taiwo," and again from a distance, insistent. "*Tai*-wo!"

She props herself up.

Sees her mother.

Fola, as if conjured, calling, "Darling!" Coming toward her. The little boys pointing, informants, behind her. Fola, out of nowhere, storming frantically toward her, white linen pants billowing, gesturing. (All but the torches.) "Kehinde said you went to the bathroom, but I looked there. The driver said he saw you walking here toward the beach. What happened, my darling?" she's saying, coming closer. "Did you get hurt? Can you stand?" She reaches Taiwo, and kneels.

Perhaps it is the proximity that overwhelms Taiwo, having Fola so close after all of these years? Something. She snaps, leaping up, startling Fola, who stands, reeling backward. "DID I GET *HURT*?!" Taiwo screams. Almost as if a thread that's been dangling gets pulled on, or catches on something, the whole thing unraveling. She is laughing and crying and screaming, "What *happened*? Mom, what did you *think* was going to happen to us?" And then, because Fola looks utterly baffled, Taiwo sneers, "I'll tell you what happened, sure, fine." Though she promised she wouldn't and hasn't for years, though she never once imagined the moment like this (empty beach in the daytime, young boys standing, staring), she tells, without pausing, how it happened, how it started:

how they shared the second bedroom, the one given Kehinde, with the creaky twin beds because hers was too big and too cold with the air conditioner, which she couldn't turn off (it was too high to reach), whereas his didn't work. That first night she came to his door in her nightdress. "Can I sleep here, Kehinde?" Her brother said yes. At first she took the one bed and Kehinde the other, but his room was too hot not to sleep by the window, so after a week they just shared, head to foot, like sardines in a can, sheets thrown off to the breeze. After two, she stopped sneaking to her room before sunrise, afraid that Uncle Femi would discover and scold them; they'd seen him only twice since they'd arrived in Nigeria, at the elaborate Sunday lunches he threw for his friends. The rest of the time he was virtually absent, locked away at the top of the four-floor apartment, accessible only by an elevator that required a code, which the twins didn't have, so an invisible world. They could hear their uncle's guests always coming and going, riding up, riding down, music playing, all hours, the raucous parties on Saturdays, women laughing, glasses smashing, muffled shouting, Niké complaining—but they never went up.

They lived on the second floor like two (wealthy) orphans in the care of Uncle Femi's large all-male staff. The houseboys would wake them and set out their uniforms. The cooks served their meals. The drivers took them to school. They'd spend the whole day there, returning for dinner. They ate by themselves, did their work, went to bed. Sardines in a can, by the window for breeze, telling stories about Boston, most involving the snow, as if by remembering the cold they might actually *feel* it, and lessen the pressure of the humidity somehow. Auntie Niké would appear in the evenings after dinner to reiterate the rules about the use of the elevator, to see that they hadn't dropped dead in the daytime, to complain about Femi, then ride back upstairs. They didn't make friends at the American International School, where their peers thought them arrogant on account of their looks. So mostly stuck to each other, eating, sleeping, doing schoolwork, watching television, playing cassette tapes, swimming, riding in cars.

When they spoke to her, Fola, on the phone at the weekends (the one call allotted them, five minutes each), they said they were "happy" so she wouldn't be worried. They weren't sad in the beginning. They were simply alone. They knew there was something not right in the apartment—different people always coming in and out at all hours, speaking Yoruba and Arabic and English and pidgin; on weekends they could see them, from the bedroom, by the pool; they saw the girls prancing in leopard-print dresses and heavy fur jackets and stilettos and wigs, and the fat men beside them, and young men in batches, all slender and handsome with dark, hungry eyes—but they didn't ask questions. It didn't seem worth it. They did what they were told to and

kept to themselves. Three months, then six, and then nine in this fashion. With the summer arriving suddenly with cool, drier air, then the
end of the school year, a change in the program, an emptiness appearing in the middle of their days.

How things changed:

that one morning. Auntie Niké, without warning. Appearing in
the kitchen as they sat down to eat. It was the first time they'd seen her
in the morning, out of costume, without face paint or wig, a silk scarf
on her head. Taiwo happened to glance up from her Weetabix and saw
her, and choked on her milk with dismay at the sight.

The woman looked like a ghost. With her beige-grayish skin and
her small vacant eyes, a white sheet in her hand. A ghost laughing.
"Surprised to see me, *ehn*? You think we don't live here? You think you
can do as you please in this house?" She was laughing very softly as she
liked to, when angry, and jabbing her finger like the tongue of a snake.
They'd observed this performance on a number of occasions when
Niké stood berating the houseboys outside: the measured opening (soft
laughter or whispered derision), one finger thrust forward on salient
points, the slow build to full volume, with rhetorical questions ("you
think we don't live here?"), the use of "my friend," then the climax, the
screaming, the invocation of the Bible, the melodramatic finale,
Shakespearean in tone. Always ranting about honor and justice and
such, before beating the houseboys, a violent to-do. To Taiwo's mind,
Nigerians seemed to *like* being angry, to derive pleasure from conflict,
some physical thrill; she would watch them in the marketplace, at
school, the way they carried on, their eyes alive with pleasure as they
screamed and tore their hair. It was hard to take seriously. She was
listening to Auntie Niké but absently, carefully mashing down her
Weetabix in milk. It was only when the woman started shouting, "It's
disgusting!" that she looked up from the cereal.

"It's *disgusting* what you've done!" In a single dramatic gesture Niké shook out the bedsheet, a white fitted sheet with a small reddish stain. Taiwo and Kehinde both stared in confusion. Niké continued, shouting, "I know what you've done! The houseboys have told me that you sleep in one bedroom, and now we can see what you do in there, *ehn*?" She pointed at Kehinde, eyes slit. "She's your *sister*. Your very own twin. You are a sinner, my friend."

Kehinde sat blinking with shock. "I-I-I'm sorry?"

A question, not an apology, but Niké raged on, "It's a sin what you've done, *ehn*? 'I'm sorry' isn't good enough! You tell me what happened. You tell me right now."

"We don't understand, Auntie," said Taiwo very calmly, though it was beginning now to dawn on her, what had happened with this sheet: not a week ago she'd woken up bleeding, just a little bit; her first period, she knew, from sex ed class last year. She'd informed the youngest houseboy, Babatunde, the nicest, who'd returned hours later with tampons and pads, a huge bag, unceremoniously. Had thus "become a woman." That was the phrase that their teacher had used. Becoming a woman. Taiwo didn't feel womanly. She felt irritable and uncomfortable (perhaps how womanhood felt?). Now here was Niké with this sheet with this bloodstain, which Taiwo hadn't noticed at the time, fair enough. Easy to explain that she'd gotten her period. Harder to explain why they slept in one bed. Heretofore it hadn't seemed odd, much less "disgusting," but now as she started to speak, she had doubts.

Two memories returned, the one faint in its details, a bit like a dream recollected at dusk: of some morning, one of many she had woken beside Kehinde, a month ago, longer, maybe months, she didn't know. All she remembered was waking from dreaming, very early, before sunrise, eyes blurred, still half-sleeping, and feeling something firm against the back of one thigh as she rolled from her back to her side, away from Kehinde. Eyes closed, barely conscious, she thought *it's his foot* and reached down, mumbling, "Move, man," to push it away. The feel of the erection in her palm was so foreign—so hard and so warm, yet so fleshy, so soft—that she didn't for a moment fully process what she was holding. Her brother stirred, snoring. Alarmed, she let go. She lay there beside him, eyes open, heart pounding, afraid for some reason, of what she didn't know. Maybe she thought she was dreaming, had dreamed it? She fell back asleep. Only remembered it now.

And the other, not a memory. A habit. "Disgusting." The thing she started doing when they got out of school, when they started spending days in the apartment, lazy hours, floating idly in the swimming pool or watching cartoons. The one day she'd come from the pool to the bedroom to shower and change, leaving Kehinde afloat. She'd pulled off her bathing suit and was looking for a towel when she found the one book she had brought here from home. A massive encyclopedia of gods and mythology, a gift from their father the Christmas before. She'd become obsessed with the Muses that winter in Classics; he'd inserted a leather bookmark at the chapter on Calliope. Some conspiratorial houseboy had placed the large volume in the last dresser drawer where they hid stolen snacks. There with the three-packs of biscuits and towels was the book she'd assumed to be stolen or lost. Delighted to find it, she'd flopped down at once on the bed that she shared with her brother to read. And was lying there naked with her stomach on a pillow when she flipped to an illustration of "The Rape of Persephone," a pink-fleshy picture of plump-breasted girls in a meadow of flowers with the accompanying text:

> Persephone was gathering flowers in a meadow with her companions Artemis and Athena. There she was attracted to an exceptionally beautiful narcissus with one hundred blossoms. When she reached out to pick it, the ground split open and from deep within the earth, Hades came forth in a golden chariot pulled by black horses. He raped Persephone and took

her to the underworld. She screamed for help from her father Zeus but he gave her no help.

Demeter also heard Persephone's cries and rushed to find her. Carrying burning torches, she searched for nine days and nine nights over land and sea for her abducted daughter. She never stopped to eat, sleep or bathe in her frantic search. On the tenth day Helios, God of the Sun, told Demeter that Hades had kidnapped Persephone. Furthermore, he said that the abduction and rape of Persephone had been sanctioned by Zeus.

Standard fare. What came as a surprise was what she felt as she read, staring repeatedly at the image of Hades's hand on the breast: a tingling pressure between her legs where the sheet was bunched up, which grew stronger and sharper until she peed on herself. She leapt up, alarmed and embarrassed, shut the book. She stared at the sheets, first ashamed, then confused. There was no spreading wet spot from where she had urinated. She patted her thighs, also dry. She hadn't peed. Squinting at the sheet, she saw the little damp spot and the liquid, almost slimy, like a drop of egg white. This is what had come from her body, not urine. She wiped it away with the towel, and showered.

But began to do this daily, after swimming, before showering: ritually peeling off her suit, then to bed with the book, always the one-page description of the Rape of Persephone, with the sheets in a ball between her legs as before, always squeezing her thighs, always listening for Kehinde, always losing her breath when the egg white slipped out. And now wondering—mashing Weetabix, Niké repeating, "It's disgusting!"—why it pleasured her to do this, did she want him to walk in? She knew she wouldn't hear him if he slipped up to their doorway in the pointy-toed ninja red leather babouches. He was Kehinde. He could do that. Appear without warning. And still she would lie there, nude, wet, while he swam.

She put down her spoon, feeling heat in her fingers. Kehinde turned to look at her, chewing his lip. Whatever she was sensing was apparent in his expression. Niké chortled, "*Look* at him!" Suspicions confirmed. "There are other stains, too," she sneered, holding up the sheet again. "You think I don't know what these white splotches are?"

Kehinde was staring at Taiwo. "What is it?" It was a question for his twin, who was looking away.

Assuming he was mocking her, Niké dropped the sheet and slapped Kehinde so hard that he fell from his chair. Before she could stop herself, Taiwo leapt up and pushed the woman, just once, screaming, "Leave him alone!" But Niké lost her balance, reeling backward in her slippers, fluffy, pom-pom–bearing slippers, landing splayed on her back. The dressing gown, parting, exposed her fat thighs to the houseboy who, entering, dropped his glass tray. Taiwo grabbed Kehinde and pulled him toward her, suddenly aware of their vulnerability, their defenselessness here. Something had broken. The casing around them. The distance between fourth floor and second had closed.

How Niké started screaming:

bloody murder. A madwoman. How she dragged them to the elevator and up to the lounge where they'd come on arrival, last seen in late August, that mishmash of marble and zebra and velour. Their uncle was reclining in his underwear and a bathrobe, Babatunde the little houseboy cutting a line on the table. Uncle Femi stroked the back of his neck as he worked, almost idly, as one strokes a pet at one's side. Two older boys, teens, were standing guard at the doorway, in white sailor uniforms, like costumes from a play. But with guns. Slender rifles, which they clutched to their chests, neither moving nor speaking as Niké stormed in.

"Well, good morning," Uncle Femi said softly, always softly.

His wife pushed the twins toward the chaise where he lay. Babatunde looked up, very briefly, then down, back to work, knowing better than to make his presence known. Taiwo and Kehinde looked blankly at their uncle, their aunt at their backs, seething, "Tell him yourselves."

"Tell me what?" Uncle Femi asked, smiling, genuinely interested. He considered the twins as if he saw them every day, as if just yesterday they'd been chatting about the weather in Lagos, as if he hadn't been missing for almost a year. Babatunde, finished, moved away from the table. Uncle Femi leaned forward and snorted the line. "*E se*," he said to Babatunde, sniffing, smiling. The boy nodded, bowed, and rushed out of the room.

"Your uncle asked a question. They think that we're stupid. And this one. She thinks she can strike me. *Odé*." Niké pushed Taiwo, not gently, between the shoulders. Taiwo stumbled forward, caught her balance, straightened up.

"Don't touch her," Uncle Femi said. "The boy doesn't like it." Now he lit a cigarette. "Isn't that what you said?" He gestured to Kehinde, brows raised, smiling brightly. "Isn't that what you told me? 'Don't touch her'? Am I wrong?"

"No, sir," said Kehinde.

"I'm sorry? I didn't hear you."

"No, Uncle," repeated Kehinde, a tremor in his voice.

"Very well then. What happened?" Uncle Femi looked at Niké, then back at the twins in their nightclothes and socks.

Niké cleared her throat as if preparing to orate, but answered, very briefly, "They were caught having sex. The houseboys discovered her blood on the sheet, and the stains from his . . . climax. I can show you the sheet."

"You're lying!" cried Taiwo, on instinct. "We didn't!" This time the blow made her fall to the ground. Niké, from behind her, halfway shoving, halfway slapping her.

"Are you calling me a liar?!" Niké shouted. "I have proof!"

Taiwo remained kneeling on the floor where she'd fallen, her ear burning sharply, too stunned to stand up. More shocking than painful, the way Niké struck her suggested more violence might follow, and soon. Their parents never hit them, never shouted, never threatened; all their punishment was issued with calm, as in court. She found it insulting to be hit by a grown-up, and trembled with anger, hands balled into fists. Intuiting her intention, Kehinde knelt down beside her.

"Don't touch her," Uncle Femi mocked, leaning down toward them. The voice remained soft but had darkened, or hardened, the sound of his laughter too steely, too sharp. A weapon.

Eyes welling with fear and with anger, Taiwo turned to look up at their uncle's blunt nose. She grabbed Kehinde's T-shirt. "Come on," she whispered nervously, pulling him up by the shirt as she rose to her feet. They stood pressed together, now facing their uncle, much closer to his body than they'd been until now. The smell of him—sweat and cologne and tobacco—was overpowering now, as was the heat from his gaze. Kehinde reached over and took Taiwo's hand, without thinking, and squeezed, fingers shaking.

"You *see!* You see how they stand so. You see how he holds her." Niké sucked her teeth, a low, long-lasting *tssssssssst.*

"Enough," Uncle Femi said. "Thank you for informing me. You're welcome to leave. I can take it from here."

Surprised and affronted, Niké turned and left them standing there, the guards nodding stiffly as she stormed out the door. Taiwo felt her heart sink as the double doors swung softly shut. Baffling as it was, she wished that Niké wouldn't go. The woman was volatile and violent and dramatic, quite likely insane, but familiar by then. Their uncle was foreign and frightening, a stranger. Too calm, too controlled, and too cold.

How it happened:

"Omokehindegbegbon!" said Uncle Femi to Kehinde. "So only you can touch her, *ehn*? Another little princess." He gestured with his cigarette to the portrait of their grandmother. "A precious little princess, *ehn*?" He stood up from the chaise. He came to where the twins were and stood just behind them. He cupped Taiwo's chin in his hands, turned her head. He held her like this, so she was looking at the portrait. "Look at her. Precious Somayina," he breathed. He stroked Taiwo's hair. She could feel Kehinde stiffen, his hand in her hand still, could feel his breath stop. She stood without moving, without looking, her eyes closed, could smell Uncle Femi's odd sweetness, his soap. "Open your eyes," he said, touching her chin again, bending beside her, his lips near her ear. "Look at her. *Look at her.* Looks just like you, no? Like you. Precious princess, that no one can touch." He took a step over so he was standing behind Kehinde. He touched Kehinde's cheek as he'd stroked Taiwo's hair. "Except you, little boy. Only you. *You* can touch her." He squeezed both their shoulders. "Show your uncle what you do."

One of the teens at the door cleared his throat. Uncle Femi looked up. "Lock the door, please," he said. The boys began leaving. "From the inside, you idiots. You two stay here." They obeyed. "There we are." Uncle Femi turned to Taiwo now. "My little Somayina." He patted the chaise, smiling warmly. "Come here."

Taiwo took a step toward Kehinde. "Uncle, please. We didn't do what she said we did."

"You're lying." Not loudly. He smiled again, patting the chaise. "Come lie here." She squeezed Kehinde's hand, shook her head, a small movement. He laughed, closed his eyes, and then bellowed, "LIE HERE!" The sound of a voice at this volume was so unexpected, so jarring, she dropped Kehinde's hand. A bit like a robot, she went to the chaise and sat down. "There. That's better. Now lie on your back." He placed a cold hand on her neck, pushing backward. Surprised at the force, at the touch, she lay back.

Kehinde stepped forward. "Please, Uncle. Don't touch her," he said through clenched teeth.

"Don't you worry. I won't." Uncle Femi stepped back, considering Taiwo on the chaise, with her arms at her side, body stiffened with fear. Still trembling from shock at his touch, and his shouting, she stared at him back, at the black, red-rimmed eyes. He looked like the drawing of Hades, the "rapist," a word that she'd heard but never seen written down. *Rape.* Flesh and flowers, golden chariot, black horses, a girl carried off. "I'm not a pedophile," he sneered.

Pedophile, pedophile, pedophile, thought Taiwo, now starting to cry. For she'd gotten it wrong. A man who loved children? Who loved his own children? *Wrong.* Who had left them, had left her, like Zeus. And where was Demeter? On the hunt for her daughter? Torches blazing, frantic searching? With Sadie at home.

The feel of defeat was a wave washing over. She felt herself slacken, her legs going loose. The tears ran out mutely from the side of her eyes to the floral upholstery beneath her neat braids. She felt her chest cave, giving in, under the nightdress, the Minnie Mouse nightdress she'd had since the man brought them proudly to Disney World, more excited than they were by this, the most American Family Tradition on earth. She felt her fists melt, fingers weaken, unclenching. She felt herself die to the hope of escape. If she tried to run now, the school-play soldiers would stop her. Her uncle would overpower her if she tried to resist. Whatever was happening would happen, she knew; there was no one to stop it. There was no one but *them.* She and her brother alone in his room with this uncle.

A pedophile.

"*You* touch her," he said. He gestured from Kehinde, who was standing there dumbstruck, to Taiwo laid out on the chaise like a cake. "She's too pretty for me." He took a drag. "*Ehn,* now, touch her." He clapped his hands, impatient. "*Jo, jo, jo.*" Hurry up.

Pedophile, pedophile, pedophile, thought Taiwo.

"I don't . . . understand," Kehinde said.

"Touch the girl."

"I don't understand," Kehinde repeated, eyes filling.

Uncle Femi sucked his teeth. "Then I'll show you. You, come." He gestured to the guards by the door, who hurried forward. "Just one of you." The older one approached with his gun. "Put down the rifle," he said. "It'll scare her." The young man set his weapon on the table. "Touch the girl." Cigarette dangling, Uncle Femi moved the boy like a puppet into position at the end of the chaise, then made himself comfortable in the armchair across, as to watch a live show, his legs crossed, his eyes bright.

"Sa?" asked the guard.

"Touch the girl. Lift her nightdress. The boy here won't do it. Unbuckle your belt."

The guard looked at Taiwo, then at Kehinde behind him. Taiwo squeezed her eyes shut, still crying without sound. With a glance at his employer, the guard unzipped his trousers.

"Stop," Kehinde said. Barely audible. "Please stop."

"If you won't do it, he will," Uncle Femi said calmly. To the guard, "Use your fingers."

"I will," Kehinde said.

Uncle Femi started clapping. "I thought so," he chuckled. He gestured to the guard, who returned to the door. With the rifle on the table. Like a coffee cup. Just sitting there. A token of the absurdity of the world in which they were. Kehinde stepped forward, looked down at his sister, his knees near her feet at the end of the chaise. Tears in her eyes, and his eyes, the same eyes. With the third pair, the portrait-eyes, watching from the wall. She looked at her brother and thought he was bluffing, perhaps that he'd hatched some sly plan for escape? She stared at him, desperately trying to read his expression. Saw nothing.

His eyes had gone vacant and dark. He looked angry. She had never seen her brother looking angry. He wiped his eyes quickly with the back of one hand.

"Touch her like you do in the bedroom downstairs." Uncle Femi looked joyful. "Pretend I'm not here." At Kehinde's hesitation, he added, "Don't worry. I won't tell your mother what your auntie told me."

How it happened:

how her uncle gave her brother instructions from his armchair, a director, the guards looking on. How her brother, not speaking, with his eyes saying nothing, removed her weekday panties, set them neatly on the floor. Put his finger inside her. The baffling sensation, less painful than uncomfortable. An opening, a tear. "Harder! Harder! Harder!" said Uncle Femi. "Faster! Faster!" With glee in his voice. Kehinde's finger, with force.

This was the first time that she learned to leave her body, just to leave the body lying there, mind wandering off. Not with effort. It simply happened: she was lying there in Lagos on a chaise longue in her nightdress when she felt herself go. Weary party guest departing. She was floating above them, then, watching the proceedings just as calm as could be, watching Kehinde in his T-shirt and his matching cotton Mickey shorts, his finger in his sister, Uncle Femi in his chair, the two boys at the door, their eyes wide with shame, pleasure, the portrait above the mantel, "Tuesday" panties on the floor—then floating elsewhere: to their parlor in Brookline, to the piano, to Shoshanna shouting, "Faster! Faster! Fast!" while she tried to play Rachmaninoff—and elsewhere: to the classroom, to the teacher's nervous laughter while she shaded in *o*'s—to her bedroom: to the window watching Kehinde in the driveway, with their father looking guilty, little light on in the car. It seemed almost impossible that she, in this body, had covered such distance, from Brookline to Lagos, from piano and classroom and bedroom and safety to *here*, to this nightmare unfolding: too far. She floated above them and wondered who was this, then, here in that body? Wasn't her. Couldn't be. Was simply a body. A body she'd left there as one drops a towel.

To which she returned.

Kehinde had finished. Slid his finger from her body. She opened her eyes. Saw the stain on his shorts. Uncle Femi was clapping. "*E kuuse!*" Well done.

Sweat, or something like it, ventured shyly down her thigh.

"You can go," said Uncle Femi. Kehinde hurried from the room, his shoulders shaking, leaving Taiwo there alone. She sat up. She looked at her uncle. She collected her panties (but didn't put them on, not yet, the gesture too abasing). She walked out the door with a hole in her body, a space where her girlhood had been, no longer crying. Babatunde was there waiting with an expression on his face that suggested he knew what had happened and how. She didn't find Kehinde in the kitchen or their bedroom. She went to her room down the hall, still too cold. She lay on the bed looking up at the ceiling for the rest of the day. No one called her for dinner. The next morning Babatunde came to fetch her. Up the elevator. For a week their uncle watched as Kehinde touched her like that. He said what the molesters say in made-for-TV movies: that he'd report them to their mother if they ever told a soul.

Then there was a party, and they were made to wear makeup and to walk around smiling at guests, boys and men, Nigerian and South African and white, of all ages. A gay man from Ghana: "I know who you are." They left without luggage in a taxi with the Ghanaian. He put them on a plane to JFK and they came home. *And . . . scene.*

Taiwo pauses, her breathing grown labored. She means to say, "Happy? Now you know," or the like, but she can't catch her breath; is weak, sweating, dehydrated; intends to storm off and instead starts to sway. Fola lurches forward, catching Taiwo as she buckles, managing to grab her by the shoulders as she slumps to the sand. The movement is instinctive—less embrace than intervention—but it puts their skin in contact for the first time in years. Taiwo jerks backward, the dizziness mounting. She tries to say, "Don't," and erupts into tears.

vi

Fola pulls the girl to her chest, clutching tightly to prevent her from attempting to flee or pull away—but Taiwo clings back, body wracked by the sobbing, too weakened to stand without something to hold. So holding Fola. Barely choking out words, as a child does attempting to give voice to its grief between sobs, "How could you send us there? How could you send us? You knew what would happen. You knew, Mom. You knew."

Of the many things Fola thinks, holding her daughter, is the thought that it's useless to love with such force, for the force doesn't travel, doesn't keep them, protect them, doesn't go where they go, doesn't act as a shield—and yet how to love otherwise? What else might she feel but this raw, desperate love as she clutches the girl, wishing only to protect her, to act as a shield, and this raw, desperate grief, having long ago failed? "I'm sorry," she whispers, stroking Taiwo's long dreadlocks, knowing *sorry* won't do, not knowing where else to start.

She's never before felt what she feels in this moment. Three feelings at war for her breath, for her strength: first the anger at Femi, the pure, crystal hatred, a rage undiluted by pity or doubt; then the grief that is Taiwo's, her shame and her sorrow, a well of it rushing beneath the right breast; then her own shame and sorrow, to know what has happened, to know what she's sensed all along in her twins, *who got hurt*, she thinks, *badly, because they didn't have their mother.* Because their mother thought they didn't need a mother like her. "I thought," she tells Taiwo, as she thinks of it, anguished, "I thought I was helping.

290

That you'd be better off. I thought that your uncle—" heaves once and continues—"I thought he could provide things I couldn't afford. I wanted you to have, I don't know, to have *more* . . ."

"More than *what*?"

"Than a single mother. Than a mother like me. I didn't know what I was doing. I never had a mother. I was making it up as I went. I was scared. I was lonely. I was a coward. I was afraid of disappointing you, of holding you back from the things you deserved. You were gifted, so brilliant, even smarter than Olu. Your teachers all said it. 'She's special,' they said. 'Make sure that you challenge her, stimulate, encourage her.' I feared I'd be the reason that you didn't excel. I was afraid that I'd fail you. So I sent you to . . . him . . . and he hurt you. And Kehinde. I failed anyhow." Fola stops talking abruptly, embarrassed. This isn't at all what she wants to be saying. Taiwo is silent, her arms around Fola, her chest quivering palpably against Fola's breasts. Fola pulls back, just enough to see Taiwo, to hold the girl's face with her fingers. "I'm sorry."

Her daughter looks back at her, blinking, eyes bloodshot, dry-raw from the salt of her tears and her sweat. *She looks like an infant*, thinks Fola. My *infant*. My baby, my daughter. *And not Somayina*. The eyes don't remind her at all of her mother's, perhaps for the first time since Taiwo was born. The clear amber eyes look to Fola like Taiwo's: the eyes of a child, not a ghost's but a girl's. Taiwo says nothing, just stares at her mother, who stares at her child, overwhelmed by her want. She wants to give healing and comfort and answers. She wants to undo what was done to her twins. She wants to find Kehinde and hold him here also. She wants to find Femi, to kill him. By hand. Very slowly. To torture him. She wants to stop crying. She wants to make Taiwo stop crying. But can't. All she can do is stand weeping with Taiwo alone on this beach in the bearing down heat, knowing someone has damaged her children irreparably, unable to fix it. Able only to hold.

She kisses Taiwo's forehead, still holding her cheeks in her palms, and is moving to hug her again when she, Taiwo, says, "Don't," thinking Fola has kissed her by way of hard stop and will now pull away.

"Don't go," whispers Taiwo, and startles her mother by grabbing her fiercely and gripping her waist. "Don't let me go yet, please don't let me go."

"I won't," whispers Fola, and doesn't.

vii

Olu is getting annoyed now. *Where are they?* His mother and sister just up and disappeared, leaving the rest of the family to receive the food offering, a beans-and-rice dish served on plates made of tin. They ate this politely, chewing, nodding, and smiling, then gulped down warm Fanta, surrendered their plates. Sadie hurried off with her newfound instructor to learn further dance moves behind some mud hut while Benson received a call on his cell and began pacing the clearing in search of reception. "Hello? Hello?" Kehinde dematerialized in typical fashion, leaving Olu and Ling with this Shormeh and Naa, the two sisters in black whom his father never mentioned, both older by the look of it, sixty or more. Naa, the somewhat friendlier, dead ringer for Sadie, asks would they like to come see the old house? "That's okay," says Olu as Ling gushes, "Yes!" and they're ushered along to the hut at the back.

He noticed the roof when they entered the compound—a triangular dome stitched of some sort of reed, five feet taller at least than the tin roofs surrounding it—but only now thinks of his father's remark. Kweku, in a ramble about renting versus owning, said something about a father having "designed his own property." Olu asks Naa, "Who designed this? Who built it?"

"His father," she answers. "Your grandfather. Come."

They duck in the door and stand still for an instant, adjusting to the relative darkness and silence. The space is much cooler than seems possible given the burdensome heat in the courtyard outside. Olu peers around at the rounded clay walls, at the sixteen-foot roof, one small window, faint light. *Intelligent construction*, he thinks. Ling takes pictures, the flash from the phone bouncing off this and that.

"There were six of us, then, with your father," says Naa. "And our mother. *Ehn*, seven. We all slept in here."

"Eight, with your father," says Olu. "My grandfather."

"No," Naa says brusquely. "That man disappeared. He wasn't our father. Just Kweku and Ekua's."

"He died?" Olu asks.

"No. He left."

"To go where?"

"Jesus knows," Naa says, shrugging. "By now he is dead. Both his children are, too. And his wife. Prideful man. That one, our mother, she loved him too much, oh. Too much. And for what, *ehn*? You came when she died. The woman was gone but he brought you to see her. He never came back here apart from that time." She laughs without joy. "Now the space is sufficient. Your father would always fuss, fuss, for the space. 'It's too small,' 'it's too hot,' always hot, like a white man." She sucks her teeth. "*Obroni*. Too hot in the shade." She is quiet for a moment, her hands at her elbows. Then, her voice breaking, "A shame, oh. So young. My own junior brother. That foolish boy Kweku." She wipes off her eyes with the back of one arm. "They say he bought a big, big house. Someplace very, very cold."

Olu nods. "Yes."

"Then he did it." Tiny smile. "You wait. I am coming." She dabs at her eyes again, shuffles to the doorway, ducks out. "I go and come."

Ling comes to Olu by the one wooden bed. "What are you looking at?"

But Olu doesn't know. He thought he saw something, a bird or an insect, flittering briskly around the window near the top of the dome, but when he points to it now he sees nothing but light spilling in full of dust to the mats on the floor.

viii

Kehinde comes tentatively to the entrance to the compound and stops by the wall, looking left, looking right. The outhouse was empty and so is the road, Benson's car left alone on its tilt in the groove. He approaches the window to peer in to see if the driver is sleeping, but no one is there. He looks up the road at the line of small kiosks and sees, just past these, one large stand-alone shack. It looks like those cabins, the square wooden cabins they slept in, in Boy Scouts, the one year he tried, age eleven, before abandoning the pretense of boyness in favor of painting and working with beads. He can make out some movement inside it, a shadow, and thinks to go ask if the person here saw either Taiwo or Fola or Benson's lost driver these last twenty minutes they've all disappeared? He walks the short way to the large wooden structure and stops at the doorway before ducking in, a low door, squinting twice in the dim of the space that is the coffin maker's workshop and a clinic in the clutch.

He doesn't see the man. He sees the one metal table bearing basic tools for woodwork and medical exams, wooden benches by the walls, single window by the doorway, rusted ceiling fan squeaking with every slow turn. Incongruously, at odds with the torture cell effect, a string of white Christmas lights blinks on one wall. The window is closed, as are three massive shutters that make up the top of the wall at the back. The only illumination is bright whitish sunlight thrown in from the door to the rough slatted floor. Even so, eyes adjusting, Kehinde makes out the coffins that hang more like boats from the beams overhead:

one a car, one a fish, one a rose by the look of it, absurd in one sense, wild, fantastic in another. The idea of it. Coffins in shapes, like kids' birthday cakes, celebratory, colorful, laughing at death. *Sangna would love these*, he thinks, with a start, caught off guard by the thought, by this flash of her face:

Sangna's narrow brown face with its ill-fitting features reviled by their owner for being "too big." An image out of context. On the backs of his eyelids. Her face on that screen in that space in his mind where such images materialize when his thoughts begin to wander, when forms replace words, like a photo exposed. (This is how paintings begin, and revelations, a form floating up out of dark on that screen, at first blurry, then detailed, then clear as a memory, as if to "create" were in fact to recall.) Here on that screen appears Sangna, lovely Sangna, whose narrow brown face passes by all the time, a flash here, a flash there, while he's working in Brooklyn or writing her texts or while they talk on the phone—but whose face he has never really properly considered, like this, out of context, on its own. In other light. As he thinks of it now, he can see that she's right, that her features don't fit in their slender-cheeked frame, that there's something too big about the teeth and the brows, a man's eyes, a man's nose, a man's mouth, a child's chin. *An exquisite imbalance*, he thinks, even thrilling, with the tension it creates when he sees her again after months and feels nervous those first thirty seconds, as if watching a juggler, afraid and amazed: *they're still there*, all in order, those huge gorgeous features at war with their borders but not yet seceding.

That face.

And her laughter.

"So you want to make coffins," he hears Sangna laugh. "You just started the Muses! You're mad. But I like it, man. 'Kehinde Sai, *Coffins*.' Materials list Monday. And please no more dirt." *A home*, he would tell her, he thinks, *for the homeless*, a home in the space after bodies, before. The thing he's been after perhaps prematurely, a home, not a coffin. His next major show. Fantasy coffins. A museum installation. When he finishes the paintings in Brooklyn of her, of his sister as each of the Muses, huge portraits—

the thought of which sends up a warm wave of grief. The image shifts abruptly from Sangna to Taiwo: the girl on her back on that rococo chaise in the Minnie Mouse nightdress, her voice in his head a faint whisper *please help me,* and after, her face. After, when he'd done all their uncle instructed so the jaundice-eyed guard wouldn't touch her instead—after, when he looked at his shorts, as did Taiwo, and saw there the wet spot—the look on her face. He hadn't been able to brook the expression, had run from the room like a coward, a fool, but can see the face now, that one glimpse of it, frozen, held steady before him as if he were there: the pure shock in her eyes at this proof of his pleasure, the strange spreading wet spot, the strange spurting shame.

This was the first time that he learned he had a body, that he was bound inside this body, trapped, an airborne being caged. In his mind he'd been elsewhere, far, farther than snow, had been floating with Taiwo in space beyond space: they were drifting in nightclothes like Wendy and Peter, her hand in his hand, not his fingers in her. He heard Uncle Femi and did as instructed, could feel the walls' smoothness and warmth and the wet, but his mind wasn't joined to his finger; was with Taiwo, perhaps where they started? Then his body began. The beginning of having a body: that moment. The feel of the liquid a snake on one thigh. The clapping, Uncle Femi, "*E kuuse*, o, Kehinde!" His mind coming back.

To that look on her face.

How could he tell her that he didn't enjoy it, when here was the proof that he had, on his shorts? When the body had betrayed him, and her, inexplicably? How could he persuade her? What could he say? He couldn't say anything. Or didn't. And hasn't. Not for the week that the thing carried on. Not when they flew to New York to meet Fola, when they got back to Boston, for the next fifteen years. He has never said anything (nor she) of the moment, has never once revisited her expression until now: at the door to this storehouse of coffins and stethoscopes, from the dim of which someone says, "You, are you sick?"

Kehinde turns, startled, to the bench by the doorway and finds here a man with a paper, reclined. The man is quite old, dressed in trousers and T-shirt and worn leather sandals and dirty white coat, short and stout, with a belly and Coke-bottle glasses, with none of the famous Ghanaian good cheer. He has lowered his paper to glower at Kehinde but doesn't get up, just repeats, "Are you sick?"

Kehinde shakes his head, caught off guard, stepping backward. "I didn't see you sitting there."

"Of course, there's no light. Too hot with the light. Me, I don't like the heat, oh. I see in the darkness. You look like you're sick." He sets down his paper and stands with some effort. "You came from Big Milly's? A rastaman, *ehn*?"

"N-no," Kehinde stutters. "We came for my father. He lived here. Grew up here, I mean. Now he's dead."

"Your father?" The man shuffles closer to Kehinde. "That one, the Sai boy? I heard that he died." Kehinde nods, silent. "It's a coffin you want then. What's your name?"

"Kehinde." He holds out his hand.

The man takes the hand, starts to shake it in greeting, then turns it face up to examine the palm. He leans in to squint down at Kehinde's raised calluses. "Rough. You are a laborer." Kehinde shakes his head. "Then why are your hands so, so rough like my own? The Sais I knew, self, they were *thinkers*." Sarcastic. "At least that, the first one, could put up a house. But the boy? Good for nothing but thinking, thinking, thinking. He thought he was smart, *ehn*, too smart to break wood. *Tss.* Your hands are good, rough, like my own. Like a man."

"I'm an artist," says Kehinde.

The man starts to laugh. "An artist." Pronounced *ah*-teest. "You *are* a Sai then." He drops Kehinde's hand and goes waddling to the shutters. He unlatches and pushes them out to rich light. Kehinde shields his eyes with one hand and squints, blinking, at the workspace now visible at the back of the hut. Half-finished coffins lie in piles by a worktable. Four men are painting what looks like a loaf. "We can't make a new one in time for the funeral—"

"What does that mean, sir? 'I *am* a Sai then'?"

The man turns to look at him, surprised by the inflection. Kehinde, surprised also, looks down at his hands. He presses them together, holding left hand with right, thumb to palm, trying to rub out the burning beneath. There is something in the smug, dismissive manner of this stranger that calls up aggression, a strange thing itself, to feel anger, simple anger, this burning sensation, this urge to do violence to some yielding thing. He is so rarely angry he finds himself nervous, alarmed by the feeling, the heat in the hands. He is certain that the stranger can sense his aggression, but the man just keeps talking, still laughing, "*Chalé.* Go and see that one, the house in the compound. The first one, he drew it. An *ah*-teest like you. Then came the boy, that your father, an *ah*-teest. His mother would send him to watch me, you see. They said he was coming to learn how to doctor, but no: he was just like his father. Just drew. Drawing and drawing, *tss*, all the day drawing. Never learned about bodies, never learned about wood. They were *ah*-teests. Like you." He looks closely at Kehinde. "You see. Now you're crying. You Sais, all the same."

Their classmates used to ask him if twins were telepathic, if the one could feel in real time what the other sibling felt. This was in high school, when they first grew their dreadlocks, when Taiwo stopped combing, he cutting his hair, when they'd walk around campus in over-sized sweaters and Doc Marten boots, clothed in black, and blank stares, when they still didn't know what to say to each other but knew even less what to say to the world, and so stuck to each other in gathering quiet like guilt-ridden robbers who'd pulled off the heist, always watching the other for signs of defection, sitting side by side, knitting a silence with breath. Of the two of them he was the slightly more approachable, would try to engage on behalf of them both, could see that their classmates and teachers were curious, very genuinely, to know whence these Sai twins had come—but they lacked the vocabulary, simply hadn't the *language*, in the suburbs, in the nineties, to know what he meant. "A year in Nigeria," in their language, was "experience," a sophomore year abroad, a vacation run long; "my father left the family" was a custody agreement, a Back Bay apartment, a stepmom named Chris. He and his sister still spoke the same language, like newborn twins babbling in conjured-up words, an odd language known only to them (and their uncle perhaps) that they spoke by not speaking at all. In this new way they were aware of their twinness, performed it in a way that they hadn't before, with their clothes and their hair and their genderless affect and constant togetherness. He knew why they asked.

But the question upset him. The tone of the questioners. As if they could sense what was wrong with these Sais, never mind whence they came. "No, we're not telepathic." He'd smile. "We're just close." Never told them the truth. That often he'd excuse himself to go find a bathroom to sit there and weep for no reason at all, only to speak with her later and learn she'd been crying at precisely the same moment for good reason elsewhere.

So it is now as he bursts into tears without warning: hard, chest-rattling, deep-water sobs. Without speaking (unable), he goes to the bench by the door and drops down as a spinning coin falls. End of journey. Bent over, his face in his palms, with his legs squeezed together, his feet curling in. He has no way of knowing about Taiwo and Fola entwined in a knot by that house on the beach but feels sorrow far greater than one heart could muster and knows not to try to abate the loosed tide. All of it comes and sits calmly beside him: the face of the woman he thinks he may love, and the face of the sister he touched though it broke him, the blanket of quiet, the body, the loss, the loose word that slipped out in New York that one evening, the word meant for Bimbo, a statement of fact, and the face of his father that night in the Volvo, "an artist like him," not a stranger at all. The whole thing is over in three or four minutes—the heart bursting inward, split, splintering apart—but it feels like an hour has passed when the last sob has risen and Kehinde looks up. The man is gone.

ix

Benson phones his driver to ask where he's gone to. The driver explains, nervously, he's here at the beach, by the path that the fishermen beat to the ocean, where he brought the pretty woman who was looking for the girl. This solves the mystery of Fola and Taiwo. Benson asks the driver to return to the car. Sadie, Ling, Olu stand waiting, bewildered. Kehinde appears, walking up the middle of the road. The driver comes jogging from the other direction. The *beep-beep* of car doors unlocked, blinking lights. Benson, Kehinde, Sadie, Ling, Olu alight, with the latter three climbing to the third row this time, as if sensing that Kehinde should be by himself for the moment; the driver starts humming again. They drive the short way to the path to the ocean where Fola and Taiwo stand waiting on the road. Fola has an arm around Taiwo's bare shoulders. Both Olu and Sadie emit sounds of surprise. Fola takes the seat between Taiwo and Kehinde and holds both their hands with the rest of her strength.

"Shall we go choose the coffin?" asks Benson.

"Can we cremate? Do they cremate in Ghana?" asks Fola.

"Of course." Benson looks stunned. "There's a place near my clinic."

"Today?"

"I'll call now." Benson takes out his cell.

The driver looks at Benson, then to Fola for instruction. "Madame?"

Fola nods. "Let's go home."

6.

Later, much later, the moon having risen, the day having died its spec-tacular death of blood reds and blood oranges, blues and magentas, a heart-stopping sunset that none of them sees—they come to the table again to eat dinner (rice, garden egg soup, minus Taiwo, who's resting), then drift to their rooms with their hurts and faint hopes drifting softly behind them, beneath closing doors.

ii

Ling is on her side when he returns from the bathroom. He stops in the doorway and stares at her hair. Usually it comforts him to look at her sleeping, to sense that there's some hope of rest in the world, to observe his heart slow from the pace of his fears to the beat of her breaths—but it troubles him now. The black of the hair on the white of the pillow reminds him of Sunday in Boston, the snow, of the dark and the drumbeat, the slick black on cotton the only familiar among so much strange. Three days have passed since he sat in that Eames chair and watched his wife sleeping, a mute to this mouth, but he thinks of it now and the moment seems further, much further away both in hours and miles. Or *she* does: this figure, her hip, waist, and shoulder, the familiar undulation too distant to touch. Or else *he* does. Feels distant. Feels far from this figure not ten feet before him, feels far from himself.

He wants to go back, he thinks, *home*, to that bedroom, to the apartment he found when they first moved for school, not a ten-minute walk from the house he'd once lived in, but in the other direction, across from MassArt. He loved it the moment the broker unlocked it: the stainless-steel kitchen and brilliant white walls and the blond wooden floorboards and oversize windows, the sun playing Narcissus, blond blinding light. But he couldn't afford it. He was just starting med school then, fresh out of college (returned from Accra, with the smell of that woman still thick in his nostrils, the taste of betrayal unnamed on his tongue). A miracle, really, how it happened, years later: he was walking out of the library at the School of Public Health when he chanced upon an advert on a corkboard, same apartment. Ling's mother had died, then, and left a small sum. He procured all the furniture at IKEA, on eBay, arranged all their photos in matching white frames, black-and-whites, he and Ling on their various adventures; he pored over copies of *Dwell* magazine; rented vans to go pick up antiques in Connecticut, did the painting himself, installed bookshelves, built desks—until the apartment was perfect, the home he'd imagined, inoculated against disorder, indestructibly clean.

He wants to go back to that order and cleanliness. He wants to go back to their tidy redoubt, to their jogs before sunrise and to-do lists on the refrigerator, their white squares of furniture welcoming them back, to their muted-toned clothing all folded and hung, to their meals of lean meat and dark greens and whole grains, to their kisses good-bye in the morning postjogging, their kisses hello in the evening, in scrubs, to the clean way they chitchat, never arguing, never lying, never asking for truths. To that place and not this. Not this tension, not Ling with her back turned toward him, not sleeping but not turning as he appears at the door to the thin-windowed room with its gray marble floor and its chipped yellow walls and its brown velour drapes (that mismatched decor he's always found, in his travels, in bedrooms in countries where sleep is a gift, where the bed needn't look like a present at Christmas with pillow shams and dust ruffles to drive the point home)—and not silence, demanding, in place of their chitchat, a large, messy silence, subsuming, like damp.

It hangs there like moisture, so thick he can feel it. There is no place to put it, and no place to go. He stands in the doorway and hears in this silence his heart beating, hard, to the sound of her breaths. He closes his eyes and he sees in that darkness, that deep, sparkling darkness that lives behind lids, like a slideshow: their flight, Monday evening, to Ghana, with Ling there beside him, her head on his chest, then their flight to Las Vegas, the chapel, October, their first night of marriage, the tacky motel. He remembers making love to her; a difference, already; to think the word *wife* of the woman below him, to place his wide palm on the side of her face and to hear her "We're married," to whisper, "I know." It wasn't the idea of being married that changed things—he'd never much cared for the language, the show—but the idea of a beginning, in which began every ending, the thing he'd been running from, for fourteen odd years.

Fola used to tease him for calling Ling "partner," for refusing to say "girlfriend" ("your lab partner," she'd joke). They had no anniversary. They had no beginning. "You're not Asian," she said, and he loved her. Fait accompli. He'd wax philosophical about the puerility of the language, "boyfriend/girlfriend," about the emptiness of "falling in love," about the physiological underpinnings of desire and attraction, the senselessness of exalting the instinct to mate, and the rest of it. Really, he was terrified of endings. He couldn't understand how people loved, then didn't love. Loved, then stopped loving. As a heart just stops beating. (Of course he knew *how*, but he couldn't see *why*.) Dr. Soto once told them that the reason for dating—the only real reason for dating as opposed to mating for life—was to acquaint oneself, viscerally and immediately and nonlyrically, with the fact of one's "personal mortality," nothing else. One of the junior attendings had just called off his wedding and was moping around the OR with a look on his face that suggested he might do himself harm with his scalpel. Dr. Soto convened them all after surgery to say:

"the only point of a relationship is to play out, in miniature, the whole blasted drama of life and of death. Love is born as a child is born. Love grows up as a child grows up. A man knows well that he must die, but having only known life does not believe in his death. Then, one day, his love goes cold. Its heart stops beating. The love drops dead. In this way, the man learns that death is reality: that death can exist in his being, his *own*. The loss of a pet or a rose or a parent may cause the man pain but will not make the point. Death must take place in the heart to be believed in. After love dies man believes in his death."

Olu listened, laughing. *But what of the opposite?* What if love never dies, what if love wasn't born? What if it had always existed since they touched pouring punch at the Asian-American Cultural Center Open House at Yale? What if there *was* no relationship to end? No boyfriend/girlfriend? No "now we are" and therefore no "now we're not" down the line? This is what he had with Ling Wei, he was thinking. The dramaless life of a love unbegun.

Then they got married on a whim in Las Vegas. After, they made love with her face in his palm. That night he lay still with her cheek on his breastbone and thought of an "ending" and wanted to cry. Many years earlier he'd vowed not to do so, teeth grit in the mirror, alone in his dorm, so just stared until dawn at the pink neon heart blinking on and off, huge, on the ceiling. In the morning he asked could they keep it a secret, not tell what they'd done, let it be "just for them." What he wanted to say was, "Don't die, don't go cold, don't stop beating," but knew it was useless. Now he stands at the door in this break in the action and thinks what he thought in the bedroom before: that he can't bear to lose her, to let her drift further, or drift off himself in the way that he's done, but that "forward" or "closer" are his only two options, not "back," as he's hoped, that they can't unbegin.

And so he begins, "I have something to tell you."

She looks, sees his eyes closed, and starts to stand up. He hears that she's stirring and shakes his head. "Please. Please just listen." (She does, sitting back, on her feet.) "You live your whole life in this world, in these worlds, and you know what they think of you, you know what they see. You say that you're African and you want to excuse it, explain *but I'm smart*. There's no value implied. You feel it. You say 'Asia, ancient China, ancient India,' and everyone thinks *ooh*, ancient wisdom of the East. You say 'ancient Africa,' and everyone thinks *irrelevant*. Dusty and irrelevant. Lost. No one gives a shit. You want them to see you as something of value, not dusty, not irrelevent, not backward, you know? You wish you didn't give a shit, but somehow you do, because you *know*, Ling. You fear what they think but don't say. And then, one day you hear it out loud. Like, your father—"

"My father's an asshole—"

"Your father was right. I didn't go to Haiti for that project at graduation. I came here to Ghana to see him. I lied. He kept sending these letters to ask me to visit, to come for my birthday, to just hear him out. He'd gotten this place, this . . . this ugly apartment. He said it was until he could afford to buy land. I don't know. I didn't stay. There was a woman, some other woman, he was living with some woman, I don't know who she was. I know what he was. He was that man. He was that stereotype. The African dad who walks out on his kids. The way that I'd always hoped no one would see us." He squeezes his eyes, shakes his head. "And I *know*. I stand in that house, in that hut he grew up in.

The man came from nothing; he struggled, I *know*. I *want* to be proud of him. Of all he accomplished. I know he accomplished so much. But I can't. I hate him for living in that dirty apartment. I hate him for being that African man. I hate him for hurting my mother, for leaving, for dying, I hate him for dying alone."

Tears. But not as for Taiwo and Kehinde, the dam giving way and the tide rushing out. They begin without noise and he stands without moving, as strange as they feel, left to flow, on his face. He leans on the doorframe, too tired to keep speaking, and hears in the silence the bullfrogs outside. He doesn't hear the creak of the bed as she leaves it. He feels her small hands on the sides of his face. "Maybe it was the best he could do," she says softly. "Maybe what he did was the best he could do." He nods, though it hurts to. He opens his eyes now. She smiles at him, wiping her tears off, then his. He touches the hand that she's placed on his cheekbone. She thinks that he wants her to stop and pulls back. But he presses his palm to her hand, to his jawbone. "I want to do better." He kisses her lips.

He can sense her surprise as she turns her mouth upward, the way that she used to when they were at school, when he'd walk her to her door on Old Campus and pause in the lamplight to consider the shape of her mouth. Feeling his gaze, the pink lips would drift up, as if moving of their volition, not their owner's, not his. He'd kissed girls in high school but never like this, with their lips playing puppet, his eyes playing string. And had never had sex (is the truth he's never told her, half embarrassed, half touched by his own lack of breadth. He always assumed that he'd want other women, come to desire other bodies as the months turned to years, but he didn't, and hasn't, as the years blur to decades. His first is his only). He touches her neck. He feels the pulse quicken beneath his four fingers. He feels his heart speed to the pace of her breath. "I want to do better," he whispers, through kisses—her chin, then her neck, down the length to her chest. Placing his palm along the curve of her lumbar and applying enough pressure to make her arch back, he kisses her sternum, the cotton-clad nipples, the one then the other, then lifts up her shirt. He presses his palm to her breastbone, five fingers, and kisses the dip of the clavicle, once. The sounds that she makes are small lights on the runway; he flats the palm down to her waist, cups her groin.

"Make love to me," she whispers. "Make love to me, make love to me." She grabs his smooth head with such force that he gasps, looking up at her face, a pale mask of pure agony, such want and such need that she looks like someone else. He lifts her up easily with one of his arms, sets her down on the bed, and removes her few clothes. She unbuttons his trousers with rushed, famished movements and pushes them down to his knees with her feet. He presses her wrists down with one of his hands, both her arms stretched above her. "Make love to me. Please."

In a moment he will: piercing body with body, pushing firmly through labia, palm to her mouth (though the moaning is his as he thrusts to her center), the slippery-pink tissue peeling willingly apart. His body will feel foreign at first, somehow larger, too large and too strong, like a thing that can hurt; for the first time he imagines himself, in his lover, as those words that he spoke, as an "African man." He will start to pull out of her, afraid he is hurting her, afraid of the noises that slip past his palm, but Ling won't allow it—and, clutching his buttocks, she'll pull him yet deeper, in, farther, down, down. For now he just kneels there and pauses to see it: Ling's body in this bedroom that isn't their own, both their faces distorted by sorrow and longing and overhead lighting and truths newly told, but the forms still familiar to his fingertips, the landscape: bones, breasts, hips, rib, pubis, navel, birthmark, flesh, hair, skin: the woman's body, a *body*, nothing sharp-edged or sterile, everything rounded and destructible and soft, and so home.

iii

Taiwo is on her side when he returns from the garden. He thinks she is sleeping and leaves the light off. He sets down his cell phone beside the pink flowers, on the small wooden nightstand, and kicks off his shoes.

"Who was on the phone?" she asks, not turning over. "I could hear you through the window."

"My assistant," he says. "We're doing a show with those paintings you saw, of the Muses, in Greenpoint. A gallery show. They're not done yet, I know, but I think I might like them. I think you might like them." He is nervous. He stops.

"They're incredible, K."

She rolls over to face him, her cheek on the pillow, her hands just beneath—but he hears something else. Three other words, in her voice, in his head, just a snippet. Her thought among his. He feels his heart swell to have heard what she's thinking, this briefest transmission, but something. Reception. Three words in silence, in the space between beds, her low voice in his head as he once used to hear. He looks at his sister, or tries, in the darkness. She looks at him back, a sad smile on her lips. They don't state the obvious: that both have been crying. They look at each other with raw, swollen eyes.

"She's pretty," says Taiwo. "Your assistant."

"I think so." He hears her breath catch, the small knot in her throat. He remembers this sensation from their early adolescence, so particular a sensation that it has its own smell: teenage lotion, kiwi-strawberry. Jealousy. Or possessiveness. Possessiveness and embarrassment, which she needn't have felt (for he'd felt the same way, that he was Taiwo's possession. A thing that belonged to and with her. Box set).

"Do you like her?" asks Taiwo.

"I think so," says Kehinde.

She rubs her eyes, sleepily. "I always kind of thought."

The knot comes untangled. She shifts her position and lies on her back with her hands on her ribs. He stays where he is at the edge of the bed, seated upright across from her, too exhausted to move. He closes his eyes for an instant and hears them again, those three words, her low voice, close to his. Almost *too* close, he thinks. Is he hearing his sister, her thoughts in his head, or just hearing himself? His heart starts to sink, a small dip of a kite. He has waited so long to hear Taiwo again. To hear anything, *any* thought, much less *this* thought that he's longed all these years to believe, dare believe. Was it his raspy voice that he heard and not Taiwo's? The three words in silence his pardon, not hers? He opens his eyes, starts to ask her the question, but finds that her eyes have slipped shut.

She's asleep.

He leans in to stare at her, elbows on kneecaps. Her face in the moon is impossibly still. When a thin film of sweat forms above her top lip, in an hour, he rises and wipes it away. He is tired. He sits on the bed by his sister. He smoothes down her dreadlocks, a tangle of snakes. He kisses her hands and he whispers, "Forgive me." His body too weak from the day, he lies down.

iv

Later, a bit later, an hour before sunrise Taiwo wakes up as one does from a dream, as one does when she's gone to sleep crying with clothes on; finds Kehinde beside her, his head by her feet. She sits up and looks at him, still in his clothing, his hand by his mouth, by the beard that he's grown. She stands up very quietly and is heading to the bathroom when, thinking he has spoken, she turns back around. He is snoring. Lips moving. Three words, she thinks, maybe. She comes to the foot of the bed and looks down. His eyes are still bulbous as a child's after tearshed. She looks at the hand, palm turned up, by his mouth. She touches the scar there, the *T*, only barely, but his hand shuts, a reflex, and squeezes her thumb. She stands there, not moving, not wanting to wake him. The birds in the garden begin their lament. She thinks it, though it hurts to, though she cannot yet speak it. His fingers relax and she slips out her thumb. She stands there and stares at his face until she sees it, fifteen seconds and not longer. A smile in his sleep.

v

In this way comes morning (death to wan gray, etc.); feeling something is missing, Sadie opens her eyes. Fola is missing, though her scent lies there lightly. The butterflies, too, have abandoned her chest. She feels with some wonder and a touch of suspicion the void in her middle, her shirt damp with sweat. She peers at the alarm by the little framed photo and laughs at the date on the analog clock. Christmas. No chestnuts, no baked beans, no sleigh bells. Pink blossoms, palms, bulbul, an Aspen chalet. She stands up the frame, tries to straighten the photo by tapping. Nothing doing. A terrible shot. But likely the last of the old family photos with all six together, she now understands. With everybody looking in a different direction, her father at the camera, she down at his head, her mother at her tutu, her brother at her mother, the twins at who knows what, all blurry, all there.

7.

Mr. Lamptey sits, silent, at the edge of the garden, his legs wet with dewdrops, his joint dwindling down, with the saffron replaced by a heavy black linen, obscured by the shadow, the more for the black. He has done this since Monday, his three days of mourning: has sat by the wall at the edge of the grass, taking leave before sunrise, unseen by the woman who comes to the kitchen at a quarter past six. She doesn't come out to the garden, or look; she just stands at the counter and fixes her drink with the frozen expression of grief before sorrow, the soft, pretty features gone hard with her shock. The dog came on Tuesday but found it too doleful and remained on the beach when he set off at dawn. The birds that he found in the fountain on Monday have yet to return, so he mourns on his own.

In a way he has come here to see the soft woman, to bid her "wake up" with his blue-bellied gaze, with the sense that his presence might send her a message, that all is not lost, that she isn't alone. (In fact it is he who is lonely, uncharacteristically. He misses the man in the sunroom he built. He misses the wave of the napkin, the glasses, the spilling of coffee on trousers, their dance.) He sits with his joint at the back of the garden and puffs with great rue, idly stroking the grass. He wonders if the man ever noticed the plant here, the lush marijuana set back from the pinks? Likely not. He laughs sadly. He closes his eyes and exhales. It is sunrise. It is time to go home.

He is thinking he'll wait just a few minutes longer to see her once more before leaving for good, when he hears someone parking a car in the driveway, the crunching of tires on the pebbles, *beep-beep*. He opens his eyes, laughs again. *What is this now?* He waits there, unmoving, amused by surprise. Someone rings the bell at the gate, a nasal buzzer. He looks at the house as if watching a film. The door doesn't open. The buzzer, for longer. The person raps once on the person-height gate. Mr. Lamptey puffs, torn. Should he wait for the woman? Should he let in the person? The man never had guests. At least not for the years that he slept in the tent or on Mondays. Only Kofi, and later the nurse.

Here she is. Nightdress and pink furry slippers. She opens the doors to the house and steps out. (The man demanded double doors— simple bamboo with a *K* on one handle, an *F* on the other—for the entrance to the gray-not-green courtyard, the main entrance, with the heatable walkway around the small square. Mr. Lamptey would have thought a *K* and *S* more appropriate but carved out the letters with no questions asked.) The woman steps out of these doors in her nightdress and walks down the path of flat stones to the gate, a straight line of gray slate through the sea of white pebbles, as sketched on a napkin in faded blue ink.

"Hello?" she says warily.

"Hello." A woman's voice.

But a different sort of woman's voice, a different sort of woman.

He has never heard her speak before, the woman-in-pink, but her voice is exactly as he'd thought it would be: very sweet, very innocent, awaiting instruction, the voice of someone used to being told what to do. The woman-at-the-gate's hummed "Hello" is a river, the bottom of a river, an echo, a tide. The voice does not wait for instruction but gives it, and gently. The woman-in-pink acquiesces. She pulls out the bar at the top of the gate, rather trustingly, and pushes it open.

The river-woman enters, her arms full of flowers. Mr. Lamptey laughs softly again, with surprise: they are the very same flowers he chose for this garden, a raucous arrangement, bright pinks and deep reds. Her appearance is arresting, the effect beyond "striking." It doesn't stir up, neither jealousy or awe. It quiets. The woman-in-pink stares in silence. He pauses his puffing to squint from his perch. Even from here by the wall, at this distance, his eyes going bad, he can see the effect. The woman laughs, embarrassed. "I'm sorry to bother. It's terribly early, I know, for a guest, but Benson, er, Dr. Adoo, he gave me this address, and I thought that I'd come by to pay my respects."

The woman-in-pink stares in silence.

"I'm Fola." She pauses. "I'm Kweku's—I was Kweku Sai's wife." She holds out the flowers. "I'm so very sorry. These are for you. I—I don't know your name."

"Ama," says the woman-in-pink, like a question. "I am Ama?" She sounds baffled, unsure what this means. She repeats Fola's words as in pursuit of a right answer, as a schoolgirl does dictation, "I was Kweku Sai's wife." She pauses to consider the words she's just spoken, the frozen-stiff features beginning to melt. "Dr. Sai isn't here," she adds sweetly, voice quivering, repeating a line clearly used on the phone. The shoulders begin trembling. "May I please take a message?"

"Oh, darling," says Fola, setting down the bouquet. She wraps both her arms around Ama's plump shoulders. She is taller, much taller. Mr. Lamptey thinks, *a tree*. ("What kind of trees are these?" he'd asked, of the napkin. The man was looking murderously at the mango. "Never mind that.")

The two women stand at the gate for some moments. When Ama can, she pulls away to wipe her button nose. "I am sorry," she sniffles.

"Never mind that," says Fola. A deep and short laugh, a small wave of the hand. "We've planned a small ceremony, very small, in Kokro-bité. You'll come with us, no? Nothing fancy. Just us."

They carry on talking, Ama receiving instruction. Mr. Lamptey watches, smiling: *so she isn't alone*. Fola says she's happy just to wait in the driveway if Ama would like to get dressed and come with? Ama insists that Fola come wait in the house, and retrieving the flowers, she leads the way in.

. . .

Fola pauses briefly at the entrance, sees the handles. She touches the *K* and the neat hand-carved *F*. Only now does she glance to her right, see the fountain, and laugh at the statue adorned with the weeds. She doesn't see the man at the edge of the garden. She enters the house and the double doors close. When they come back outside, she and Ama together, the garden is empty. Mr. Lamptey is gone.

ii

They return to the beach, Ama riding with Fola, the others with Benson, a small caravan. No one quite knows what to say to this Ama; they all smile politely and leave it at that. The sisters stand huddled together, suspicious. They exchange a few greetings with Ama in Ga. Benson produces the urn from an official-looking container and hands this to Fola with an official-looking nod. She had it in mind to toss his ash to the sea breeze, to let the man free, end at the beginning and that. But now as she twists off the top, she can't do it. The idea of him scattered seems wrong in some way. *We've been scattered enough*, she thinks. Broken pot, fragments. *Keep him inside*, she thinks, *let him stay whole*. She twists the metal top on and kneels by the water. She doesn't face her children, afraid that she'll cry. "*Odabo.*" Good-bye. Puts the urn in the water. A wave washes in but doesn't take the urn out. It rolls to the side, sort of drifts a few inches. Another wave comes, but it still doesn't go. She stands up and watches, an arm at her middle. The urn turns in foam, drifts a bit farther out. As if waiting for something. She thinks but can't say it. *I love you.* A wave with some promise appears. Ama makes a squeaking sound, a bit like a bulbul. Fola watches Kweku bobbing, bobbing out of view.

iii

Now she is back in her chair by the fan palm. Amina is busy with the dinner inside. Olu and Ling are very dutifully helping her; Benson took the baby and the twins to find a tree. There are conifers in Ghana, she knows, but not fir trees. She started to warn them, then just let them go. They want to keep busy, she knows, not to say it. Not to let there be stillness or silence or pause. Not to say that they've done it. Sixteen years in the making, they've lost him. Whatever else, Kweku is gone.

The sun is going down; there will soon be mosquitoes. She takes a long drag, leaning back in the chair. She thinks of plump Ama's round face, and she chuckles. Just barely a "woman," how possibly "wife"? Then laughs at her chuckling. Is she jealous? Yes, maybe. Or more so embarrassed, for not moving on? She remembers meeting Benson in the lobby at Hopkins. The skin of burnt umber, black soap, velvet voice. Does Benson rather like her? she wonders. Yes, maybe. She laughs at this, too. Takes another long drag.

Mustafah is hanging up the lights with a ladder. She remembered that she had them and asked him to try. Mr. Ghartey is chewing sugarcane, watching with amusement. All of them start at the bell, at the gate. Fola looks over. "Must be Benson," she tells them, though wonders why he didn't honk his car horn instead. Mr. Ghartey opens both of the gates to let the car in. Ama stands there nervously, a taxi behind.

"Madame," she says shyly, seeing Fola in the beach chair.

Fola scrambles up. "W-w-what a pleasant surprise." She thinks to hide the cigarette but just can't be bothered. She goes to greet Ama. "Is everything okay?" They'd dropped her back home when they returned from Kokrobité; Fola invited her to dinner, but Ama refused. She thinks that perhaps she's changed her mind, and is happy. There is something about the woman that cries out for care. She wouldn't mind having a new thing to care for, the other things appearing to have all fluttered off.

But Ama shakes her head. "I won't stay, please," she says, voice staccato and steady. "I brought these for you." She holds out a bag, a plastic Ghana Must Go bag, her smile and raised eyebrows belying her pride. Her movements as before seem to replicate Fola's: she presents the plaid bag as Fola presented the flowers. The mimicry is touching, almost paining. Fola smiles.

"*Thank* you," she says. "Are you sure you won't stay?"

Ama glances back at the taxi. "I won't, please." Mirroring Fola's pained expression, she smiles, then she leaves. Fola, surprised by the sudden departure, holds up one hand as the taxi drives off. She cradles the plastic bag, pulling on her cigarette. Mr. Ghartey steps forward and closes the gate.

She returns to the chair. She peers in the bag. She laughs with such force that Mr. Ghartey looks scared. Cigarette in one hand, she retrieves with the other the slippers: battered slip-ons, thin, worn to the soles. She stubs out her cigarette to free both her hands up and only now sees the face drawn in the dirt. Kweku, however gestural (it must have been Kehinde). She looks at the mouth, at the angled-up eyes. "There you are."

Here I am.

"Your wife's a bloody genius. Slippers." Starts to laugh, picks them up from her lap. "I mean, really."

Genius. He is laughing. She is laughing. *Why did I ever leave you?*

"I also left you." She breathes in the smell of forgotten familiar. She presses the soles to her dampening cheeks. "We did what we knew. It was what we knew. Leaving."

Was it?

"We were immigrants. Immigrants leave."

Not good enough.

"Cowards."

We were lovers.

"We were lovers, too."

Couldn't we have learned? Not to leave?

"I don't know." She is quiet for a moment. She knows that they're watching, the staff, from the gate, with confusion, alarm. But still can't be bothered. She thinks but doesn't say it: one can learn only so much in one life. "Still there?"

Yes. Forever.

She laughs. Yes, most likely. "We learned how to love. Let them learn how to stay."

How are they? The children?

"They're here," she says, pointing. "I got what I wanted. You sent them all home. They're all here for Christmas. We're roasting a game fowl. Your Olu insists upon carving, of course."

My Olu.

"Well, yes. He was always your favorite."

Your Sadie.

"Then whose—?"

They're each other's. The twins.

"The twins . . ." She trails off. Hears a car engine idling. The honk of the horn. "They've come back. I should go." But doesn't. She sits, slips her fingers in the slippers as if they were mittens and covers her face. "You should go," she says softly. She squeezes her eyes shut. The gate rattles. Tires turn. "I know, I know, I know." Then there is quiet. Car doors open, shut. She slips out her fingers and opens her eyes.

A dawn-colored sunset.

"We found one!" calls Sadie.

She watches them hauling out the tree from the trunk. Benson smiles, waving. Waving back to him: "Coming." She places one toe on the mouth on the ground. The sketch is remarkable, unmistakably Kweku. She stares at it, waiting to hear something else. Then laughs at her waiting. There is nothing to wait for. She picks up his slippers and brings them inside.

ACKNOWLEDGMENTS

I am so very grateful to God, and (in alphabetical order, from the bottom of my heart) Andrew Wylie, Ann Godoff, Anne Carol Edelberg, Anthony Campbell, Ashish Bhatt, Auntie Allison, Auntie Ertharin, Auntie Gail, Auntie Harriet, Auntie Joy, Auntie Judith, Auntie Renée, Auntie Simi, Carlos Watson, Avery Willis Hoffman, Catherine Coker, Charity Hobbs, Cheryl Faye, Cousin Alex, Damon Darryl Hamilton, Dan Urman, Daniele Novello, David Adjaye, David Holloway, Deborah Holloway, Dela Wosornu, Derrick Ashong, Dr. Juliette Tuakli my beloved mum, Dr. Lade Wosornu my brilliant father, Dr. Wilburn Williams my dearest dad, Edem Wosornu, Edward Williams, Elaine Markson, Eliza Bentley, Elizabeth Janus, Elizabeth Shipman Lee, Ellah Allfrey, Ernest Marshall, Eyi Williams, Fabio Berardo, Fiorhina Perez-Olive, First Corinthians Baptist Church, Ford Morrison, Francesco Aureli, Francesco Clemente, Gabriele Paoletti, Gabriella De Ferrari, Garry Bromson, the Geezer Gang, Genevieve Dadson, Genevieve Helleringer, Gianna D'Amore, the Harlem Arts Alliance Creative Writing Workshop, Heather Charisse McGhee, Ileane Ellsworth, Ingrid Barnsley Juratowitch, Jamakeah Barker, James Connolly, Jamin Gilbert, Jeanine Pepler, Jenny Calixte, John Earl Jelks, John Freeman, John Kuhn, John Reed, John

Pepper, John Simms, Joy Hooper, Joy Sacca, Judas Hicks, Julia De Clerck-Sachsse, Kamin Mohammadi, Kate White, Kathryn Getty-Williams, Kathy Trotter, Keith Davis, Kendrick Forte, Kevin Quinn, Khadija Musa, Khameron Juttla, Kirsti Samantha Samuels, Kofi Owusu, Kristina Moore, Kurt Gutenbrunner, Kyle Juttla, Lanita Marie Tolentino, Laura Armstrong, Lauren L. Messelian, Lauren Zeifman, Lexa Marshall, Lindsay Whalen, Lord Patten of Barnes, Lou Gutenbrunner, Mai Gianni, Margaret Yee, Maria Manuela Enwerem Bromson, Mary D'Amore, Masao Meroe, Matthew Jacobson, Maureen Brady, Melanie Harris Anderson, Michael Ryan Robinson, Michaeljulius Youmanli Idani, Monte Harris, Muina Wosornu, Naima Jean Garvin, Nike Jonah, Nonking Eheh, Olukemi Morenikeji Abayomi, Omar Hakim, Pablo Mukherjee, Paola Pessot, Patricia Nelson, Patrick Marber, Paulo Perez Mouriz, Peggy Broderick, Pier Francesco Grasselli, Piero de Mattia, Pino Scarpato, Pradip Krishen, Rachel Watanabe-Batton, Raman Nanda, Rayya Elias, Rekha Thakrar, Renee Epstein, Rita Pacitti, Robin Holloway, Roszella Turner-Murray, Sadia Shepard, Saffron Juttla, Sangna Karir, Sarah Chalfant, Saskia Juratowitch, Sékou Neblett, Sergio Taranto, Sheila McKinnon, Shelby Nicole Washington, Slice( ) Mango, Sukari Helena Neblett, Suketu Mehta, Tamara Juttla, Taneisha Berg, Tawan Davis, Teju Cole, Thembi Ford, Professor Toni Morrison, Uncle Ade, Uncle Kojo, Uncle Remi, Uncle Yinka, Venetia Butterfield, Victor Magro, Vivian Kurutz, W. Watunde Omari Moore, Wilfred Finn, Yemeserach Getahun, and, above all, the first person I ever loved, Yetsa Kehinde Adebodunde Olubunmi Tuakli-Wosornu, my extraordinary and eternal journeymate.